Kirby Jonas
6/7/03

Lady
Winchester

Books by Kirby Jonas

Season of the Vigilante, Book One: The Bloody Season
Season of the Vigilante, Book Two: Season's End
The Dansing Star
Death of an Eagle
Legend of the Tumbleweed
Lady Winchester
Disciples of the Wind*
The Devil's Trail* (a revised version of the two Season of the Vigilante novels)

Books on audio tape read by James Drury, The Virginian
(Available through the author or Books in Motion)

The Dansing Star
Death of an Eagle
Legend of the Tumbleweed
Lady Winchester

*Forthcoming

Lady Winchester

Kirby Jonas

Cover art by author

HOWLING WOLF PUBLISHING
POCATELLO, IDAHO

Howling Wolf Publishing
P.O. Box 1045
Pocatello, Idaho 83204

Kirby Jonas
kirb@ida.net
www.kirbyjonas.com

James Drury "The Virginian"
www.thevirginian.net

For more information about this and other Kirby Jonas books or about James "The Virginian" Drury's tape recordings of the books, or to be included on the author's mailing list, email Kirby at kirb@ida.net or send a request via postal mail to Howling Wolf Publishing at the above address.

Jonas, Kirby, 1965—
        Lady Winchester / Kirby Jonas.
        ISBN 1-891423-06-1

Library of Congress Catalog Card Number: 00-109635

First edition: November 2000

Printed in the United States of America

Acknowledgments

Every time I begin one of these, I feel like an award winning actor accepting an academy award: "I'd like to thank my mother, my father, my sisters, my brothers . . ." You know the routine. But here I go again anyway because, in fact, I would be nowhere at all without my friends and colleagues and the many people across the country who love a good book and who love to see fiction that reads as true and as accurate as it possibly can.

There are a number of people within the pages of this book who are real. Not necessarily real to the time period of the book, but real just the same. First, we have the beautiful Geri Berg. Although I changed her name I tried to stay as true as possible to her character and her persona and still be true to my story as well. Geri became, of course, Kathryn Winchester. It is her you see on the front cover.

Then we have the list of those who appear within the pages of this book under their own names: Clyde Hall, Arch Hess, Cheyenne Jonas, Roger and Susan Sievers, Beaver, John and Janet Webster, Curtis and Annette Selders, Keith and Caroline Perkins, Michael, Braden, Christian and Hunter Perkins, and Bob Lynch.

Clyde Hall's mother also appeared briefly in the book, under the name of "Elk."

And there are again those who appear only behind the scenes, without whom this book would have gone nowhere at all, or at least would have been so embarrassingly full of errors that I wouldn't have dared put my name on it. Here are those people: Actor James Drury is a master of guns and horses and common sense. His brand is burned into many pages of this book. Shawn and Laura Curtis, who put themselves through a little physical abuse to bring to light the impossible and then mold it into the possible. A teacher and a friend, Cleve Morgan, who didn't have much chance to help with this book but tremendously with *Death of an Eagle* and somehow escaped my mention. Wallace and Marlene Reid, whose own story should be a book of its own. Rocky and Dawn Moldenauer, who have cared enough to take me under their wing. Chris Taft, whose .44 Colt-fast and Winchester-true inspiration helped a jumble of ideas become a plot. Candy Moulton and Sherri Campbell, whose careful research on feminine styles of the day lent its perfect touch of reality. Dr. Jim Shaw, whose knowledge of firearms and unexpected generosity were indispensable. To Dell Mangum, whose love of the past shows up in his every word. And to Thornton Waite, whose knowledge and documentation of Idaho's railroads made those sections of this book real down to such tiny details as when the trains were scheduled to arrive and depart. To Dan and Jim, Todd and Quin Gilbert and Todd Fitch for letting me live a huge part of my dream and re-live a little of our rugged past. The folks at the Lucy P. Boyle Library, the Blackfoot City Hall and Bingham County courthouse, as well as the Blackfoot Historical Society and all of those I have talked to briefly and whose names I might have forgotten but whose help I never will.

I know I sound like a broken record, but I must thank: Debbie and my mom. No two people have meant more in my life. Loui and Alice Novak, with love and undying gratitude. Kandy and Jamie, Jody and Marqueta, for believing. Cheyenne and the boys, for making this all such an adventure. They are watching TV even as I write—what else but a Western?—and riding their rocking horses to the ground while their cap guns spit smoke and flame. And here sits Debbie, taking care of all my fan mail and book orders and taxes. Who could ask for a better life than I have here with five people as close to perfect as they can be?

Author's Note

I am a writer of fiction. Most of you know I try to keep things as close as I can to the way they were. But because I am foremost a writer of fiction, once in a while I use the name of a mountain range or a road or a stream before it was actually named, simply for reader benefit. In this book, there is a strong possibility I not only named a road but *created* one before its time. Little Indian Road, east of Blackfoot, may or may not have existed in 1885, but for aesthetic value it does exist within the pages of this book.

Scab Mountain, mentioned on page 206, is now Scout Mountain. It was named in the late 1880's after a disease of sheep, because sheep were kept there in huge flocks before they could be fitted into Henry Harkness's dipping vats, at McCammon. The good citizens of the area decided Scab was not a fitting name for this beautiful landmark, and so early in the 1900's it was renamed Scout. See? The annoying phenomenon known as "political correctness" began many years before our time!

The town of Blackfoot I faithfully re-created as nearly as I could, but for a town without the infamy of a Denver or Tombstone or Virginia City it was hard to find all I needed to accomplish that. In cases where I couldn't pinpoint the original location of a business, I put it where it best suited my needs. Yet every business listed in the book did exist in 1885. That much we know. And the doctor's office really was located inside the Commercial Hotel, just off the railroad tracks. The big new courthouse sat on the outskirts of town, like it does in the book, and the insane asylum was purposely placed far away from the rest of the population and stood there like a mysterious fortress, looked at with awe by local children and citizens.

As for the locations in the book, the side-canyon off of Wolverine Road and such, they are all real. As a family, we picnicked in that particular side-canyon and waded in the creek there in the 1970's. My own family now carries on that tradition. There was a time those rocks were infested with snakes, although humans with little knowledge of their impact on ecology have managed to nearly wipe them out now. We can thank them for the mice that come to visit in the night!

The Irving Wolfe ranch in the book sits where Wallace and Marlene Reid's place is now, just off Reid Road. Farther west up the road can be found a yellow two story home that sits on the property where the Winchesters fictionally resided.

In 1984 I came up with the idea for *Lady Winchester* while working in French's potato factory, in Shelley, Idaho. I had a picture in my mind back then of how she would look. But I never could find her. I began writing the book, wondering how I would ever locate this woman who had to be so precisely beautiful and yet strong. Then one day in a fabric store my eyes fell upon Geri Berg. I knew instantly that here, at last, was Lady Winchester. I was an unpublished author at the time and didn't dare walk up to her and ask her if I could paint her portrait. She probably would have called the police. But miraculously enough I ran into her on duty on a medical call a few years later and had the chance to meet her first, then later spring the proposal on her. To my delight, Geri said yes.

Several long years later, the book is done. Geri is not only on the cover but it is her inside as well, as far as I am concerned. I hope she agrees, at least a little bit. Here is to her family for being so patient with me. They let me borrow their "lady" for a few years, and I couldn't have found a more fitting lady.

Foreword

by James Drury

If you have become a fan, as I have, of Kirby Jonas's work as a novelist from reading some or all of his earlier books, you are in for another wonderful example of his compelling, arresting, consuming style. If this is your first experience with his work, you are in for a rare event: the first reading of a new author who will, I predict, become a lifelong favorite of the reader.

In *Lady Winchester* Kirby writes with a deep and telling insight the story of one woman's struggle to keep her family and her life from being destroyed by forces beyond her understanding or control.

Kate Winchester, the lead character, is a woman of great strength and passion. She is a woman who has suffered almost unbelievable losses as her life has unfolded before the story begins and seems certain to lose her battles with the forces arrayed against her as the story opens.

This could be a damsel in distress kind of tale that would have us nodding at predictability if not for the continuing revelation about Kate's character and beliefs that show her evolving into a force that must be reckoned with. Kate is tempted often by circumstances to abandon her principles and take the easy way out, but she defines for us by her actions the true meaning of the words "She's a lady," and she is a lady you won't want to miss. She sets high standards and lives up to them, and we see at last the values she holds are the ones that make all civilizations from her time, to long before her time, to this time we all must live in now, the sticky stuff that holds it all together.

James Drury
Houston, Texas
February 19, 2000

To three ladies: Mom, the one who put up with my lazy, good-for-nothing childhood; Geri Berg, who submitted to a man she hardly knew to be thrown into the Wild West for better or for worse; and Debbie, who, unlike Mom, made a conscious decision to be saddled with this maverick and has stuck it out like a champ through more rough spots and land mines than most women would have stood for from *three* rascals.

Chapter One

The first shot cracked hollow and faint, out of place in the still afternoon. The pesky black-tailed jackrabbits ornamenting the road flicked their ears and took nervous hops forward. Kathryn Winchester's team pointed their own ears toward the disturbance.

Another shot exploded on the wind, and Bob, the near horse, shied and tried to run, dragging Tarnish, the red roan off horse, with him. Kate managed to hold the animals in check, leaning back hard on the long black ribbons of leather and bracing her feet against the dash.

Who was out here shooting this time of day? Maybe someone had run into a rattlesnake. Or maybe it was only Ira shooting at rabbits, which had overrun the country so badly this year that the county auditor had offered five cents per scalp or for a pair of ears. But even with the reward Ira wasn't a man much taken with shooting. He hadn't done much of it since the end of the war, twenty-one years ago. In fact, he had sold or traded off all but one of his guns, an ancient Sharps carbine. Rather than hunting, they lived mostly off their own beef and hogs.

Kate had had her one long look at the house after they crossed the new log bridge over the Blackfoot River and before they turned onto the main road that led to the ranch. She had taken Little Indian Road that day as a way to break the monotony. It wasn't the way she normally went. But since they had built the bridge there it made the trip a pleasant one, and it gave her a little extra time to think. That day, after an argument with Ira which culminated in her taking the trip to town alone, there was plenty to think about, and she needed the time.

At that point the house had still been more than two miles away. But from that distance much of the yard could be seen clearly. There was no movement.

Kathryn put a hand to the broach at her throat, fingering it the way her children said she did when she was nervous. She knew Ira would be home. She had left right after their argument, at eight o'clock that morning, with two of their horses pulling the wagon. Ira's mare, Ginger, had cut a fetlock on barbed wire and wasn't in riding shape yet. And her husband wasn't a man to walk much, especially on a July afternoon like this one when it topped out at a blistering ninety-five degrees in the shade. Worry crept into the edges of Kathryn's mind, though she tried to ward it off. This was range country. It wasn't unheard of for someone to shoot at a snake, a coyote, a wolf or bear—any number of animals most self-important humans considered pests, especially the rampaging jackrabbits of that year. But something nagged at her stomach, an unexplained sensation that this was something more. She forgot all about her argument with Ira, about the stupidity of it.

Her worry had its way. She clucked Bob and Tarnish into a long trot, letting the white ribbon of road fall away behind them. She stood up in the wagon, trying to get a glimpse of the house and outbuildings but knowing she wouldn't see them again until they topped the big rise.

Nagging worry transformed into a strange fear as she drew on. She allowed her emotions to get the best of her. It was only gunshots, certainly nothing out of place in country where most travelers still went around armed. But something sent her a warning. Something unspoken, confided only to her heart. She had had similar feelings before and ignored them; always she had lived to regret it. And even if her instincts were giving her a false alarm, the sooner she reached home the sooner she would know for certain. She could wait till then and laugh her feelings off if it proved to be a laughing matter.

Kathryn slapped the ribbons against the horses' necks, driving them harder than any prudent teamster would have chosen to do. There were five hundred pounds of grain in the back, along with other dry goods and a month's supply of staples for her, Ira and the children. The right wheels dropped into a rut, then careened back out of it. She heard things shift behind her and glanced back. For the moment the load seemed secure.

At nearly a mile and a half they came over the top of the rise. She could see the house and barns, and all appeared to be quiet. There was still no sign of life there of any kind. But the gunshot worried her. She didn't slack her speed.

It was at a distance of half a mile from the house that everything changed. Suddenly, a group of horsemen appeared from behind the house. Surprise made Kate's heart leap into her throat. She watched the riders gallop up the curving lane that led down to her yard, then surge onto the main road. They skidded to a halt, a huge, whirling cloud of dust enveloping them until most of them became a mass of shapeless images. The foremost rider sat a buckskin horse, and another rode a gray. The rest were too vague to make out.

Before Kate's wagon had come much nearer, the man on the buckskin waved the others back. They spun their mounts and spurred east toward the holdings of the Twin Wolfe Ranch and the Blackfoot Mountains and Wolverine country. By the time she came to the ranch turn-off, they had disappeared in a cloud of dust.

Kate wheeled the horses onto the down-sloping lane. She yelled at them, sending them careening recklessly along the ruts. She no longer cared what happened to the goods in back of the wagon. Something was wrong at the ranch. She had to reach Ira. They tipped up on the right wheels as the wagon came around the first turn, then up on the left ones as it made its last curve. The weight in the back slammed the wheels back against the ground as the wagon straightened out.

Bob and Tarnish slowed when they neared the house. By the time they reached the north side they were at just over a walk and breathing heavily, stamping their feet and tossing their heads. Their hides ran with dark fingers of sweat and froth gathered at the corners of their mouths. Warily, Kate drew them up in the yard alongside the house. Except for the chickens and the snuffling of the hogs in their pen, all was quiet.

The memory of the fleeing horsemen scared Kate, but even more terrifying was Ira's absence. He would never leave her to unload the wagon herself.

Kate took a deep breath, then forced herself to take another. It was difficult to breathe against the tightness of the corset she had donned to make herself presentable in town. She cursed, as she often did, the unwritten rules of society that made such a hindrance necessary at all.

Her eyes swung back and forth. The door to the house hung open, as well as the one to the barn. Wiping beads of sweat from under her eyes with a gloved fingertip, she jumped from the wagon, nearly turning an ankle. Absently, she patted Bob's rump, causing him to shift his weight. When she dropped her arm, a soft cloud of dust sifted from the ruffles of her light blue cotton dress. Bob blew through his nostrils and shook his head, stomping a foot.

She brushed a strand of dark hair from her cheek. Dust that had stuck to it where it wasn't covered by her hat filtered away on the dead air. She forced herself to take another breath, looking toward the house. Panic had nearly closed off her throat, so she had to fight for that breath. The corset squeezed her lungs down deep, only letting her fill them partway.

3

Curse women's fashion! She tried to calm herself.

"Ira?" she called tentatively, then once more.

Ira didn't answer. The only sound was a hen digging for grubs and clucking to its chicks among the red roses along the side of the house. She looked back up the road. She didn't know why. There would be no one else around except perhaps R.M. and Susan Sievers, who were half a mile away across the valley toward the river—unless some of the riders had remained . . .

With a ragged sigh of despair, Kate lifted the hem of her dress and her petticoats off the ground and took the three steps up onto the porch. Her eyes roved the yard once more, not wanting to go into the house. Where was Ira? Who were the riders she'd seen? And a more important question—did she really want to know? She had experienced enough heartache in her life for three women, but it never got easier. In spite of the fact that she and Ira had started arguing frequently, the thought of something happening to him tore her apart. Her heart couldn't have beat any harder. It felt like it would explode in her throat. She steeled herself and moved along the porch.

When she reached the door, she peered around the side of the frame. The first thing she saw was the chair lying on its back. She caught her breath and brought her hand to her mouth. Gaining control, she took a quick step inside, biting the insides of her cheeks so hard she nearly bit them through.

The curtains hadn't been drawn, so the interior was well lit. But after peering at the brightness of the road so long, the room seemed very dim. She let her eyes adjust for several seconds. As they came to the divan, she saw Ira's flat-heeled boots. Her ears began to ring with terror. Her eyes dimmed. With her teeth clenched, she forced herself forward, trembling all over, nearly stumbling over the throw rug.

Ira lay motionless on his face, a puddle of blood around his chest. He had grabbed at the cover of the divan as he went down, pulling it partially with him and smearing it with blood. Kate dropped to her knees, not caring if she soiled her dress in the blood. Taking off the leather gloves she wore for driving, she threw them aside, struggling to roll Ira onto his back. With fear tearing at her, she put her fingers to his throat. The faint mutter was almost weaker than her fingers could detect.

Putting her hand under her husband, Kate found the hole a bullet had made in his shirt, and she used that weakness to tear the garment open. She touched the bullet wound in his ribcage. One of the ribs was broken, and the wound still seeped. The bullet had gone through.

4

Dabbing at her eyes with the backs of her hands, Kate stood up and ran out to the well. She drew a tin bucket full of water and spilled half of it on the way back inside. Gathering linen sheets from the bedroom, she returned to the main room to drag the old bear rug near. She had never liked that hideous thing. Maybe the bloodstains would give her the reason she had always wanted to throw it away. She told herself to be calm, but still her hands shook.

Kate tore off a long section of sheet, folding it over several times. She pressed that firmly against the wound, stanching the flow of blood. Again she picked up the sheet and tore off a larger strip its entire length. She wound this strip around Ira's torso as many times as it would go, then at last made a knot in the center of his chest.

Kate had one thought in her head, and that was to save Ira's life. Nothing else mattered—not whether they still loved each other, not who had done this to him, or why. She only wanted to see her man smile at her again and speak her name. If he died he would be the fourth husband she had lost. That was too much to ask a woman to take, even a woman as strong as Kathryn Winchester.

Strange old sensations flashed across her mind as she tried feverishly to stop the bleeding. The look of the wound; the biting rotten egg smell from black powder smoke still in the room; the slippery feel and crimson appearance of blood on her hands; the sickeningly sweet smell of it pooled on the floor; the taste of cold fear in her throat. Everything brought her back, forced her mind to the military hospital at Shiloh, Tennessee . . .

It wasn't really a hospital. It was only an old farm house and barn, and rows and rows of tents with the sides drawn up to circulate air. There in that man-made hell, men and boys in blood-soaked bandages screamed in agony and lay dying. Behind the barn hulked a grisly pile of severed arms and legs, sawn from these poor boys, these fathers and husbands, sons and brothers. The appendages had lain rotting in intermittent rain and sun until Kate broke down and begged for someone to at least cover them with a tarp. Colonel Trivitts, the senior surgeon, complied with that until they could be carted away for burial. But the smell remained. It lingered all around her, suffocating in the closeness of the house where she went to try and catch an hour's sleep between amputations.

She thought of how she had left the home of her Quaker parents to run away with handsome Dan Lauder. They had been bound for his father's steel mill in Philadelphia. And then the war broke out. She begged Dan not to go, but he claimed it was his duty. And now here they were.

Outside, the day was sullen. Raindrops pattered like mice feet across the shingles. Puddles gathered in the yard and at the corners of the buildings. Men came and went with blue greatcoats and pants blackened by the rain and faces paled, beneath their beards and smudges of gunpowder, by the unending pall of death.

There were other smells Kathryn could never chase from her mind. Laudanum, whisky, chloroform, unwashed bodies, excrement, urine . . . fear. She shuddered to think of it all. She pictured a young man staring at her, not screaming or crying like most, just gazing like an abandoned house, vacant behind filmy windows. She thought of an older man with no forearms, only stumps wrapped in bloody linen. He cried forlornly until he was crying without tears, his voice pitifully hoarse. He repeated a name over and over and over and over. Janie . . . Janie . . . Who was Janie? A wife? A daughter? Whoever she was, she seemed the only hope he had left.

Kathryn Winchester had seen all of that through the horrified eyes of a sixteen-year-old, but the memories these twenty-four years later hadn't waned. She could still see the blood on her hands, on her dress, smeared on her cheek and splattered in her hair. She could hear the screams, the not-so-distant boom of cannons, the popcorn crackle of muskets. She could see the broken-topped trees at the edge of the trampled cornfield and the drizzling gray sky gulping up plumes of billowing smoke. She could smell the black powder smoke that drifted in on the afternoon breeze, later to be wetted down by the pattering gray Tennessee rains.

Shiloh. The name was branded forever in her soul, in her nightmares. There her first husband, Daniel Lauder, had taken a bullet in the thigh and suffocated to death beneath a pile of his comrades. She was resting against the outside wall of the makeshift hospital the day they carried his lifeless body by. All she could do was stare. Her eyes could form no tears . . .

Clamping her teeth, Kate shook her head and closed her eyes, then opened them again to look down at Ira. No time to think of the war. She had to care for Ira, and to do that she needed all her senses, needed to steel them as if this man meant nothing to her. Weak women didn't survive long in this land, and Kathryn Winchester had many times proven herself one of the toughest of a tough brand, although born into a meek family of Quakers.

Kneeling down, Kate shoved the bear rug as close to Ira's side as she could, stuffing several inches of it underneath him. She shuddered at the thing's gaping mouth and tiny, crusted eyes that stared up at her. Again, she swore it wouldn't come back to this house. She put one hand on Ira's shoulder and the other on his hip and rolled him toward her until she could pull the bear rug out on the other side. As she straightened the rug out underneath him, it struck her that pulling with the grain of the bear's hair would make her struggle to the wagon much less strenuous. Pulling with the bear's long slick hair as a kind of runner on the smooth wood floor would be akin to using a sled. With a flustered sigh, she went through the entire process again, moving Ira off the hide and turning it over so that he lay at last on the flesh side. By the time she was done, she was gasping for air, and her sides were soaked with sweat.

Frustrated tears swam in the shadows of Kathryn's eyes when she finally stood, letting her gaze sweep the room. But she couldn't cry—not yet. Her job wasn't done. Somehow she had to get her husband into the back of the wagon, then drive him to Blackfoot, to Doctor Sims's office.

As Kate glanced down again at Ira, something caught her eye. From underneath the cover Ira had pulled off the divan, the corner of some unfamiliar object protruded. Absently, she bent to scoop it up. It was a little leather coin purse, beaded all around. On one side of it, in white beads on dark blue, were the initials, "I.W." Snapping it open, Kate was taken aback to see a roll of cash along with several double eagles. Perhaps this had belonged to whoever had shot Ira! With the vague thought that this might be used as evidence, Kate took the purse outside and threw it into the wagon box.

Climbing into the wagon, Kate brought it around to the front of the house and backed it up as close as she could to the porch. With strength as much earned as inherited, she dragged the grain sacks out of the back and onto the porch, then hustled the other goods into the house, trying not to look at Ira as she passed. She returned to look at the wagon. It was as close as she could bring it to the edge of the porch, but even so, she would have to lift Ira up two feet to get him in back. Even as strong as she was, she had the sickening realization that it could not be done. Ira wasn't a huge man, but he was solid—he probably weighed one hundred eighty pounds on his most sickly day. The heaviest grain sack was only one hundred. And if she dropped one of those or bent it the wrong way it would do it little harm. The same mistake might kill Ira.

Her initial thought was of R.M. Sievers. She knew he would come running if he had any idea of her plight. She thought of going to get him, but she couldn't leave Ira alone as long as there was any chance the killers might come back.

For several moments, she looked helplessly about the yard. The long, slender fingers of her bloodied hand brushed a strand of dark hair from in front of her face. Her eyes lit upon a pile of planks at the side of the barn. She had pleaded with Ira so many times to move those boards or cut them up for firewood. There were mice living under them. And what this place didn't need was one more shelter to aid in the infestation of vermin. But now she realized those planks were her answer.

Running in her anxiousness, Kate nearly turned an ankle thanks to the narrowness of her shoe heels. Fortunately, their laced tops were tall enough for support. She carried two of the eight-inch planks from the barn to the house, hardly noticing the tiny splinters left in her soft hands. Gasping to catch her breath, she leaned the boards side by side from the porch to the wagon.

"I need your help, old fellow," she beseeched Bob. She felt like a fool, like she was talking to a rock. But the old bay nickered softly and flicked each ear in turn, touching her shoulder with his long-haired upper lip. His huge brown eyes looked at her with the appearance of understanding, and she smiled and patted his neck. She climbed up and took off the brake and led Bob forward just enough to flatten the planks out to their full length, then set the brake again. Going back to look at the planks, even at their full length she saw it wasn't going to be easy to get Ira into the wagon.

Forcing it out of her mind, she returned to the house, coming to a stop at Ira's head. There was no point in putting off the job. She summoned all her strength, reached down and took the bear rug by its matted shoulders, rolling wads of skin into both hands to use as handles. Steeling herself, she began to pull backwards. When she tried to breathe, it was immediately obvious the corset had to go, and she didn't care what they thought in town. She took off the broach she was wearing, and just for a moment it made her stop and stare. The broach was one Ira had given her not long before, a beautiful piece of jewelry yet a constant reminder that something was wrong between them. Wishing she hadn't worn it that day, she dropped it down between his legs.

Undoing her dress and taking the bodice down, she unhooked the corset and flung it gladly aside, sucking in a deep breath that felt very good in spite of the stifling air inside the house. She breathed deeply again and closed her eyes. The air felt cool against her damp skin. She almost regretted buttoning up the bodice again.

Making another start with the bear rug gripped in her hands, Kate pulled Ira the ten feet to the door, then eased him across the threshold, gasping for breath. Even in her discomfort, she was unable to parry the memory of the way he had teasingly carried her over that same threshold five years ago.

Dampening the sleeve of her dress across her brow, Kate stopped to rest for a moment, turning to look at the wagon bed. It seemed so far away. Biting her lip, she glanced past the barn toward town. Ira had to make it. She almost looked down at him, then decided better of it.

Steeling herself, Kate took several lung-filling breaths, then shifted folds of her dress up higher around her hips. She bent at the waist, took the bear rug's shoulders again, and started backward. One step. Two. She gasped. She was feeding this man too well. Three steps. Four. She forced herself not to look at the wagon but glanced back to check on the ends of the planks. One more step.

Now she was almost there, and the distance was less, but on an incline. She renewed the air in her lungs and said a little prayer. Then she started up the ramp. It was an inch at a time now. An inch—a rest. Another inch—another rest. A couple of times her heels slipped and she nearly fell. She was thankful her common sense had convinced her to turn the bear hide over. It would have been nearly impossible for a woman of her size to drag a man of Ira's with the rough flesh side of the hide dragging against the splintery planks.

With her last ounce of strength, Kate took a ragged breath and heaved her burden over the lip of the planks. With Ira's legs still hanging out of the wagon, Kate collapsed. Her lungs burned horribly, and she tried to catch her breath. She nearly retched as she crouched there, her head spinning, her eyesight dim. Over and over, she gasped, trying to draw in air that never seemed enough. She wanted to give up, but she knew the worst of her job was over, if she could only get her wind back.

At last she stood, with her muscles crying out against the strain, and dragged Ira the rest of the way into the wagon. Then she fell onto her knees and took his hands. She stared searchingly at his pale face, her lungs still heaving.

"You've—come out—of worse things, Ira," she lied to ease her mind. She sucked a deep breath. "If you leave me over a stupid—thing like this—I'll never forgive you." She caressed his cheek, leaned over and kissed it. She stood up with hardened jaw and made her way gingerly down the ramp onto the porch. With her strength and her wind slowly returning, she pulled the boards away and dropped them into the dust below.

Kate hurried into the house and picked up her gloves, slipping them back on. As she was turning back toward the door, a warning rang in her head. What if the men came back? Maybe she had startled them the first time, but what if they decided they had to return and make sure Ira was dead? What would she do? What could she do? She looked over at Ira's old Sharps carbine, leaning behind the door. She could take it, but what good would it do if she were attacked? She had never used a firearm in her life, and this one was cap and ball! Even if she wanted to know how to shoot it would take her years to become proficient with it. Two of her husbands before Ira had tried to talk her into learning to shoot, but she still held to some of her childhood teachings against killing another human being. She would just have to outrun anyone who came after her, that was all. She had no other choice.

Shaking those thoughts out of her head, she picked up her black reticule—another of Ira's recent gifts, as were the beautifully crocheted white string gloves inside it—and stepped back outside. Before getting onto the wagon seat she stopped to look again at Ira. Faithful Ira. Yes, they had argued of late. They had argued often, and he had been very distant. But she still loved him. Why would anyone want to hurt such a caring man?

He looked so unstable on the rug that Kate packed four of the sacks of grain back into the wagon and laid them alongside him so he wouldn't roll around. As she was bending over to set the last sack in place, she saw her broach lying there between his legs and picked it up. The broach, to Kate, was the symbol of whatever had gone wrong with Ira in the last months. She wore it almost every day, as a reminder that something had to be done if things were ever to be right between them again. With a grim countenance, she fastened the broach once again at her throat.

Winded, and her throat now raw, Kate climbed onto the wagon seat, pulled off the brake, and started Bob and Tarnish back toward Blackfoot. She felt sorry for the horses. It had been a long day for them, and it was over fourteen miles from the Winchester ranch to town. It was going to seem an eternity.

Kathryn Winchester was a handsome woman, far more so than the teamsters, cowboys and farmers of Blackfoot were used to. She stood taller than most women and many men of her day, a good seven inches over five feet, and carried this height with the grace and poise one might expect of the high society ladies of Boston, Philadelphia or Washington

City, or the belles of the South. Certainly uncommon for a rural Idaho homemaker. She didn't even need to wear her corset to look trim, and after her bad experience with it that day would probably continue to wear it only because it was commonly thought the proper thing to do. Kate dressed modestly, like her parents had taught her, in petticoats and in dresses that left only her face, neck and hands exposed. But some women can't hide beneath a dress, and Kate Winchester had too often been made uncomfortably aware that she was one. When she walked the streets of Blackfoot no head was left unturned.

In public, her dark brown hair was always well kept, usually topped by a hat. In the western custom, it normally hung long, settling in soft, lustrous waves below her shoulder blades. She took pride in that hair, though her parents claimed pride was a sin. She took further pride in her hands, wearing gloves whenever she could, and keeping the skin supple with lilac-scented lotion. Most men, taking one of those hands in greeting, would never have guessed how hard this woman worked—throwing hay, branding, mending fence. She did what she had to do to help Ira keep up on the ranch, but she took extra care of herself when the work was done.

Yet even considering her other attributes, it was Kathryn's face that drew men to her. It was the dark, fathomless eyes capable of revealing any emotion or none at all. It was the arched brows, the soft, faintly smiling lips always so ready for a laugh; the aquiline nose which gave her beauty an edge of handsome maturity with far more character than the oft-admired button nose. It was how she looked straight through a man, or deep into his heart, then, if she chose, touched his hand with a lingering electricity that sent shock waves through his body. There was many a man who would have stolen Kathryn from Ira Winchester at the drop of a hat had she given them a reason. But she was completely devoted to her man.

The wagon rattled south past the cemetery and at a good clip down West Main Street to the imposing brick walls of the Commercial Hotel, where Doctor Sims had his office. By now, Kate had control of her nerves. She had convinced herself, at least momentarily, to accept the inevitable. She jumped down off the wagon seat with a crowd starting to gather near the wagon and went into the hotel, hurrying through the dining room and parlor and down the hall to the doctor's office.

Doctor Sims was a middle-aged man with a connected mustache and goatee and straight eyebrows that slanted upward at the outside at such a severe angle he would have appeared perpetually angry if not for the

11

kindness swimming in his gray-green eyes.

Doctor Sims was the only man in Blackfoot who called Kathryn by her given name (besides Ira, whose favorite name for her was Katie). He took that liberty with all his patients, male and female alike. As much of Kathryn as the doctor had seen she would have felt foolish if he had addressed her any other way.

With his usual calm wits intact, Sims had some men bring Ira in and lay him out on the operating table. Then he summarily invited them out of the office with the briefest of thanks.

Kate was glad Sims dispensed with any questions about the incident. He went straight to business, and after an initial appraisal of Ira's bullet wound he turned and looked her squarely in the eyes. "Kathryn, you might not wish to stay in here, and that's fine. But I'll be perfectly straightforward with you. If you walk out of this room, you must be aware that it may be the last time you see your husband alive."

Chapter Two

The Commercial Hotel sat just off the tracks of the Utah and Northern railroad, with West Main and Pacific Street intersecting behind it. It boasted being one of the finest lodging establishments in the state. It was built as a Keeney House, the railroad's tangible boast of opulence and first class accommodations. Kathryn Winchester took up a room down the hall from Doctor Sims's office and paid the higher-than-normal one dollar and fifty cents per day. But she didn't have much chance to utilize their hospitality nor their fine bed. She left her belongings in her room but stayed most of the next five lonely days and nights in an armchair beside Ira's bed. She had debated staying at the Hogan Restaurant, which was also a lodging house and only charged five dollars per week, but having Ira just down the hall was worth the extra cost.

Sitting for hours in the doctor's office, for Kate, was somewhat like reliving the past, except the medicine of the Civil War had been almost medieval compared to Doctor Sims's modern knowledge and skill. Part of the gap in quality, of course, stemmed from the overwhelming workload the surgeons had faced during the war. Many more of those men and boys could well have been saved had the doctors been able to devote all their attention to one of them at a time, rather than the multitudes who arrived each day, bloody and screaming out their anguish. The nerve-racking atmosphere of the war hospital had appalled Kate. Amputation was the order of the day, not because it was always needed, but because it was the quickest way to save the most lives. But it certainly didn't save them all. A bullet wound in that war was as likely to bring death, quick or lingering, as not.

Shortly after bringing Ira in to the doctor, when Kate had found the strength to go back outside and move the wagon, she had remembered the little leather coin purse and looked for it. To her horror, it was gone! The wagon box was tight, so it couldn't have fallen out. Someone must have come by, seen the purse and made off with it. Kate was sick about losing it. It was possibly the only thing that could be considered as evidence against whoever had tried to kill her husband. But she had to go on and forget about it. The most important thing right now was nursing Ira back to health. If he lived, he could point out his attackers. They would have no need of the purse.

The first two days in Blackfoot, Kate sat beside Ira while he remained still. A huge lump had swollen up on the side of his head, dangerously close to his left temple, where Doctor Sims informed Kate her husband had been struck. Doctor Sims said the blow alone, had it struck closer to the front of her husband's skull, might very well have killed him.

Kate tried not to think of Ira's wounds. She channeled her thoughts to other places, other times—places of joy and beauty, times of passion unbridled. She didn't allow her thoughts to wander to Ira's present predicament and the reasons behind it. She couldn't—not yet. What good would it do? There wasn't a thing she could do about it.

After the third and fourth day, when Ira began to turn in his sleep, to whisper—and sometimes scream—delirious words and mysterious phrases, she caved in. Once she did, her mind began to rove over many things, looking for any hint of who would want to kill Ira and why.

A constant reminder of her troubles with Ira was the cameo broach at her throat. Often, in quiet moments, she would remove it to look at it and wonder why it held such a fascination for her. At any other time in her life, the broach would have been nothing but a source of enjoyment for her. It was beautiful. It could be worn either at the throat, as she normally wore it, or as a necklace. It was two inches tall, with a black stone base surrounded by a frame of hammered metal lacework and all-encompassed with a rope twist border. The cameo was the face of a beautiful woman, turned to the right, her hair put up with a band the way Kathryn sometimes kept hers, on special occasions. Set on the metal lacework were eight even clusters of tiny metal balls, forming the shape of flowers, whose centers were seed pearls.

Kate would hold that broach, and sometimes her string gloves and black reticule, and wonder where Ira had suddenly begun to come up with the money to buy these things. It wasn't like any of them were so expensive, in themselves. The crocheted gloves had a lace look to them. The reticule was also crocheted, with a drawstring opening and lining of beautiful black silk. It wasn't as if either of them could have cost Ira the price of a cow, but they were just three in an endless stream of gifts. It had never been like Ira to spend money frivolously. Until he had become distant, in fact, he had brought her gifts only to mark a special occasion, which was as it should be.

On the afternoon of the fourth day, Kate sat with Arch Hess—who had become sheriff of Bingham County upon its creation in January of the year before—and her fears gushed forth uncontrolled as she held Ira's pale hand.

"Sheriff, they will come back, won't they? If—when—Ira starts to heal, if I take him back home they'll try again . . . won't they?"

Sheriff Hess was a big, solid man with a square face and wide, expressive mouth. He held his narrow-brimmed hat in his hands and studied it for a moment before looking back up to center Kathryn with a frank gaze.

"There's no sense in lying to you, ma'am. I'd sure like to say you have nothing to worry about, but here's a plain fact: somebody tried to kill your husband, and you say you had nothing to steal. So, ma'am, I would venture to say that yes, you and Ira are still in danger. If my guess is correct, those fellows meant to kill your husband, and since they didn't get it done, they've got all the more reason to make sure of it next time. Whatever their reasons were before, now they can add to it an attempted murder charge if he is able to point a finger at them."

Kate nodded and pursed her lips, looking down at Ira's hand, folded tightly in hers. Tears came into her eyes, but she forced them back. She was long past weeping like a little girl, and she wouldn't show any weakness now.

Swallowing, she looked up at Sheriff Hess. "What do I do, Sheriff? I can't stay in town much longer. I don't have enough money. Besides, I need to go back and take care of the stock. I have R.M. Sievers taking care of them now, but he can't do it forever. He and Susan have their own place to take care of. But what am I to do if those men come back to finish what they started? And what about our children? They'll be back within the week."

Thoughts of the children, visiting Ira's Aunt Betsy and Uncle Nat in the northern Utah town of Brigham, made tears again push to Kate's eyelids, but she spoke quickly to drive the children from her head.

"I'm at my wits' end. I have no way to protect myself or Ira, but I'm at the point I have to return home." Suddenly, Kate gave a little laugh, letting her shoulders rise and fall. "I'm sorry. I don't mean to burden you with my worries. I know you have a big jurisdiction."

She stood up and let go of Ira's hand, walking across the room to the little north-facing window with its lace curtain. She heard Sheriff Hess stand up behind her. In the street, the citizens of Blackfoot went about their business as if nothing had ever happened. In front of D.H. Biethan's furniture store, a rancher helped his wife up into a buckboard, and she smiled lovingly down at him. Three young boys stood in the shade of Warren's notions store, dividing a sack of candy. A young girl and her mother walked away from Mrs. Holbrook's Emporium of Fashion, the girl holding up a bundle of blue gingham cloth thoughtfully in front of her. Her mother squeezed her shoulder and smiled.

Life went on outside, and people were happy. The trains still arrived like clockwork, four times a day. The Blackfoot and Challis Stage still pulled out promptly at eight o'clock every morning. Everyone came and went and did as they always had. A terrible thing happened in their county and they as soon forgot. But life had to be that way. A person couldn't go around worrying all the time—it wasn't healthy. It was Kate Winchester's place to worry in this case, and Heaven knew she would do enough for them all.

She dropped her hand from the curtains and turned back around. Sheriff Hess made a sorry attempt at a smile. "Things'll be all right, Mrs. Winchester. I'll send a deputy out now and then to check on you. And your neighbor R.M. Sievers—he's a good man. I know he'll look out for you. You just do what you have to do and don't worry about those men. We've got our noses to the wind, and I'm sure some clue will turn up."

Kate smiled, grateful for the reassuring words. She knew the sheriff felt badly for her, but she also knew he didn't believe those words any

15

more than she did. He proved it when he spoke again.

"Just the same—and I know you don't believe in violence—but you should maybe get a good gun and learn to use it. A shotgun would be best for you. If nothing else, the racket might bring Sievers running."

Kate quickly shook her head. "No, Sheriff. That's not the way. Men—or women—can't go around killing each other. I'm not going to be drawn into murder."

Hess looked down and nodded as if he had already known her answer. He sighed and glanced over at Ira before looking back at her. "If you need to go back out to your place to get anything, ma'am, you just let me know. I'll have a deputy watch your husband and I'll ride out there with you. That's the least we can do."

"Thank you so much, Sheriff. I'll let you know."

"Well . . ." Sheriff Hess stood a moment longer, then turned and made his way to the door. He opened it, then turned back momentarily to Kate. He gave her a long, searching glance, then put on his hat with a nod. "Ma'am," he uttered by way of farewell, then closed the door softly behind him.

Kate stood there in front of the window until she heard his footsteps fade. She was left with only the sounds of the street, muffled by the walls and curtains.

Wearily, she walked around and sank back into the chair beside Ira. While Doctor Sims finished his noon dinner in the dining room, she meant to make the most of this moment alone with her man. She looked over at him and studied his sweaty brow, his pale cheeks. His dark hair was neatly combed, his face freshly shaven. She saw to that every day. Even unconscious she insisted he remain presentable in the event of a surprise visitor.

"Oh, Ira." Her own voice in the shadowy room startled her. She reached out and took his hand again, feeling its clammy chill against her skin. "Who would want to hurt you? What have you done? Men don't come and just shoot a man down for nothing. We're not at war anymore. What is it? I wish you could talk." At that moment he emitted a soft moan. "But you wouldn't tell me anyway, would you?"

She knew it was true. It had been over the past year they had grown increasingly distant. He had become secretive, always tending to some business he would tell her nothing about. And then there were the poker games. Sometimes they lasted all night, and she could never learn where all the money came from for him to play so much. Was he that good at poker? She didn't imagine he was—it didn't fit him. The games just served to keep him away from her more, and sometimes she found herself wondering if it was poker that kept him away, or something—some-*one* else . . .

But even while she realized how far apart they had grown, she didn't really believe even for a moment he was seeing someone else. Not Ira. And then there were the little things he had started buying for her. For years, she and Ira had had nothing but their deep love for each other, and it was all they had needed. Yet in the past few months he had started bringing her things like the broach, reticule and string gloves—other pretty things she didn't really need to be happy: music boxes, glassware, lacework furniture dressings, frilly hats. He seemed pleased being able to offer these gifts, but they didn't fill the void between them. The fact was—and she didn't understand why—these gifts served only to estrange Kate still further from her husband. She couldn't abide his hiding things from her, yet he left her to wonder where all the newfound wealth came from. It certainly wasn't profits from their ranching operation.

In her pondering, one certain answer came to Kate. The attempt on her husband's life was connected somehow to the mysterious appearance of all that money. But how? Those men hadn't come to the house to steal; they had broken into nothing. It seemed plain they had come there for one reason, and that was to kill. Had Ira cheated someone out of money at poker and been caught? She doubted if he was skilled enough in the game to pull that off in the first place. As far as she knew he had never played poker—or cards of any kind—until half a year or so ago, when he began to disappear with his secret companions, using the game as his excuse. Besides, if he had cheated someone, why hadn't they tried to get the money back? No one had ransacked the house as if looking for something.

For the last several months, she had wondered and worried about where the money came from. Now she knew her concerns had been founded. But she didn't know any more than before. If she could find how Ira came upon the money she would also find why someone tried to have him killed. But she had no clue where to begin.

The turning of the doorknob pulled Kate from her thoughts, and in a moment Doctor Sims peered carefully inside. When he saw her smile he came on in and shut the door.

"You're a loyal guard, Kathryn," he said with a wink. "Do all wives feel so strongly about their men?"

Kate's eyes welled up with tears, and she tried to hide them with a soft laugh. Its strangely melancholic ring drew a concerned glance from

17

Doctor Sims, who pulled off his glasses and looked at her fondly. "Ah, Kathryn, I think you can relax. I'll give Ira the once-over again in a minute, but I don't think it's premature to say he's going to recuperate just fine. He had me worried the first day, but . . . well, so far he looks good. You're entitled to worry a little, but I do miss your smile."

Kate swallowed and gave a little nod. She stood up from her chair and placed a hand on the doctor's sleeve. It was one of those rare touches so many men hoped for and few ever received, and Sims looked down at her hand thoughtfully then placed his own over it, giving it a pat and then just resting his there. He looked back up at the woman searchingly.

Kate suddenly let her hand fall away from his arm, but rather than move away she took his hand in both of hers and squeezed. "Thank you, Doctor Sims. Thank you so much for your friendship."

Before tears could come back into her eyes, she let go of his hand and spun away, walking briskly again to the window to stare out at the street. Clearing his throat softly, Sims turned to Ira and drew a stethoscope from a shelf above his head, wiggling the tips of its stems into his ears. With a deep breath, he leaned over the unconscious man.

The Blackfoot train depot sat directly south of the Commercial Hotel, so Kate was always well aware of the movement of passing trains. Three days later, when the single long blast of the nine-fifteen express signifying that it was about to come to a stop reached her ears, Kate hurriedly tied on her hat and left the hotel.

She walked along beside the narrow gauge tracks of the Utah and Northern even as she listened to the train coming up fifty yards behind her, gushing steam. The sun was only a red hump in the west, and dusty clouds glowed gold and orange and rust against a backdrop of the palest green. The street lay in shades of purple, but the tops of the roofs were still bathed in gold light. The Blackfoot Mountains were lit brilliantly, turning a drab, almost desert-like land of sagebrush and juniper into a gilded kingdom where sorcerers and dragons, knights and fair maidens should mingle.

Evening brought with it the hordes of gnats and mosquitoes that plagued Blackfoot, venturing off the river. The insects swarmed all around her. But because Kate, like her family and many pioneers, was in the habit of drinking a cup or so of vinegar every day, beginning a few weeks before the onslaught of the mosquito season, the little pests seldom made any attempt to land and taste of her blood. Even as the insects whined about the street, bats made their appearance, swooping

18

and dashing and looping little acrobats, worth their weight in gold for the mosquitoes they destroyed.

By the time the train chugged up to the platform, Kate was standing there looking anxiously from car to car, swatting now and then at the mosquitoes and gnats that drew too near. The sickly yellow shine of the lamps glowing from the eaves of the platform overhang, and the wash of pale orange and yellow coming from the station windows backlit Kate as she waited.

She saw her oldest daughter, Vala, after the girl had already spotted her and was hurrying along the aisle toward the door. But the first one out of the car was four-year-old Cheyenne. The girl carried a tiny valise in her right hand, but as soon as she saw Kate this fell from her stubby fingers. With a shouted, "Mama!" she ran as fast as she could and fell into Kate's outstretched arms. Kate hugged the little girl for a long ten seconds before holding her away and looking her up and down.

"You're growing up so fast, Cheyenne. Look at that long hair!" she exclaimed. The children had only been gone two weeks, but Cheyenne was proud of her hair, and Kate couldn't resist the huge smile that broke out across her face whenever anyone mentioned it. She hugged the girl again, then stood up to meet the others.

Kate's other three children, her daughter, Vala, and sons, Marshal and Ellis, were all from a previous marriage, to Tom Briggs. All of them, though they loved their new guardian, had chosen to retain the last name of their father.

Kate proudly looked the three of them over, a real smile lighting her face for the first time in days. Vala, now seventeen years old, had grown into a beautiful young woman in the last couple of years, after a frightful period of adolescent awkwardness Ira still teased her about. She wore her dark hair long like her mother's. And, also like her mother's, it was covered modestly today by a cornette—a bonnet tied beneath the chin.

Marshal was fifteen, and a stronger lad of his age she had never seen. He was broad across the shoulders and chest like his father had been and nearly able to keep up with Ira when it came to throwing hay or calves. As far as looks went, he was the black sheep of the family, although in this case the black sheep was blond. Only Cheyenne's hair even came close to Marshal's, hers being a light honey brown.

Ellis, younger than Marshal by two years, looked Kate up and down with fetching dark eyes and a dimpled smile and took his turn at hugging. He was the most sensitive one of them all, and he had developed a deep fondness for his stepfather. Almost even more than Cheyenne, who

19

wasn't old enough to understand, Kate was going to hate telling Ellis what had happened.

When the luggage had all been unloaded and set on the platform, Kate helped the children gather it together in one place. She noticed Ellis searching the gloaming of the street and the dim-lit platform. When he looked up at her, disappointment swam freely in his gaze.

"Ira didn't come with you?"

"Oh, son." Kate placed a hand on his shoulder, steadying herself as well as him. "I didn't want to worry you children while you were away. But something has happened to your father."

The children shot glances at one another. Vala, one hand to her throat, reached out with the other to touch Kate. "What, Mother?"

Kate cleared her throat and forged on. "Your father was shot."

Shocked silence hung between them. The children just stared at Kate, their jaws slack.

It was Marshal who spoke first. "Is he . . ."

"Is he alive?" Kate finished the thought the way she hoped it would have been worded. "Yes, and recovering. But we don't know who shot him, and we don't know why."

Almost as if speaking of the attack had broken some spell, a rifle shot suddenly crashed from the direction of Idaho Street. The five of them whirled toward the sound. Two more shots followed, and then an excited hum of voices exploded among the people gathered on the platform.

Kate stood still. She had started to bring her hands to her mouth, then dropped them to Cheyenne's tiny shoulders instead, pulling her tight against the front of her dress. She didn't consciously bring it on, but the first thought that naturally came to her was of Ira.

Chapter Three

Terror clutched Kathryn Winchester's insides like a cold hand. She was surprised to see Sheriff Hess come hurrying past her from inside the depot. He cast her a glance of despair but continued along the porch without a word, almost running. Kate heard a voice rise above the others, and the words froze her in place.

"They killed somebody at the hotel!"

She turned to the children, her jaw clenched. The memory of the shots still stung her ears. Her eyes swept the children. She took Marshal and Ellis each by a shoulder. "Your father's in the doctor's office in the hotel. I'm going to check on him, and you have to stay here. Whatever happens, don't try to follow me. Go over to the Star Restaurant." She pointed toward the restaurant; like the Hogan, it was open late in keeping with the train schedule. "Wait for me there," Kate said.

"Yes, Mama," she heard Vala's words far back in her head as she started up the street.

As she neared the hotel, she hesitated, awed by the crowd gathered there in the lamp-lit shadows. She forced herself to continue on, trying to keep from running. Oh, Ira. Please, Ira. God, please don't let it be. She wished the words in prayer fashion, feeling the blood drain from her face. She lifted her long skirts and held them up to let her walk faster. She saw Arch Hess pushing through the crowd. He looked dismally at some bystanders and spoke quietly as he passed. The sheriff's face had gone gray, and his wide lips turned down at the outside. He stood there with blood on his shirt and hands. His hat was missing, and a shock of reddish gray hair lay across his forehead.

At a glance Kate took in his weary eyes and the smudge of blood across his cheek. Without her realizing it, both of her hands had come to her mouth. She stared at the sheriff, not wanting to hear what he had to say. She had lost three husbands, all of them violently. It couldn't happen again. It just couldn't!

When Sheriff Hess spoke she continued to stare in silence. She barely

21

grasped his words through the hum of the voices around her. The news she had thought would make her a widow didn't come. But because the message surprised her so, a feeling of nausea, of faintness perhaps even worse than she had expected, washed through her stomach. She stood on the porch in the dying light, four feet away from the big-boned lawman, and his words pounded at her until somehow, at last, they soaked into her consciousness. Her knees nearly collapsed, and she had to grasp the awning post to hold herself up.

"Ma'am, Ira's fine," said Hess. "He's fine. It's Doctor Sims. Poor Martin. They just killed him. Just killed him."

The skin of the big sheriff's face was pale and drawn and full of despair—the way Kate's heart felt.

Kate Winchester sat beside her sleeping husband in Doctor Sims's office, with Cheyenne on her lap and the other children gathered around her. In the corner, the big grandfather clock ticked unceasingly, and its hands read ten o'clock. Sheriff Arch Hess met her gaze and minced no words in discussing the prior evening's murder.

"I haven't known you long, Mrs. Winchester, but I judge one thing about you. You're no fool. You know as well as I do why Doctor Sims was shot. Somebody must've heard your husband was recovering and didn't know how far along he was. When they saw the silhouette of the doctor through the window, they thought it was your husband. A murder that's totally unconnected is just too bizarre to believe. You know it, and I know it."

The sheriff stood there and looked at her for several seconds, his face aching with the need to help her out.

"Ma'am, you knew they'd come back. Now we know they're desperate. I don't want you to go back out to the ranch. These people are serious, and they're far from through."

Kate stared at the fresh bloodstains on the softwood floor. Someone had tried to wipe them up, but they had soaked into the wood too quickly. She shuddered. That blood was there because of her husband, because someone had wanted him dead. Because of him, a good life had been taken away.

Her hands rested on Cheyenne's thighs, and she squeezed, raising her eyes soberly to meet Arch Hess's. "You've done your best, Sheriff. I can't fault you for this shooting or anything else. There's only so much you can do. And I trust you to protect us, I honestly do. But we just can't stay here anymore. My money is gone. I can't afford to stay in the hotel.

And now there isn't any reason to keep Ira here, with no doctor."

"Ira's still unconscious, ma'am," said Hess. "He isn't out of the woods yet. I've heard good things about Dr. Blickensderfer and Dr. Davis, in Pocatello. Why not send Ira there?"

"Like I said, Sheriff, I can't afford it anymore. Anyway, Doctor Sims told me it's only a matter of time and rest now. I can care for my husband just as well at home."

Hess pursed his lips, cutting a glance at the children. "Are you sure you want them here?"

The children looked at one another, and Marshal reddened at his collar. He bunched his jaw muscles but said nothing. Kate cleared her throat and looked at her oldest son. Then she turned her eyes back to the sheriff, lifting her chin as she met his gaze.

"I want them here, Sheriff. Vala is a full-grown woman, and these two are more men than boys. If we are to weather this together, it is only fitting they know what we face."

The sheriff shrugged. "That's your choice, ma'am. I just don't want to scare someone needlessly. But back to what I said. Sure, I know you can care for Mr. Winchester at the ranch. You're a brave lady, and you've told me you nursed in the war. But ma'am, it's not just the nursing. It's the fact . . . well, you don't even believe in guns. Now, how're you going to protect yourself if those fellows come back looking to finish this business? You just can't go out there with these four kids. I can't order you not to go back, but . . ." He paused and looked up helplessly at Vala.

Kate sighed, then stood and set Cheyenne down. Out of courtesy, Sheriff Hess sprang from his chair, almost upsetting it. "Sheriff," said Kate evenly. "I told you, we don't have any money. The only thing we have is that ranch, and there we have food, water and a place to sleep. It isn't as if we had a choice where to go."

Hess ducked his head then brought it back up, rubbing vigorously at his chin. "Ma'am, I know this is a rough town, and the boys do like their fun. But I think you're selling Blackfoot short. The folks here aren't cold-hearted. We can come up with a place for you and the children to stay, at least till we find some clue who's after your husband. Now don't make me sweet-talk you. We like you Winchesters. And I don't want to see anything happen to you in my county. It makes a man feel worthless to be in charge of people's lives and not be able to protect them. Just let me try to round up a cottage or something. At least give it a week."

Kate breathed deeply. She avoided looking at her children. She had to make a decision on her own this time. The children usually had an equal say in any major decision, but not this time. She knew what the three oldest children would say. They had learned their fierce pride from her. Like their mother, they were frightened, but they wouldn't want charity. She had no doubt they would choose to go back to the ranch. But Hess was right; she knew nothing about guns, nothing about defending herself and her loved ones. On her own, she would have gone, but she couldn't endanger these children.

"All right, Sheriff. I hate charity, and I won't take it. But if you find someone I can work for to pay for our keep, we'll stay—for one week. Maybe you'll find out something about the killers by then." She felt Marshal's angry stare, making her skin flush, but she ignored him. She had made up her mind, and she was more strong-willed than he.

Sheriff Hess went straight from the Commercial Hotel to the office of C.O. Sonnenkalb, Blackfoot's mayor, to ask for assistance. Together, the two of them gathered men to spread the word. In less than three hours, more than a score of citizens had lined up to make donations to the hapless family, among them a number of toughs from the saloon crowd. The spirit of the West drove men to stand up for those in need.

But there were no empty cottages available at the time. Instead, John and Janet Webster took them in to their home on the corner of Francis and West Main Streets. John had been a shipbuilder in Seattle before moving to Blackfoot. He had saved enough money to have a good-sized, comfortable house with a second story balcony and three wood stoves. The house was immaculate. The Winchesters crowded into the Webster parlor and set up camp, with Ira to sleep on the davenport and everyone else on the floor.

John Webster was a stocky man with a trim mustache and thinning brown hair. He always had a gleam in his eye and a ready sense of humor, and Kate and the children liked him right away. He and Janet made it plain to Kate from the very first that they would be there if she or the children needed anything at all.

Kate wasted no time in putting out the word she was willing to do washing, mending, house cleaning or any menial chore that might earn her enough money to pay their keep. And it wasn't long into the afternoon she had a customer.

Kate was wearing a drab green dress decorated by deeper green rosettes. Its hem brushed the floor, hiding her slippers, and its sleeves were pushed up while she worked. A large white apron covered the dress and made her look like a housewife. She was finishing up the dishes from noontime dinner, wiping a damp cloth across a porcelain plate, when she heard three sharp, distinct raps on the door. Janet Webster answered the door, and in a moment her voice came floating back to Kate in the kitchen. "Mrs. Winchester, you have a visitor."

Surprised, Kate glanced at Vala, who stood beside her with another dishrag. She hurriedly dried her hands, untied her apron and pulled it off. She laid the apron across the back of a chair as she walked out of the room and into the home's entryway. Janet Webster smiled at her and quietly vacated the room.

Ward Brassman, president of the First National Bank of Idaho, stood in the doorway holding a brown nutria hat in one hand and a valise in the other. When Kate's eyes fell on him, her heart faltered inexplicably, but she shook off the feeling.

Brassman was a fine figure of a man, with slightly thinning dark hair pulled straight back from a high, smooth forehead. Even after being a resident of Blackfoot for a number of years, the banker was still a frequent topic of conversation during many a feminine gathering. He was dressed today in the finest brushed wool suit, with impeccably polished ankle-high shoes and a gold chain trailing out of a buttonhole in his vest.

He had a square face and precisely cut features, full lips, a dark, heavy brow and umber eyes that stared out at his world with more confidence than any man ought to make obvious. Since their first meeting, Kate had found Brassman an attractive man, his manners gracious and polished. But as a married woman, she was ashamed his appearance moved her at all.

"Ma'am." Brassman tipped his head in a bow. "I heard about your troubles and came to express my regrets. I'm upset to hear something like this happened so close to home. And your husband, ma'am—Mr. Winchester. How is he?"

Kate shrugged, walking closer but stopping just out of reach. "Thank you for asking, Mr. Brassman. He's recovering, but very slowly. Doctor Sims seemed to think he would fully recover in time."

Brassman smiled, revealing deep-cut creases below his cheeks. "Well, that's good news, anyway."

"Thank you again, Mr. Brassman." Kate dipped her chin, clasping her fingers together in front of her. "Was there anything else?"

"Uh . . . oh, yes, ma'am. I'm sorry." He looked down at his valise and gave it a little shake. "I regret I can't tell you this is full of money to help your cause, but I did hear you were taking in washing, so . . . there is some money in it for you. There are five shirts here, and a pair of trousers I would like washed and pressed for Monday morning. And a little extra starch in the collars, if it wouldn't be too much trouble."

Kate forced a smile. "No trouble. The customer is always boss."

The banker snapped his chin in a vigorous nod. "Now, that's the spirit. Could you bring these to the bank then, when you've finished?"

Kate took the valise from him. "Certainly. Is Monday morning soon enough, or do you wish them back by this afternoon?"

"Monday morning is fine, Mrs. Winchester. And again, I wish your husband the best." His long-fingered hand, brushed with fine, dark hair, came out between them, startling Kate. She looked down at it for a moment, then placed hers inside. One firm squeeze, and then the banker's fell away. But his deep brown eyes lingered on hers. "Good day to you then, ma'am. And good health."

With that, he clamped on his hat, turned and shut the door behind him. Kate stood staring at the door for a long minute after the banker left, one eyebrow raised in thought and fingering the cameo broach at her throat, which she wore that day out of mere habit. At last, she turned to see Vala standing in the kitchen doorway.

"He is such a handsome man, isn't he, Mama? How old do you suppose he is?"

Kate took a breath and let it out. "Now, why do you ask, honey? He's much older than you—that much I know."

Vala blushed. "Perhaps. But just how old do you think?"

"Thirty-five, maybe. I really don't know."

"Do you really think so? Still, he certainly is handsome, don't you think? And I heard he's never been married."

Kate cocked her head to one side and cast a serious regard at her daughter. Setting the valise down, she walked to her and placed both of her hands on Vala's slender shoulders. "And that should be sign enough something's wrong. Now, you're not serious about this, are you? What makes you suddenly notice a man so much older than you?"

Vala blushed fiercely, looking down at the floor and shuffling her feet. As her hands came up to rest on her hips, her eyes rose and met Kate's. "Now, Mama! If he's thirty-five he's only eighteen years older than I am. And I'm a full-grown woman—you said so yourself. Besides, I didn't suddenly notice him. I noticed him the first time I saw him. Wouldn't you be happy if I married a banker? I could really help you and Ira then."

Kate gave Vala's shoulders a firm squeeze. "Honey, I don't mind you

26

marrying a banker. It's that banker I'm not sure of. He has . . . a way about him."

"I know he does, Mama. And I like his way." Vala giggled, and the dimpled creases appeared in her cheeks, reminding Kate of Vala's father, Tom Briggs.

"Oh, go finish cleaning the kitchen! I have enough to worry about." Kathryn spoke teasingly and gave Vala a slap on the backside as she walked away, which brought a glance of mock reproach. But when the girl was gone into the kitchen, Kathryn forgot about the valise on the floor. She walked over to a burgundy colored settee leaning up against the wall, straight across from the davenport where Ira slept. Wearily, she sank onto it, resting her elbow on one of its arms and once more touching the broach, letting her fingertips react to each of its different textures. Her heart still pounded. Avoiding looking at Ira, she stared at her black reticule and string gloves, which lay on the console table, near the door. Her mind churned. Her eyes came to focus at last on a vision of Vala walking hand in hand with Ward Brassman. It wasn't a frightening spectacle, yet somehow disquieting. To a Quaker, money was supposed to mean little, so that had no bearing, good or bad. What she saw in Ward Brassman was a man with good looks and a shrewdly prying eye. A man she wasn't sure if she should put her trust in not only because he handled large sums of money, a pursuit that never lent itself to integrity, but also because of the uncomfortable way he made her feel when he looked at her. Maybe more than that—and she hated having to admit this—it bothered her to see her daughter interested in a man who had turned her own head. To her, Vala was still no more than a child.

There was no longer a question in her mind. She would give Sheriff Hess one week to find who had shot Ira and Doctor Sims. Then she would take her family back to the ranch. Vala was too close to trouble here.

Feeling the sudden urge for fresh air, she rose from the settee and walked to the front door. Almost desperately, she pushed down on the brass handle and swung the door wide, stepping out onto the porch and pulling the door shut behind. She sucked in a deep breath, not realizing until then that she had been holding it. A feeling of claustrophobia had taken hold of her in the house. She felt so closed in, so locked up. This house, this town . . . the circumstances.

She sucked in another breath. It was a deep breath, like it might be her last. It smelled sweet—slightly of dust and sagebrush, and of the yeasty smell of baking bread from the Star Restaurant and the earthy scents of livestock operations . . . but mostly of freedom. That was the sweet part. It smelled of open country, and if she closed her eyes and ears she couldn't see the people, couldn't hear the traffic rattle by in the street. Oh, how she wished she were back at the ranch! Why, why had this happened to them? What had Ira done?

Even as the question entered her head, she looked north up the street and saw a buggy approaching, flanked by several horsemen and followed closely by a wagon. Just to the right of the buggy driver rode a man on a stout buckskin horse with a thin strip of white down its face.

Kate Winchester's breath stilled without her knowing when she saw that the man to its left rode a gray! She stared as if dumbstruck, her lips parted. She had to tip back against the doorframe to keep from falling over. It wasn't just the two horses. Buckskins and grays were plentiful enough that their presence proved nothing, especially when many cowboys rode a different horse every day. It wasn't the horses alone that made her stop and stare, speechless. They simply added to a jigsaw puzzle whose pieces had all just slipped together: the buckskin and gray horses of the assassins at the ranch; the mysterious beaded purse left lying on the floor, obviously belonging to whoever had attacked her husband. The initials? I.W. . . .

Irving Wolfe! He was the man driving the buggy, one of Bingham County's most powerful and ruthless men. He owned the Twin Wolfe Ranch, fifty-five hundred acres of what might have been the best deeded cattle range around. A piece of ground that, coupled with untold public acreage he ran his stock on, at one time had come close to monopolizing the entire cattle industry in Bingham County. But unforeseen events had conspired to put a stop to the growth of his empire.

Unfortunately for Wolfe, when the Desert Land Act had been passed in seventy-seven he, in his smug self-assuredness, had been unprepared and strangely uninformed. The act was put in to encourage the settling of some of the country's more inhospitable pieces of land. It allowed a homesteader to take up six hundred forty acres of ground at twenty-five cents an acre, prove he could irrigate it, and then pay off a balance of one dollar per acre within three years. It was a law for the west, where the earlier Homestead Act, with its meager allowance of one hundred sixty acres, had done little to encourage productive settlement in dry farm country.

The chance for settlers to take up good, arable land for a dollar and twenty-five cents an acre cut Irving Wolfe's ranch by two thirds, down from over fifteen thousand acres. When the settlers surged in so unexpectedly Wolfe's lack of planning had allowed them to take up much of the land between his ranch and Blackfoot, land that he had previously used to run his cattle on. Several years later he had an even larger blow to his empire when the three sections of land adjacent to the Twin Wolfe came up for sale and were bought right out from under his nose. At the time, he had had the money to purchase them himself, but the sale had been kept a secret from him until it was too late. Banker Ward Brassman had been the cause of that, with the fervent wish to populate the county and to fill his own bank account in the process. The banker had been pretty much solely responsible for the Winchesters buying the beautiful piece of land where the ranch sat now.

Wolfe still had plenty of river frontage himself, but much of the Blackfoot River on the white man's side ran beneath steep, jagged basalt cliffs, and that was where most of the Twin Wolfe lay. Without leasing land from the Shoshone and Bannock Indians on the other side of the river, his cattle could only reach the water now in a few treacherous places. By far the majority of the best river access on white man's land was now legally in the hands of the Winchesters and their neighbors.

The Winchester holdings bordered the Twin Wolfe, which made their place the most likely for Wolfe to try to procure. Owning it would provide his herds the perfect access to the river without completely over-grazing the banks directly behind his own ranch house. Irving Wolfe had come to the Winchesters no less than eight times over the years, asking to buy back "his" land at what he termed a "fair" price. The land was prime, and their reply was a firm "no," but each time he returned he became a little more insistent, and a little more angry before he went away.

It all seemed shockingly simple to Kate. Wolfe hadn't even entered her mind before. But now she was certain he was the man who had tried to kill Ira—just for a piece of land!

Wolfe's buggy was drawing nigh, and the moment she looked at his face he glanced her way and saw her standing on the porch.

Wolfe sawed his beautiful gray horse to a halt, causing the riders to pull up in confusion and the two horses drawing the wagon behind him to almost run into the rear of his buggy.

Coolly, he looked into Kate's eyes, a close-mouthed smile barely tipping up the corners of a perfectly curried mustache.

"Good morning, Mrs. Winchester."

Stunned to hear the man speak to her, she nodded. She started to raise her hand in acknowledgment but changed her mind. Her eyes darted to the left, to the man on the buckskin, then to the right, to the one on the gray. The morning of the attack they had been too far away for her to recognize either, as if that mattered. Her eyes returned to Wolfe and leveled on him.

A man in his late fifties, Wolfe lacked the rugged looks she had once expected of a cattle baron. He was on the small side, not over five-foot-seven and with narrow shoulders, distractingly wide hips, and soft, age-spotted hands that had surely never felt the burn of a rope. His face was unusually round but small, and his eyes much too large for it, like two dimes stuck to the side of a peach. But those eyes looked out at the world with a shrewd savoir-faire that only hinted at how he had come to be the affluent man he was. They were blue eyes, blue and chilled like February afternoon skies, and they could drill right through a person's head like they now did Kathryn's. She forced herself to hold them, to not be cowed.

Wolfe cleared his throat when he realized Kate wouldn't return his greeting. "I almost asked what brings you into town, ma'am, but it would be foolish to pretend I haven't heard what happened out at your place. I hope you'll accept my condolences."

Kate stared unspeaking, her lips still parted as she searched for words. But nothing seemed appropriate.

Again, Wolfe cleared his throat, at last dropping his eyes away, for only a second. He tugged at his tie, then attempted to straighten it inside his vest. "How is Mr. Winchester, if I might ask?"

"He's alive. Very much alive."

Kate Winchester heard the words as if someone else had spoken them. She straightened away from the doorframe and folded her arms across her chest.

"He's alive, no thanks—" She stopped, the rest of the sentence hanging up inside.

Wolfe tilted his head questioningly to one side. When he could see she didn't intend to go on, he said, "Ma'am, I know we haven't been on the best of terms, but I really hope your husband will recover. I am not a spiteful man. We are rivals, in a sense, because of your land, but still I wish your husband no evil." He paused again, ostensibly searching his head to be sure he had said all he meant to. Then he touched his hat to her. "Ma'am. Good day to you."

Obviously expecting no response, Wolfe set his eyes back on the street before him, flipped his horse with the reins, and the buggy started forward. Kate watched the man's profile until it disappeared behind the vehicle's sleek black sideboard. As she started to turn away she caught other eyes on her. She swung her gaze back to the man on the buckskin. He was twisted around in the saddle, watching her. Her immediate reaction was one of revulsion mixed with fear. He had the face of a coyote, long and leering, with a pointed beard that gave it an even longer appearance. His eyes were an odd shade, indistinguishable at this distance, but not like any others she remembered seeing—at least not in a human face. When the man started to turn back to the front, Kate caught his crooked smile, and her insides turned cold.

As the buckboard pulled past, its driver, a man by the name of Harvey Manfred, lifted a hand hesitantly in greeting. He quickly looked away, reddening around the collar. He made a point of turning his head to scan the opposite row of businesses, and he and the other riders in the cavalcade followed Wolfe on up the street, none looking toward Kate.

The air no longer pulsed with the mild pleasantness it had held for her when she first stepped outside. It seemed like evil demons danced nearby, floated all around her in the breeze. Oh, but Irving Wolfe was cool!

Kate dropped her hands and placed one on top of the other behind her, leaning back against them and the doorframe. She breathed deeply and stared after the shiny buggy, her mind churning. Irving Wolfe didn't have the face of a killer. Or did he? Had she ever really known any killers? What made a killer? Desperation? Wolfe was desperate for better land, for better access to water to quench the thirst of his cattle. Without that access, the vast tracts of land he owned were nearly worthless, and in the few places where his cattle could reach the water they had destroyed the range. Ira and Kate had long since been forced to put up barbed wire fence between Wolfe's property and theirs, clear down to the riverbank.

Kate's mind raced. She could run to Sheriff Hess right now and tell him her convictions. She could probably have Wolfe questioned, so he would know he was under suspicion. But she hesitated. What if she was wrong? The thought was almost absurd, but what if? Ira was the only one she knew of who could really say who had tried to kill him, and he was unconscious. Until he woke up or died, did she dare go to the sheriff about Wolfe, with possibly false accusations? And on the other hand, did she dare not? She began toying absently with the broach. What if they came back today? Or tonight? Or any other night? What if the killers returned and this time finished their job? It horrified her to realize it, but once again the killers knew Ira's whereabouts.

With a weight like a cannon ball dragging at her stomach, Kate turned back into the house.

Kate sat on the burgundy settee for a good twenty minutes, massaging the broach at her throat with her thumb, before her heart ceased racing. Some powerful thoughts had filled her head since seeing Irving Wolfe pass by on the street. Some powerful thoughts, coupled with some powerful doubts. She had been so certain of Wolfe's guilt not very long ago. Yet if Wolfe had tried to kill Ira only to put Kate in the position of having to sell her land, how did that explain Ira's strange behavior of the past months? Why the late night poker games? How did he come by the money for all the gifts? And why was he so distant? Kate still couldn't force herself past the feeling that Wolfe was to blame, but it must go deeper than the man's simple desire to regain his land. After all, killing Ira didn't necessarily mean he would end up with the land. No, Irving Wolfe was guilty. There were too many coincidences for him not to be. But all of his reasons were as yet unfathomable.

Later, she stood in the parlor over a large tub of scalding water, stirring the sudsy mixture of soap, water and white shirts with a broom handle and watching Ira sleep. Thoughts of dread and uncertainty filled her head. She was thinking about the boys, whom she had sent out to the ranch earlier to talk to the Sievers and to see after the stock and the house. She was worried, but she wasn't sure if there was reason to be. After all, she knew whoever had attacked Ira had probably wanted just him, and now that he was in town there probably wasn't any reason for them to return to the ranch. But what if they did? The feeling nagged at her until she felt sweat beading on her forehead and soaking the sides of her dress under her arms.

Ira's eyes fluttered open so suddenly Kate didn't even realize it until he spoke, though she was looking right at him.

"Hello there."

She started and clutched the stick closer to her. The voice was so quiet and weak—not the voice she had known eight days ago. But the room had been silent, except for the softly sloshing water, so the voice seemed loud to her ears.

Dropping the stick, Kate walked to her husband, her eyes brimming with tears and her steps uncertain. When she stopped beside him, looking down, he attempted a smile and blinked groggily. "Woman, you look like you've seen a ghost." He smiled again, this time with only one side of his mouth, and feebly raised a hand to her. Ignoring the hand, Kate fell forward, catching herself just short of landing across his torso, and squeezed him. When she straightened up she took his hand in both of hers and held it tightly.

"Oh, you poor sweet man," she whispered, looking his face over tenderly. "I love you so much."

Ira looked to left and right, then glanced back at her quizzically. "Where are we?"

Kate's heart fell. She had longed for him to say he loved her too. She would have given almost anything to hear those words again, for it had been so long. But she couldn't reveal her disappointment. Instead, she steeled herself and told him about John and Janet Webster, about the children's return, and about the murder of Doctor Sims.

Ira just nodded throughout the telling, his expression varying little except for a pursing of his lips when he heard about the doctor. Kate's mind churned with a hundred questions, but she lacked the strength to broach the subject of his attack.

When she had finished recounting all that had happened since she found him, Kate fell silent. Ira lay there with his eyes shut, his forearm draped over his face. She hoped he was thinking about Doctor Sims, whose death he had been the cause of.

Finally, Kate couldn't wait any longer. "Ira, you are way too quiet to make me happy. The children aren't in the house. I think now is the time to tell me why this happened."

He dropped his arm and looked up at her tiredly. "Why what happened?"

"Ira!" she said angrily. "You know what I mean, and I think I deserve the truth. Who shot you?"

"Now, Kate—"

"Ira . . ." she said warningly. "The truth."

"I can't tell you anything. Anything I say would make it worse right now. You'll have to trust me."

"Trust you? Ira, you have been hiding something from me for— I guess I don't even know how long. What is it? You've committed some crime, haven't you? What did you do that was bad enough to be shot for? Did you steal money from Irving Wolfe? Is that how you were able to buy me all those things?"

Hurt washed across his face, and he turned his eyes away.

"Don't you dare look away from me!" she said, wanting to curse him. "Ira, you look at me. Have you stolen someone's money?"

He looked back, his jaw set. "Kate, I'm not a thief. You should know me better than to even ask that."

"Then what?" she raised her voice angrily. "What could make those

33

men try to kill you? Those late night poker games—have you cheated someone gambling?" she pressed on. "Is that it? Did you cheat Irving Wolfe?"

"Just stop it!" Ira growled, trying to sit up and failing. He took a deep breath, grimacing against his pain. "I can't tell you anything. I won't tell you. You're wasting your breath."

"Is it Irving Wolfe?" Kate asked doggedly. "It's Irving Wolfe, isn't it? But it can't be just the land. There must be more."

Ira looked at her angrily. "You don't know anything you're talking about." He sighed and looked away. Then his eyes snapped back. "Where are the children?"

Kate threw up her hands and stood away from him. She rested a hand on her hip and put one to the broach. Damn this man! She thought the curse and didn't even regret it. Her husband must hold the answers to all the puzzles, yet even with him awake she knew nothing more than before.

"Vala and Cheyenne are here," she responded irritably. "Vala's cleaning the house, and I expect Cheyenne's playing in the back." Ira's face stiffened at that, but Kate didn't notice and went on. "I sent Marshal and Ellis out to check on the ranch and see the Sievers. They're feeding the animals while we're away."

Ira's eyes widened, and he looked at her anxiously, glanced toward the door, then back into her face.

"Kate, I have to go after the boys! They're not safe out there!"

Chapter Four

Irving Wolfe pulled his buggy up in front of the feed store and directed the driver of the wagon and two outriders to purchase supplies and load them. Then he drove on with his other two riders and pulled in at the First National Bank, two blocks away.

Wolfe wore a white hat with a scarlet band and a brim that was much too big for him, bound in a narrow scarlet silk like the band and curved slightly up on one side as if to give him some dashing quality his soft, unmanly features never could. He wore a three-piece wool suit, dusty now from the drive, with wide alternating black and herringbone gray stripes. Unlike most men who rode into Blackfoot in 1886, Irving Wolfe had no gun in sight.

The rancher climbed down in front of the bank, but for a moment his two men sat the saddle, scanning the street. Wolfe glanced from one to the other of them almost mockingly. "Are you going to get down or just sit there and look dangerous?"

The coyote-faced man, Case Deckan, shrugged and cast his lopsided grin toward his partner, Dunn Yates. "Guess we getta go in where the important folks go." Wolfe blew derisively out his nostrils, swinging his big round eyes away from the two.

Yates, a bony-cheeked, dark-haired man with narrow eyes slanted upward at the outside, tipped back his hat with a knuckle and grinned at Deckan, revealing a gap where he was missing three of his top teeth. Yates didn't say anything, just slipped a leg over the saddle and bounced into the dust, again turning to look over the street. Deckan followed suit.

Deckan and Yates both wore short-barreled Colt Peacemakers, one with ivory ox-head grips and the other with mother-of-pearl. From the guns, to their tooled gun leather and boots and their brushed hats, to the fine silk scarves draped down their shirtfronts, it was plain the two prided themselves on their appearance. Each wore a shiny gold watch chain dangling from a vest pocket, and that in itself made it plain that neither of them aspired to be a run-of-the-mill cowpoke.

Case Deckan, now standing beside his partner, looped his horse's reins around the hitching rail and waited for Yates to do the same. Wolfe had gone on into the bank, and, with the swagger of men who liked to be noticed, they pushed through the green-shuttered bank door.

Irving Wolfe stood before a barred window at the counter. In a moment, the clerk stepped in, with bank president Ward Brassman on his heel holding a sheaf of papers in his left hand.

"Good morning, Mr. Wolfe," Brassman greeted politely. "It's a fine one for a ride, isn't it?"

Wolfe smiled briefly, closing his eyes tightly and letting them flutter back open. "It is a bright one, that's for certain."

"Mr. Lynch tells me you wanted to see me," continued Brassman. "What can I do for you?"

"Well, I'd like to step into your office, if we could. It's a . . . a private matter, shall we say."

Brassman's eyes showed concern, flickering quickly to Deckan and Yates, then back to Wolfe. "Why, certainly. Step right this way. I hope there's nothing the matter," he said as the rancher followed him around the counter.

Wolfe made no answer in the time it took them to reach Brassman's office. Not until the banker had invited him to a leather-upholstered chair in front of his ornate, wide-topped mahogany desk and seated himself in the chair behind it was there another word spoken of the reason for Wolfe's visit. It was once more Brassman who spoke.

"I'm worried now." Wolfe raised his eyebrows in a questioning manner. "You didn't respond when I asked if anything was wrong," Brassman pointed out.

Wolfe waved a hand dismissively across the front of his face. "Do you mind if I smoke?"

He was already drawing a long brown cigar from inside his coat, and Brassman's eyes flashed across it distastefully before he answered. "By all means—my office is yours." As Wolfe's eyes met his, he smiled and reached in his desk for a match, striking it and holding it across the desk for Wolfe to light his cigar. Smoke wafted away from Wolfe's lips just as he closed them, pulling them slightly inward as if to trap the smoke inside. Brassman politely suppressed a cough. Nonchalantly, the banker got up and stepped behind his chair to draw up the blind, throwing daylight harshly across his office. He raised the window three inches, then returned to his chair and settled into it as if he had never left.

Watching the banker shrewdly, Wolfe let a little, derisive smile touch his lips and released a long streamer of smoke from the corner of his mouth. His words followed quickly. "I seem to be experiencing some problems with getting my hands on hard cash this month. I certainly have the funds in my account to cover any problems, but I don't like to deplete that if it can be avoided."

"I see," Brassman said hesitantly. His eyes flickered down to the papers on his desk, then back up. He half smiled and cleared his throat softly, waving at a fly that buzzed too near him. "Maybe you could tell me a little more. I'm not certain what your troubles are. I don't mean to pry; that's your affair. But exactly what is it you need of me?"

Irving Wolfe stood up suddenly, forcing his chair backwards. He stepped to the side, puffing furiously on the cigar, then turned and walked back. Plucking the cigar from between his lips and holding it between the first and second fingers of his right hand, he leaned forward on the desk, resting his weight on both hands.

"Let's not be evasive about this, Brassman. I'll lay it all out, though we both know where I stand. Due to a lack of access to the river," —by the way he emphasized the words, it was plain he was aware of the rumors concerning Ward Brassman's involvement in skirting him on the land deal— "I've overgrazed certain sections of my land. I'm down to burrs and sagebrush at all my best watering sites. It's hurt me. To feed the cattle I have now, I'm using hay I'd rather use for winter. Granted, I do have funds, but they are by no means endless. I can't imagine the Idaho ranges are as bad as I hear they are in Montana and Wyoming, but they aren't good. Another winter like the last one, and . . . Well, you see where I stand."

Brassman nodded his understanding, looking at Wolfe compassionately while he vented his woes. He was aware of two thin trails of sweat that had crept from under the brim of Wolfe's hat and were making their way down over his cheekbones. Somehow, that knowledge gave Brassman great satisfaction. When Wolfe stopped talking, Brassman cleared his throat again. "What can we do, Mr. Wolfe? Your business is important here, but . . . if it comes to letting payments slide—something of that nature? I just can't do that. The board is strict. Very strict." He gazed at Wolfe apologetically, waiting for a response that came only in the rancher's disapproving expression.

"I can stretch my power so far as to give you another loan, however," Brassman bore on. "It might be foolish in the minds of the board, but you have always been a worthy client. If another loan would help somehow . . ." His voice trailed off, allowing Wolfe his moment to speak.

Wolfe sighed and sank back into his chair, putting a weary hand over his eyes to shield them while his emotions flooded past. At last, his hand fell away, and he sighed from deep in his chest. He straightened back up in the chair, leaning slightly forward and pulling the cigar out of his mouth with a gush of smoke. "All right. If I had some extra funds, I could lease some of the land from those cursed Indians across the river until I get this next herd sold to the mining camps up in the Lemhi country. I suppose that's what it has come down to now. What must we do, Brass-man? What do I have left that would be accepted as collateral? And don't say the house. You know how I feel about that. My wife—Judith . . . she loves that place. It's all she has. The house and our son."

Brassman shrugged. His face showed embarrassment—something his closely guarded front wouldn't normally allow. He wiped a hand roughly down his cheek and across his broad jaw. "I won't delve into your records, Mr. Wolfe, but I believe you have four thousand acres of land under mortgage with us already—and most of the land is, I must frankly say, in rather poor shape."

"I know what I have! And it is in poor shape. Forty-five hundred acres of it on your papers, to be exact. But the grass will grow back. It's been good land, Brassman."

Brassman's lips tilted down almost indiscernibly. He never referred to this haughty ranch owner in any way but Mister Wolfe. But the man refused to show him the small courtesy of the same title. Only his last name, like he was some piece of alley trash.

Quickly, he forced a businesslike smile to tug the frown away. "My greatest concern, Mr. Wolfe, is your current mortgages. You realize, of course, there are three of them. Three fairly stiff payments you're obli-gated to make each month. We both know the cattle market now, and it's not good. It's saturated, to say the least. The range is overgrazed—all of it. As you say, one bad winter and . . . Well, we can both read into the future, and it's not promising.

"I can give you more money for the year if you need it, Mr. Wolfe. Ask and the paperwork will begin. But Mr. Wolfe, the money in your account? Well, frankly, there is very little of it left. Your assets now lie almost solely in your holdings, until you can put through a fairly major cattle sale. That is what both of us must hope for."

Irving Wolfe set his jaw, but the resolve quickly faded from his eyes, and his jaw muscles relaxed. "All right then. What can you do for me?"

Brassman smiled. "Now that's the spirit. How many cattle are on your land? Your land and the government land? Over two thousand pairs, by your last count," he answered his own question. "If you'll put, say . . ."

The banker wasn't allowed to finish. Wolfe stood up from his chair again, raising his hands to call a halt to the banker's words. He reached down and snuffed out his cigar in an ashtray on the banker's desk.

"I won't talk about cattle. I don't want them as collateral. Listen, Brassman. I have fifty-five hundred acres of land in my name. Fifty-five hundred! For hell's sake, I know it's been overgrazed. But it's good land, nonetheless. If you'll give me one month—just one—I have this sale set up in Salmon City. A very large sale, mind you. By a rough calculation, I will be able to pay off the majority of my debts after that. I just need good graze and hay right now, and some grain and corn to fatten these beeves up. I need your money, Brassman, but instead of cattle, put land down as collateral. I'll need five thousand dollars."

Brassman sat silent for a few thoughtful moments, toying with a long, smooth pencil as he waited patiently for Wolfe to be seated again. At last, he gave up the wait. He spread his hands, then clasped his fingers together, his pencil between them. "I haven't seen your land in the last two weeks, Mr. Wolfe, but prior to that it looked bad. To be blunt, you don't have enough land to cover that kind of money. I can give you three thousand dollars, Mr. Wolfe, but you'll have to include five hundred pairs of the cattle to pay for it. If your sale is as certain as you tell me, that should be no problem. Just think about it."

"Five hundred pairs!" Wolfe looked angry. "And how much land?"

Brassman gave an apologetic shrug but went straight to the point. "For that money you will have to put down everything. All but perhaps half an acre where your headquarters sit. I'll leave you that."

Irving Wolfe's face went white, and he sank resignedly into his chair. "Do what you have to do, Brassman. Put it down. Put it all down! It doesn't matter. By the saints, I swear to you I'll sell enough cattle in September at seventeen dollars a head to pay off your mortgage—in toto! So start your blasted paperwork."

Two hours later, when Irving Wolfe had downed a couple of whiskys at the Gem Saloon, he returned to the bank with Case Deckan and Dunn Yates, who stationed themselves at either side of the door. Wolfe walked right past Robert Lynch, the teller, and stepped brazenly into Ward Brassman's office.

Brassman looked up at the sound of the opening door. His eyes fell on Wolfe as he stepped inside, evoking Brassman's most professional smile. "You're right on time, Mr. Wolfe. I was just finishing up the fine details."

"Good." Wolfe's demeanor had changed. His smile was amicable, relaxed. "Are we ready to sign?"

"Just one moment," Brassman replied. He was conscious of the change in his client—glad for it. He started to pen in one last set of numbers when Wolfe spoke again.

"You sure look familiar to me, Brassman. Remember, I told you when you first came to town I had seen you somewhere before? I'll come up with it one of these days. You can be certain of it. I've a memory like a trap—always have."

Brassman looked up and laughed. "I guess I just have one of those faces. People have told me that all my life. I always look like someone they knew before, from somewhere else. All right, Mr. Wolfe. Sign here."

With his face set grimly, Ira Winchester struggled to his feet and dressed himself, Kate arguing with him all the while. John and Janet Webster had come into the room at the first sounds of a disturbance, but Kate begged them so pitifully to leave her alone with her husband that they went outside to wait.

"You can't go out there like you are, Ira!" Kate almost screamed after they had gone. Vala stood there staring at them, but Kate didn't even notice her. "You aren't well enough yet! You can't ride that far."

"I have to go, Kate!" Ira growled, punctuating his words with a curse. "I have no choice. Get out of my way. You're killing our boys!"

Kate Winchester stared at Ira, her face red with anger and despair. He wouldn't answer any of her questions, wouldn't tell her what was going on. His secrets weren't important right now. What was important, he insisted, was to go and find Marshal and Ellis and make sure they were all right. They were in grave danger at the ranch by themselves!

Kate was close to tears, but she wouldn't let Ira know that. She was discouraged, beaten, worn down. But she knew Ira wouldn't lie about the boys. She had to let him go find them before something happened. Or she had to go herself.

"Ira, you stay here. I'll go for the boys. I can ride faster."

"No!" Ira growled angrily. He grabbed her by a wrist, shaking her arm. "Woman! You stay here! Don't go out there. I won't let you."

She forced herself to be calm when she spoke again. "Ira, you are deeply into something illegal or immoral—or both. You can't deny that for one second. But I can't argue with you all day. I can't even go to Sheriff Hess, because of your stubbornness. And I want you to know if anything happens to anyone in this family it's on your head. All of it. I hope that satisfies you."

Ira clenched his jaw muscles and started to speak. But something seemed to seize him, and he dropped to his knees. Even as she reached to catch him, he flopped over, the side of his head slamming hard against the corner of the coffee table.

Kathryn whirled toward Vala, trying to fight panic. "Go tell the Websters to come back in. Hurry!"

Without a word, Vala flew out the door. John and Janet Webster hadn't gone far. Within moments they were back inside the house. After helping lift Ira back onto the davenport and stanching blood that flowed from a gash on the side of his head, John Webster rushed to saddle his horse, promising to return with either Doctor Blickensderfer or Doctor Davis, from Pocatello.

When Webster left the house, Kate turned to Janet and Vala. "I'm going to the ranch." Her voice left no room for argument. "I have to bring the boys back. But I can't leave Ira here. Mrs. Webster, you've been very kind, and I want to thank you for everything. But I'm afraid the man who is after Ira has learned where he is, and they'll come here for him. Vala, run to Sheriff Hess and ask him to try to find a new place for Ira to stay. A place no one knows about. I'll be hitching the team."

The home of Curtis and Annette Selders, on the corner of Shilling and Alice, was a humble one, but the Selders were gracious enough to allow the Winchesters in. And Sheriff Hess himself said he would trust them with his life. So they made plans to carry Ira there in the dark that night, then leave him without anyone knowing except Hess and his deputy, Luke Weaver, and of course the family.

Sheriff Arch Hess never said much during the time new plans were made. It was obvious Kate was distraught over something, but she would tell him nothing. He must have put her fears down to those of an irrational woman, a woman cracking under pressure. Kate said nothing of her plans to go to the ranch. She didn't have time to listen to the sheriff's arguments.

If she kept Bob and Tarnish to a decent clip, it was two hours out to the Winchester ranch by wagon. All the way there Kate could only pray her boys were all right. Between her worry over the boys and over Ira, it was the longest two hours of her life. What if the boys were hurt? She couldn't imagine living without them. Marshal, the strong one—the fighter. Ellis, the loving one—the peacemaker. Both of them were so dear to her. And Ira, her fourth husband, the man who had saved her from the blackest depths of her life . . .

They were still living in Bozeman, Montana when the money ran out. It was her and the three children, and Ellis was only seven years old. All of them were gaunt, especially Kate. She had passed up far too many meals, saving the food for her children.

After Tom was killed, rustlers quietly moved in and cleaned up the ranch. Predators took their toll, too, until the Briggs family didn't have a steer left that Kate could have spotted on a leisurely ride across their land. The neighbors were no help. They had their own problems to deal with. And the Briggs' Diamond B Ranch slowly ceased to exist.

Kate ended up in town with the children, living on what meager savings they had put by over the last two years of struggling with the ranch. She tried to take in washing, but the Chinese had that market cornered. She contemplated opening a sewing business, but she didn't even have the funds to buy needles and thread. It wasn't until the tall blond woman dressed in the red gown trimmed in black lace came to see her that she had her first real chance to make any kind of money that might tide her and her children over and fill their stomachs.

The woman had introduced herself as Lace Hardin, and she discreetly told Kate she had a house in town where women with looks like Kate's could make themselves a healthy living while helping Lace out, too, incidentally. It would, of course, be somewhat uncomfortable in the beginning. But Lace Hardin claimed the profits of this profession were so lucrative she had never hired a woman yet who didn't quickly forget the disagreeable side of her work.

Kate Winchester was a little naïve. But she wasn't so naïve she had to wait for Lace Hardin to tell her exactly what this profession entailed. Without any need to contemplate, Kate had thrown Lace Hardin out. And from then on she and her kids had nothing—less than nothing. But Kate always had her pride, and she had her virtue. There were some things money couldn't buy.

Every day grew worse from the time Lace Hardin walked out the door. It was as if she had cast some spell on the Briggs family. Kate could find no work. She even tried to beg odd jobs for her children to do to bring home a little money for food. All of them had to quit school and scrabble for any way to earn a dime. That, perhaps, was the worst part of all for Kate. As a Quaker, she had grown up knowing how important education was, and it made her sick to see her children going without it.

Kate's clothes sagged from her once beautiful body that had become little more than a covering of skin over bones. The children's eyes became sunken, with dark circles under them that never went away.

And then Ira Winchester rode into town.

From the very first, there was something about the dark haired "Mr. Winchester," as she had called him then. Every other man in town seemed to want her only for what they could get from her immediately. None of them wanted to have anything to do with her children, and it looked like all of the decent men were long since married and raising families of their own. But Ira Winchester was different. Ira Winchester was a gentleman. He was also in mourning.

He had come from North Dakota most recently, running from the memory of a wife and two children swept suddenly away from him by a prairie fire that burned twenty thousand acres of tallgrass before it was through. He had come to Montana looking for good land, land that could be planted, land that could be stocked with cattle. He wasn't interested in another wife, and yet he treated Kate Briggs and her children as if they were saints. He looked after them like nothing was too good for them, like he had nothing in the world better to spend his hard-earned money on than them. Everything Ira did was for her and her kids, even when he told her he didn't know if he could ever leave behind the memory of his dead wife and children. He was so kind, yet he never made advances toward Kate. He never let on that he had any physical desire for her whatever. But somewhere during the time that he decided to take the Briggses under his wing, he and Kathryn fell in love.

She could never forget Ira's loving touch, his soft caresses. He treated her for so long like she would break. Even Tom Briggs didn't have the time to treat her that way, between rounding up and branding and driving cattle to market. Or perhaps he didn't have the instinct. The first time Ira kissed her it was so soft, like a butterfly landing there on her lips, quiet and serene, ready to flit away at the slightest scare. And the first time he took her in his arms he shook like the leaves of October aspen.

Forever, the memory of Ira taking her to his bed the night of their marriage would live with Kate. She had known men—three of them. And they, with the exception of Conn Scarbrough, had had their virtues. But of them all, Ira was the softest, the most gentle. He did nothing without making sure it didn't bother her. He caressed her, kissed her lightly, then passionately, made sure she was satisfied long before he worried about himself. Dan Lauder had been young, too young to fully care about another person. Conn Scarbrough had quickly proved he cared for little more than his own satisfaction. Tom Briggs was a good man, and he took care of her, but he was always tired from working the ranch. And Tom knew little about the intricacies of romance that pleased a woman. Ira was the one who made her feel like a woman, no matter what the cost to him, no matter how worn-out he might be. He was the one who constantly told her how beautiful she was. The one who brought her little things—wildflowers, pretty fabrics—the only things they could afford by the time they had been married a couple of years and were homesteading in near poverty along the Blackfoot River. Until perhaps a year past, in fact, he had been the perfect mate. And then something had changed. And her loving, caring Ira seemed to fade away . . .

Kathryn touched the broach as she thought of Ira and of their good times. But the closer she got to the ranch, the more her thoughts were drawn back to her boys. And the more she thought of those boys in peril, the more spears of anger at Ira stabbed through her heart. How could he let this happen if he cared so much? He loved his family, or she had been convinced he did. What had he done to place them in such danger? Was it something that could send him to prison? She had little doubt of that. If it was, he had to pay. But why should the family suffer? Her anger rose in her breast until it pounded inside, writhed like some living, breathing evil. She wanted to . . . to . . . She didn't know what she wanted. She just wanted to strike out. At Ira? Maybe. To strike out at him for doing something that threatened to destroy their family. They had never raised a violent hand against each other, not even when things had become so bad the morning of the attack, when she had gone to town alone. But they had never before been up against the threat of violence. And she had thought if they ever were they would face it together.

But Kate Winchester was alone.

And not just physically. Of course Ira couldn't be with her now—couldn't defend her. He'd been terribly wounded, scarred for life. But he wasn't with her mentally or emotionally, either. Whatever he was involved in must be wrong, for someone to try to kill him over it. And whatever it was seemed more important to him than their children's lives! More correctly, *her* children's lives.

That realization made her almost sick. Right now it was her children in danger—not his. His only child was safe in Blackfoot, thank Heavens. Kate's stomach churned, her face burned hot, her limbs trembled. At last, the tears came to her eyes, and they rolled down her cheeks without her trying to stanch them. What had become of the Ira Winchester she loved?

Then she saw the smoke.

It rose in a muddy gray cloud at first, chugging into the sky in spurts, and she knew it came from the vicinity of the ranch. What would be burning? The last she had talked to R.M. Sievers, he had said he had some brush he wanted to clear and burn, but the July heat seemed a frightening time to do it. Sievers had seen his share of rolling smoke clouds up in the Blackfoot Mountains and out on the Big Desert west of Blackfoot. It was not an uncommon sight, and always a terrifying one for anyone who lived nearby. Fire was good for the land; it kept the sagebrush down and new grass coming in. But it wasn't good for the cattle caught out there in it! Sievers wasn't foolish. He would take the threat of range fire seriously.

Kate's heart caught in her throat as the wagon drew nearer. She forgot her tears. That smoke was at their place, not the Sievers'! It came now in a heavy black cloud, blotting out a large swathe of sky as it shouldered upward in great, dark humps of soot and gases.

Fear clutched her heart, digging in its icy talons. As she came over the rise and saw the ranch, she gasped in horror. The barn was totally engulfed in fire! She slashed brutally with the ribbons and sent the horses into full gallop, and still it seemed to take ages to cover that last mile and a half. By the time they veered down into the lane, nearly upsetting the rig, the horses were breathing heavily and jerking against their harnesses. They rolled their eyes and balked at passing within a hundred scorching feet of the barn.

Frantically, Kate leaped down from the wagon seat. She stared at the flaming barn and knew nothing could be done to save it. She was thankful Ira had had the foresight to clear the yard of sagebrush. But by the height the burning brands whirled into the air she was afraid some of them would reach the brush anyway.

Kate was in shock. She held up her forearm to guard her face against the blistering heat, watching helplessly as the flames licked out the loft door and caught the eaves. The smell of the smoke burned her nostrils, made her cough violently. She tried to steady the horses by talking to them between coughing, but they continued to fidget and jerk away from her.

Where were the boys? She yelled their names. No answer. She called again, as loudly as she could. The only sound was the pop and crackle of the barn wood as voracious flames consumed it and boards clattered against the inner walls.

With dread gripping her heart, Kate took the reins at Tarnish's mouth and led the horses at a run to the back side of the house; there they would be sheltered from the withering heat. As she ran back around the house toward the well, the heat flung itself against her like a wall of molten lava. It pounded against the front of her house, seeming to cook the side of her face as she ran by. She had the horrible picture of her hair bursting into flames if she got too near the barn. She was thankful for all her petticoats now, for they kept her legs from burning. But not much protected the rest of her.

With a rush of hope, she saw R.M. Sievers gallop into the yard on his horse, a rifle in one hand. His horse screamed in terror. Sievers cringed and ducked, holding up his arm like Kate had done to shield his face as he raced past the licking flames. As he rode toward her, Kate noticed his hat already lying in the yard. She had only the briefest of moments to wonder why he had already been here. Sievers leaped out of the saddle and lost his rifle in the process. He gave his horse a hard slap on the rump, which it really didn't need to send it running, and rushed toward Kate and the well.

Sievers was a lean, wiry man. His face was baked by the sun and wind and creased by forty-five years of struggling with the land. There was no man Kate would have trusted more with her life, and now she almost cried with joy to see him.

Not far after Sievers came a wagonload of settlers. Kate recognized the McLaws, Perkins and Dederscheck families, all of them carrying buckets. No sooner had the wagon swerved up next to the well than they all piled out and began drawing water, throwing it almost frantically at the front of the house. The team and wagon raced away and disappeared beyond Kate's line of sight.

Sievers only glanced fleetingly at Kate and then joined the group, drawing water alongside Kate as fast as he could. The heat blasted against Kate and the others like the insides of a furnace, burning their skin, turning it bright red. It felt as if they would ignite beneath its onslaught.

There wasn't a thing to be done for the barn, so every effort was concentrated on the house. The water that wetted it now rose up in a steady drift of steam from the walls and from the wooden shingles. But the barn fire had begun to die as fuel was consumed.

Kate was thankful there was no wind to carry it on to the dry grass and sagebrush, so vulnerable there in the sun. She worked until she felt she would drop. Her arms and back and shoulders, even her hips ached. But always she found some miraculous strength deep inside.

Sometime during the excitement Susan Sievers showed up. She battled the heat alongside the rest of them, her bodice soon soaked with sweat. Kate had looked for Marshal and Ellis, hoping it was they who had gathered the neighbors and that they would be back with more. But something nagged at her brain: the rifle R.M. Sievers had been carrying, his hat left previously in her yard. And the fact that neither he nor Susan would meet her eyes. Something was wrong.

When Kate finally caught Sievers' eyes again, he deflected his glance toward the barn. The fire was lying down. He glanced at the McLaws, Dederscheck and Perkins children and their parents, so bravely fighting the battle. Then, with a sigh, he dropped his shoulders, and the bucket fell with a clunk from his fingers and rolled away. He and Susan came toward Kate. R.M. had a drawn, scared look that said the loss of the barn meant nothing. He stopped before Kate and grasped her by the right arm with the callused fingers of his left.

"Kate! Ah, Kate. They took the boys!"

Chapter Five

Kate stared at R.M. Sievers. He stood with his head bowed, unable to keep eye contact. The sparse hair on his head that was pale from almost always wearing a hat was sticky with sweat, dust and ashes now. His clothes were wet and smeared with soot.

Behind them, flames still crackled. Now and then a charcoaled board would shift in a pile, causing a flurry of sparks to sail into the air. Dozens of neighbors stood around weary, their faces, hands and clothes blackened. Sometimes they glanced at Kate and at the Sievers, then at each other. Thirteen-year-old Liza Dederscheck was crying, holding onto her mother. No one spoke.

Kate at last drew in a deep, ragged breath. She glanced at Sievers, then at Susan, who stood next to him. Susan, whose blond, red-tinged hair and cotton-blue eyes failed to reveal the Shoshone blood in her, had the face of an angel. In her gentle way she seemed the strongest of them

47

there. She looked at Kate with a soft smile, as if everything would be all right. And looking into Susan's eyes Kate almost believed it.

"There wasn't nothin' you could've done," Sievers offered. His eyes darted to Kate's face and away. He waved his hand absently about the yard. "They all came wearin' masks, wavin' guns. A couple had shot-guns. One of 'em took Ellis an' had 'im up on his horse before anyone could move, an' after that Marshal just did what they said. They didn't say much, Kate, after tellin' 'im to come with 'em. They just rode around the yard a couple times, threw their torches into the hayloft, and then stayed till it was goin' good. It was just me an' McLaws here, an' neither one of us with a gun."

Kate nodded weakly and looked toward the barn. All that work—for nothing. Ira's planning, his labor—his sweat and blood. Only the house and the other outbuildings left to show for it now. She thanked God Siev-ers was able to chase old Ginger, Ira's lame sorrel, out of her stall, before heading back to his own place for his rifle. She also thanked God these people had successfully doused the spot fires that had cropped up in the sagebrush from burning brands. If there had been any wind, the hills would have soon been black as far as the eye could see.

Wearily, Kate sank back against the well housing. She hid her eyes with her right hand and hugged herself about the midsection with her left. Why, God? Why? The barn could be rebuilt. Just a couple hundred more hours of work. Its loss was only an avenue of drawing her mind from darker thoughts. The boys! Where had they taken them? And what did they plan to do with them?

Her self-control went away before she had any warning. She began to sob and pushed away from the well, almost falling into Susan Sievers' ready arms. The tears came like a gush of backed-up water. Kate didn't try to stop them. As Susan Sievers and she held each other tight, Kate felt the woman's husband pat her back a couple of times. Then he walked away toward the others.

Howard McLaws was a stocky man with cheeks so wide they made his gray-flecked mustache look like only a dot above his lip. He looked at R.M. Sievers as he took off his hat and wiped a hand down his sweaty cheek. Sievers swung his eyes over the settlers gathered there, the farm-ers and small ranchers—the newcomers to this land. Last, his eyes met those of McLaws.

"You thinkin' what I am?"

McLaws nodded. "I reckon. This Wolfe's doin', you think?"

Sievers shrugged. "He's been pushin' awful hard for this land—awful hard. An' what're we gonna do? We're not gunfighters. You think the sheriff can help? I wonder. Irving Wolfe's a powerful man around here. Prob'ly owns the sheriff."

"What about the boys?" Keith Perkins asked. Perkins was a handsome man in his mid-thirties whose sly grin and quick sense of humor made him a favorite of everyone whenever they gathered together for social events. "You don't think Wolfe would go so far as to have them killed. Would he?" Perkins's wife, Caroline, and their sons, Michael, Braden, Christian and Hunter, had gathered close to their father.

Sievers bowed his head and let out a long breath. He looked back up, swinging his eyes tiredly about the yard. They came to rest on the last standing timber of the barn. It was only six feet tall now, and a wispy cloud of smoke curled from its upper end, dissipating in the hot afternoon.

"If it's Wolfe, I hope not. But we can't even swear it's Wolfe, an' that's the devil of it."

"If it was Wolfe's men," offered McLaws, looking carefully over the group, "he'll be coming for the rest of our land, too. Whadda we do then?"

"Fight." That was the common answer. Fight. But what if they did fight? R.M. Sievers spat into the dust. He had said it all when he spoke before. These men weren't gunfighters. If they fought, they would die. But maybe Irving Wolfe had decided the West was still wild enough for him to do as he pleased without any repercussions. Maybe they would die even if they didn't fight . . .

At last, Kate calmed herself and dried her tears on her sleeve. Susan Sievers stood before her, waiting patiently and lending her strength. Kate looked into Susan's eyes, and they took each other's hands.

"Thank you so much, Susan. For being here."

Susan smiled, and tears flooded her own eyes as she hugged Kate again. "I know you'd do the same," she replied, stepping away.

They decided Susan would stay with Kate that night, for Kate refused to leave her home unguarded. R.M. wanted to stay, too, but someone had to watch their own family, and reluctantly he returned home.

Kate and Susan sat across from each other at the table that evening, and uncertainty filled the room. Kate had tried to eat, but she had no appetite, and Susan only picked uncomfortably at her meal and watched her friend.

"You have to tell the sheriff, Kate." Her voice had a firm edge. "You can't be bull-headed, not with your children involved."

Kate just stared at her plate, playing endlessly with the cameo broach. It was such a habit now she didn't even know her fingers were there. She couldn't explain why she was being stubborn. She just had a feeling. Something whispered to her not to tell the sheriff. Not to tell him anything. There was no doubt word would reach him eventually, even though she had begged everyone to keep quiet about the kidnapping. But her neighbors didn't make it into town any more often than she normally did, and that might still give her a few days. But a few days for what? She couldn't even answer that question. She just had the gnawing feeling her boys were safer if she didn't run to the law. There was still a chance they wouldn't be harmed.

Kate could think of only one explanation why her boys would be kidnapped. It must be due to whatever Ira had done. If only Ira knew what had happened now! But she had opted not to tell him. Not for now. The men who had taken her boys had taken them for a reason, and that reason was not to kill them. They wanted something, and they would use the boys to get it. Ira? That was the most likely answer. Money? Kate laughed inside. They had none of that, and if that was their goal they had their hands in the wrong purse. The Winchesters' money was all in their cattle and land.

And of course there was the answer. The land. It always returned to that. It was all the Winchesters had and all anyone could want from them. They had never shown any signs of wealth, anything that would lead someone to believe they had money. But Irving Wolfe knew they had land—his land. Kate no longer had any doubt the man would stop at nothing to have it back in his name.

The door swung open, and Kate whirled even before catching the look in Susan's eyes. There in the doorway stood Marshal.

In her haste to rise, Kathryn knocked her chair over. She spoke the boy's name with a rush of gratitude for his safety and hurried to him and threw her arms around him. He responded in kind. As quickly as she had taken him in her arms, Kate pushed herself away, scanning her boy up and down. His blond hair was disheveled, his clothes rumpled and dirty, and a bruise was forming on his right cheek. But otherwise he appeared unharmed. Kate kissed him—on the cheek, on the forehead—then held him to her again. She kept repeating his name over and over, unable to believe he was actually there with her and somehow knowing Ellis must be just outside.

"Ma, they're going to kill Ellis."

It took these words to pull Kate Winchester away from her son. With her hands gripped tight on his shoulders, she shoved him away from her and stared into his eyes, the horror unmasked in her own. She wanted to speak, but her tongue wouldn't move.

But Marshal Briggs was a strong boy, and he had had plenty of time to think about the imminent death of his brother. "They sent me back to tell you if Ira doesn't come to meet them in three days Ellis will die."

Kate felt Susan's hand soft on her shoulder, and she shuddered. Cold fear gripped her heart and seized her limbs. A shadow seemed to fall across the room—a black picture of death marring her family. Taking her loving Ellis away.

Susan Sievers stood silent. All she could do was look from the boy to his mother and wait.

"Marshal . . ." Kate Winchester whispered the name. It came out slightly louder the second time. "Marshal, where are they?"

"I—" The boy stopped and glanced at Susan, then went apologetically on. "I can't tell anyone but you and Ira. They said they'd kill Ellis if anyone else came."

Kate turned to her friend, and Susan must have seen the lost little girl in her eyes, for now she took her hand again.

"Kate, I'm so sorry. I'll leave. You have Marshal to stay with you now."

Kate nodded, overwhelmed by her friendship. As tears flooded her eyes she took the blonde-haired woman in her arms and held her tight. At last, she forced herself to let go, but she said nothing.

Susan just smiled and squeezed her hand. "I'll come back in the morning. First thing." She turned then to Marshal and took him by the arm. "Keep your eyes open, Marshal. We'll come running if you need us. Or you run to us. Be careful."

After Susan was gone, Kate and Marshal sat alone. Marshal told his mother the awful story of his and Ellis's kidnapping, how the boys had both thought they were going to be killed and left for the coyotes.

Four rough men, one of them large and speaking in an accent that was strange to Marshal, took the boys at a gallop up into the Blackfoot Mountains. Every time one of the boys said anything, they were rewarded by a backhand across the face from one of the men. They learned quickly.

The kidnappers took them up along Wolverine Creek, which lay east and north of Blackfoot by a good fifteen miles. They rode into the Narrows, where they originally intended on hiding out in Forty Horse Cave. But when they tried to get their horses up the steep ascent, amid a cloud of dust, a lot of grunting by the horses and swearing by the men, they decided it wasn't worth the trouble. They ended up instead in a narrow little side canyon not far west of Forty Horse Cave, where the little band of kidnappers secreted themselves and the boys in the rudest of camps.

One little man had decided to lord it over the boys, and it was he who had inflicted the most abuse on them. Finally, the big man with the strange accent stepped in and put a stop to it. It wasn't long after that he decided to send Marshal with his message. The closest Marshal came to breaking down was when he had to tell Kate about riding out of the canyon and not knowing if he would ever see his little brother again.

After Marshal had to choke back his tears, talk came to a standstill. He had told his mother most of what happened; there didn't seem much more to say. They stared at the pine table, at the earthen dinnerware with its scarcely touched victuals, at the floor, at the empty windows that showed nothing but the black beyond. Once in a while they would look at each other, but only to quickly look away.

Kate's thoughts tore her apart. What could she do now? She was just a woman, and she knew as well as Marshal did she was helpless in a world of men, at least in their physical realm. Not that this was so for all women. Kate had heard of women—even met a few herself—who stood strong in a world of men. One woman from Missouri excelled in hand-to-hand combat. Several were expert with firearms. Some were just plain tough—in all ways. She had even heard about a Negro woman in some Colorado mining town who had been elected sheriff and ruled the town with an iron fist and with no need to resort to gunplay.

But Kate was not like those women. Sure, she had branded calves, even been kicked by more than a few and survived. She had built fence, and that hardened a woman. She could drive a wagon, haul water, beat the tarnation out of a pan of bread dough. And most of all, she had borne children. But she was, in spite of it all, a woman. Not only a woman, but a lady, she hoped. Neither her hands nor her spirit were made for brawling. Her fingers weren't made to work the mechanisms of a firearm. Her heart wasn't made to fight. She was a peace lover.

Silently, Kathryn Winchester prayed for strength, prayed to keep herself sane. And one thought kept barging in among all the others. Ira couldn't go to her son. He had collapsed that morning without even making it to the door. Besides the blow to the head he took from the coffee table, she had no idea what might be wrong with him internally from the previous assault, or if he was even still alive. He had hit the table hard, and with no doctor immediately available he might very well have died, although she preferred not to entertain that thought. But either way, there was no chance he would recover enough in three days to ride. They had said if anyone else came the boy would die. But if no one came at all he would die, too.

It was Marshal who broke the silence. He cleared his throat and looked at her. His eyes were scared, but his jaw muscles were bunched, and his voice was husky when he spoke. "I don't know if that spot up Wolverine has a name. I'll have to take you there."

Kate allowed a tight smile to move her lips. Her boy wasn't stupid. He knew the two of them had to go.

"Don't tell a soul, Marshal. Absolutely no one. I'll ask Mr. Sievers to ride into town and tell Vala and Cheyenne we're all right out here, and then we'll go. We can't allow the girls to find out anything has happened."

R.M. Sievers raised his voice. "You can't go through with this, Kate." Sievers didn't often get angry, and perhaps he wasn't now. It was more uncertainty and helplessness that filled his voice. Standing in the Winchesters' living room three days later with Susan, Kathryn and Marshal, he swung his eyes away and drew a callused hand across the lower part of his face, as if to draw the tension from it.

Kate watched him and held back a smile. She could sense her friend's frustration. He wanted to protect her. But she couldn't risk her son's life. She had her own way to go, and no one must interfere.

She reached out and touched his sleeve. "I know what I must do. I promise you, I'll be fine."

Sievers raised his eyes and looked at her, the furrows deepening across his brow. His eyes shifted back and forth between hers for a moment, and it was plain he was searching for an argument. At last, he just waved his hand and turned away. He walked into the kitchen area and slumped into a chair, staring out the window at the sagebrush and juniper hills.

Kate looked over at Susan apologetically, then put a hand on Marshal's shoulder, squeezing it. "We'll be fine, Susan."

Kate and Marshal made the dusty trail in silence. They had watched their backtrail for two hours, from up in the junipers north of Dutchman's Curve, where the road ran close to the top of the cliffs along the Blackfoot River. Kate had sat Bob, and Marshal, Tarnish, while the two horses fidgeted, swatting flies with their tails and nipping at each other now and then out of boredom.

Now that they knew no one had trailed them, there was a deep, empty loneliness about the Wolverine Narrows. It was just the two of them, with unknown enemies up ahead. Kate had never dreamed she could call a man her enemy, but stealing her son and threatening to take his life had opened a new place within her chest, a place to be filled with hate.

The Wolverine Narrows was a deep, rocky gorge with walls of ochre and gray rock rearing straight up on both sides, sometimes no more than forty yards apart. Green bushes, trees and grass gave fresh life to the place, in particular abundance on the south side of the road, where in spring gushed Wolverine Creek, a cold mountain stream sometimes ten feet across. Now, in July, the creek was still full but wandered listlessly. Kate had heard of Wolverine before, imagined from Ira's and her sons' descriptions its towering ramparts, deep-slashed crevices and hidden caverns. It had become, the newspaper and word of mouth claimed, quite a spot for families to come to get away from town. She had planned to come here one day herself—perhaps for a picnic, perhaps just to see the spectacular sights.

She could never have dreamed she would come here for this.

Kate felt no need for conversation, and Marshal must have agreed. He scanned the rocks around them, his eyes full of the same awe she felt at this mysterious canyon. The constricting cliffs fell quickly behind them, leaving only the creek gurgling along nearby, shaded by chokecherries and red birch. But even out of the maw of the close-hugging, sharp cliffs, both sides of the road boasted impressive stone masses farther back, rocks broken and jumbled in heaps or upheaved and grinding battered knuckles into the sky. Natural bouquets of white chokecherry blossoms lined the sides of the trail, especially along the creek, and the service-berry bushes already sported hard green fruit. Along the hills grew juniper and sagebrush, whose scent mingled with the soft perfume of willow. On their right, matted Douglas fir banded together in scattered ranks, as it did along the ridgeline to their left, mingled with the olive-white trunks and whispering deep green leaves of quaking aspen.

Kate sensed her son's horse beginning to slow, and she checked Bob's speed to match. She looked over at Marshal, whose eyes were fixed on a branch canyon ahead and to their left. His eyes flickered meaningfully her way, then back to that canyon, where they remained until he reined his horse to a stop.

Kate's heart thudded against the wall of her chest, and each beat seemed louder, faster. She drew in beside her boy. He didn't need to tell her where the trail would take them. Fear enshrouded her like a cold grave. What was she doing here? She was a peace-loving woman—the daughter of Quakers. She had never had anything to do with death, at least not violent death, in all of her childhood. So why, the moment she walked away from home, it seemed, was she bombarded with it at every turn? Was it God's way of telling her she had made a mistake in leaving Pennsylvania, leaving home?

First, Shiloh, and her young husband, Dan Lauder. Dead at the age of twenty. Then her second husband, Conn Scarborough, gunned down while "bucking the tiger" at a faro table in Abilene, Kansas. Granted, he had been a drunk and abusive both mentally and physically. But he had been her financial support—protection from becoming something neither her religion nor her heart could abide. And then there was Tom. Soft-spoken, determined Tom Briggs, with hands that were scaly with calluses and a heart soft as beaver fur. They had had such far-reaching dreams. Such a beautiful family and ranch. And then the bloody vulture of death swooped again, and Tom was gone—shot down like the other two.

Kate couldn't help but believe she had done something wrong, committed some unpardonable sin in her youth. She felt she lead a righteous life. She tried to be humble. She prayed to have faith. But somewhere all this killing had to stop, or she didn't know how she could go on. Somehow she had to find out, once and for all, what real peace meant. Its distant, shadowy image swam always one length ahead of her, elusive in the dark currents of her life.

Marshal reined his horse past Kate and started up the smaller canyon, and Kate fell in behind him. She watched the way he sat the saddle, the wary way he scanned the canyon sides around them. Marshal was only a boy. Fear must perch tightly on top of his heart like it did on hers. But he didn't show it on the outside, and his strength made her proud.

From up the canyon, a three-foot-wide creek ran down to cross the road and join Wolverine Creek. It was a tight little canyon packed with junipers and big gray rocks jutting out of the earth. Along the right side were shale slides dotted with grass and brush, and along the left grew chokecherries and fir, making the canyon seem serene.

The sudden blast of a rifle shot racketed back and forth across the canyon, causing both their horses to swing their heads and saw against the bits, trying to back down the trail or turn and break. They held them in check, and Kate turned her head as she heard rocks rolling down the slope to her right.

Two men wearing bandannas up to their eyes came down the hillside, pistols drawn. A quick glance revealed another perched on a boulder midway up the ridge, his rifle covering Kate and Marshal.

Brush crackling to the left drew their attention that way, and they saw a big man duck to brush past a juniper, slip on a loose rock and almost fall. He only saved himself by reacting quickly enough to grasp a branch. Kate instantly regretted seeing that and having him know she had seen it. The embarrassment couldn't be good for his mood.

The big man, his face also hidden, behind a mask of blue calico, stopped in front of Marshal and looked from him to Kate, his eyes narrowing dangerously.

"You little pup! I told you only Ira Winchester was to come. What is this?"

Marshal snapped a glance back toward Kate, whose motherly instinct took over when she saw the fear that filled his eyes. Her eyes flashed toward "Calico."

"I would appreciate you talking civilly. And please—don't talk to the young man at all. I'm the one you want to see." Her dark eyes bored through the man, whose pistol swung loose in his hand. Kate didn't feel the strength she tried to show. Her insides were bound in knots of fear. But no one would talk to her boy that way.

The two men who had come down the hillside came to a halt beside Kate and Marshal's horses as Calico stared at Kate for a moment, his eyes narrowing still further. Then he laughed, a noise beginning deep in his throat and ending in a high-pitched humph. "All right, lady. I'll talk to you. And you just may be the one I want to see." Brazenly, his eyes scanned her body. "But yer sure not the one I was told to see. Now both of you—" His eyes turned hard. "Get off the horses."

Kate could see in Calico's cold, slate-colored eyes that he was not to be trifled with. Marshal almost fell from Tarnish in his haste to dismount. With deliberate care, Kate slipped from Bob and held firmly to his reins, turning her eyes to the big man and trying to meet his gaze steadily but without challenge. She didn't wait for the big man to speak again.

"My son brought your message—exactly as you sent it. But thanks to—I presume you—Ira Winchester wasn't able to leave his bed. He's still unconscious. So I came in his place. What is it you want?"

The big man emitted a laugh—a dirty, evil sound behind his mask. "We won't discuss that with all these ears around. But what I'm directed to ask for is a confab with Ira Winchester. And if I can't get it—a certain boy is to die. Understand?"

A shiver ran along Kate's spine, and her scalp tingled. Who was this man? What was he capable of? Murder? Of a helpless boy? Her mind raced. She tried to place this voice, this hulking form. The accent was undoubtedly from New York, though faded by a lengthy sojourn elsewhere. The voice meant nothing else to her. So he must be a stranger. A New York accent in Blackfoot would have stuck in the memory of a Pennsylvania girl.

"I understand what you're saying." Kate forced herself to sound calm. "But if my boy dies Ira Winchester won't come."

One of the other men suddenly stepped forward, grabbing Marshal by the neck and shoving him roughly to the ground, pointing his pistol at the back of his neck. The man's eyes turned back darkly to Kate, obscured between his hat brim and bandanna mask. "So what if we kill this one and keep the other one? Will that bring Winchester to see us?"

Kate took a step forward, then stopped herself. She stared at the man with the gun, then swiveled her eyes to the big man again. She was a proud woman, but she knew her eyes were pleading, and she couldn't help it.

The big man turned his head toward the other and growled, "All right, let 'im up! We've already seen what you can do to boys."

A grudging gratitude rushed through Kathryn, but she kept it to herself and turned again to the smaller man. So he was the one who had bruised her boy, the brutal one Marshal had told her about. She gazed him up and down, concentrating to settle every detail of his body and clothing in her head. His holster had a star stamped on it, with one on each boot to match.

As "Star" stepped back, Marshal pushed to his feet, forcing himself not to look at anyone. He just stared at the ground. *Good boy,* thought Kate. He knew he was the vulnerable one here. Only a brute would harm a woman, but Marshal was a big enough boy to draw their punishment— deserved or not.

"Where's my other son?" Kate directed her query toward Calico, who was obviously in control here.

By the sudden twist of the big man's bandanna, she could tell he smiled. He jerked his finger toward the matted junipers behind him. "He's up there. Safe and sound. When Ira Winchester comes, you can see 'im. See 'im, heck! You can even have 'im back. Him and maybe his teeth—in a can."

That vision caused nausea to rise in Kate's stomach. "I would think you were a big enough man without trying to scare helpless people."

Calico's eyes widened. He started to step forward then stopped. "Don't even bring that boy close to here!" he growled at the man next to him. His slate eyes turned immediately back to Kate. "You send the man, you can see the boy."

Kate stood frozen for a moment. She had only one chance, and she meant to take it. "I want proof he's alive. You show me the boy—I'll send the man."

Even as she spoke, Kate's eyes were drawn inexplicably to Star, the man who had pushed Marshal down. His nervous glance had flickered to the big man, taking on a hint of fear. When she saw that, Kathryn's heart also filled with fear. Maybe these men couldn't prove Ellis was alive. Maybe he wasn't.

Chapter Six

Kathryn stared at Star, her face a mask. Her eyes darted back to Calico, who still watched her, calculatingly. "You're not in much of a position to give me orders, woman. The way you talk, a man would think you had us surrounded."

Kate could think of no reply. What possible response could a Quaker woman raise for this common ruffian? A harsh, inhuman criminal who held a loved one's life in his hands—unless he had already taken it. She ended up just staring into his eyes, trying to mask her fear with a challenge.

"What do we do?" It was Star's voice. A hint of uncertainty in it lent further ammunition to Kate's horrified imaginings. Had they indeed killed her boy?

Calico's growl belayed her fears. "Just go get 'im. What are you afraid of?"

The smaller man eyed him for a long moment then turned and walked into the junipers, trying to show his independence through slow, deliberate movements.

Half a minute later, Star returned. Ellis was in front of him, his face and neck wreathed in bruises. Both eyes were black, and scabbed blood marked a spot where his lips had been split, but he still managed a feeble smile when he saw Kate and Marshal.

"Ellis!"

Without permission from the kidnappers, Kate dropped Bob's reins and ran to him. She threw her arms about him and hugged him to her, and for several seconds there was silence. Finally, Calico spoke up.

"All right, that's enough. Now step away from 'im, woman. You've seen 'im, and that's more than I was told t' let you do."

Kate pushed away from Ellis, holding him by the shoulders. Her eyes searched him up and down, then snapped to the big man. For a long moment she studied his eyes, then swung hers back to Ellis. She didn't know why, but she knew the big man wasn't the type to do any of this to her boy. Even without Marshal telling her, she would have known it was all Star. Perhaps it was the reason he had seemed so worried to let her see the boy. She turned slowly to Star, one hand still on Ellis's shoulder. Her voice came out cold and steady, nothing like she felt.

"You're a very brave man—when it comes to boys."

Star's eyes narrowed. "I'd like to've killed him. He's got a smart mouth."

"And I'm sure you don't," she said acidly. "I hope you feel big, for such a little man." Kate's eyes snapped against the man like a quirt. He met her gaze for a second, then swung his eyes away to the third man, who stood near Marshal.

Calico's throat erupted with a laugh, puffing out the front of his bandanna. "All right, ma'am. You've seen the boy." The exchange of the word woman for ma'am surprised Kate. Had his estimation of her grown? "Now I'll tell you this," he continued. "You've crossed me once, and I'll give you that one. Because you're a tough lady, 'n' I like that. But I have orders, an' I already went against 'em once. You send the man next time. Or I'll let these wolves take care of your kid. It's that simple. Just send the man."

The last sentence came to her more as a friendly caution than as an order. It was something in the tone of voice, a softening of the eyes. But as quickly as Kate caught it, it was gone, and the growl returned. "Now get out of here, and I don't wanna see you back. I *don't* wanna see you back. Next time it's just the boy and Ira Winchester. If it's you, you'll hear just one shot, back in those trees. Then the boy's all yours to do with as you like. Ten days, ma'am, an' your man should be healed enough to ride. Boy?" He turned toward Marshal. "You bring 'im here and wait for us. Ten o'clock at night next time. If there's anyone else with you, you won't get another chance."

Marshal nodded, his eyes darting toward Kate, who forced a brave smile.

Kate had the presence of mind to look the rest of them over before turning toward Marshal and her horse. Besides Calico and Star, there were just the two others, the one who had fired the rifle and the nervous man who had come down the hill with Star. He wore a black slouch hat, California plaid pants, and a bright red neckerchief that hung nearly to his waist.

Kate turned her eyes back to Ellis, unable to hide the worry in them. He tried to wink, and she could tell that hurt him, but not as much as his lopsided smile did, twisting the bruises and scabs on his face. She reached out and placed a gloved hand on his cheek.

"Ira will come, Ellis. Don't you worry. You'll be home before you know it."

"I know he will, Mama. I'm not worried." The boy tried to stand a little straighter, and tears pooled in both their eyes. Kate stepped forward and kissed him softly on the cheek, then turned and started stiffly toward her horse.

As she passed Calico, the big man reached out and grabbed her by the wrist, his grip powerful. He turned her to face him and let his eyes pass boldly over her. "You better hope Ira Winchester's strong enough to hold you, woman. When this is all over, I might just pay a visit."

Kate forced herself to meet his eyes, the stench of his unwashed body reaching her across the still July air. She should be scared of him, she knew. He meant to kill her husband if he could. He hadn't said it, but she was no fool. They had tried to kill him once, and there was no reason they wouldn't again. Still, for all the man's size and strong talk, he didn't scare her, at least in regards to herself. But as for his threats toward Ellis, she believed them. Calico would kill the boy—or have it done. He would go through with what he was here for. That hard truth shone in his slate-colored eyes.

With a firm, steady pull Kate drew her arm away from the big man, and he dropped his hand back to his side. "Go on, get out of here." His tone was subdued now, but raised again when he turned to Marshal and jabbed a blunt finger toward his chest. "Remember, boy. Ten days. Ten o'clock at night. Just you and Ira Winchester."

Kate finally cried as they rode out of the Narrows. It took the fifteen minutes of riding through the gorge for the tears to fight their way past her eyelids. Before that there was no talk. Marshal tried to be brave. He sat tall and straight in the saddle, glancing now and then at her. But he must have been hurting like she was, and no words could struggle past the tightness in his throat even if he wanted them to.

It felt good to cry. It started as silent tears coursing in rivulets down her cheeks, across her jaw, making dark splotches on her gray-blue riding habit. And it felt even better when she relaxed and stopped fighting the tears. She didn't want Marshal to see her like this, but he was here, the tears had won, and there was no sense hiding it now.

When she began to sob, Bob flicked his ears and tried to look back at her from the corners of his eyes. He shook his head and swished his tail. She fixed her eyes straight ahead and let him pick his speed and follow the road on his own. She couldn't see to direct him anyway. She didn't look toward Marshal. She just cried and prayed quietly and let the tears wash down her cheeks in torrents. *God, please don't let Ellis die,* she whispered in her head. *Please, please, please. Three husbands, and now perhaps another—and a son? What have I done? Why did You forget me? Why hast Thou forsaken me?* The Bible quotation slipped into her head like part of a jigsaw puzzle, a piece that fit so perfectly she couldn't deny it. Was this how the Savior had felt? All alone? Forgotten? Small? *Please, God, spare my son.* She imagined her words lifting off toward Heaven, then slowing, slowing, turning to mist, finally burning away long before they neared the throne.

They sat in the home of John and Janet Webster, silent, unmoving. The Websters had already retired. Ira lay in bed at the Selders' home, but Kate, not wanting to draw attention there, had chosen to leave herself and the children at the mercy of the Websters, who had been so kind to them. They sat about the room, stared at the walls, at the floor, at the furniture—at anything but each other. When one of them did look at another and was caught, they glanced quickly away.

Marshal didn't cry. Tears weren't his way. He just stared, his eyes unmoving—a statue. A statue full of pain and anger and fear that couldn't release itself because fate had chosen him to be a rock. Rocks lay quiet, full of sleeping energy. They were hard, cold when exposed to cold, hot when exposed to heat. But when they came loose, they flew with unstoppable fury, with power to crush whatever lay in their path. That was Marshal. Or it would be when he was old enough to meet his destiny.

Kate was sorry for her oldest son. At least her other children could release their emotions, and they had—all evening and into this night. All

Marshal could do was steam and be silent. Even as she thought that, his eyes turned to her, and his lips moved slowly.

"Ma? You need to buy a rifle."

For a long moment, Kate just stared at her boy, and so did Vala. Cheyenne looked from one to the other of them, lost in her own innocence.

Kate searched for words. Marshal knew how she felt about guns. He knew how she felt about killing. It wasn't man's place to kill—only God must take that responsibility. Her children weren't Quakers, and neither was she, anymore. But she held to certain principles with which she'd been indoctrinated, and she had raised her children to these beliefs. With Ira, it had been easy. He didn't even hunt anymore.

When Kate made no response, Marshal cleared his throat. "Did you hear me? You've gotta buy a gun. We have to defend ourselves."

"We already have a rifle," Kate said halfheartedly.

"That's no rifle, ma! That old thing is rusted up and ready to fall apart. It doesn't even shoot cartridges anyway. I've seen Mr. Perkins load an old one like that of theirs, and you'd be dead before you could fire a second shot."

"Marshal . . ." Kate tilted her head to one side, letting her disappointment seep into her eyes. "I know that rifle isn't much good, but you know how I feel about guns."

"Damnit, Ma!" He had anticipated her answer, and he sprang to his feet and glared at her across the little room. "Open your eyes! We're defenseless. You think they won't come back? Even if Ira doesn't go meet them, they'll come and find him. They'll kill Ellis, and then they'll kill Ira!"

Kate stood up, trying to hide her disappointment. "I taught you better than to curse."

Marshal met her gaze challengingly then dropped his eyes at last. "I'm sorry, Ma."

Kate sighed. "Son, guns kill people. It's not our place to kill. Even if we wanted to, I can't use a gun. Can you?"

Marshal shrugged and avoided looking directly at her. "Well, sure. I've gone rabbit hunting a couple times with some friends."

Kate was surprised by that revelation. "So you have used a gun once or twice. But, Marshal, how do you think you can fight those men? They get paid to use guns."

Marshal blew a disgusted breath out of his nostrils and stared into Kate's eyes for a moment. "Oh, to hell with it," he said angrily. He turned and left the house, slamming the door behind.

Vala and Cheyenne turned shocked eyes to their mother, and she met their glance. "Stay here, girls. I'll go get him."

But on the street Marshal was not in sight. Kate wore no shawl, no jacket, and a cool night breeze rushed along the street and tugged at her insistently. Folding her arms against the chill, she looked up and down the street, guessing Marshal must have dashed between some buildings or through a vacant lot.

Marshal's disappearance left Kate no reason to remain outside, and she turned toward the door. Then she paused. She didn't want to go in yet. She didn't want to face other hurt eyes, other lost voices. She just wanted to be alone and think—or be alone and not think, just let her mind drift away and leave her like a statue here, staring at the dim lights along the street and the stars sprinkled like distant lamp-lit windows across the sky.

She turned absently and found her way to the bench at the front of the house. She sank into it with a sigh, closing her tired eyes.

When she opened them, they fell as if by design on the dark windows of the Idaho Trading General Merchandise store kitty-corner across the street. There was no gunshop in town. Blackfoot wasn't large enough to support one. But the merchandise store and Henry Curtis's hardware store served the purpose, housing a considerable collection of firearms and weapons of all kinds.

There were plenty of other items in the stores, of course. But most intriguing, because they were so foreign to Kate, were the guns. They lay in their finger-smeared glass case, in all their assorted makes and varieties. She didn't know any of the names—except for Colt, and, of course, Winchester. That one had been drilled into her head, as well as anyone else's who had ever set foot on American soil—or in a score of foreign countries. And her recognition wasn't just due to the association with her own name. No, the Winchester was the "Gun that won the West," they said. With a Winchester rifle and a Colt's revolver, it was said a man could face any odds—*except maybe several other men with Winchester rifles and Colt's revolvers,* she thought wryly.

Kate drew a deep breath and let it out as she squeezed herself tighter around the midriff. She couldn't lie to herself like she might to others. Marshal wasn't the only one whose thoughts had turned to guns. In spite of all her preaching, and her beliefs that used to be so firm, guns had crossed her mind once or twice—no, that was a lie. They had crossed her mind numerous times since the attack on Ira. She was so helpless, so small in the face of the odds against her.

But she would be helpless with a gun, too. It would just be something they could take away and use against her, for she didn't think she could shoot a living thing with it.

Final memories of her third husband, Tom Briggs, flashed violently across her mind. Splashes of orange light in the dark; rotten egg smoke hurled against her senses by the night wind. Tom crying out, choking, bleeding on her hands and on the porch. Dying in her arms.

Conn Scarborough, her second husband, and Dan Lauder, her first, had died by the gun, too. But Conn had died away from home, in a gambling hall, and was carried to her on a board. And Dan had died amid the thunder of guns, among the blue and gray rush of sweat-soaked men and boys grunting with exertion and fear, dying to relieve themselves of their pain and exhaustion. But that was war, and they were soldiers. Soldiers were expected to die.

The reason Tom's death stood so clearly in her memory was the vivid scene born out in front of her very eyes. She would never forget that August night outside of Bozeman, Montana. The year was 1878, and they had just made five thousand dollars in a cattle deal . . .

Kelly Doyle and his brother owned a ranch right next to the Briggs spread. She never knew the brother's real name; everyone just called him Tracker. The Doyles were usually friendly enough when sober, but pure hellraisers when drunk.

They had had a run-in with Tom over the cattle sale that afternoon. They claimed one of the calves he'd sold was theirs and demanded payment. It only ended when Tom knocked Kelly to the ground.

It had been a long day, and the children went to bed early. That evening, at dusk, Kate heard the faint sound of hooves drumming in the road that led to the house. Looking out upon the hazy lane, she couldn't tell who was riding, but she could see there were two of them.

When she told Tom riders were coming, he pulled her roughly away from the window and ordered her to stay low, then blew the lamp and went to stand just outside the door. Kate went back to the window.

From there, she remembered the conversation as if it had been only minutes ago.

"Who's that?" Tom spoke over the steady chirp of crickets.

"That you, Briggs?" came a friendly sounding voice.

"Yeah. Is that Tracker?"

"Sure is."

"Is Kelly with you?"

"I'm here," came the slurred answer.

Tom's face set in hard lines, and Kate's heart jumped when he touched the butt of his belt gun.

"I think you lost a cow," Kelly Doyle bellowed.

Tom sighed and waited several seconds. "What cow, Kelly?"

"I dunno." Kelly laughed, a crazy sound, and Tracker fired from the saddle, an orange flash jumping from the muzzle of his gun. Tom went down, groping for his pistol, as Kate ran to the doorway and smelled the acrid smoke whirl around her.

Kelly was off his horse and running for the house, laughing crazily, and Tracker warned him back and fought his frightened horse. He fired another round toward Tom. The bullet whined past Kate like an angry bee and thunked into the back wall. More powder smoke—tickling her nostrils, stinging her eyes.

She screamed.

Tom fired twice from a kneeling position, and Kelly crumpled to the ground. They found later he'd died instantly, a bullet through the forehead.

Tracker Doyle was sliding from his saddle when Tom shot him in the back, and for the next two hours they listened to the slowly weakening sound of his voice pleading from the yard. With a bullet in his liver, Tom couldn't walk to Tracker. And Kate didn't care to. An hour later the crying ceased, and they knew there was no need.

The next morning, at the breaking of a beautiful golden sunrise, Tom Briggs died . . .

It all left a cold, vivid picture in Kate's head. The man she had loved, dead. Lifeless like a pile of corn stalks, to be carried away, disposed of. Nothing had saved him. Not luck, not fate, not a guardian angel . . . not even God. And not the pistol he had always carried on his hip.

Yet it had given him a chance.

And now, thinking back on it, Kate couldn't help but think that pistol—and Tom's skill with it—had saved her life, and perhaps the children's, even if his own had been taken away.

But there was that one word, and that word meant everything.

Skill.

She didn't have it, Marshal didn't have it. And there was no one else. Even if Ira recovered, he had no skill with a gun, either. He never had. He had never been in any of the battles of the war, never fired a shot at another human being, and had given up hunting years ago. At best, his gunmanship was rusty. At worst, it was worthless.

Kate suddenly slammed her eyes shut and covered them with her tightened fists, bending forward to place her elbows on her thighs. She gritted her teeth, trying to will all thought of guns away from her mind. She just couldn't give in. She wasn't the kind to own a gun. Guns were foreign to her, and they always would be.

Kate thought suddenly of Blackfoot's new insane asylum, which had just opened its doors on the second of July. An impressive brick building three stories high, Kate had felt an inexplicable fear the first time she looked on the place. Already they had twenty-six male patients and ten women they had brought in from Salem. If things continued on as they were, it wasn't going to be long before they had eleven women! Kate smiled tiredly at that ludicrous thought. In truth, she might not have been the strongest woman alive, but she knew her mind would never let go of reality.

At last she returned to the house, and the lamp had gone out. Vala was asleep on the davenport, as was Cheyenne, with her head cradled against her sister's shoulder. Kate carefully laid a blanket over the two of them, then picked up one for herself and returned to the porch, wondering what had become of Marshal.

Her son had disappeared before, and she had never worried much, after the first few times. He went to walk, to think, to pull himself together. Only this time it was different. Now there were those about who would use him against Ira. She didn't think there was any danger of that while Ellis was being held hostage, but she didn't know anything for certain anymore.

Wrapping the blanket around herself, Kate sat down on the bench and watched the quiet, starlit street. A sliver of moon rode high in the sky, but it didn't give much light. Just a mysterious silver sickle, waiting in the dark for day to come and banish it.

She thought of Ellis, out there with those hard men, lonely and cold. Then she forced the picture from her thoughts. She had to in order to stay sane.

Staring at the Idaho Trading store, Kate dozed off, and her chin dropping against her chest woke her up. All the houses were dark now. Shadows blanketed the town. And from these shadows across the way came Marshal Briggs, his face apologetic, and all the more so when he saw her sitting there waiting for him.

Even when Marshal had gone off to bed, Kate remained outside. Her cheeks felt stiff now, and her lower legs, too, where the night air made its way up her dress from below.

She was thinking of Ellis and Ira and the other children, and out of the darkness came the answer for which she had been searching. She might save Ira's life and Ellis's—maybe all of theirs—before this nightmare was over. It was simple. Money talked, and land was money. All she had to do was reach the rancher, Irving Wolfe, while there was still time. If Ira had stolen from him, there was a way to pay it back. If he had tried to kill him only as a way to gain the Winchester land, the answer was the same. It was an answer that would break Kate Winchester apart. Their dream would be gone, and the Winchester family would be left without a home. But she had no choice.

She would sell Irving Wolfe their land.

Chapter Seven

Kate Winchester hadn't been much for riding horses in the last several years. But today she chose that mode of travel for its speed. She put on bloomers instead of her petticoats, slipped on a split riding skirt, and rode Bob seated astride. She wouldn't have even thought of sitting astride a horse to go to town or to anyone for whom she had any respect. But Irving Wolfe was not someone she respected.

It wasn't yet eight o'clock when they approached the Twin Wolfe Ranch.

Kate had never had reason to go to Irving Wolfe's ranch headquarters, though it was a mere mile up the Blackfoot River. She had seen it the once, in passing by on the way to Wolverine to meet the kidnappers, but there had never been a reason to go any nearer than that.

Compared to the Winchester homestead, the Twin Wolfe headquarters, set fifteen feet below the road grade among its cluster of fruit trees, was a mansion. It sat in the same beautiful valley of the Blackfoot River as the Winchester place, and from the turnoff she could see the course of the river snaking along through the expanse of good pastureland. Its sparkling waters were visible only in one place, two hundred yards or so beyond the back of the house.

Along both sides of the lane leading to the house grew a row of cottonwoods. They stood fifteen feet tall, lending the final approach to the ranch headquarters a shadowed stateliness. The peach, apple, cherry and plum trees added their own elegant touch, shading the decorative three-foot-high rock wall that ran fifty feet to left and right, twenty yards from the front of the house. A flagstone path led from the rock wall right up to the house. It all gave the meadow estate a secluded feel, with the Blackfoot Range's shoulders hovering over it.

As for the house itself, it was built in southern style, three stories high, counting its attic, with the ground floor far taller than that of any house Kate had ever lived in. Four gray-painted steps ran up to the fully surrounding portico, sporting a balustrade whose rails were dark gray, with white balusters. The six grooved columns supporting the verandah and iron-railed balcony above it were also painted dark gray. They perfectly contrasted the house's immaculate white walls, which took on a cloud-like glow in the early morning sun. Above it all slanted a gray hip roof. Kate could never have dreamed of having a tenth of the windows in her house that the Wolfe house flaunted. The outbuildings and corrals, which sat off to the right of the house, weren't much less impressive, all of them built of the best wood and painted white, standing like a fortress against the sun's slanting rays.

Irving Wolfe had made his money through investments in transportation and express companies, mostly stagecoach lines. He had since detached himself from those businesses to put everything he had into his ranch. If the residence was any indication, it was apparent he had taken out his money while stakes were high. One thing the Wolfe ranch did not lack was opulence.

Harvey Manfred, the bone-thin ranch hand whose nose looked like a Brazil nut stuck to the side of a dried apple, swaggered toward her from one of the barns. He wore a narrow-brimmed hat hanging over his eyes, a useless attempt, along with a half-layer of thin, fine brown hair, to hide over-large ears. Manfred looked Kate up and down as the tip of his tongue came out beneath a bristly mustache and rested against his lower lip.

"Can I help you?" he asked. In spite of the courteous words, he had an obnoxiously teasing set to his round, dark brown eyes.

"I came to see Mr. Wolfe."

He tugged the battered gray hat from his head to scratch a thinning hairline and replaced it just as quickly. "He prob'ly ain't even up yet. What's the problem with talking to me?"

Kate raised an eyebrow. "You're the one who suggested there was a problem with it."

Before Manfred could think to offer any help, she slipped off the saddle and landed lightly on the ground, holding her reins in a gloved hand. Manfred stood leering at her, a half-grin on his face like he wanted to make some joking remark but wasn't bright enough to think of any. Finally, he shrugged and jerked a thumb toward the pillared house.

"Like I said, I ain't sure Wolfe's even awake, but I know he's still inside. Let me give you a hint: he doesn't like to be bothered this early in the morning. But if it'll make your day any better, I'll go get 'im."

"I'm certain it won't make my day better," replied Kate with a cool glance. "But then pulling a thorn out of one's heel doesn't necessarily feel good—it's just something that has to be done."

Manfred stared at her stupidly, the analogy apparently lost on him. With an upward tilt of his chin as his only reply, the man turned and swaggered up into the house. After a few minutes, he returned to where Kate stood at the front porch. "Mr. Wolfe was in his robe. He'll be out in a minute."

Accepting Manfred's information with a nod, Kate asked, "Where may I water my horse?"

Manfred led her around to the watering trough, swallowing his pride enough to pump the water for her. She watched him and wondered why his rail-thin arms didn't break in doing it. When they walked back around the house, Irving Wolfe was stepping out onto the porch, his eyes full of sleep. He had tried to slick back his dark, thinning hair, but one strand poked stubbornly out to the side.

"Mrs. Winchester! What on earth brings you out at this ungodly hour?" He dabbed at his prim mustache with two fingertips. Then, before she could reply, he waved his hand peremptorily. "Never mind, never mind. I forget my manners so early in the day. Won't you please come inside for a cup of coffee? Or tea, if you prefer? Perhaps a biscuit?"

Looking up at him on the porch, Kate shook her head as she wrapped Bob's reins twice around the hitch rail. "I have no wish to accept your hospitality, Mr. Wolfe. I came only to make you an offer. If you will promise to leave my husband alone and set my son free, I will sell you our land."

Aside from the sparrows screeching out their morning gossip in the fruit trees there was no other sound. Wolfe just stared at her, and Manfred glanced with unbelieving eyes back and forth between the two of them. Wolfe seemed about to bluster a reply when his wife, Judith, a tired looking woman in her early forties, with freshly combed stringy blond hair, stepped onto the porch. Her puzzled eyes went from Wolfe to Kathryn. Their son, Arthur, stood beside her, his face dusted by its normal pallor.

"Why, hello, Mrs. Winchester." A question in Judith Wolfe's eyes remained unspoken.

Irving Wolfe stepped suddenly off the porch and strode to within four feet of Kate before coming to an abrupt halt. "I find serious offense in your words, Mrs. Winchester. I realize you are under a great deal of stress, and I will make allowances for that. But please . . . Mrs. Winchester, do come inside. It is imperative that we talk."

Kate's eyes flickered toward Judith. She felt sorry for the woman. Judith was a quiet person, a reserved melancholy locked in her green eyes. She didn't associate with other women much, was never seen at church or social or civic gatherings. It seemed a sad life she lived, to be imprisoned here with a man of Wolfe's overbearing character. Kate didn't think the woman deserved it. And Arthur, that poor boy. It couldn't be a healthy existence for him. He looked over-protected, seldom permitted to venture out into the sunlight.

Her sympathy quickly burned away beneath stronger emotions as Kathryn turned her eyes back on Irving Wolfe. "I will not be bullied, Mr. Wolfe. I have met with your henchmen. They treated me and my sons like common trash. But they will not intimidate me, nor will you. What are your terms for the land?"

Wolfe's face hardened into angry lines. "Mrs. Winchester, I refuse to talk to you while you are in this accusing state of mind. If you would like to sit down to a polite cup of coffee with me and Judith and discuss our differences like adults, my house is open to you. I hold nothing against you and your kind for buying land that is rightfully mine and was placed open for purchase without my knowledge. But I will not be accused of being a villain in front of my wife and hired help."

Under her cold exterior, an almost paralyzing fear built in Kate's heart. She feared she would lose this chance to ransom her son and her husband, if this was even a chance at all. Yet she couldn't let her fear show. Wolfe's demeanor was convincing, but she had no doubt he was responsible for the attack on Ira. And Kate knew it was his orders that held her son captive. But how could she prove any of it? And what if he tired of her accusations and had Ellis killed out of spite?

"What if we just give the land to you?" she said on a whim. "Will that save Ira and Ellis's lives?"

"Madam, I cannot help you," said Wolfe in an angry tone.

Clenching her teeth, Kate choked back a rush of hot tears. "So you refuse to release my son?"

"Mrs. Winchester, I'm afraid I must insist that you leave my property." Wolfe shook an angry finger toward the road above. "I suggest that you go see the sheriff. Come back when you are in a rational state of mind, but be gone with you now." He turned to his hired man. "Harvey, see that Mrs. Winchester is escorted safely off the property. Immediately." With that, he turned on his heel and stalked into the house, leaving the door open behind him. Judith tried to meet Kathryn's gaze but failed. She put a hand to Arthur's shoulder and meekly followed her husband inside, nudging the door closed.

With tears burning her eyes, Kate fumbled with Bob's reins until they fell loose from the hitching post. Whirling as Harvey Manfred came toward her, she climbed into her saddle with Bob as a shield between them. Manfred stepped up beside her right leg. He looked up uncertainly, and she raised one hand to straighten her hat, which didn't need straightening. "I know my own way off this ranch, thank you."

Before the hired hand could see her tears, Kate whirled the horse and flicked him with the reins, putting him into a trot toward the cottonwood corridor.

The more the exchange with Wolfe ate at her, the more furious Kate became—and the more frantic. An unquenchable hatred burned within her, a hatred for Irving Wolfe and all of his men. If she had a gun right then . . . Her anger got the better of her, and as she reached the main road she put the big bay into a gallop, leaving the Twin Wolfe headquarters behind.

Kate rode hard for half a mile toward home before slowing down. She kept Bob, who was blowing excitedly out his nostrils, at an easy jaunt for another two hundred yards before spotting riders in the road ahead.

Pressing a gloved knuckle to her eyes to dry them, Kate slowed the horse to a walk, patting her hair to straighten it and brushing at her riding skirt. Almost the first thing she noticed about the group of horsemen, before she could discern who they were, was that the lead man was riding a buckskin. And beside that man rode another on a gray.

Kate's immediate instinct was to run. To run Bob off the road into the sagebrush and flee, or else run him right up the road and through the lot of them. Either way, it would keep her from facing them. But Kate Winchester was tired of being afraid. And even more than that, she was tired of others seeing her fear. This brought a determination that kept her from lashing Bob with the reins.

The closer Kate drew to the riders, the more it became clear the rider on the buckskin and the one on the gray were the same two she had seen ride into town with Irving Wolfe's cavalcade five days before. But there was another man, a bigger man, who rode a strawberry roan to the gray's left. Kate's attention was drawn to him, particularly when he dropped to the back of the troop after the man on the gray turned to say something to him. And then, contrary to cowboy custom, he pushed the hat off his head so that it hung from a rawhide thong. This Kate watched from only seventy yards away.

With all her might, Kate was hoping she could ride by without so much as a how-do-you-do. She had no words to exchange with these men, especially with knowing what they had done to Ira.

When the six riders drew near, they fanned out across the road almost casually, all but the big man, who stayed behind them. They stopped their horses, and Kathryn was forced to do the same. Something kept drawing her attention to the mysterious big man at the back of the bunch, but the voice of the man on the buckskin forced her to meet his gaze.

"Hah-dy. Yer that Winchester woman."

Kate just nodded, stunned by his eyes. She recalled the first time she had noticed him, the other day when he rode into town beside Irving Wolfe's buggy. She remembered thinking how odd his eyes looked, and now, up close, she saw why. They were yellow. Yellowish brown, really, but closer to yellow than Kate Winchester had ever seen in a human being. Again, looking over his long face and pointed beard, she pictured the coyote his features had called up before.

"Yes, I am Mrs. Winchester," Kate said, summoning boldness to her voice. She didn't give them the satisfaction of saying her Christian name. "I would like to pass."

"What's yer hurry?" It was the man on the gray who spoke now. "We ain't been innerduced proper, an' we may's well start, since we're neighbors." He smiled, revealing a large gap between his teeth. "I'm Dunn Yates, and my pardner, here, is Case Deckan. Trouble shooters on the Twin Wolfe."

Trouble shooters? This Dunn Yates spoke the words with a large measure of pride in his voice. Trouble *makers* was more likely, Kate thought.

"Now we've met," she said coolly. "I would like to pass." Involuntarily, her eyes fell away from their leering gazes. They lit on the belt and holster of a small man who sat a shaggy bay horse next to Yates. The man's hand rested conspicuously over the holster, so she couldn't see much of it. But the belt buckle was scalloped in such a memorable way that . . . Her eyes dropped to his boots. The pants were pulled over them besides the stirrup leathers being in front of them. Frustrated, her eyes scanned quickly to his, and she paused, startled. It didn't matter whether she saw the holster with the star or not. It didn't matter if she saw the stars on his boots. This was the man she'd seen up Wolverine Canyon with Ellis, the one she had dubbed "Star."

Kate's eyes went over the other two men in the group, and she recognized them by their hats and by the one man's huge neckerchief as two of the others who had been up Wolverine Canyon.

Case Deckan was uttering words she didn't even hear as her gaze jumped beyond the other riders, back to the big man on the roan. He had removed his hat, probably in hopes of looking different to her. And she couldn't see the tell-tale blue calico bandanna. But he couldn't conceal his eyes, nor could he erase them from her memory. She caught them on her for just a moment before they fell away. They were the deep gray color of slate. The big man was the one she called "Calico."

Kate's eyes darted away from the big man, who was slouched over in his saddle, probably hoping to look smaller than he was. They fell back on Deckan, who had just finished speaking. He was watching her as if expecting a response, but she had none to give him.

"She never heard a word you said, Case," Dunn Yates said with a leering grin. "She's got her mind drawed by some'n' better lookin'." Laughing, he took his watch chain and gave its pen knife fob a twirl.

Kate glanced at Yates's face. His narrow, slanted eyes watched her from beneath his hat with just as much intensity as any predator. He and Deckan were cut from the same mold.

Kate Winchester had been in the West long enough not to fear harm from any group of men, even ones she knew as murderers. It was a rare man who would assault a white woman. She doubted this many men could be gathered on one ranch who would be depraved enough, especially when sober, to lower themselves so far. But even if they were, she had the feeling it would amount to nothing. She attributed this feeling to the big man on the strawberry roan. Perhaps he had no chivalry. Perhaps he only wanted her for himself. But as long as he was in this group she felt no threat.

rom this instinct ate drew strength. She lifted her chin and s uared her eyes with Case eckan 's, who she decided was the closest thing to a leader here. Either you men move out of my way or I will ride through you, she said. I'm tired of sitting here in the sun.

Star's eyes flashed angrily, and his face reddened. But she saw Cali co's eyes lighten, and a grin cut briefly across his face. ates and eckan just stared at her belligerently, and the other two men were only mean ingless shapes in the back of her mind.

Case eckan touched his hat brim, resting his thumb and forefinger there for a moment. Be seein' you, ma'am. Be seein' you soon. eeah

e lunged his buckskin forward with a slap of the reins and galloped up the road. The others followed, and, after calming Bob down, ate started west. She glanced back to see Calico's face turned toward her, and she noticed something else, too. is right arm, which had been hidden from her view by the other riders and by his being turned to the side, had a bandanna wrapped and tied around it . . . a blue bandanna that appeared to be soaked with blood.

With her heart pounding, ate turned her eyes to the road before her, and to Bob's tirelessly twitching ears. She hardly even noticed the ranch as they drew past it at a trot. There were six killers behind her seven, counting Wolfe. It was frightening, now that it was over, to think how close she had been to six men who had already tried to kill once, and at least two she felt would kill her son without any compunction. It was within the power of one man to stop it. et Irving Wolfe had flatly refused by denying involvement.

ate mulled over many thoughts as her blood slowed down and allowed her mind to clear. or one, what had happened to Calico, that he should be wearing a bandage on his arm It was only an idle thought, compared to her others. ore importantly, where was Ellis, and what was happening to him ow was she going to save his life It should have been obvious to her, if she'd really been thinking, that saving Ellis's and Ira's life wouldn't be as easy as selling the land to Wolfe. She had been dreaming to expect anything to come of that. But she was glad she had tried, for in leaving the ranch, happening into Calico and Star riding with Wolfe's gunmen, she had proven to herself beyond any doubt who the true killer was: Irving Wolfe. It wasn't just by chance that those men had been riding together toward the Twin Wolfe. They all worked for Irving Wolfe.

Kate had to force herself to put Ellis out of her mind. Thoughts of him being alone and hurt were slowly driving her insane. Instead, she thought of Ira. There could be no further doubt that her husband was involved in something that made Wolfe want to kill him for more than just their land. In Kate's mind, the rancher's refusal to talk about the land clinched that. Wolfe probably figured he'd end up with the land anyway, after Ira was dead. He wouldn't expect a lone woman to stay on, with only her children to help her through the loneliness and toil.

There was no way to fight a man as ruthless as Irving Wolfe except on his own terms. That was the fact which ate deepest into Kate's soul. She had no intention of leaving her land if Wolfe wouldn't deal with her, and to stay meant to risk her husband's life. Surely, the killers wouldn't miss again. That left only one option, and that was to fight Wolfe the way he had asked for it. She didn't know how. She had no plan—no plan, that was, beyond saving the life of her son and holding onto the land she had come to love. And protecting a husband who, although he had grown distant, was her last hold on sanity. No woman could be expected to recover from having four husbands die violently.

Tears built and rolled down Kathryn Winchester's cheeks as she came to her final decision and mulled it over and over again. *Kate, you are on this land to stay. If you do not wish to see your husband, your children, and perhaps yourself die, you must ready yourself to kill.*

In her heart she could find only that answer. She must hire someone who was able and not afraid to fight a gun battle. Someone who would be willing to risk his life for money. Case Deckan and Dunn Yates, as well as Calico and Star, were proof that such men existed. And although the fact embarrassed her, it would be nothing to find men who would be glad to work for a woman with the beauty people thought she possessed.

When Kate drew off of Francis Street and onto Shilling Avenue, where Curtis and Annette Selders lived and where they had placed Ira for refuge, it was immediately obvious that something was wrong. Her mind had been preoccupied, planning the wording of an advertisement she would place in Salt Lake City, Denver and Cheyenne newspapers asking for an experienced, courageous gunman to take the part of a persecuted woman. But these ponderings were torn from her by sight of the mass of people along the street looking toward the Selders' house.

Urging the bay to a faster walk, she soon found the majority of the people thronged around the Selders' home. She put Bob into a canter and arrived at the house with fear gripping her in a way that had become all too common. Sheriff Arch Hess was standing out on the porch of the little house talking with his deputy, Luke Weaver, and Curtis Selders, a man almost bigger across the shoulders than some men were tall.

Weaver, a greyhound lean, whiskered man with over-large hands and narrow-set eyes, happened to look her way and pointed. Sheriff Hess whirled, then stepped off the porch and strode across the yard to meet her. She jumped out of the saddle before he could reach her.

"What's happened?" She wanted to sound brave, but the words came out breathlessly.

"No one's hurt. I want you to know that first," assured Hess, placing a big hand on her shoulder.

Glancing toward the house, Kate noticed splinters of wood along a fresh gash on one of the posts that supported the awning. "What's wrong?" Kate demanded. Her fear turned almost instantly into unintended anger, and she ducked her shoulder to shake his hand loose.

"Mrs. Winchester . . . I don't know how they found your husband, but they came after him again, two hours ago. If Curtis Selders hadn't been here with his scattergun, I'm afraid they would have got him. There's no man around here better with a gun than Selders."

Kate's eyes flashed angrily. "How could they have found out where we moved him? We didn't tell anyone!"

"I had Deputy Weaver guarding the front porch," Hess replied. "They must have figured it out from seeing him there. It's my fault. The minute Luke went for a bite of breakfast, two men came riding up with rifles. But it turned out all right. Selders drew blood on one of the men, and I'm hoping we can locate him when he tries to look for a doctor. I don't know how bad he's bleeding. Bad enough to leave drops on the street."

Kate's heart leaped. Calico! An urge to tell the sheriff welled up in her chest, and she almost gave in. But something more powerful closed her throat off and warned her against saying anything. She had to think first, before she could tell anyone what she had seen. She couldn't do anything that would endanger Ellis . . . or send Ira off to prison.

"How is Ira?" she asked, moving numbly toward the porch.

The sheriff stepped to the side as if to let her pass but stopped her with his words. "He doesn't even know anything happened. He hasn't woke up yet. Ma'am? If you don't mind my saying so, I think you ought to send him on the train to Salt Lake City. They have good hospitals there—real hospitals. They can take proper care of him, and we can't. You ought to consider that before he gets worse. Or at least send him over to Pocatello Junction. Davis or Blickensderfer would be better than what you have here now that Martin's gone."

Kate drew her hands up into fists, beset by many thoughts at once. This nightmare was going to drive her to the grave if she didn't stop it. She wouldn't even have time to bring in help if Wolfe found her husband again. And until she knew what Ira was involved in she didn't dare tell the sheriff the many things she'd learned. She didn't want to send her own husband to prison if there was some other way out of their predicament. And worse than anything was her fear of making the wrong move and getting Ellis killed.

But one thing she knew, even amid all her blurred anger and terror. No matter how long it took to bring someone in to help her, she had to defend herself in the meantime. It had been proven too many times that she could not rely on the law until she dared tell them everything she knew. For now, if anyone were to end this nightmare, it would be Kathryn Winchester herself. Marshal was right. She had to arm herself.

Chapter Eight

The red-headed, freckled clerk in Henry Curtis's hardware store on West Main Street had a condescending way of speaking to anyone he felt inferior to himself. Kate had seen it in his dealings with her sons and with others who had been in the store while she was present. She had never experienced it herself because normally Ira was the one doing the dealing, and most people respected Ira. Although not a man of large stature or strong voice he had a calm self-confidence that commanded respect.

The minute Kate walked up to the counter without Ira there, she felt the clerk's scrutiny. She had almost no knowledge of guns, but she had no intention of letting the redhead know that.

"I would like to purchase a rifle," she said.

The clerk seemed taken aback. She doubted he often heard respectable ladies ordering firearms. "A rifle, ma'am?"

"Please."

With a bewildered shrug, the clerk turned, and with a sweeping motion of his arm indicated the long rack of rifles, carbines, muskets and shotguns. "There are at least forty rifles in stock, ma'am. New and used and engraved and plain looking. What's your pleasure?"

Now that she was in front of the impressive rack of weapons, Kate was bewildered. All of the weapons looked the same to her. Trying to sound intelligent, but knowing instantly she had failed, she said, "Why don't you tell me about them?"

The clerk cleared his throat, glancing uncertainly toward the weapons. "Uhhh . . . Yes, ma'am." He took a deep breath and turned toward the long line of mated metal and wood. It wasn't long after he began to speak that Kate could see someone had attempted to arrange the rifles in alphabetical order. "There are three Ballards," he said, "and one used Bullard. Not much good, as far as I can see. There's this strange Chaffee-Reese, too. Wouldn't waste my money there. We have our Colt Lightnings. Both of ours are forty-fours, but there are other calibers. A Colt-Burgess. Three Marlins—a good gun there. We have a .32-40, a .45-70, and one in .45-85." He continued down the line, pointing at the Remington rolling blocks, the Sharps, Spencers, Springfields, Stevens, Frank Wessons, what he called a Whitney-"Laidley," and four other different Whitney and so-and-so's she couldn't have remembered if her life depended on them.

Kate's head had begun to spin before the clerk was halfway through the line. She felt herself sinking in despair. She might has well have walked into a medical school and tried to catch up after classes had been in progress for several months. What was she going to say to this man? Her mind began to fade into a daydream stage until she wondered if the red-headed clerk was even speaking her language.

"There's a Ward-Burton," he was saying. "It's a strange one. A rifle with a bolt action, in .50 caliber. And then of course the Winchesters."

Kate's heart nearly shot through her throat. At last, a name she knew! She would be saved from total embarrassment. Trying to look calm, she nodded. "I think I'll look at one of the Winchesters."

The clerk's face seemed to harden, and he looked back down the line of rifles he had just gone through. He looked back at Kate, and she had the feeling he was wishing he had listed them all in reverse alphabetical order.

Kate ignored the man's obvious irritation. Picking a rifle from the Winchesters he had indicated, she pointed to it. The clerk leaned in to touch its forearm. "This one, ma'am?"

Upon her affirmation, he withdrew the rifle and held it toward her with both hands. "That's the Centennial model. It's a powerful rifle."

In side view, the weapon looked massive. The part where it must be loaded—Kate had no idea of any technical name—was by itself as big as her extended hand. She pretended to look it over, reading on the round barrel that it was of .50-95 caliber and designated Model 1876. That meant nothing to her, but the bore looked like the inside of a cannon, and she imagined it might kick like one.

With a confident nod, she handed the weapon back. She deliberately chose a smaller model the next time, and the clerk handed it over with a smile. "This is the best of them all, in my opinion," he said. "A good rifle for any light game, deer-size or smaller." Kate took those words into account as she read the caliber of .38-40. Shortly, she handed it back. The bore seemed small, even to her. Working in a battlefield hospital, she had been too close to action too many times not to hear stories. She had heard of men carrying eight or nine lead balls in vital parts of their body and continuing to fight on will alone.

An involuntary shudder coursed through her at that image. What in the name of all that was sacred was she doing? Kathryn Winchester—kill another human being? It wasn't possible. But these particular human beings were murdering her, in a sense, if they succeeded in killing her husband and children. If she had to kill, it would only be to protect the innocent.

Taking a deep breath, she pushed the thoughts of killing aside, realizing the clerk had spoken to her. "I'm sorry. What did you say?"

"I only asked if you would like to look at anything else," the clerk said, unable to hide his irritation at having to deal with her.

With a set to her jaw, she met his eyes. Her gaze was determined enough that his own soon fell away. "Yes, I would," she said. "I'm sorry if I'm taking too much of your time. But I do not spend money frivolously."

She didn't mean to sound irritated, but she must have. The clerk quickly stammered, "Oh, it isn't any trouble, ma'am. I'm only here to help. I'd be careful, too."

"Thank you." Kate turned her eyes back to the rack. "What about that one?"

For verification, the clerk pointed at the weapon she had indicated. "This carbine?" She nodded. "It's a used one, ma'am," he said.

"It doesn't matter," she said. "Show me that one."

The weapon she had chosen was another Model 1873, the same as the .38-40. On its barrel it read, "Winchester's-Repeating-Arms New Haven CT," along with some patent information. Then, behind a sight that appeared to elevate for different ranges, it read, "44 W.C.F.," which Kate guessed might mean "Winchester cartridge firearm." She only learned later, while reading the literature that came with the weapon, that it meant "Winchester centerfire."

The rifle's stock was long and red and smooth like silk, except for a few blackened scars. Black grains stitched their way the length of the wood, enhancing an overall look of elegance. The barrel, unlike the other two, was round and appeared to be possibly four inches shorter. On its left side was a metal ring that swiveled back and forth. She wondered what that was but didn't want to make herself look foolish by asking. There was a faint brown look about the weapon's metal, but severe wear only where the metal ring met the body of the rifle. Everything else looked to be in good condition.

There was something about the carbine, something fascinating in its deadliness. It was lighter than the Model 1876 and felt good and smooth in her hands. The wear of its metal and of its wood gave it an oddly warmer feeling, if it was possible for something so cold to feel warm. There were certain functions of the carbine that appeared obvious. Taking a chance, Kate tentatively opened the lever, watching a round shank of metal retract from inside the carbine and thrust back the hammer. This also slid a metal plate back on top of the weapon and opened to view some brass parts inside, as well as the rear opening of the barrel. Fascinated, Kate peered in. It was all a mystery to her how something so cold and quiet could turn so deadly. But it was a mystery she had to unravel.

She looked up at the clerk, whose eyes flickered when caught looking at her. "I know an Indian who claims to kill elk consistently with one shot from one of these," he uttered, to hide his embarrassment. "He told me he once killed a grizzly bear with it, too. That's a lot of gun."

"How much is this weapon?"

"Eighteen dollars, ma'am, since it's used. And it comes with its original cleaning kit and loading tools."

Kate raised the carbine uncertainly and placed its cold crescent butt to her shoulder, sighting along its barrel to the door of the potbellied stove at the back of the store. Being a tall woman, the stock fit her well, like it was meant for her. But that was the devil's thinking. Her hands were never meant to kill.

"The case is of the finest walnut, too," she heard the clerk say. "And I would be glad to throw in a box of cartridges. I'll even tie a little bow on the case, if you're buying it for a birthday present or such. I'm assuming this is a gift?"

Kate looked up and met the clerk's eyes. He had a naïve, expectant look on his face that forced the corners of her lips to turn up. "The weapon is for me," she said.

"Oh. You seem . . . That is, you don't look like the kind to shoot a firearm."

"Do you shoot any firearms, sir?" she asked, forcing politeness.

"Why, yes, ma'am."

She just nodded, looking him up and down. "I'll take the rifle."

Marshal Briggs sat and fingered his new 1883 Colt double-barrel shotgun. He looked back and forth from it to his mother, but it took some time for him to come up with words. Kathryn waited in silence until he finally spoke.

"Why'd you change your mind, Ma?"

Kathryn looked at the shotgun she had purchased along with the carbine. She felt the weight of the carbine in her own right hand. Instead of looking at Marshal's face, her glance fell away. "They're going to kill Ira if they can, Marshal. And they aren't past killing Ellis, too. The sheriff hasn't been able to protect anyone. It's up to us to stop it."

"But . . . Ma, you said yourself you don't know how to shoot. I don't much either. I was mad yesterday, and the guns were my idea. But I wasn't thinking. What could we do—really?"

Kate pursed her lips, trying to drive away the thought of even pointing a weapon at another human being. "We have to do something."

Vala and Cheyenne were also in the room. Both of them wore the gravest of faces, and neither spoke. By the silence, it was easy to forget they were there. Finally, Vala came and put her arm around her mother, and Cheyenne drew strength from that and hugged Kate's leg.

Kate looked at Vala, then down at Cheyenne. She knew that in a few days this could be their entire family. But she was ready to kill if she had to, to save Ellis's life and see the family remain whole. She was tired of being a peacemaker while her loved ones fell around her.

The telegraphed advertisement went over the wires to Cheyenne, Denver and Salt Lake City in these words:

Persecuted lady rancher seeks fearless man to fight for her rights stop *Husband shot son kidnapped* stop *Must have help soon* stop *Come with weapons and credentials* stop *Pay one hundred dollars* stop *Bonus of two hundred if husband remains alive and son returns safe* stop *Contact Kathryn Winchester in Blackfoot Idaho* full stop

Banker Ward Brassman was glad to grant Kate a loan. She had told him it was to pay medical costs and living expenses until Ira was back on his feet. The loan was against fifty of the four hundred head of cattle on the Winchester ranch, and Kate had to bite her lip when she signed the paper. But as long as she had the land and her family, they could start again.

When the papers had all been signed, Kate remained sitting, feeling awkward in front of the big cherry wood desk in Brassman's office. The banker stood up and leaned across the desk, offering his hand. Caught off-guard, Kate gave him a questioning look, then took his hand and shook with a firm grip. She stood and waited as he walked around the desk.

"Mrs. Winchester, you're a brave woman," Brassman said. "To be frank with you, I envy Mr. Winchester his good fortune. I wish there were more I could do for you and your family, something more . . . personal."

Unable to summon an answer to that, Kate just looked at him, then cleared her throat. "You've been very kind, Mr. Brassman. I hope somehow to repay you. I know you didn't have to carry this loan."

Brassman dipped his head, the creases along his mouth deepening with a close-lipped smile. "Mrs. Winchester, you and your husband have been good customers. I'm happy to help you out in your time of need. So . . . where will you take your husband now? Back to your ranch?"

Kate shrugged. "I'm at a loss right now. Wherever we might go we're in danger. I don't know how to fight it. I don't know what Ira has done. I don't know why someone is after him—not for certain, anyway."

"Well, I suppose it's all in God's hands," replied Brassman. "And the sheriff's, of course. It seems, however, that God has played the greater part in your husband's salvation."

"It seems," Kate agreed.

He held open the office door for her, and she walked to the outer lobby. After stopping at the teller's station to draw her loan, she smiled gratefully and moved toward the street. Brassman continued with her to the front door, stopping by the hat rack. It wasn't until he had already plucked his brown nutria hat from its hook that he gave Kate a half smile and said, "I'd be pleased to walk you back safely, if you'll allow me."

"Oh, no, I— You don't have to—"

Brassman raised his hands. "No, no. I insist. I have to protect my interests, you know."

Kate laughed, looking down at the brown leather sheaf in her hand. "Yes, I suppose you do. I'm not a very good risk."

Brassman placed his hat on his head and brushed his fingers along one side of its brim as if to straighten it, which it didn't need. He then opened the door. Kate hesitated, reaching hurriedly into her reticule to pull out and draw on her white string gloves. As she turned and passed in front of Brassman, he nonchalantly placed a hand on her back. Through the gingham dress his palm felt warm, yet it sent a shiver through her.

On the boardwalk, Brassman offered her an elbow. She looked down at it and paused, shooting a glance along the street. Her instinct was to put her gloved hand daintily inside the crook of that elbow. It seemed natural somehow, a feeling she didn't understand. But she shook her head with an apologetic smile.

"I'm sorry, Mr. Brassman. I— I have my things," she said lamely.

Brassman smiled and dropped his arm to his side. If her reaction disappointed him, it disappeared in the amiable greeting he offered an acquaintance just then passing them.

"The Old Farmer's Almanac claims fall will come early this year," the banker said when he turned back to her.

Kate forced a smile. "I hadn't heard that."

"Do you have cattle you're planning to sell?"

"I believe we do. Ira was very secretive about the ranch in the weeks before he was attacked. I can't say for sure what plans he was making."

Brassman nodded. "That's too bad. Irving Wolfe is building up a big herd for sale. A very big herd, I've heard." He laughed at the sound of his own words. "Herd, I've heard? To listen to me talking, you'd think I was the village idiot."

That made Kate laugh, and she looked up to catch his eyes studying her. He had a beautiful smile with perfect white teeth and little wrinkles that caught up the outer corners of his eyes. She blushed, and her eyes flickered away.

They made the remainder of the stroll in silence. When they stopped on the Websters' porch, Brassman removed his hat, taking care not to disturb his hair. "Is your husband here, Mrs. Winchester? I'd like to pay my respects, if I could."

"He isn't," she replied. "He's sleeping in a jail cell now—like a common drunk." Kate laughed, but there was shame in her heart.

"Kathryn, I—" Brassman halted his words quickly. "Mrs. Winchester. My apologies. I do wish there were some way I could help you. You bear a heavy load."

Feeling a rush of bold gratitude, Kate reached out and squeezed the banker's hand. She was immediately embarrassed and dropped her hand away as heat flowed into her cheeks. "Mr. Brassman, you've been very kind to us—not just now, but ever since we came to this area. I assure you, if there is anything you can do, I'll let you know."

"Please do." He spoke with such soft, utter sincerity, such gentle, truly caring eyes that for a moment— Kate halted her thoughts there, turning abruptly into the door.

"Be careful about the door," Brassman warned. Embarrassed, she looked back and caught his teasing smile. In two seconds, his look became serious. "Really—please do be careful. You're too fine a lady to be left alone."

Kate pondered the banker's words long after he was gone. Too fine a lady to be left alone? What exactly did that mean? The banker was certainly a smooth man. So full of compliments, and seeming so sincere. She had known many men, four of them intimately. She had never been able to bring herself to trust one who was wealthy, but for once she felt that prejudice losing its powerful hold. Yet rather than being a reason to ask for Brassman's help, it was a reason to avoid him. Becoming too close to a man so kind and attractive was dangerous—dangerous to a woman whose vows had been made to another.

The next step in Kathryn Winchester's plan was to remove Ira as far from danger as she possibly could. That meant sending him away to stay with his Uncle Nat and Aunt Betsy in Brigham, Utah. She spoke with R.M. and Susan Sievers, and it was agreed that R.M. would escort Ira to Brigham. It was also agreed the word must be passed along to Nat and Betsy that absolutely no communication must pass between them and the Winchesters until Kate sent a wire that everything was safe. Kate knew she could trust no one—not the postmaster, not the telegrapher, not even the men on the train. No one in a position to pass word on to the assassins of Ira's whereabouts. Kate had even thought far enough ahead to purchase Ira's original train ticket for the Battle Creek station, near Preston, rather than for his actual destination. At Battle Creek, Sievers would purchase tickets to take them the rest of the way. Thus, even the conductors on the train wouldn't know where Ira was headed as they left Blackfoot.

It was going to be a lonely time for Kate Winchester, and she had to hold back her tears when she made the decision. It would be as if Kate were alone once more, alone with only her children for comfort. But it had to be that way. Nat and Betsy couldn't contact her until she told them the assassins had been captured or until . . . until Ira died. Kate couldn't let herself forget there was always that chance. The possibility of it made her ache deep inside. She loved Ira more than any man she had ever known. In spite of whatever had happened to them in the last year, that was still true.

The next morning by seven o'clock Kate and Susan Sievers put Ira and R.M. on a train bound for Brigham. Tears filled Kate's eyes as the Utah and Northern caboose faded to a tiny dot along the tracks. She wasn't sure Ira loved her anymore, yet she still loved him. He was Cheyenne's father, after all. She wondered if she would ever see him alive again.

R.M. Sievers rode beside Ira's bed. He carried a twelve-gauge shotgun, which Kate knew was deadly in his hands. Kate had been embarrassed to have him travel all that way, leaving his own ranch vulnerable. But Sievers could not be dissuaded. He was as stubborn in some ways as Kate herself.

Four hours later, Kate Winchester stood at the riverbank, as she had for the past hour and a half. Her fingers were tired. With Marshal beside her, she worked the lever of her new carbine and fired imaginary shots at make-believe targets. With her son's help and the information in the Winchester Arms Company brochure, she had learned how to load the carbine, how many cartridges it held and how to clean it. From Marshal she had learned how to line up the sights by placing the tip of the front sight into the valley of the rear one, then centering the front sight just beneath her target. But she had yet to fire a shot.

Putting beeswax in her ears to guard against the noise, Kate now slid three cartridges into the magazine, glancing apprehensively at her boy. With an almost hungry look he watched the brass cartridges slide inside, then cast a longing glance at his shotgun, leaning against a sagebrush branch. He turned back to watch his mother.

"Well, Marshal, I guess this is it. See that white rock on the other bank? That's my target." She took a deep breath and raised the weapon to her shoulder. Her stomach felt empty, oddly reminding her of the same queasy feeling she'd felt at sixteen the first time Dan Lauder took her into his arms to kiss her. Stalling, she wiped at her eyes to clear her vision. When she aimed she closed the wrong eye. She'd done the same several times when first trying the carbine out empty, but the regression angered her since she had thought she was over it.

Closing her left eye, she squinted down the barrel, which glinted in the sun. It wavered drastically while she tried to line the sights, then find her target. When she found it she worked the lever clumsily, cringing as she felt the slightest nuance of change in the action. That must have meant a shell had entered the chamber.

She had to relocate her target, and by the time she did she was forced to let out with a gust the air she'd been holding in. Frustrated, she lowered the carbine.

"Watch your finger, Ma," Marshal warned. "I almost shot Michael Perkins's dog once, doing that."

Kate smiled, trying to appear calm. Steeling herself, she raised the gun again and this time found the rock more quickly. The rock was there, but the sights wouldn't stay on it. They moved everywhere with the rocking of the carbine. But she determined to go ahead. The next time the sights came near their target, she closed her eyes and pulled the trigger.

The punch of the crescent metal butt plate into the bone of her shoulder made Kathryn wince. She lowered the carbine and opened her eyes against the acrid smoke wisping around her face. Her gaze went automatically to the rock. It was still there and seemed untouched. When she glanced over at Marshal he was watching her with a concerned frown.

To the question in her eyes, the boy shook his head. "I don't even know where you hit, Ma. But it wasn't anywhere near that rock."

Kate sighed and dropped the butt of the carbine to the grass at her feet. She raised a hand and brushed at the strands of hair and the beaded perspiration on her forehead. "Oh, Marshal, what am I doing out here?" She reached up unconsciously and rubbed the front of her shoulder. "Does it always hurt like that?" she asked.

Marshal shrugged. "It doesn't hurt me." He walked to the shotgun and picked it up. As Kate watched, he cracked it open and pushed in two brass-cased twelve gauge shells. Looking over at the rock, he slung the shotgun to his shoulder, held it for a moment and let go with one barrel, then the other. Smoke clouded around him as the rock rolled to a stop several feet away.

Kate looked over at her son with new hope in her eyes. "That was good, son. We aren't lost yet, are we?"

Marshal shrugged, obviously proud of himself but not wanting to be boastful. "We'll see what happens," he said, looking toward the rock rather than at her. "Maybe you should buy you another shotgun."

Kate Winchester was wearing Ira's pants today. She wore one of his shirts, too, a white one with a half placket and thin black stripes, and his hat tied under her chin to make up for its being too large. She sat on old Bob, and Marshal rode Tarnish. It was dark, and the sky was clouded over, without so much as a star to light their way. The Wolverine Narrows made it darker still.

Kate had stubbornly kept practicing with the carbine the day before. Once she figured out how to settle the butt of the weapon against the soft meat just inside her shoulder she found the recoil surprisingly meek, compared to that first walloping kick to the bone. She still couldn't hit what she wanted, at least not any closer than half a foot off at fifty yards. But it was an improvement. She had fired forty rounds through the carbine. That was forty more than she had fired during the rest of her life.

Kate and Marshal had decided to ride out to Wolverine and see if they could get a glimpse of Ellis. Kate had to know if her boy was all right. She knew she had no hope of winning a gun battle with the kidnappers, and she didn't intend to engage them in one. But she couldn't sit at home. She had to be doing something. She had to at least try to form some kind of plan.

Before they reached the side canyon where Ellis was being held, they turned right and dropped over the steep edge of the trail, splashing across Wolverine Creek. They hid the two horses well back in the shelter of chokecherries and birch trees. The air, besides sagebrush, juniper, fir and cottonwood, was tinged with the rosy scent of the chokecherry blossoms, but Kate could draw little pleasure from it. She felt very little but the fear that almost paralyzed her heart.

In spite of the awkward feeling of unfamiliarity, they carried their new weapons when they left the horses. Somehow, knowing the weapons were with them made them feel like someone else was along with them, watching over them. Carefully fording the creek and soaking their legs to their knees, they crossed the road once more. They hunkered down in the shelter of a clump of junipers and waited for better light, listening to the sound of the little stream that gurgled down out of the canyon toward its meeting with Wolverine Creek. On a cloudy night such as this, it was one thing riding the road through Wolverine Canyon. It was an entirely different thing trying to make their way up through the jagged, snake-infested rocks.

With the first hint of daylight, diffused by the cover of cloud, they started up the steep juniper hillside. It was good neither of them had any undue fear of snakes, for they startled three of them into rattling before they had climbed two hundred feet. Fortunately, it was too cold at that time of the morning for the snakes to do much but rattle. By then it was well into dawn, and they were able to plan their route without much backtracking. Only now and then were the Douglas firs and junipers thick enough to hide some rock escarpment they had to go back and skirt around. The clouds had broken up, and in the east they burned with pink flames. A faint wind hustled wild, luring scents up out of the dark canyon.

Stopping now and then to catch their breath, they warily scanned the canyon below. When they reached the two hundred-foot-high crest they believed to be above the kidnappers' hideout, they crouched low down in the junipers and sneaked carefully forward. Behind them, gnarly firs and tall clusters of jagged cliff choked a much higher ridge. Over the eastern hills the sun exploded between the clouds, pouring down warm light on them at last. It should have been comforting, yet to Kate it brought a feeling of doom.

In the canyon below, it was still shadowed, but they could see the boulder-studded place where they had come to meet the kidnappers before. No movement. Marshal glanced over at his mother, and she just gave him a brave smile. Her heart pounded like a goat trying to hammer its way out of a wooden box, and even in the cool air her temples glistened with sweat. She scanned the trees and rocks below, staring at particularly dark places until her eyes hurt. A time or two she thought she saw movement, but each time it proved to be her imagination.

They continued looking, down the hill and at each other. They looked but saw no movement. It wasn't until they had climbed higher up the ridge and scanned the remainder of the canyon that they could see it continued on still farther. Unfortunately, the firs and quaking aspen had become too thick to see anything that way. They tried to climb carefully down the canyon, but ended up slipping and sliding down the steep slope more than they remained in control of their speed. At last, they entered its narrow passage and began making their way up into the cool shadows of the trees. Kate expected at any moment to come around the corner and see the kidnappers, but some strange, morbid curiosity kept her walking. At last, the trail came to an end. There was no sign that anyone had gone on farther.

Ellis was gone.

Fear soaked her sides with sweat as Kate walked back down the steep trail to where it started to level out. Not long after that, they found a fire pit, the site of several fires. Its ashes were cold. Kate sat down on a big gray boulder that was half buried in the dark soil and stared. Marshal took a seat Indian-style beside her, the shotgun resting across his legs. Since leaving their horses, neither of them had spoken. First it was out of fear and anticipation and a sense of strange excitement. Now it was out of dread. Where were the kidnappers? Where was Ellis? What did his disappearance mean?

It didn't take long to sort it out.

Kate knew the kidnappers had been riding near the Wolfe ranch the last time she had seen them. If there were only the four of them, would they leave their captive alone? What about predators? If they had left Ellis trussed up so he couldn't run, how would he defend himself if a mountain lion or a bear happened along?

Kate was trembling as her thoughts darted from one possibility to another. What if Ellis had been killed by animals? What if the human kind had killed him before leaving him here? For her own sanity, she forced those thoughts aside. They must have moved her son. There were other places to take him. Irving Wolfe wouldn't be foolish enough to let them keep him here, now that Kate and Marshal knew the location. Kate could easily have informed Sheriff Hess, in spite of their warnings, and he could have come here with a posse. Besides, Wolverine Canyon was beginning to be known as a place for townfolk to get away from their cares on camping excursions. The kidnappers wouldn't be stupid enough to remain like so many doves on a limb. If Kate had been more familiar with the criminal mind, she would have thought of that before.

As to where they were, they could have gone to a hundred different places. But the sensible one was somewhere on Wolfe's ranch. It wasn't far from here. It would be good shelter. And who would seek them there? No one except Katherine knew Wolfe was involved in the kidnapping, and who would believe her? Wolfe was a respected member of the community, and Kate had nothing but supposition on her side. Besides, like Ward Brassman had pointed out, the law had done little good protecting Ira from attack.

Now that she was certain there were no kidnappers here, Kate settled into her position, pushing her tears far back inside. On a whim, she raised the carbine to her shoulder, resting her left elbow on her thigh. She sighted down the barrel to a dusty patch of shale on the east slope of the canyon and pulled the trigger. It was only a shot out of anger, but it did her heart good. With pounding pulse, she continued to jack the lever and fire until she had emptied all twelve shots. Then she lowered her head and cried.

Clyde Hall was a métis, son of a half-French father and a Shoshone mother. The white men on the reservation called him True Shot. The name didn't necessarily have anything to do with his marksmanship but was simply a typical American mutilation of his grandfather's French name, Truchot, pronounced "true show."

It was well known in town that Hall was friendly toward whites, inviting them openly to attend Indian ceremonies, expressing his desire for different peoples to understand each other's cultures and religions. Kate had never met Hall, but in her desperation to find her boy, it was to the métis she turned. Even to a Pennsylvania Quaker, the tracking skill of Indians was legend.

It was twelve miles from Blackfoot to Ross Fork, the headquarters of the agency for the Fort Hall Reservation. Alone, Kate drove her buggy there. At the government trading post, dressed once again the way a proper woman should be, Kate asked about Clyde Hall, and she was directed out to a low hovel west of the town site. Major Gallagher, the Indian agent at the post, happened to be in the store, and he suggested Kate take a gift with her. That was Indian custom. She ended her visit to the store with five yards of red flannel under one arm.

The Hall dwelling was half a mile from the post, with a lone tepee nearby, a quiet place until the silence was broken by five or six barking dogs. Kate had no idea what to expect, but she urged Bob to pull the buggy on past the dogs and up near the front door. Unsure of herself, she sat the buggy for a moment, looking around. She felt safe up high on the buggy seat, behind phlegmatic Bob. She wasn't altogether sure of the intentions of one red dog who stood nearby, wagging his tail but barking in a deep voice. He looked like a little red lion.

The moment Kate gathered her nerve and stepped out of the buggy, she heard the door creak open. She turned to the house to see a giant of a man. He stood six-foot-two but couldn't have weighed much more than two hundred pounds. His shoulders filled the doorway to the house, and his chest looked wider across than two well buckets set end to end. But his face was gaunt, and the padding of his cheeks was missing, making them look like sharp edges of stone. His hair was short and black, and his face was the deep reddish brown of tarnished sandstone.

"Can I help you?"

Startled by the sound of the soft voice from this giant Indian, for a moment Kate only stared. "Uh, yes, I— Actually, I was told I could find a man by the name of Mr. Hall here. Clyde Hall."

The big man let his eyes go up and down Kate, measuring her. In spite of his giant stature and thick hands, he didn't seem the threat she had first pictured. This was due to a curious, friendly glow to his black eyes, a glow that bade her no evil.

"I am Clyde Hall," came the soft, almost musical reply. "Won't you come in?" He noticed her glancing nervously at the dog and smiled. "And don't worry about Red Dog. He's very friendly."

Stunned first by his size, now by the idea that Clyde Hall, the métis, actually looked more like a Shoshone than a Frenchman, as she had for some reason half expected, Kate just stood there for a moment more. At last, she shook herself past this hesitation and looked down at the buggy reins in her hand. "Yes, of course. Is there somewhere safe I could tie my buggy?"

"You can tie it to the tree, right there," Hall said. Kate quickly complied. Hall shifted his big frame to one side of the door and nodded toward it, waving a hand. "Come in, please."

Kate walked quickly across the close space and past the big Indian, going inside the house. It was dark inside and filled with a sweet-flavored smoke. Everywhere lay beaded and painted Indian objects, moccasins, shirts, lances and such. A large-boned woman with as little meat on her as the métis sat on the floor against the far wall, threading a needle, and three thin young girls sat beside her, staring with wide black eyes at the white woman. Clyde Hall introduced the woman as his mother, Elk. He gave the names of the three girls, too, his nieces, all of whom had English names. Kate forgot them all in her astonishment at their English sounds.

Looking around, Kate saw that the blankets and the clothing worn by Hall and his mother and the girls was all threadbare and beyond repair. Most white women would have thrown it all away long since, but Kate didn't imagine the Indians could afford to. It was a hard time for the Indian people. Remembering the flannel, Kate took it from under her arm and held it out nervously toward Clyde Hall. "This is for you," she said, nodding at it.

Hall made an appreciative face as he looked down at the offering, then back up at Kate. "You know Injun ways," he said. "This is a good thing. Thank you." He took the material and laid it aside, and Kate saw Elk smiling happily at sight of the flannel. "I am sorry we have no white man chairs," Hall went on, pointing to a legless seat made of willow branches that sat on the floor against the wall, similar to the one on which Elk sat. "Please sit there."

Kate did so, and when Hall had sat across from her on his own willow backrest, rolling and lighting a cigarette, he squinted through the smoke at her. "Madam, tell me what makes you come here to see me."

Kate gave an uncomfortable smile. "I have come to you for help in finding my son. I need someone who can follow tracks."

Hall began to laugh, a soft, fun-loving laugh. He looked over at his mother, who laughed too. The girls giggled at the laughter of their elders. "I am sorry," said Hall, looking back at Kate. "I am no tracker."

Kate shrugged. "I didn't know. But I thought you might know someone who is."

"I do know someone," he said after a moment's thought. "There is an old Choctaw man who came here a long time ago and lives out beyond the river. His name is Beaver."

Beaver was in his eighties, with a stooped back from years of living, leathery skin from years in the sun, and a broken, scarred face from years of war. His wrinkle-shot smile was genuine. He wore a black top hat with one eagle feather protruding from its band, and he came from his tepee to meet them supporting himself on a cane of cured longhorn phallus.

"I follow tracks," the old man admitted to Kate, after listening to Hall reveal their mission. "I follow tracks good—you see."

A few minutes later, the three of them were seated on willow backrests inside the tattered tepee. The old man started tamping tobacco into a long-stemmed pipe whose bowl was shaped like an eagle's head. Clyde Hall watched him patiently, and Kate Winchester looked back and forth at the two of them, her heart pounding with nervous tension. Didn't the old man understand she wanted to find her boy as soon as possible?

Hall looked over at Kate and nodded almost imperceptibly. He glanced upward at the sunlight coming through the smoke hole of the tepee. The sun was almost at its zenith now. Most Indians, even though forced to live in white man-style cabins, still kept a tepee nearby if they could. Only there could the spirit survive, Clyde Hall had told her.

"When a man is old he grows wise," Hall observed, watching Beaver's pipe smoke drift skyward but speaking to Kate. "Beaver, he will find your boy, Madam. But you must learn to be patient."

Kate's breath caught for a second. It was as if Hall could read her mind, and the realization was shocking. What other thoughts had he read?

Beaver sucked deeply on his pipe stem, squinting his eyes and forming his mouth in such a way as to hold onto the smoke as long as possible. He watched Kate with laughter in his eyes as with two hands he held the pipe out toward Hall like the sacred object it was. Graciously, Hall took the offering as he bowed his head and leaned back against his backrest. He sucked the smoke in and let it seep out slowly through large nostrils, a peaceful look coming over his features.

Kate had to force herself to be calm, afraid of her anxiety being read the wrong way. She played with the broach at her throat and tried not to look at either of them, hoping they wouldn't notice her, either.

"Father, he wishes his childs to move . . . to move with wisdom in their footsteps," Beaver said suddenly. When Kate raised her eyes to him, his body was canted to the side and he leaned on one hand as he searched her face. He waved his free hand slowly in front of him. "No hurry, you. Go slow, see all. Things gonna happen, hurry or not. Maybe hurry make bad things happen."

Kate's eyes flickered involuntarily to Clyde Hall, perhaps hoping for some kind of guidance as to how she should respond. Because of the peaceful wisdom in the old man's voice, or the knowing, self-confident humor in his eyes, she had the urge to call him "your Honor" when she spoke again.

"Sir, my son is a captive. Bad men are holding him. I have to hurry, or he might be killed."

Beaver took the pipe Hall passed his way. He didn't look at Kate for several moments, but down at the pipe stem as he inhaled deeply of the smoke. When he looked back up at her, his eyes were almost laughing, but his wide, wrinkled lips were straight. "Because I no hurry, I live and am old. You think first. Think long time. Then you hurry."

Chapter Nine

Although he walked feebly, Hall and Kate had to concentrate to stay up with the old Indian called Beaver once they had stopped by the ranch to pick up Tarnish for Hall and they were all mounted. Kate watched the old man ride ahead of them, his long white strands of hair glistening yellow in the morning sun, tossing to and fro with the movements of the horse. He didn't seem to pay any mind to the country around him, yet on description alone the old man rode straight to the Wolverine Narrows. That surprised Kate, for Beaver was not a native of this country. She guided him up the little side canyon, and Beaver had her and Hall tie their horses down in the first huddle of junipers, then walk with him up to where the main camp had been. They went cautiously at first, in case someone had returned since Kate and Marshal's visit the day before. But it wasn't long before it became clear Beaver had decided from the tracks that no one was in the canyon.

For several minutes the old man walked about the area, stopping now and then to study the ground. When Kathryn tried once to approach him, he just waved her back without looking up. He picked up and studied a whisky bottle and the shards of another one. He peered at the stubs of cigars and cigarettes as if minuscule directions were printed on them. At last, he came to a stop near where Kate had seen Ellis the last time. There, he squatted down on his heels, and for three or four minutes he made no move. Eyes narrowing, he held his cane in both hands, out in front of his shins, and just stared down the canyon.

When Beaver stood up there was a new spring to his steps. He still used the cane, but it seemed more of a decoration now as he made his way back down to the horses. He led his old white gelding to a big rock, which he climbed up on before struggling onto the horse's back. Hall and Kate followed him. As he made his way down the canyon, Hall motioned for Kate to stay well behind and to the side, and he did the same. He told her it was in case the old man had to backtrack. He didn't want their tracks to interfere.

At the road, Beaver glanced down and then started west without hesitation. In this country, there were few places the kidnappers could veer off. In the few where they might chance a change in route, Beaver always slowed. Otherwise, he continued in a straight line.

Once out of the Narrows, the old man became more careful in watching the road, getting down once or twice to study out something only he seemed able to see. Then he would ask Hall to boost him back up into his saddle, and they would ride on.

They rode for perhaps three miles this way, past Dutchman Curve. The canyon of the Blackfoot River fell away off to their left as the river swung south. Finally, Beaver jerked his mount to a stop and stared north across the rolling sagebrush hills—the opposite direction from where the river had gone. Holding onto the saddle horn for support, he slid off his horse and hunched over to peer at the road. When the old man had stood up and had Hall boost him into the saddle, he turned his horse off the road and started north—away from the Twin Wolfe headquarters.

Beaver never appeared to look down after that. His face pointed always straight ahead. But somehow he seemed to know right where he was going. Kate was ten yards to his rear, and after half an hour Clyde Hall dropped back to her. It was late afternoon, with long shadows seeping out of the sage and bunchgrass and fat juniper trees. Hall smiled at her, his eyelids heavy with fatigue.

"You see his head, how it does not move?" Kate nodded. "If you could see his eyes, you would see they never stay still. He watches and sees everything. Maybe he watches through the eyes of others," Hall said cryptically, glancing skyward.

Kate followed his glance to a red-tailed hawk that swung from the bottoms of cloud wisps far over their heads. She looked back at Beaver thoughtfully.

After some time, Beaver brought his horse to an abrupt stop and motioned the two of them to do the same. He stared ahead intently, but Kate could see nothing that would draw his attention.

Sliding from his horse, the old man took his cane and started forward at a loose, ambling walk. He was headed for the low crest of a juniper-covered hill, and when he neared it he bent into a stealthy crouch and tugged off his top hat, letting the white hair fall around his face. At the crest of the hill, he went to one knee.

Several minutes later, he came back to them, seeming like an old man again as he leaned on the petrified phallus.

"Over that hill is house. Men are livin' there. Men from canyon go there."

"Is my boy there?" Kate asked breathlessly.

Beaver shrugged, his expressionless eyes taking in Hall. "Don't know that. But . . . You wanna go there, not go now. Too much sun. You wanna go there, you wait night."

It was the longest two hours Kate had endured since hauling her husband to Doctor Sims's office. They sat and gnawed on jerked deer meat while they waited, and drank warm water from two canteens shared among them. Finally, with a band of rust still pooled over the far-off Big Desert, a thin sliver of moon knifed its way into the eastern sky, like a fat smooth bolt of lightning rising back up out of the Blackfoot Mountains. Rather than lighting the sage, it seemed to bring darkness on its tail, and by the time its sharpened lower point cleared the hills only dim images remained of the landscape.

"A good moon for sneakin'," said Clyde Hall, nodding knowingly at Kate. "Are you a good sneakin' woman?"

Kate allowed herself a weary smile. Coming from a white person, those words might have sounded offensive. Hall intended it only as a light joke. "I'm a good sneaking woman."

Hall gave his soft laugh and turned to eye Beaver. The old man was watching them both, his face void of emotion. "You wan' me go? You stay?"

Kate shook her head. "I want to see my son."

Beaver nodded as if he had known what she would say. "You follow then. What I do, you do."

Kate had no words, only a nod. The old man went into his crouch, and Kate followed. Clyde Hall did the same, moving in silence in spite of his size. His moccasins and his skill made his feet like those of a cat, and once Kate had to turn around and look to see if he was still there.

A light shone in the house when they crept over the hill. That light made a dim outline of the house, but Kate could see nothing of the yard around it. She trusted Beaver and followed him closely, her heart seeming to beat louder and faster the closer they got to the house—no more than a shack, really.

As if there were no danger involved at all, Beaver led Kathryn and Hall straight toward the lighted window, the only one Kate could see from that angle. Fear knifed through her chest, but she walked on, praying fervently.

When at last they were within ten feet of the house, Beaver went to his hands and knees, bringing the cane with him as he crawled forward. Kate realized suddenly that her carbine was back in its scabbard beneath the stirrup leather. She didn't know if she felt more relief or worry. She didn't want to use the carbine, but what if someone caught them here? It came to her that neither Beaver nor Clyde Hall had brought any type of weapon with them, at least not any that she could see. What did they intend to do if caught? It was obvious they simply didn't intend to get caught, for even in 1885 a white man could still shoot down an Indian with little repercussion, especially an Indian who was sneaking up on his house. There was even still a ridiculous law on the Idaho Territorial law books making it legal to shoot down any Indians seen in groups of three or more if a man was riding in a wagon when he spotted them.

Suddenly, a horse whinnied, seeming to be right on top of them. Kate looked into the darkness in horror, now able to see the dim shapes of several horses in a corral. The three of them fell onto their bellies and lay there in the sagebrush. Kate was breathing dust into her mouth, and she started to cough. She stifled it just as the door creaked and a long rectangle of light fell over the yard. The house was silent, and Kate didn't dare look toward it. They were right out in the yard, in plain sight if it had been daylight. Kate's heart pounded heavily and began to pick up speed. She knew they would be dead if the kidnappers saw them there. Why was it so quiet?! Had they seen them, or were they just waiting?

Whoever had opened the door finally spoke, to the horses. "Shut up out there." Then the door shut again with a dull *clump,* and for several long minutes they remained there, unmoving. Finally, Beaver raised his head a little and looked toward the house, and then he looked back at Kate and nodded. They got back up on their hands and knees and crawled forward again. Kate was shaking like spring grass.

The walls of the shack were very thin, for as Kate crawled she could hear voices from inside, voices of men apparently engaged in a game of cards. One man laughed boisterously, and another swore.

Crawling behind Beaver, Kate almost bumped into him when he came to a halt at the wall. She sat back on her legs, bent over in fear someone would happen to glance out the window and catch her there.

Beaver motioned with his hand for Kate and Clyde Hall to stay low. Kate was not inclined to argue. The old man pushed up slowly along the wall and slipped along it until even with the windowpane. Slowly, he eased past the wood, Kate watching him intently. Now and then she could hear an exclamation or a growled curse from inside the cabin walls.

Beaver returned with gravity in his face and hunkered down against the wall. "You boy, he there," he said in a low whisper. "You boy and four man."

Tears flooded Kate's eyes at those words. Mostly they were tears of joy, for her worst fears had been that Ellis would be dead somewhere, half-buried in some lonely canyon. Knowing he was still alive brought her more joy than she had known in weeks. She brushed roughly at her eyes and stood up against the wall, unable to contain herself any longer. Beaver stopped her with a hand on her sleeve. She turned to meet his look of narrow-eyed concern, and he hissed a warning. "You move slow. Not look long. You boy, he is hurt." She accepted this last hushed statement with knowing gravity as Beaver's way of preparing her so she wouldn't lose control of her emotions.

Edging along the wall, Kate reached the window. There she froze. She didn't have the strength to pivot her head the small distance it would take to get Ellis in her sight. She glanced over at Beaver, and he gave her a reassuring nod and a smile, motioning her on.

Breathing so deeply it seemed to set her ears ringing, Kate eased around until with one eye she could see past the window pane. First to meet her glance was the cruel little man, Star. As proof she had pegged him correctly when she saw the group riding toward Wolfe's ranch, Star had his boots lying on the floor by his chair, and the stars on them showed plain in the lamplight. The little man was leaned back in his chair with a smirk on his face, one hand behind his head, and cards fanned out in the fingers of the other hand, which rested on the table edge. Another man sat across from him, a man with unruly blond hair and a mustache that curled down toward his jaw. Somewhere in the back of her mind she heard Star call him "Dub." The man with the huge neckerchief was seated on the left-hand side of the table, watching the other two, and Calico lay back on a bunk, his arm now bandaged with white cloth.

Then Kate's eyes were drawn away to a shape that seemed so small in the shack . . . Ellis.

The boy was trussed up on the floor, seated with his back against a bedpost. His left arm was in a sling, and there was a bloody bandage around his head, his hair poking over it in unruly wisps.

Kate's entire body started to shake. The more she looked at her forlorn boy the more violent the shaking became. Was there a God above, a God who would allow something like this to happen? She ground her teeth together, wanting to do something, to scream, to curse.

Looking at Beaver, she knew her eyes must have blazed fire, but she couldn't help it. She wanted so badly to have her carbine with her at that moment, but at the same time she was very thankful she didn't. Number one, she didn't know how to use it well enough. Number two, she would have killed the four men in that room if she could, and she wasn't ready to have blood on her hands.

Kate realized Beaver was motioning her away from the window, and she went hesitantly. She was still shaking, and she walked brazenly across the yard behind him. She gave no thought to how vulnerable she was in the open yard.

When they were deep enough into the shadows away from the shack's light, Clyde Hall straightened out of his crouch and put an arm around Kate, guiding her along behind Beaver. The big Indian was so kind, so soft-spoken and gentle that Kate had the sudden, strange sensation that she had known him for years. She leaned against him and began to sob as hot tears streamed down her face. She didn't care if he heard.

Kate and Clyde Hall made the decision together to go for help and come back. Beaver was done in, so he returned to Ross Fork alone while Kate and Clyde rode on toward the ranches along the Blackfoot River.

When Kate and Clyde reached the river, they turned west along it and rode past the Twin Wolfe Ranch and Kate and Ira's property toward the Sievers ranch and that of the Perkins, Dederschecks and McLaws. While they rode, Clyde Hall did his best to persuade her to go to the sheriff. But without knowing what Ira was involved in, she told him she couldn't go to the law. Besides, the lawmen of Bingham County had already twice proved themselves incapable of adequate protection. She couldn't afford to tell them anything, not with Ellis being held captive, and his life possibly hanging in the balance. No, Kate had to do this alone. She was far past the point of turning back, and past the point of wanting the law to help her. The men who had taken Ellis away from her were a brutal lot. She could see the proof of that in one glance at her boy. Her retaliation must be just as ruthless.

It wasn't until Kate had come to the boundary of the Sievers' land, and she and Clyde sat looking across at the quiet ranch yard for ten or fifteen minutes, that Kate came to another realization. As much as it hurt her, she had to stick to her original plan. She couldn't drag the Sievers or Perkins, the Dederschecks or McLaws into the nightmare her life had become. She could never forgive herself if anything happened to them. No, she had to wait and see what her telegram brought. If it brought her a worthy champion, that would be ideal. If not, she could come to her neighbors, but she swore it would be the very last resort.

Turning to Clyde Hall, Kate put a hand on his shoulder. "Mr. Hall, I have to apologize to you."

"For what?"

"You have been so kind to me, but I've taken you on a fruitless search. I can't ask these people for help."

"You don't think they would help you?" he asked, surprised.

"No, I know they would. But who knows what would happen to them? So far they've escaped Irving Wolfe's wrath. But if they join me in this fight, they'll be just as vulnerable as I am. Well, perhaps not completely. Ira has done something bad to draw Mr. Wolfe's anger. But still it isn't fair to expect these family men to risk everything they have. I have advertisements out in several big newspapers asking for a man to hire for protection. Let me see what that brings. After all, I still have a week before Ira was supposed to go get Ellis."

"You are kind to your friends," Hall said. "And you are right. Perhaps a spirit warrior will come to you," he said with a little laugh. "And if not, I will be your warrior."

"What do you mean?"

"I don't have no plans. I am a free man—even if I am an Injun. I will bring Red and stay at your place. Then, if you need protection from your 'protector', you will have me near. I am not a gunman like you need against Irving Wolfe's ranch, but against one man who comes as your protector—and turns out to be something else—I will be your ally."

Just for a moment, Kate forgot her grief, her pain and her fear. Clyde Hall, this big, affable man she hardly knew but trusted completely, was the friend she had prayed for. With a tender smile, she leaned close and kissed him on the cheek.

The next afternoon, the stranger stopped before Kate and Clyde Hall as they scanned the station platform of the U & N Railroad. They were waiting for the man Lang Gutterage, who had wired from Utah to say he was on his way in answer to Kate's advertisement. For Lang, recognition was easy. A beautiful dark-haired woman was how her reply to his query had described her, and she would be waiting at the station with a very large Shoshone Indian and a stocky red dog.

The big man rocked to a halt, jerking off his eagle-feather bedecked, ragged excuse for a hat and thrusting his thumbs behind his belt. "You gotta be Kate Winchester. I'm the man what wired yuhs. Lang Gutterage is the handle. You c'n call me Lang."

The unusual name seemed to fit the man. He was a burly ox with tobacco-stained teeth and an oft-broken nose, hair that parted down the middle and hung over his ears as if pressed there with glue. His tremendous belly hung over a gunbelt covered with rattlesnake skin, and from various parts of his dirty frame hung the largest array of weaponry Kate Winchester had ever seen on one man. His buckskins were so filthy they shone blackly, and little bits of vegetation and the corpses of hapless insects were caught as if glued into the layers of grease that begrimed him. Gutterage wasn't quite as tall as Clyde Hall, but the cruel set of his face made him seem larger.

In spite of the bad taste immediately forming in her mouth, Kate strove for cordiality. She forced herself to meet Gutterage's eyes with a cool glance and gave him a polite look but no smile. She sensed that smiling would be the wrong thing to do with this one.

"I'm Kathryn Winchester, and you may call me Mrs. Winchester." Gritting her teeth, she forced herself to hold her hand out to him. With a grin that lacked several teeth, he took her hand, his paw swallowing it. His fingernails didn't appear to have been pared or cleaned in months. She gave him the firmest handshake she could muster, cringing at the gritty, oily texture of his skin. A musky animal stench lifted off Gutterage in the slightest breeze. She smelled it this close and suspected Clyde could smell it from his position five feet away. It was pretty bad for a man to smell rank enough to notice it especially in a day and age when as a rule a man might go for days, weeks or longer without a formal bath.

"And this is Clyde Hall," she told Gutterage.

Gutterage gave a nod, passing his eyes with open scorn over the Indian. "I'll jist have two rifle cases 'n' one bag, Injun. It's made o' beaded buckskin. Yuh can't miss it."

Kathryn cleared her throat, drawing Gutterage's eyes back to her. "I'm afraid you have mistaken the nature of my relationship with Mr. Hall. He isn't my employee. He is my friend. He didn't come to carry your luggage."

Lang Gutterage's gaze shifted back to Clyde, and he looked him up and down disdainfully, then belted out a laugh. "Hell, t'ain't nothin'. Hold a minute, 'n' I'll git it m'self."

With that, Gutterage snugged his hat back down over his hair and swaggered off to the baggage car, where two men were off-loading trunks and bags. Hitching his overloaded gun belt around on his hips, he leaned down and hoisted a large buckskin bag to one shoulder. Then he reached down to scoop up two cased long arms in one big hand. The fringe on his blackened buckskin pants and one of the firearm cases joggled as he walked back to Kate and Clyde.

"Wal, shall we go?"

Realizing she had a bull by the horns, Kate decided to take the tiger by the tail—a backwards-seeming analogy, perhaps, but a bad predicament in either case. She wouldn't let this situation go any further without stating her case to Lang Gutterage flat out.

"Please understand, Mr. Gutterage, that what I said in my telegram still stands. You are guaranteed twenty-five dollars and a repayment of travel expenses for responding to my advertisement. But if I am not satisfied after one day with your performance and carriage, your employment is terminated. I did make that clear, I hope."

Gutterage's cat-like eyes narrowed, and there burned a flame in their depths that Kate didn't like. But he just smiled and spat a stream of tobacco juice off the edge of the platform onto the rail bed. "I understand that, lady. One day. 'N' I want my money now."

Before Kate could respond, she was surprised by a voice beside her. "Hello, Mrs. Winchester. Won't you introduce me to your friend?" It was the banker, Ward Brassman.

With relief flooding over her, Kathryn turned to look at the banker. "Oh, Mr. Brassman. It's so nice to see you!" Her eyes flickered back to Gutterage, and she felt momentary embarrassment, not knowing quite how to introduce the man. "Um, Mr. Ward Brassman, this is Mr. Lang Gutterage. Mr. Brassman is the bank president," Kate added. She was confident that Ward Brassman's sense of etiquette wouldn't allow him to press her further as to her relationship with Gutterage.

The banker nodded, hesitant. Instead of offering a hand, he just touched his hat brim to Gutterage, repeating his name with forced grace. Then he turned his full attention to Kate. "Your daughter said you had returned to the ranch."

Kate paused. Why had Brassman been talking to Vala? It concerned her, but she instantly wondered why. Was she jealous?

Kate smiled. "I did go back to the ranch. I had to take care of the animals." As her mind churned further, rolling on its own wheels, she said, "Mr. Gutterage will be working for us for a while, looking out for the stock." There—that explanation should ward off any further questions Brassman might harbor.

But Brassman's curiosity wasn't quenched, and Kate saw his eyes make the quick trip over Gutterage's form, noting with studied disinterest his display of weapons. To a man of Brassman's perception, it would be apparent Lang Gutterage was more than just a stock tender.

Brassman looked back at Kathryn with concern mounting in his eyes but a smile parting his lips. "Well then, I'll wait until you are settled in at . . . at the ranch? Assuming that's where you'll go. And then I would be pleased if you'd allow me to pay you a visit. I heard you sent your husband away, and I'd like to check on you to make sure everything is all right."

Kate's voice faltered. How quickly word flew in a little town! So everyone would know now that Ira was gone. She wondered if that would change anything. What would the kidnappers do about Ellis now? The thought horrified her, and she choked back tears.

She blurted out almost harshly, "I would rather you didn't come out for the time being, Mr. Brassman. You've been very kind, but . . . Well, we'll be busy out at the ranch with Ira absent, and I don't believe I'll have any time to receive callers."

"Very well then." Even as Brassman replied, his eyes said he would ride out anyway. She wished there were some way to stop him, but at the same time it comforted her to know he intended to. It also made her heart pick up just a little.

"I'll take the liberty of calling on your children again, Mrs. Winchester," Brassman said, doffing his hat to her with his most gracious smile. "Please at least allow me the comfort of knowing I can do that much; I'll feel helpful if I can allay their fears in some small fashion."

For a moment, Kate felt the urge to reach out and touch Brassman's hand. She could still feel the electricity of that earlier touch, which was why she didn't do it again. If only she could somehow let Brassman in on her strategy. Clyde Hall was becoming a good friend, but Brassman was . . . he was . . . like a knight in shining armor. She smiled at that childish thought, and Brassman smiled back, oblivious to her schoolgirl imaginings.

"Good day, Mrs. Winchester," Brassman said. "Mr. Gutterage." Before parting, he nodded at Clyde Hall. "Nice to see you, Mr. Hall." The big Indian only nodded.

An hour later, as Kate, Clyde and Lang Gutterage sat the Winchester wagon, en route to the ranch, they lost a wheel. While they were standing at the road edge, Hall and Gutterage attempting to jack up the wagon and replace the errant wheel, they were approached by a shiny black buggy. When it drew near, Kate recognized with a quick intake of breath the square-shouldered silhouette of Ward Brassman. He wouldn't dare be coming out to visit her already! Against her wishes?

The buggy hesitated, but then it came on, pulling up next to them. "Hello again, ma'am. Mr. Hall, Mr. Gutterage. It looks like you have that well in hand."

"Yes, thank you," Hall said, huffing. "What a day to have this happen. It's too hot."

Brassman smiled, forcing his eyes away from Kate to rest on Hall. "Yes, it certainly is that." He seemed momentarily uncomfortable with some thought, looking up the road toward the Blackfoot Mountains. Then he looked over and smiled at Kate. "Nice day for a ride," he said. "I just had to get away from that office for the morning. I'll be on my way, then, if you're certain I can't be of any help." Casting a glance at the wheel, now back in place, Brassman touched his hat and slapped his horse with the reins, making the buggy lurch forward and go on at a good clip. Kate watched the rig fade away in its own cloud of dust.

Ward Brassman grimaced and spat past the side of the buggy, wiping at the dust that collected on his cheeks. He thought of the woman behind him, with Clyde Hall, the métis, and that ruffian. It was pretty plain this Gutterage was not just a stock tender, as she had told him. He was disappointed to know the woman would lie to him. But he had to understand. She didn't want him to know where the money his bank had loaned her was going. But seeing Lang Gutterage, all loaded down with firearms, it was pretty obvious she had hired him as a gunman.

It was a foolish thing for the woman to do, but he understood her desperation. Her husband lay dying, and as far as he knew she had no idea who had tried to kill him, or why. To make matters worse, further attempts had been made on her husband's life. Brassman could see why she had become desperate and sought help. He had offered her his own, but he was no gunman. He was the last man who could help her protect her husband.

The shameful part was he didn't want to protect her husband.

Ward Brassman squinted against the dust his horse kicked up. He thought ahead to the lover that awaited him. She had always been so good to him, and he had even started to feel like she could make a man a good wife. But she was no Kathryn Winchester. A woman of such beauty and charm came along only once in a man's lifetime. And she was a fighter, too—a woman of strength. He couldn't help but think that if Ira Winchester died, Kathryn—Mrs. Winchester—would certainly be looking for another man. In spite of his lover—he thought regretfully of the sad-faced woman he knew affectionately as "Tiger"—he planned to be the first man on Kathryn Winchester's doorstep if her husband died. Having seen her beauty and known her charms, however briefly, he didn't believe he could ever be completely happy without her at his side. And Ward Brassman was no slouch himself. He had seen Kate Winchester look at him with a look that said she was intrigued, whether she would admit it or not . . .

A thin skiff of clouds milked over the moon. Kathryn Winchester crouched near Clyde Hall, watching the lonely shack in the shadows of the Blackfoot Mountains. They had found it before dark, for Kate didn't trust her own sense of direction after the sun went down. Then they had proceeded to wait, a wait which proved eternal under the onslaught of Lang Gutterage's stench and foul, crude mouth.

But as much as she detested the sight, sound and smell of Lang Gutterage, he had more than proved himself with his arsenal back at the ranch. He could consistently place a bullet into a head-shaped target at two hundred yards with the big Sharps rifle he carried, and the four pistols he wore had cut a pumpkin in two with their twenty loads. His ability could not be faulted. But still Kathryn could barely stand to wait until she could pay him off and shoo him out of her sight forever.

When it was well after dark, Kate peeked over the hill, and her heart leaped. She knew the cabin should be there, yet there was no light. Had the kidnappers already bedded down? She cast a concerned look toward Clyde Hall, but in the cloud-dimmed moonlight the only thing she could tell for sure was that he was looking toward the house, not her.

"Well, let's go git 'em." In spite of the dark house, Lang Gutterage's coarse voice remained full of confidence, raising Kathryn's optimism in spite of her dislike for him. She had to admit he had proven himself a very able man, at least in handling firearms. She hoped he had the intelligence to match.

In the darkness, Gutterage walked straight forward, not bothering to be discreet about his arrival. His weapon of choice, the one he held in his hands, was a double-barreled Remington shotgun, backed by the four revolvers and an immense butcher knife.

Gutterage's first moment of hesitation was at the door of the shack. He paused, as if suddenly realizing he had no plan from here. He could rage right on in the house, but without any light if he started shooting he might kill Ellis. Kathryn was about to utter a warning when Gutterage turned to her.

"Just stay right here." Then he was gone into the night, around the corner of the shack, and Kate and Clyde Hall were left standing at the door, completely vulnerable if the kidnappers happened to step out.

It was several minutes before Gutterage returned. Seeking out his lumbering silhouette, Kate saw a match flare in his fingers, illuminating a bundle of grass and small sagebrush branches in his hand. He touched the match to the bundle, and the grass burst into flames, licking into the branches.

Without warning, Gutterage threw a big shoulder into the door, and it gave against his force. The big man stumbled into the house, and before Kate could gather herself together to follow, she heard him curse.

"Nobody here!" he growled. "Not a soul."

In another second, Kate saw light flicker and burst. Her heart leaped as she realized he had set his makeshift torch to one of the two beds in the cabin.

"Don't be a fool!" she cried. "You'll set the whole country on fire."

She ran through the doorway toward the bed. A big hand caught her arm and jerked her around, pulling her much too close to the hot stench of Gutterage's breath. "We gotta let 'em know we mean business," he growled. "'Sides, it's too late."

Kate tore her arm from his grasp, whirling again into the room. The bed was engulfed in flame.

Chapter Ten

Kate ran to the bed and tore the blankets from it. She threw them on the dirt floor. With Gutterage looking on in amusement, she stomped at the flames, soon joined by Clyde Hall. The room quickly filled with smoke. Both Kathryn and Clyde were choking against lungs full of soot and gas before it was safe to back away from the blankets.

When the world had again fallen into near-complete darkness, the harsh sound of Gutterage's laughter shook the little room. "You're both fools. We shoulda struck a blow ag'in' 'em whilst we could. Shoulda skeered 'em a little an' let 'em know some'n's after 'em."

Kathryn just stared at the big foul man while her anger churned hot inside her. "Only a fool would do that."

It was too dark now to see Gutterage's reaction, but she could feel it. It was like a burning rush of hot wind, coming toward and over her, yet leaving her cold. In a low, calculating voice, Gutterage called Kathryn a foul name and spat hard against the wall. "You hired me t' do a job, woman, 'n' I intend t' do it right. Yuh can't go pussyfootin' in on men like these er yer gon' lose the fight. I kin tell yuh that right now. So you tell me what the hell yuh wan' do. Either you let me handle this my way, er I'll take my money 'n' go."

Maybe it was the darkness that made Kate brave. Maybe it was the big Indian standing silently behind her. But her instincts told her this would be her only chance to rid herself of this man she knew without a doubt now she had made a mistake in taking on.

"I'm afraid you force me to choose that course, Mr. Gutterage. Your methods are not ones I will brook from someone I employ."

There was silence for several seconds, but it was silence so loud it hurt. "Then t' hell with yuh," Gutterage said at last. With that, he was gone into the dark, and Kate could hear his lumbering feet crunch the brush for half a minute as he stalked away from them toward the horses.

Kate laughed to relieve her fear. She looked toward the big shadow of Clyde Hall. "We don't need his kind," she said.

Hall's tone was grave. "That is a bold thing you did. But I hope you are ready for the consequences."

It was black in the Winchester yard, black and filled with the fresh scent of summer dust. Stars seemed to bulge and recede intermittently in their distant stalls, and one shot brilliantly across the sky and into the juniper horizon. A horse nickered beyond the house, and crickets made their bold, loud music all around.

Toward the front porch, there came an arc of dim red light that matched the falling star, only this one landed in the dust of the yard and burst into dozens of tiny bright sparks that instantly died, leaving only the acrid odor of cigar smoke.

Kate saw the big form of Lang Gutterage unfold from the edge of the porch as she and Clyde Hall climbed down from their mounts. Gutterage stepped forward and stood in front of Tarnish as Kate worked the latigo of her saddle loose to let the horse breathe.

"I'll take my twenty-five bucks and travelin' expenses t'night, lady," Gutterage said around a mouthful of tobacco. "I'll be gone when yuh wake up t'morra."

Kate felt nothing but relief at the words. "Mr. Hall, would you mind taking care of Tarnish for me? I'll pay Mr. Gutterage what I owe him."

Hall complied silently, and as Kate made her way up the dark porch she heard Gutterage following her. She turned on him abruptly. "Would you mind waiting here for me?"

One corner of the big man's mouth twitched with a look of perverse humor. "No, thank you, lady. I'll just go inside away from the skeeters."

With a strange chill running up her spine, Kathryn turned on her heel and went inside. Then, while Gutterage stood by, she took the lamp from its customary place on the shelf beside the door and struck a match to bring its wick to guttering life. Wanting as much light as she could get, not to better see Gutterage but to put off the feeling of him watching her from the dark, she then went around the room and lit three other lamps, putting a soft yellow glow on everything.

"You may sit at the table if you wish," Kathryn said to Gutterage, waving him toward it. She would rather have asked him to leave the house while she went for his money, but she had tried that once with no success. Doing it again would make him suspicious of just how much money she had. She had had the foresight to put fifty dollars up in the cupboard, away from the remainder of her loan money, which was hidden in a metal case under the floor of the outhouse. She went to the cupboard now.

After standing on her tiptoes to retrieve the money, Kate turned with forced boldness to Gutterage and looked at him levelly. "What did it cost you to come here, Mr. Gutterage?"

The big man's eyes flickered to the money, resting there before they came back to her face. "I come a fur piece, lady. A fur piece, right enough. It cost . . . Well, it cost more'n yuh got there, no doubt. But I'll take that 'n' be gone—for now."

Another shiver passed up Kate's spine as he spoke those last two words. She had the sudden feeling it wasn't going to be so easy ridding herself of Lang Gutterage. "There are fifty dollars here, Mr. Gutterage. Take it and go."

Gutterage's eyes dropped to the money in her outstretched hand as he pushed indolently to his feet. He looked at her face, and then his eyes flickered to the cupboard from where the money had come and made a cursory sweep of the room. "You give away fifty bucks like it's an ever'day thing. Wisht I had money like that there myself. Come in mighty handy on a cold night. So would you."

The fear hadn't yet had time to fully seize Kate when she heard Clyde Hall's footsteps on the porch, and the clicking toenails of Red. The two came through the doorway together and stopped just inside.

"I'll sleep in your little shed with Red Dog. Then I won't be no trouble to you," Hall said. "But a blanket would be nice." His eyes landed on Gutterage, then purposefully slid away.

Kate drew in a quick, silent breath, forcing herself not to look at Gutterage. "No, Mr. Hall. Mr. Gutterage will be sleeping in the shed, and there isn't room for two."

Gutterage looked boldly over at her, then back at Hall, laughing loudly. "'t's right, Injun. You'll have t' sleep out in the sagebrush."

"Mr. Hall, why don't you and Red Dog stay here on the floor? It may rain tonight."

A deadly silence engulfed the room. At last Lang Gutterage walked close to Kate to take his money from her hand. She could feel the hate rolling out of his eyes at her. "I shorely didn't figger you fer that kind o' woman, lady. I shorely never." Sliding the coins off her palm, he let them fall with a jingle into his pouch and strode wordlessly out the door.

A minute after he was gone, Clyde Hall broke the silence. "Spirit told me about him before he even came. It's funny how your protector can turn against you without no warning, like a rifle with a barrel full of dirt. You have an enemy now, Mrs. Winchester."

Kate didn't know what woke her in the morning, but she awoke with a start. For a long moment she stared at the whiteness of the ceiling, trying to get her bearings. When she realized where she was, she swung her feet to the floor and stood up to dress hurriedly, running a brush through tangled hair.

There was a nagging worry in Kate's mind, and she had no idea what it might be over until she stepped into the main room. There, one foot on the floor and a thigh perched across a corner of the table, was Lang Gutterage. A quick glance across the room showed Clyde Hall lying on the floor, a few spots of blood near his head. Red was nowhere to be seen.

A little smirk ticked up one corner of Gutterage's mouth. "Hell of a couple o' watchdogs yuh got there, lady. That dog, he just slicked on out the door when I opens it. 'N' the Injun, hell, he ain't no more'n a papoose. But one stroke o' my rifle butt done fer him."

"What is it you want?" Kathryn said, trying to force boldness into her voice and fear for Clyde Hall from her mind. Without thinking about it, she had folded her arms across her chest.

"You give away money too easy, lady. Where's the rest of it? I come a fur piece t' git here, 'n' I ain't leavin' with on'y fifty bucks in my pouch t' show fer it."

"It's all I had, Mr. Gutterage. And I'll ask you to leave only one more time."

Anger flashed across the big man's face, but it turned almost instantly to a look of mirth. He began to laugh, leaning back his head and letting his laughter roll out from deep in his throat. He had just stopped laughing and stood up from his perch when they heard the dog barking in the yard, barking the way dogs do to announce a new arrival.

Gutterage pointed a blunt, threatening finger at Kate. His eyes were full of warning. "You go 'n' see who's out there. 'N' nothin' funny. You try anything, I'll kill whoever's out there 'n' have my way with you later. You know I c'n do it, too."

With her feet frozen in place, Kate stared at the big man for a long moment in which he looked blandly back. Then his look changed instantly to one of fury, and he yelled at her, his face turning red.

"Git t' that door now!"

They could hear the rattle of a lone horse's hooves now. Pulling herself out of her trance, Kate gave Gutterage a wide berth and made her way to the door, fearing for whoever was on the other side of it. At the door, she waited until the beating hooves stopped. There was a pause before boot heels sounded hesitantly on the porch. The first man she thought of was Ward Brassman.

The knock, unlike the footsteps, was a sharp set of confident raps, a pause, and then three more raps. Kate waited a prudent amount of time, then placed her fingers on the door handle. She eased it open reluctantly, making sure Clyde Hall's form was out of sight of whoever stood at the other side of the door.

The man on the porch was not Ward Brassman. He was no one familiar to her. The man had a chiseled face, on the point of being handsome, with hazel-green eyes and sunken cheeks, a brazen mustache curling past his lip corners and a dark tuft below his mouth. Reaching up, the stranger tugged off a white planter's hat, letting early morning light fall across a forehead that was white in contrast to sunburned cheeks. The man's green eyes flickered expectantly past her shoulder at the quarter-open door, and then again met her puzzled gaze.

"Mrs. Winchester, my true apologies for riding out so early. I hoped to catch you up alone, though, and I was told you had young ones that may be about."

Kate turned her head a little to the side, her eyes traveling quickly around his face as if searching for some hint who he was.

"I'm afraid you have the advantage of me," Kate said nervously, wondering what Lang Gutterage was doing behind her and trying to keep her eyes from betraying her. "And I don't have the children with me today. But I'll have to ask you to leave and come back later. I'm—I'm in the middle of something."

The man was obviously taken aback, from his long pause and questioning search of her face. "Ma'am, I'm Lain McShannock. I came in response to your ad in the Salt Lake Tribune."

His eyes dropped for a moment to the dust-speckled white crown of the hat in his hands. Kathryn let her eyes pass down and then up McShannock's frame. He was a slender-waisted man, a couple inches over medium height. He wore a tailored gray suit over angular shoulders and a gaudy vest of silver silk brocade. Her first guess was that the man was some type of town dandy, judging by the outfit. The butt of a revolver nudged at the right inside of his coat, destroying an otherwise sleek silhouette.

The stranger must have seen her looking over-long at his attire. "They called me Vest McShannock when I was in Kansas," he said. "They still do, time to time." He said it with a look in his eyes like he expected her to recognize the name, but it meant nothing to her.

"Kansas," said Kate. "I lived there some years ago myself."

"Uh . . . yes, ma'am." He stopped and studied her for a long moment. "You don't— I thought— I was under the impression you knew me from Abilene."

Kate gave him a bewildered look. "I'm sorry. Should I know you?"

Seeming to gather himself up, McShannock just shrugged. "Well, ma'am . . . That is, I reckon not. No matter. But as to your advertisement—has it been answered yet?"

Kate stared at McShannock, lost in indecision. Her greatest emotion was fear of the man who stood in the shadows behind her. Yet a small measure of relief played into her feelings, too, if only she could use this unforeseen rescuer. The problem was how to plead for McShannock's help without getting him and herself killed in the process.

Even as she asked herself that, she knew she had to try. It was obvious Vest McShannock had been sent by God or angels in Heaven, and she couldn't let him get away. She had the awful feeling he was the only thing that stood between her and death . . . or worse.

"I— It hasn't," she stammered, in answer to his query. "But I'm afraid I'll still have to ask you to call back later, Mr. McShannock." Even as she finished speaking she mouthed the words "Help me" emphatically and flickered her eyes toward the room behind her.

Every bit as quick as Kate had perceived, McShannock's eyes began asking questions even as his lips voiced words. "When may I call again, then, ma'am? I have some more of my things in town that I need. If you like, I'll go after them and come back."

She again signaled him with her eyes that danger lurked in the house, and with the finger and thumb of her left hand she made the sign of a gun. As McShannock nodded, she said, "Why don't you do that, Mr. McShannock, if it's no trouble. I believe we'll be able to talk then."

"Thank you, ma'am," McShannock replied, lifting his hands in a silent signal for her to stay calm. He made his way to a palomino horse ground-reined near the porch and climbed on board, turning to ride out of the yard as Kate shut the door.

As Kate was turning, her heart jumped to see Lang Gutterage nearly upon her. But instead of touching her, the big man lurched past and to the window, parting the curtains with the fingers of his left hand. From that window, the road could be seen for a mile before it disappeared over the hill. Kate waited and held her breath, hoping McShannock had the sense to ride on until he was well out of sight.

Finally, Gutterage turned back to Kate. "You done good, lady. Real good. You done a real good job a-gittin' 'im gone. I'd a kilt yuh both."

"What do you want, Mr. Gutterage?" Kate asked, her voice weakening under his bold, leering stare.

"Lady, you know what I want. 'N' then I want yer money, too," he replied with a guffaw. His eyes scanned her up and down, then went serious. "Now first jist tell me wh'r the money is, 'n' mebbe I won' even hurt yuh. That is if yuh gimme what I want. Got a feelin' I c'd stand t' stay here fer a awful long time 'fore I got tired o' gittin' some o' that."

Kate shuddered and averted her eyes, not wanting to anger the man. "I'm afraid we're going to have to search for the rest of my husband's money. He isn't very trusting with anyone, even me. The only thing I know is that he keeps it in a strongbox somewhere in the house. I wasn't lying to you: that fifty dollars was the only money I had access to."

"Wul mebbe a little sidetrackin' c'n he'p yuh remember," Gutterage said, grinning as he grabbed Kathryn by the arm.

Kate struggled to pull away. Gutterage only laughed and grabbed her other arm so he had both of them in the grip of a vise as he whirled her around and shoved her backward toward the divan. When Gutterage let go of Kate's arms, it was too late for her to catch herself. She felt the backs of her legs hit the edge of the divan. Then she was going down.

Kate landed and rolled to one side almost in a single motion as Gutterage threw himself toward her. She hit the arm of the divan and forced herself past it. Even as she struck it, the divan's wood frame cracked and groaned under the new strain of Gutterage's weight. A gust of stale sweat stench bit into her nostrils. As she was shoving away from the couch, Kate felt something grasp the back of her dress, but Gutterage was too slow. She had gained the momentum she needed, and she pulled away just as his hand must have been closing.

Kate ran for the kitchen. Her thigh slammed into the corner of the heavy table, knocking her to the side. A searing pain shot through her leg, but she felt it only in the back of her mind. She had no time to even contemplate the agony.

The thump of Gutterage's boots told Kate he was behind her. She didn't dare look back. She sprang toward the cook stove. Her fumbling fingers laid hold of a big cast iron skillet. She felt Gutterage's arm encircle and lock around her neck. The fingers of his other hand clawed a hold into the back of her bodice. She heard the awful sound of its tearing. She struggled against him, choking, as he next got hold of and tore her camisole nearly to her waist. She felt the rush of air against her exposed skin.

Kate fought with the instinct of a wild animal. She drove down and back with the sharp, pointed heel of her shoe. Gutterage groaned with pain and loosened his hold on her neck just enough for her to turn her head and then, her chin freed, to drop down out of his grasp. He threw his weight forward to pin her against the stove, but she had already pushed away from him and now whirled to face him.

Lang Gutterage was good with a gun, and he was plainly a powerful man. But speed was not among his assets. He was just turning as Kate raised the big pan and swung with it. The pan weighed perhaps five pounds, but Kate had spent years working the ranches with Tom and Ira. The weight of the skillet didn't even slow her down. Its bottom edge caught the side of Gutterage's face at an angle. It jarred his shaggy head sideways. Its dull clunk filled the room.

The big man staggered and fell against the counter. His hand went instinctively to his face. It was that move which saved him. The pan was making its desperate arc again. It struck Gutterage in the back of the hand before it reached his face. But the blow still stunned him, making him stagger backward. Then, taking the pan handle in both hands, Kate drew back again.

Gutterage snarled a curse at her and reached for a gun.

Chapter Eleven

For a moment, Kate felt frozen. She watched the big hand close over a pistol. Then she reacted. She didn't know what she was about to do even as she did it.

With the uncommon strength bred of fear, Kate threw the pan. As it was making its strike she whirled for the door. She had the vague perception that the pan struck Gutterage high in the chest. She had aimed at his face.

The room had never seemed so long to Kate.

She reached the door expecting to be grabbed from behind.

Even as she threw it open and lurched out onto the porch she thought she heard Gutterage's heavy breathing still coming from across the room.

In hopes of gaining herself some time, Kate slammed the door behind her. She stumbled from the porch, nearly falling. Her first delirious thought was of the pitchforks in the barn, but one shocked glance reminded her of the fire.

At that moment, Kate heard a noise at the side of the porch. She whirled. Her eyes fell on Vest McShannock. But before she could feel any relief she heard a heavy crash against the inside of the door. McShannock made a lunge across the porch. He reached the door just as it flung inward and spewed forth Lang Gutterage.

In the ensuing confusion, Kate saw Gutterage's gun in his hand. As it came to bear on her, she saw a blur from the corner of her eye. Her glance flickered to see Vest McShannock with his own pistol in hand. He struck down with crushing force against Gutterage's wrist. The bigger man growled in pain and surprise. He whirled to accept this new challenge, but the gun slipped from his useless hand and landed on the porch at his feet.

Lack of weapons was one problem Gutterage didn't have. But even as he reached for one of his other guns it was obvious the blow to his wrist had damaged him. At least for the moment all dexterity was gone. The other hand, the one Kate had struck with the skillet, was balled up in a contorted-looking fist.

Gutterage seemed to forget Kate even existed. The big man spat a string of curses at McShannock. He lurched forward as if to grapple with him. McShannock stepped lightly back and planted the barrel of his gun alongside the bigger man's head. It was a move that seemed almost casual, with such a lack of effort as to appear no more than a tap. But Gutterage hunched his shoulders and rammed his eyes shut against the pain. He tried to raise his hands to his head. Then he fell to his knees and tipped forward. McShannock sidestepped and cracked him again across the back of the head with his gun, and the blow seemed to drive Gutterage's face into the boards of the porch. He started to draw himself up, then relaxed and lay in a heap like a pile of discarded buckskin clothing.

Kathryn Winchester stared at Gutterage, then at last forced her eyes to look up at Vest McShannock. He stood spraddle-legged over Gutterage's motionless form, his gun still poised in one hand as if he wanted the big man to try to rise again. Without warning, tears flooded Kate's eyes, and a shiver ran through her entire body. She felt suddenly very cold and very vulnerable and very alone.

What had Ira done to her family? This should have been a peaceful place to live. What had her husband done to destroy it? She thought of Ira's gaze upon her, and the image left her more empty than before. She was looking through blurry eyes at a stranger, and she was thinking of Ira. But nowhere could she find any love.

At last, Vest McShannock stepped away warily from Gutterage and holstered his gun. He came off the porch with practiced grace and stopped before Kate, opening his mouth to say something as he saw her dab at her moist cheeks. That moment was the first she had read any uncertainty in his eyes. He looked uncomfortably away from her until she cleared her throat. Then he looked back, and their gazes locked.

"I don't want to be the one to bear the news at a time like this, Mrs. Winchester. But there are more like him in town."

Her eyes flickered to Gutterage. "Like—like him?"

McShannock shrugged uneasily and brushed the back of a finger across the lower edge of his mustache. "You can't print a notice like you did without expecting riffraff to reply. And, ma'am? They're here."

Kate forced a little smile and held his gaze. "You're here with them, Mr. McShannock. What does that make you?"

Vest McShannock smiled gravely. "I'm your guardian angel."

Kathryn Winchester ticked up an eyebrow and met McShannock's eyes with a level gaze. McShannock stared back. He couldn't take his eyes off the woman. It had been years since he had seen her, but she had lost none of her beauty. Fact was, time seemed to have matured her good looks—solidified them. Signs of fatigue lined her eyes, but that was understandable, considering what they had told him in town. Her cheeks seemed a touch gaunt, too, but those were both things that could be cured by decent sleep and a few good meals. Pushing aside his conscience, he let his eyes quickly scan the length of her, noting the odd, loose sag to her bodice, as if the back of it had not been done up.

Kathryn Winchester was gazing at him now with questioning eyes, and he read the questions in them but couldn't find his tongue. The memories of years ago had seized him. He was half glad the woman didn't recognize him. And really, there had been no reason that she should.

"You're a long way from Kansas, Mr. McShannock."

McShannock realized he was staring. Half a smile tilted his mustache. "Yes, ma'am, I suppose I am. I've been living in Salt Lake." He forced his eyes past her to the man on the porch. He hadn't moved in all that time—maybe he was dead. It wasn't unknown for a pistol barrel to crush a man's skull, and he had certainly made no attempt to be gentle. The man was far too big to treat his head like a china cup.

"We'd better see to your friend," McShannock said dryly. "I would just as soon he didn't get back up."

Kathryn Winchester started to turn, and he glimpsed the reason the front of her bodice hung so loosely: the entire back of it, along with the camisole she was wearing beneath it, had been ripped. It hung down in loose flaps. The skin of her back, though obviously not habituated to sunlight, had an olive cast to it and glowed provocatively in the morning sun. The gentle valley of her spinal column, between its smooth layers of flesh, lay subtly curved, the skin looking soft as a beaver pelt—and Vest McShannock knew of nothing softer than that. McShannock hadn't come to Idaho with any intention of becoming involved with Kathryn Winchester, but the sight of her bare skin stirred him. His thoughts shamed him, and he nodded toward the front door.

"Mrs. Winchester, if you'll kindly pardon my saying so . . . perhaps you'd like to change out of that dress. I'll see to this."

Kathryn Winchester's face flushed, and she turned fully to him once more, her eyes filled with pride that strove against the obvious desire to look away. To save them both further embarrassment, he stepped past her and up onto the porch, noting the rise and fall of the big man's chest. As he rolled him over and started removing pistols and knives from him, he heard the woman move up the steps behind him.

The animal side of him, the base male instinct, told him to turn his head for one last look at her bared skin, but he kept his eyes on the fallen man until he heard the door shut. He closed his eyes and cursed his own manhood. It was beyond any doubt providence that he had arrived here when he did. He had helped out Mrs. Winchester, which was why he came there in the first place. But maybe he should leave now. Maybe he had already done enough. Maybe his plans here amounted to only a fool's errand.

After removing every weapon he could find from the unconscious man, he took piggin strings from his gear and lashed his hands to an awning post, then tied his feet together with two more of the leather thongs. This was one man who wouldn't be going anywhere.

Stepping away, McShannock went to the door and knocked. He heard the woman tell him to come in, and when he did he was shocked to see her back still bared to him. She was crouched over a man on the floor. It wasn't as if Vest McShannock didn't know anything about women. He was a veteran gambler, and it was a profession that kept him in almost constant contact with women—mostly free-living single women who didn't care for the idea of a permanent relationship any more than he did. He had seen bare backs before—and more. But not of a lady like Kathryn Winchester—not of the only woman he had met since he was twenty years old who had moved him beyond physical desire. The fact that he couldn't put himself beyond these feelings for Kathryn Winchester disturbed him deeply. He had told himself from the beginning he was coming here for honorable reasons. But the truth that had been thinly hidden in his consciousness was rearing its ugly head now. He had never been able to erase Kathryn Winchester from his thoughts; he had come here to find out why.

McShannock lent the woman a hand without comment while she explained who the big Indian was. It was not until they had bandaged his head and laid a blanket over him that Clyde Hall began to stir. His eyes flickered open, coming to rest on McShannock. Immediately, he struggled to rise, looking around disconcertedly.

"It's all right, Mr. Hall," Kathryn Winchester said. "He's a friend."

The words caught McShannock by surprise, and his eyes jumped to the woman, then back to Clyde Hall. "My name's McShannock—Vest McShannock. How do you feel?"

"I remember feelin' better," Hall said with a little smile. "What hit me?"

"Mr. Gutterage hit you with his rifle," Kathryn Winchester replied. "And Mr. McShannock repaid him in kind."

Hall started to nod and then groaned. "I guess my head don't agree with rifle butts."

A silent procession made its way into Blackfoot later that day. Kathryn scanned the street, looking for sign of Irving Wolfe or any of his hired men. Lang Gutterage rode beside her, his red-rimmed eyes making him look like a bear just out of hibernation. And Vest McShannock sat his palomino behind Gutterage, the big man's bag and leather rifle cases across his thigh and a gunny sack weighted down with pistols and knives jouncing from his saddle horn.

They passed through town to the south and came to a stop before the courthouse. Two rows of tiny "Mormon poplars" on both sides of the big brick building hung their leaves languidly under the summer sun. A ditch alongside both rows trickled with water right then, keeping the little trees alive. It had been dug because these poplars, the first trees planted in Blackfoot, were the county's pride. Their cultivators had no intention of letting them perish.

Kate left McShannock and Gutterage outside at the steps and went into the sheriff's office. She caught the big lawman in the process of cleaning out his desk. While Hess shuffled a sheaf of papers quietly, Kate told him about Lang Gutterage. Hess didn't say much while he listened to the story.

When she finished, he laid the papers down and went outside, holding back what Kate thought was a look of deep anger. She wasn't certain who the anger was leveled at. He stopped in front of Gutterage, whose hands were tied. Taking the big man ungently by the arm, he shoved him inside and led him downstairs to a cell. When the big man was safely locked up, the sheriff climbed the stairs again and stopped in front of Kate, who had returned to the office. He leveled his gaze at her.

"We talked about you buying a gun to protect yourself, Mrs. Winchester. I'm glad you chose to follow that advice. But I've heard about the advertisement you placed in the papers. I haven't seen it, but to be honest with you I think you're walking on dangerous ground."

Kate just looked at him, so he went on.

"I think you see exactly what I mean, since your experience with Gutterage. I don't know about this McShannock fellow. Maybe under the circumstances he really is your guardian angel. But in my experience that kind of thing only leads to danger. As a general rule, men like that aren't any better than animals. They're going to take money any way they can get it. That might mean turning against you the second they have a better offer."

Kate shrugged. "I can't argue with you, Sheriff Hess. I've never done anything like this before. But I can't see that I have any other recourse."

"I know you're in a bad position, Mrs. Winchester," the sheriff said, shaking his head. "But I hate to see you make it any worse. I'm doing all I can, ma'am. I hope you understand."

"I do understand, Sheriff. And I hope you understand why I have to do this."

Hess looked down at the floor, rubbing the back of his neck. "Well, what about this fellow outside? This McShannock? What do you know about him?"

"I know that today I owe him my life. And more. And, Sheriff, having a personal protector is the only way my family and I will make it through this trial."

Hess nodded. "All right. All right." His face was full of exasperation. "I know I haven't helped much."

Hess cleared his throat and sat down on the corner of his desk, putting his attention on the papers he had dropped there. Finally, he looked up. "It makes a man feel pretty worthless when someone comes to him for help and he fails. I hope for your sake this fellow pans out. But don't let me down, ma'am. I have faith that you know the law. If you break it—you or this man you've taken on—you'll be prosecuted just like any criminal."

When Kate left the sheriff's office, McShannock was nowhere to be seen. She started to look around for him and spotted him walking out of the El Dorado Saloon, quite a ways up the road from her. She met him halfway, looking at him questioningly.

"You probably think I just couldn't wait to have a drink," he said with a chuckle. "Actually, I just started to spread the word that you're no longer looking for gunmen."

Kate looked McShannock's face over with one eyebrow raised.

"You're very confident."

He laughed. "You didn't want those men, ma'am. And before we leave town you'd better place another advertisement telling folks you're no longer in the market."

With that thought in mind, they went first to the telegraph office and sent out a telegram to that effect. Then they went to the dry goods store, where Kate bought herself a new dress and camisole to replace those Gutterage had destroyed. Kate figured on sewing up the others and wearing them while she was on the ranch, but she couldn't very well wear them on visits to town. She and Ira were by no means well off, but she had her pride.

McShannock hung in the background of the store, picking out two new pairs of socks and a cravat. He made his way quickly to the counter when he saw Kate stop in front of it. "I'll pay for the lady's things, too," he told the clerk.

Kate glanced at McShannock, then leveled her gaze at the clerk. "Mrs. Filer, I will pay for my own goods."

The storekeeper quoted Kathryn her total, and Kate counted the money out to her. It wasn't until then she turned to look at McShannock. He was watching her with an amused look on his face, and when she caught him he just shrugged blandly. He turned with a smile for the storekeeper and paid for his own things.

They stepped into the porch's sunshine, and Kate started to turn to McShannock, planning to mildly berate him. After all, he had come to her to make money, not to spend it. Before she could open her mouth, her glance fell upon a short, dark-suited man standing across the street in the shadows of the barbershop.

It was Irving Wolfe.

He was in conversation with Sheriff Hess.

Kate's heart picked up its rhythm, and she found herself staring. Wolfe had as much right to talk to the sheriff as she did. And it might have been nothing at all—nothing more than the two of them exchanging pleasantries. But several seconds' observation made it plain it was more than that. This was a serious conversation. At one point, Wolfe jabbed his finger at the sheriff's chest to punctuate something he said. Hess stood his ground, but his face didn't appear very self-confident when he replied. That made Kate wonder even more.

Then the conversation seemed to soften, and suddenly Irving Wolfe reached into his coat and drew out a pocket book. Counting out several bills, he passed them to Sheriff Hess. The sheriff looked back and forth between him and the money. At last, he held out his hand and accepted it.

McShannock's voice startled Kate. "Is anything the matter?"

She turned to look at him and blinked her eyes, more to clear her thoughts than her vision. "I, uh— I don't know. That's the sheriff over there. The man he's talking to is Irving Wolfe. He's the man who tried to kill my husband."

The moment she returned her eyes to the pair, Wolfe happened to turn, and his glance fell upon her face. He was still speaking to Sheriff Hess, but he paused in mid-sentence. He said something to the sheriff, and the lawman's glance also leaped her way.

There was something in the sheriff's face—the look of a startled fox caught in the chicken coop. An altogether different quality was in the flat, measuring glance Wolfe threw her way. Hess pried his eyes away from Kate and said something to Wolfe, hurriedly folding the bills Wolfe had given him and tucking them into his vest pocket. Then the big lawman turned on his heel and walked away. Wolfe, too, tore his gaze away from Kate and made a beeline away from the barbershop to where his rig was parked down at the hardware store.

Kate Winchester was left standing on the porch of the dry goods store, her fingers wrapped around the awning post. A feeling of illness had erupted inside her stomach, paralyzing her. All she could do was stare toward where the sheriff and Irving Wolfe had stood in conversation moments before. And all she could think was that she had been betrayed. The look in Sheriff Hess's eyes could have been nothing but guilt. What could he have been doing but telling Irving Wolfe that she had hired Vest McShannock as a protector? And what could Wolfe's money have been for but to pay for Hess's information?

Kate's thoughts spun back to what Hess had said about not being able to trust people. Now she knew he was right. She couldn't even trust him.

Chapter Twelve

Not much was spoken after Kate and Vest McShannock picked up the children from where they had been staying with the Websters and started back toward the ranch. The kids must have seen there was something wrong. They sat silently in the wagon and watched the grass and sage roll by.

McShannock knew something was wrong, too. Kate could feel him studying her, and he came across as a man who liked to indulge in conversation. Yet he never said a word. In all that time back to the home place, only Cheyenne tried to carry on any kind of a dialogue, and Kate didn't offer her enough feedback to keep any communication alive. Cheyenne finally fell asleep in Vala's arms. It made Kate feel horribly guilty, but there were so many other things on her mind right then.

As Kate's fingers mercilessly stroked the broach at her throat, she couldn't stop thinking about Sheriff Hess and Irving Wolfe and Vest McShannock. Had the sheriff actually warned her to get rid of McShannock? She didn't recall his exact wording, but that seemed to be his message. And why? Because the sheriff was under Wolfe's thumb? Anyone could talk to the local law. That in itself meant nothing. What bothered Kate was the exchange of money and the way both Hess and Wolfe had reacted when they caught her watching them. Sheriff Hess was one of the people in Blackfoot Kate had never doubted. He was the only man besides Doctor Sims in whom she would have confided—except, perhaps, for Ward Brassman. But now she no longer could be sure. After all, what did she know about Arch Hess? It wasn't as if she had ever dealt with him before Ira's attack. He was just someone who greeted her on the street and asked how she was. And what elected official didn't do those things? Who was to say he hadn't been in Wolfe's pocket all along? Wouldn't that explain how they always found Ira? After the money Hess had openly accepted, the answers seemed obvious. Wolfe was a powerful man, more powerful than Kate had ever guessed.

Kathryn brooded over these thoughts the entire way back to the ranch. She almost wished she had left the children in town. She could have thought more clearly without them underfoot. But then, were they safe in town? She couldn't say anymore.

Before they arrived at the ranch, Kate had made up her mind. The first thing she had to find out was exactly what kind of man Vest McShannock was. What did he expect from her? And were he and Clyde Hall and Ward Brassman to be her only true allies?

What about Fred Dubois, the United States marshal for the territory? Did she dare go to him if she couldn't trust Hess? The Mormons in the area had good reason to mistrust Dubois. He had declared an all out war on them—a political war. But Kate was not Mormon, and she knew many others in Blackfoot who would have trusted their life to the charismatic Dubois. She had just started entertaining thoughts of wiring the marshal to ask for his advice when she remembered his term was going to be up just that month. Not knowing who would succeed him, she dropped the notion of turning there for help.

Clyde Hall and Red Dog were sitting on the front porch when they pulled into the yard, and they walked out to greet them. Kate introduced Clyde to Vala, Marshal and Cheyenne, and asked Marshal and Vala to begin preparing supper. They all went into the house, and Kate went to the bedroom to change out of her town clothes.

When she came back out, McShannock was standing looking at the shelf Ira had mounted in the corner of the room near the bedroom door. There, in a dry vase, stood three roses, their stems tied together with a piece of lace. The roses had once been red, but they had all been dead and dry for a long, long time. Now they were nearly black.

McShannock looked up at her and met her eyes, and her own eyes touched the roses before coming back to him. "There is one there from the coffins of each of my husbands," she said simply. "Maybe that will help you understand why I placed that advertisement."

"I understood before. You have to protect yourself however you can."

Kate took a deep breath, her gaze holding his. He had deep, pretty green eyes full of a kindness even a gambler couldn't hide. "Would you take a walk with me, Mr. McShannock?"

McShannock hesitated, and his eyes swung over the children. At last, he shrugged and glanced toward the corral. "If you need to talk, we'd just as well do it while we're brushing down the horses. I won't leave them out here uncared for. If you'll excuse us a moment, Mr. Hall . . ." he said to the big Indian standing nearby.

As they walked back outside, McShannock paused, and Kate saw him looking over at the roses that grew along the wall. Most of them were red, but she had some white ones and a few pink mixed in. McShannock walked over and leaned down to sniff at one of the white ones, closing his eyes. When he straightened back up, he looked over thoughtfully at Kate.

The heat of the day had begun to subside, and the smell of warm, powdery dust rose in the cooling air of the corral. As the two of them walked into the corral and shut the gate, McShannock watched for a moment as his palomino stamped its foot, raising a little cloud. Pulling his saddle off, he rested it across the top rail. He turned to Kathryn, and she supposed he intended to offer her a hand, just by the way he paused and looked at her. But she had purposely hurried with her saddle to avoid that. She hefted it herself and set it on the ground, tilted on its horn with the cantle supported against a corral post. She wanted the man to know he was dealing with a self-sufficient woman.

When Kathryn straightened up, she found McShannock staring at her. He didn't look away when caught. A smile formed on his lips, making his dark mustache spread and thin at its cleft. It was the kind of smile a brother might give a sister in time of trouble, a smile of fond concern.

The man turned away, digging into his saddlebags to come up with a battered bristle brush. He tossed it to Kate, and she caught it easily in her left hand and raised the right one to rest on the top pole of the corral. For several more seconds, they stared each other down. Kate tried to read behind McShannock's eyes, and by the way he watched her she guessed he was trying to figure her out, too.

"Why did you come here, Mr. McShannock?"

"I . . . Well, what do you think? You placed an ad offering money. I answered it."

Kate dipped her head. "All right. That's fair enough. And after this morning I wouldn't feel bad about paying it all to you and letting you go. You've already saved my life once."

"That may be, but you aren't out of the briars yet."

She looked at him squarely. "This affair may be much deeper than I thought when I placed that advertisement, Mr. McShannock. I couldn't expect anyone to stay and help if it's as bad as I believe it might be."

"I came to help you," McShannock said with a shrug. "I'll stay until the job's done."

"Mr. McShannock. I have to be frank with you. I've seen the way you look at me. If you're here for my money, you'll be well paid. But if you're here for anything else . . ."

"Is that what you think?"

Kate's eyes flitted briefly away, then back at him. "I don't know what to think of anyone anymore. I trusted Sheriff Hess."

McShannock turned and dug his curved fingers like claws into his horse's mane, giving the knots a firm, steady pressure until his fingers pulled clear. He ran them a couple more times through the same section of mane and looked back over at Kate, leaning his arm across the horse's back. "From where I stood the sheriff was carrying on a conversation with this other fellow. I don't know as that makes him a bad man."

A sigh escaped Kathryn. "It's not the talk. It's the money Irving Wolfe gave him. And the way they both looked at me and then stopped talking and walked away from each other. Wasn't it obvious they were talking about me?"

"Now, Mrs. Winchester," McShannock said, letting an amused chuckle escape his lips. "It seems to me when the chips are down people are always quick to assume everyone's talking about them. I've learned over the years it's mostly imagination. Those two could have been talking about the weather."

"You know better than that. That wasn't a casual conversation. And why the money?"

"Maybe he was buying his underwear."

"That's not funny," Kate said.

"No, maybe not. But maybe Wolfe was paying some fine or something, maybe for something one of his ranch hands did. Hired help is always causing headaches for employers. As far as their talking, there are a hundred things they could have been discussing. Maybe the sheriff was telling Wolfe to stay away from you."

A sudden glimmer of hope sparked and died in Kate's heart. "He wasn't telling him anything of the kind. I've never told the sheriff I suspect Wolfe of anything."

McShannock drew a deep breath and worked his fingernails across his horse's sweaty side until Kate saw what he was doing and held his bristle brush out to him. He looked at it a long moment, then finally took it from her and sighed. "I assumed the sheriff knew your suspicions. I guess that might throw a different light on their talk. But it still doesn't prove anything."

Kathryn felt a surge of stubborn pride and spoke without knowing what she was about to say. "I could have done all right here, you know. I have Mr. Hall, and the banker in town, Ward Brassman. He offered to help."

McShannock stared at her quietly for a long moment, his face expressionless. "But they're not enough," he said frankly.

"How do you know they aren't?"

"If they were, you wouldn't have placed that ad."

Kate frowned. She looked at McShannock, not liking the way he watched her. His gaze made her uncomfortable, like she was under glass.

"Your help was welcome this morning, Mr. McShannock. I'm glad you came when you did. But I'm not sure if I can trust you."

Watching the gambler's face, Kate didn't know if she read hurt or surprise—or both. All sign of friendliness left his face, and he slapped his horse on the rump and sent it trotting across the corral with only one side curried. "Fair enough, ma'am. You just say the word, and I'll be gone."

With that, he turned and left the corral, walking off across the flat toward the river. Kate didn't have the heart or desire to call him back.

Vest McShannock didn't come back for supper. Without Kathryn's requesting it, Clyde Hall walked off with Red Dog the way the gambler had gone. He found him sitting on the bank of the river, looking at the blue water roll slowly past with his Colt pistol in his hand.

McShannock glanced back once, to be sure of who approached, and then he put his attention, at least outwardly, on the Colt.

Clyde Hall stopped just behind McShannock's left shoulder, and Red, after sniffing at the white man's shirt, rambled off to explore the water's edge. Hall rested his fingers in his waistband and studied McShannock and his Colt, then the quietly whispering river and the yellow-green hills beyond.

"Mrs. Winchester, she don't know what she wants," Hall said while he studied the gentle lift of the grassy Blackfoot Mountain foothills. "She has a boy who has been taken away from her. He is a part of her spirit. They call me True Shot, but I'm no good with a gun. That name just comes from you Americans playing around with a language you can't speak. The name on the French side of my family is Truchot. Americans saw how it is written and thought it should be True Shot. So they called me that.

"That lady there, she needs you to get her boy back, but I don't think she *wants* to need you. She doesn't want to need anybody. Too many other people have died and disappointed her."

"You talk pretty well for an Indian," McShannock said, studying the cylinder of his pistol as he spun it around and around. "You're educated."

"Sure, I'm educated. I'm what you whiteys call a Progressive—a good Injun. If I was a bad Injun I could get that boy back myself. My old friend, Tongue Eater, he could have got that boy back. But one of you whiteys killed my friend."*

McShannock stood up, holstering his gun and dusting off the seat of his pants. "I'll get the boy back. I came here to help that woman, and I'll stay until it's done. I hope that 'True Shot' name comes through for you. I'll be asking you to go after the boy with me."

The ten-day deadline Calico had given them came at last, and Kate met it with dread in her heart. Her stomach was already torn up inside from all the days of wondering what the kidnappers might have done with Ellis if they had heard about Ira being sent out of town. But she had to go out to Wolverine. She had to do something.

Before dawn that day, Kate stood beside Marshal. In the light of the full moon he looked like a frail little boy. And he was, after all, just a boy in the eyes of many. But they didn't know him like Kate did. Fifteen-year-old Marshal had proved himself a man.

Down in the birch trees, the horses milled around, their fidgeting drowned by the gurgling waters of Wolverine Creek. Kate, Marshal, Clyde Hall and Vest McShannock tied the animals by their lead ropes to the stoutest of the birches, separating them by enough distance so they wouldn't get tangled in each other's ropes or fight in the absence of their masters.

There was little talk among them. Only the creek and the wind and the sound of hands tampering with leather broke the night-quiet. They deposited their saddles among the roots of a gnarled tree and turned their eyes toward the steep, jumbled rocks across the road.

The Narrows were black and lonely in the moonlight, their angular blocks of stone blotting out packs of stars and blurred by the high-up fringe of Douglas firs. Marshal knew the way best, and with his shotgun clutched tightly in his fists, he led out. On Clyde Hall's suggestion, they had ridden a few hundred yards past the side canyon where Ellis was to be held. If the kidnappers somehow managed to break away with Ellis, they wouldn't discover the horses on their way back to the Twin Wolfe

*Tongue Eater appeared in *Death of an Eagle*, Howling Wolf Pub. 1988

and be able to put their pursuers afoot.

Kate and Clyde took up the rear of the procession. Kate felt the almost numbing weight of the Winchester carbine held awkwardly across her thighs. It smacked first one, then the other as she walked. Why had she brought the weapon with her? She couldn't trust herself with it yet. But McShannock had spent a couple of days showing her the finer points of its handling, and her confidence had grown. She knew to squeeze the trigger instead of jerking it, to count each shot aloud as she fired in order not to lose track amid the excitement. She knew the importance of keeping both eyes open to aim and of keeping the crescent butt tight to her shoulder between shots. That saved the precious time of lowering and raising it each time she jacked the lever and also saved the pain of its slamming back into the shoulder bone. She understood follow-through and lead, and she was prepared for the awful feeling of dead men on her conscience.

That last was a lie. Even McShannock admitted there was no way to truly prepare for that anguish. But she had no doubt she could kill to protect her family. If only her hands agreed.

McShannock's plan could have been no bolder—nor any simpler. Clyde and Kate would skirt the edges of the canyon, one on either side. McShannock and Marshal would slip up the middle and right into the midst of the kidnappers, hoping to reach them just when there was enough light to see. With any luck, they would still be sleeping. After all, they didn't expect to see anyone until ten o'clock that evening.

They reached the side canyon, and Kate bit her lip as McShannock turned to look at her, smiling reassuringly. "They think they have you scared," he said in a whisper. "They won't be expecting a strong move, not when they have your kid. That's our hole card. You find one man there, and you put your sights on him when we move in. Same for you, True Shot. Sounds like there are enough of them to go around.

"Marshal?" He turned to the boy and put a hand on his shoulder. "Don't think about this as killing—it'll weaken you. Think about it as protecting your father's and brother's lives—and your mother's, too. If you even think they might be going for a gun, you shoot them." He emphasized his words by pounding his chest with his fist. "Shoot them dead-center with one barrel, and then look for another target. You won't need to shoot them again."

Before Kate knew it, she was alone. The others had moved on. She eased her way along in the dark. She went from tree to tree as slowly as she could. She tried to be silent the way Clyde had shown her. Not much light filtered down into this hole in the world. That forced her to go slower, feeling her way with the toes of her shoes. She went silent as rabbit feet. Other than the wind occasionally blowing across her ears she heard no sound.

Then she became gradually aware of one disturbing noise. It was the sound of blood pounding inside her head. It seemed to rattle against her hat brim. It made her ears ring. She wasn't a woman prone to sweat, but her blouse under her arms and on the back of her neck was soaked. She kept wondering how she was going to know when to stop. How would she know how close was close enough? What if she walked right into the middle of them?

She was surprised she couldn't hear the others. She knew how narrow this canyon was, and even Clyde, on the other side, couldn't be any more than thirty or forty yards away.

Finally, she reached a juniper with several trunks jutting up together into one massive crown. She stopped and hid behind the tree, facing the center of the canyon. Then she listened. There was no sound.

How far were the kidnappers? How far were Marshal and McShannock? Why didn't the kidnappers' horses make any noise?

The thought hadn't occurred to her before because she had been so concerned with the idea of shooting someone, but it came to her now. It came so strongly that it made her start to shake, only partly because of the pre-dawn cold. What if they weren't here at all? Sure, they said they would come, but they had had a long time to change their minds. Maybe they had seen the burned blanket in their shack and realized someone had followed them. Maybe they knew Ira was gone out of Blackfoot and wouldn't be coming to meet them. Maybe she would find nothing more here than the crushed body of her boy.

Again, Kate shivered, leaning her forehead against the tree for support. Why had she been chosen for this trial? Certainly other people went through worse than she, but still . . . four husbands? Why Kathryn Winchester? She had lost too much to justify. Was God working on a new Bible, and she would be the female Job? Kate shook herself free of that blasphemous thought. Fate had served her these trials, not God. But He hadn't pulled her out of them either. She was meant to gain strength by dealing with it alone. Perhaps this time Fate would make Kathryn Winchester a murderer.

A feeling of utter terror gripped her heart. She could hardly breathe. Between the fright and the cold, she couldn't stop shaking. Her eyes would blur, and she would dab them dry, only to have her sight dim again almost immediately. The scents of the nighttime mountains that she normally would have enjoyed brought her no pleasure now, when she even stopped to notice them.

Kate wanted to give up. She wanted to sit down right here and cry and will this nightmare away. She had been born a Quaker, not a killer!

Gritting her teeth, Kate forced her mind back to the present. She strained her ears to hear something—any sound that might mean she was not alone. Her pulse was the only sound, beating in her ears like two heavy straw brooms being slapped together rhythmically. She heard only that pulse and that mischievous little wind that would come down the canyon and whisk past her ears, shuffling her hair around.

The nightmare became complete when the landscape lightened enough to see. Kathryn, her eyes strained from peering into the dark, could see there was no one around. And she was right on the main trail now. The terrain had forced her there, becoming too steep to go along the hillside any longer. So where were the others? Was there some place farther up the canyon? Had McShannock and the others gone on ahead? Somewhat farther, surely, for she couldn't see them here. Unless she had gone past them and they were behind her.

Her heart took a leap, and she started forward, holding the Winchester out in front like McShannock had taught her. It wasn't too long before she heard, then saw, the others coming back.

Clyde was in the front, and when he saw her looking at him he grimly shook his head. They came together, and Kate could see the despair in Marshal's face. If her son could cry, he would have. She could see that. Had they found Ellis? Found him . . . dead?

McShannock scanned the canyon slopes as Clyde reached out and squeezed Kate's arm. "I followed the tracks. I'm not much good at trackin'. But I can see all the tracks here are old. No one has been here since before, when we came with Beaver. You're sure this is the day they said to come?"

"I'm sure," Kathryn said in despair. "I'm sure it is. Marshal?" The boy only nodded, clamping his jaw and looking quickly away.

Vest McShannock sighed. "What about that old Indian? He could track them from the cabin, maybe. Give us some idea where they went. Or what about the cabin itself? They weren't there the night you went, but they might have gone back. Whatever we do, it'd better be today."

"But— They said to meet them here," Kate protested. "Why wouldn't they come?"

"They did say ten o'clock at night, ma'am," McShannock said. "It's a good bet they don't plan on coming out themselves until later. It gets too hot to spend the whole day lounging around up here. I'll ride to the cabin, ma'am. They won't know who I am. Maybe I can get close enough to see if they're there."

"They'll know who you are," Kate corrected him. "Irving Wolfe saw us together, remember? And I'm sure the sheriff told him about you."

For a long moment, McShannock held her eyes. His glance took in Clyde Hall as it slid away. "I could sure use a cigarette."

Having said that, McShannock pulled a sack of Bull Durham with its attached packet of papers from his coat pocket and worked with them as he turned and started back along the little stream toward the road, his rifle under one arm. When he had finished rolling the cigarette, he reached into his pocket for a match. Kathryn was trying to keep up with McShannock, with Marshal at her right rear and Clyde Hall to the left.

Without warning, four horses rounded the corner to come into the canyon. Their riders were talking among themselves. One of them let out a laugh. It echoed unusually loud in the early morning. She instantly recognized the laugher as Star, who rode a little grulla. One of the others was Calico, seated on his strawberry roan. She recognized "Mr. Neckerchief," too. He rode a sorrel.

Puzzled just for a moment, suddenly Kate realized there were five riders, two of them on a dark bay together. The one in front was Ellis!

Kate was stunned to see the riders appear. Clyde must have been too, for he made no move. But McShannock's cigarette and match went tumbling, and his rifle came from his armpit and into his hands like a living thing. He raised it to his shoulder, and Kate jumped at its bellowing roar.

The horses erupted into action. Star's grulla whirled and slammed into Neckerchief, knocking him over the side of the sorrel. Even as Kate saw this, she heard Clyde Hall's rifle roar, and the dark bay carrying Ellis stumbled. It went down like its legs had been shot out from under it, throwing Ellis clear and landing on the leg of the man in the saddle, who Kate guessed must have been the man she had heard Star call "Dub."

Shaking, Kate raised her carbine. She realized Ellis hadn't moved from where the falling horse had thrown him. She heard McShannock fire again. Neckerchief's sorrel let out a scream yet didn't fall. Then Clyde Hall's rifle belched its second cloud of smoke. Kate hardly even heard the shot. She didn't see what he hit. Everything seemed to move so slowly. The gunsmoke hung forever in its bush-shaped puffs. Kate's eyes were dimmed by tears of terror at the smoke and sound of firing and men yelling and horses screaming out in fright. The grunting bay on the ground squirmed and kicked, rolling half over to crush Dub against the road. Neckerchief's horse turned back the way it had come and ran until it disappeared in the Narrows.

Calico had ridden over the far side of the road and down toward the creek. Neckerchief ran after him. No one fired at him before he reached two junipers at the road's edge and dove down behind them. The only other man left in the saddle was Star. He whirled his horse and rode straight for Ellis. The boy suddenly leaped up from the middle of the road and started in a run toward the creek to Kathryn's left.

Star drew his pistol. In spite of his head start, Kathryn could see her son would never make shelter. The rider was almost on top of him. He leaned over the side of the horse and aimed his gun.

Chapter Thirteen

McShannock's rifle roared again, and then Clyde's. Both were aimed at Star. Kate flinched. Her carbine, which she didn't even remember cocking, erupted smoke and flame. It kicked like a fist against her shoulder. She hadn't had to jack the lever; McShannock had her do that before they started up the canyon.

Star drew himself up in the saddle. He flew sideways off his horse. He slammed into Ellis,and they both went to the ground in a swirl of dust. The horse turned and ran up the road the way the first one had gone, its stirrups flopping loosely.

The fallen bay had struggled to its feet. It stood now with head bowed, but Dub lay on the road. As McShannock started toward them a shot cracked. Kate heard the bullet wing past, a sound like the slice of a willow switch too near her ear.

The carbine was frozen in Kate's hands. "Ellis! Run!" she heard herself scream.

"Stay there, Ellis!" McShannock countered. "Tell him to stay!" He yelled the order at Kate out the side of his mouth.

Without thinking, Kate obeyed. In spite of feeling immense relief at the sound of Ellis's reply, her angry eyes shot to McShannock. "He's too close to them," her voice hissed.

Without a reply, McShannock pushed hard at her shoulder. The pressure drove her to the ground even as he dropped to his knees and then flat to his stomach. Kate's cheek pressed to earth. She tasted dust in her mouth and looked over at McShannock. This was too much like the war, only then she had been but a heartsick observer. She wished fervently she had taken her children and run with them. It wasn't worth being here amid this violence.

She choked on her next breath and coughed violently. Then she lay there spent, clutching her carbine. McShannock's rifle cracked, too close to her face. She couldn't see his target, for she was looking at him. But she rammed her eyes shut at the sound of the shot, slapping a hand over her ear.

Suddenly, she felt McShannock's hand rest on her shoulder. Her eyes flew open, and her head came up. He gave her three comforting pats, then returned his hand to the forend of his rifle.

And the morning was still.

Kathryn felt numb. She raised her eyes to look toward Ellis. All she could see was a dark mound at the edge of the road. The shape was mostly Star, but somewhere in the pile lay her son.

The thought reminded Kate of Marshal, and she looked quickly around, seeking him out. She found him lying down behind her, staring back at her, his face scared in spite of his best attempt to look brave. Clyde Hall was at her left side, and he, too, was quiet as death. He didn't even look her way.

"Hey!" a voice called from beyond the far side of the road. "Hey, I'm done fightin'. Let me pick up my pardners, an' I'll ride out of here."

McShannock lay there silent until Kate looked over at him. He was sighting down his barrel, pivoting it ever so slowly as he searched out the source of the voice. Finally, he gave up and raised his head a little.

"Come up out of there holding your guns high so I can see them."

Neckerchief scrambled up from his hiding place, his rifle held high above his head in one hand. He stood a mere ten yards away among the branches of the two junipers. "I'm reachin' for my Colt now," he said, and with the free hand he pulled out his pistol and held it with his rifle toward the sky.

"Now walk across the road toward me," McShannock ordered. "I've killed two men in my life—maybe three, after today. Don't make the mistake of thinking I'd mind chalking you up, too."

Neckerchief came toward them, nearly stumbling in his haste. McShannock eased up to a knee to keep from being towered over. "Don't shoot, man," Neckerchief begged. "Don't shoot. I tell you, I'm done. I'll leave the country today."

"Hold your shotgun on him, Marshal," McShannock spoke over his shoulder. His eyes narrowed at the kidnapper, then began to scan the area behind him. "I'm a gambler, friend, and you must be, too. You gambled I wouldn't blow a hole through you, and you've almost lost. Where's your friend? You realize if he tries anything you die first."

Neckerchief shook his head emphatically. "You got it wrong, mister! He's gone. He rode down into the creek bottom and never quit goin'. Believe me, if he was in there I wouldn't be comin' out here to bait his hook."

McShannock nodded, still on one knee. He read the truth of the man's words in his eyes. "All right. Empty those guns and throw them behind me. Throw them high and hard, like you're playing Annie-I-Over."

The man complied, and McShannock's face made a little grimace when each weapon struck the ground. He hated to think of good weapons being damaged. "Now go out in the road and lead that horse toward me, away from your friend," he ordered.

Again, Neckerchief did as told. Then he returned and crouched near Dub. "How is he?" McShannock asked, coming to his feet.

There was a long silence until McShannock repeated the question. Then Neckerchief whipped his head around. "He's 'bout near dead. He's bleedin' inside. What do I do with 'im? I ain't got no wagon."

Ignoring the plea, McShannock looked toward Ellis Briggs. "Hey, Ellis. How's the man with you?"

After a long moment of silence the boy struggled to a sitting position and replied, "I think he's dead."

Kate stood up, and her eyes jumped toward McShannock. If she had expected to see any change in him, she didn't. But he was a card player, practiced at hiding his emotion.

McShannock turned to Marshal, who had stood up behind him. "You and that shotgun come with me. If the fellow in the road makes any move, I might need you to back me up." Then his eyes shifted to Clyde Hall and Kate. "You two watch the other side for the fourth one."

Swallowing hard, Marshal looked over at his mother. He followed McShannock toward the road. When they were almost there, McShannock stopped. "What's your name?" he asked Neckerchief.

The man hesitated, but looking at McShannock's rifle he thought better of it. "Rolfe. Sid Rolfe."

"All right, Rolfe. Kneel down there and pick up whatever weapons he has, and I want to see you unload them and throw them just like you did yours. Over the far side of the road."

Rolfe knelt down and pulled a pistol out of Dub's holster. He took out its shells and lobbed it toward the grass on the other side of the road. McShannock, keeping his rifle leveled at his hip, walked to within six feet of Rolfe and the fallen man. Kate looked at them for a moment longer. Then she turned and hurried toward Ellis. Her son rose to his feet, but he didn't come toward her. He stood there shaking, looking like he was ready to burst into tears. Kate had nearly reached him, but a strange, distant warning stopped her. Something she couldn't explain warned her, *Go no farther.* Was it the look on Ellis's face? The mortal fear in his eyes that should have been a look of relief, at least to some extent? Here was her most sensitive child, standing not fifteen feet away from her, but making no move toward her. Ellis, not coming to her for comfort?

Star, lying on the ground behind Ellis, must have realized something was wrong. He had lain perfectly still, as if he were dead—like Ellis had told them he was. But now he started up, pistol in hand. There was a moment of hesitation. Was Star actually loath to shoot a woman? Was he gaining his bearings and judging his chances at killing her without in turn being killed by McShannock or Clyde?

Without thinking, Kathryn Winchester leveled her rifle barrel.

She moved like a machine.

She looked at the man's pistol.

She looked at the expanse of his chest.

Then she fired.

It wasn't an aimed shot. It was one of instinct. She felt the weapon lunge back in her hands. The barrel struck upward at an angle. Even as she saw the man drummed backward, she raised the weapon to her shoulder and fired again. This time she sighted down the barrel toward his narrow chest.

It all seemed to take an eternity. Her mind moved forward so fast that everything else seemed sluggish. The man rolled over onto his face. His legs kicked. He started to come to his knees. His pistol was pressed underneath his palm, apparently forgotten. Ellis had stumbled to one side. In the back of her consciousness, Kate felt his presence but couldn't see him. Her mind had been seized as if by some power. She fired her

135

carbine again, with no doubt where the bullet would strike. It hit the man underneath the right arm. It drove him over onto his side. His pistol lay in the dust where he had pressed it in pushing himself up.

The man struggled for a moment, churning his blood into mud. At last he rolled over onto his back, his arms flinging up over his head. Giving one last spasmodic kick, he relaxed. With his arms and legs spraddled, he looked like a big misshapen X scratched against the powdery dust.

Kate stood alone—at least it seemed that way. She felt nothing, no one around her, not even her sons. All she could see was a dead man—a man she had killed. She didn't even know his name, other than "Star." He lay with his eyes turned to the sky, red mud smeared on his face and vest and shirt.

Again, Kate pictured the big X made by the dead man. She started to laugh at the ludicrous thought, but her laugh turned to a sob. Her carbine falling to strike the ground and her foot was the first sound she remembered hearing since before firing the first shot. With that sound came a full, numbing realization of what she had just done. With the realization came the tears. She hugged her arms close to herself, her eyes instantly so full of tears she could no longer even see the man on the ground.

She didn't see Ellis come toward her, but she felt his good arm close around her. Unfolding her arms, she threw them around him, and Ellis, too, began to cry. Then, for many minutes, there was no other sound. To Kate Winchester there was no one else in the world but Ellis Briggs.

They sat in the junipers until the sun rose high in the sky. Kate had been forced, most likely to her benefit, to put off thinking about the moral gravity of what she had done that morning. More important things were on her mind now, like what to do with the bodies and whether to let Sid Rolfe go or take him back to Sheriff Hess with the story.

The matter wasn't easy. Had they been able to trust Sheriff Hess, that would not have been the case, but they *couldn't* trust him, not anymore. If they knew Hess was upright, they could go to him without fear of recourse. They could take Rolfe to him as a prisoner, along with the two bodies now side by side on the road—the second body was of Dub. He had died after an hour of screaming for help from everyone from Doctor Sims to God to his mother. Kate couldn't help remembering he had taken part in the kidnapping of her son, but that had given her no comfort as she listened to him die.

With their distrust of the sheriff, McShannock reasoned they could let Rolfe go and send him out of the country—if he would indeed go. They could leave the two bodies buried somewhere in Wolverine country, and who would ever find them? Wolfe might miss them, but he would probably surmise they had run out on him. Even if he guessed anything different, he could never prove it. Even Calico had run before anyone died, and he wouldn't dare testify even if he had seen something. That would incriminate him on the kidnapping charge.

But as much as Kate's harried mind seized on that idea, she knew it wasn't possible. She might have killed a man, but it was to defend herself and her family. She felt no shame for the killing, only a sickening realization that she had lost whatever innocence had remained to her. But what happened from here on *was* within her control. She couldn't allow herself to break laws that she had a choice in. She had to take Rolfe and the bodies to the sheriff, even if he was working for Wolfe. She had originally kept the kidnapping a secret from the sheriff out of fear for her son's life. But there was no longer any reason to keep the secret, as if there ever had been. The sheriff probably knew about the kidnapping from the beginning. At least he couldn't blame her for hiding the killings. Hess could only do so much. There wasn't a jury in the state that would convict Kate for anything she had done so far.

When Kate came to her decision, a huge load was lifted from her. No matter what happened now, her conscience was clear.

Clyde and Marshal had brought the horses. To keep anyone from having to ride with the prisoner, Kate and Ellis rode double, as well as McShannock and Marshal. Clyde rode his own horse, and Rolfe rode Tarnish.

As they rode, McShannock kept his rifle across his saddle. His eyes tirelessly scanned the creek bottom and the rocks and trees on both sides. Once, he turned to look at Kate, and his glance was full of apprehension that she didn't figure he would ever admit to. But she felt it, too, and she knew why he was looking. No one knew where Calico had gone.

A shiver passed through Kate, and she squeezed her boy tightly to her. "No matter what else happens, we're going home, Ellis."

It didn't take long for Vest McShannock's watchfulness to eat away at Kate's sense of relief. She had been of the notion the violence was over, but was it really? Would a man like Calico actually run away from a battle and keep going? Something told her no. He seemed too brave, and his pride would be hurt. He would wait somewhere here in the Narrows to avenge himself.

Fear began to take hold of Kate's heart with a vengeance. Soon she could feel her heart making its crashing beat against Ellis's back. With the skin tingling along her spine, she scanned both sides of the road. She knew at any time a shot would crash out. Calico might not take them all on, but did he actually have to? Couldn't his revenge consist simply of killing her? Or Ellis?

Reaching down, she absently let her fingers caress the butt of her Winchester, feeling sweat run into her eyes and down her sides. Bob blew out his nostrils, scaring her and making her swear. Everyone turned to look at her, and she felt herself redden.

Kate couldn't seem to pull in all the air she needed. She tried again and again and failed. She thought about carrying the carbine in her hands instead of in its scabbard. But at long distance, from where Calico would most surely fire, she would be no good. She wasn't experienced enough, and she was sure Calico was. Besides, by the time she had any warning, either she or Ellis would likely be dead.

Kate Winchester suddenly tasted blood, and her tongue flicked across her lower lip. She had bitten it through.

To Kathryn Winchester it seemed a miracle when they rode out of the Narrows without being attacked. It came as even more of a miracle when they rode up to the ranch house steps, the same silent cavalcade that had ridden into the Wolverine Narrows with the threat of certain violence hanging over them. What had become of Calico?

After an emotional reunion between Ellis, Vala and Cheyenne, Kate went outside to where Marshal and the others had hitched up the wagon. They put Sid Rolfe in the wagon box, and then, with Kate and the girls on the seat and the rest of them mounted, they headed for Blackfoot.

They rolled into Blackfoot a little over two hours later, with no sign of Calico anywhere. Kate wondered if they had seen the last of him. With the great empty void ballooning in her stomach once more, she led the way directly to Sheriff Arch Hess's office. She didn't want to have to look at that man. She didn't want to have to speak to him. But they had to straighten out this matter now, before all of them became outlaws. Even if Hess was being bought out by a murderer, he was the county official. Kate wasn't going to give him anything to hold against her.

Sheriff Hess wasn't in his office, and Kate came back outside to see McShannock and Hall lowering the two bodies onto the landing. He wasn't there when they tied their prisoner by his hands to the hitching rail. But word of such matters travels fast, especially in a town of less than a thousand people. It wasn't long before the lawman strode purposefully down the road, away from the town and toward the courthouse.

Kathryn saw him come, and her heart did a little dance. Then the anger welled up inside her, and she stepped forward, placing Vest McShannock behind her left shoulder.

Ellis was just behind her other shoulder, and Marshal was to the rear of them both, with Clyde Hall and the girls. None of them made a move when Sheriff Hess stopped before them.

For a seemingly endless several seconds, Hess stood there looking at the two bodies on the porch. Then his eyes shifted to the man tied like an animal to the hitching rail. The man had slumped over the rail and just stared at the ground.

Finally, Hess raised his eyes to Kate, and she stared at him, trying to hold back her hatred. "Mrs. Winchester, I don't know if I want to hear this, but what happened? What did you people do?"

"It isn't what we did, Sheriff," she said, the calmness of her voice surprising her. "It's what you did. And didn't do."

Startled, the lawman searched her eyes. "I don't follow."

"These men and one other kidnapped my son. They were hired by the man who tried to have my husband killed. They wanted to trade my husband's life for my son's. Oh, but of course you already know that."

Sheriff Hess's neck reddened. His eyes scanned the others as if seeking for a clue to what she meant. "Mrs. Winchester, I can see you're agitated about something. Can we go in my office and talk for a moment? There are a lot of ears out here."

"What do you want me to do about these men, Sheriff? That's all I need to know. I don't need to hear anything more from you. I know enough about you already. I killed one of these men in self-defense, and the other was killed by his horse falling on him. The man tied to the rail surrendered, and another escaped. You probably know him."

It was as if a gate had broken in Kathryn Winchester's soul. The words flooded out of her without control. She despised this so-called lawman, and she knew it must show in her face and in her tone of voice and in her words. But she didn't care. She was glad to know he would no longer believe he was getting away with something.

"You'd better just stop," said Hess in a louder voice. His face had gone bright red. "Just stop right there. I don't know what you've heard about me, or what you think you've learned. But, Mrs. Winchester, I have enough evidence right here in front of me that I could place you under arrest and throw you in a jail cell for murder. Maybe you would be released, in time, but that would do you no good now. What I'm telling you is I don't like the way you're speaking to me. I can see you're angry with me, ma'am, and I have no idea why. I thought we were friends. If that's true I would appreciate you telling me what's made you so upset."

"You know as well as I do," Kathryn snapped. "Now, either throw me in jail or tell me what statement you need me to fill out. But whatever you plan to do, do it. I'm sick of looking at a man I can't trust."

"Mrs. Winchester," Hess growled, "I'm placing you under—" He stopped. His eyes danced uncertainly across her sons and across McShannock and Hall. All of them stood in shocked silence, staring at Kate.

The sheriff's eyes swung back to Ellis, and he glanced at the bandage on his head, stained with dried blood, and the sling on his arm. He suddenly sucked in a great breath, and the old softness soaked back into his eyes. He looked at Kate Winchester. "Ma'am, it's plain you have no intention of it, but I wish you'd change your mind and talk to me. I feel bad about whatever happened, and I'm sorry I couldn't stop it. But nobody told me, ma'am. Why don't you go over to the restaurant and feed the family. Think about talking to me. One way or another I'll need a statement from you, and I would just as soon it be when we're both on the legal side of the bars. I'm asking you not to force my hand, ma'am. I don't want to see your family get hurt any worse than they already have. And murder is a charge you sure don't want on your head. One way or another, ma'am, I'll come for you in one hour. Or meet me here before then. Until that hour's passed, I'll be in my office."

With that, he turned and took out his jackknife and cut the ropes tying Sid Rolfe's hands. He marched him up the courthouse steps and inside.

After leaving the courthouse, Kate decided to take the sheriff's advice and take everyone over to the Hogan Restaurant. From the restaurant window where Kate Winchester sat rubbing the broach at her throat, she watched Thornton O'Toole, the local undertaker, hurry down the road from his parlor toward the courthouse. Like a vulture, O'Toole must have been running to the smell of death.

They ordered their dinner, and then the five of them sat there silently waiting for its arrival. For Kate's part, speaking wasn't in her. Sheriff Hess's reactions had created too many new doubts, and her mind was sorting through all of the crooked paths of her anger and the bent suspicions that now, in spite of her earlier conviction, seemed so hazy.

Sheriff Hess was a public figure. That was true enough. And as a public figure he was bound to be able to put on a good front for his constituents. Yet he had seemed so genuinely shocked and even hurt by her accusations that Kate was deeply troubled. She found it hard to believe he was acting.

Yet maybe she was comparing the sheriff's actions to what her own would have been in his situation. Maybe she needed to realize the sheriff was cut from a different bolt of cloth. He had to be to have hired on as a peace officer in the first place. Naturally, the sheriff wouldn't be as emotional as she was. It wasn't good to compare his actions to what hers would have been. She wouldn't be able to pretend, especially not about something as serious as this. That didn't mean the sheriff couldn't.

Still, even with all that argument by her darker side, Kathryn found herself leaning toward at least talking to Hess, telling him all she knew and what she believed. It certainly couldn't hurt. If he wasn't working with Wolfe it would be good for him to have the information. If he was working with him, he already knew everything she would tell him anyway. Either way, her life couldn't be in any greater danger than it already was.

Thirty-five minutes later, with a meal inside her, Kate felt better. They all went to the Websters' home to freshen up, and the Websters greeted them with gladness. They were more than happy to allow them the use of their home. Kate took off her husband's hat, straightened her hair, and started back toward the sheriff's office. McShannock, Hall and the children stayed at the Websters' at her request. She was ready to tell the sheriff everything. She felt sure she would know from his reactions if he was truly an honest man.

Feeling better than she had felt all morning, she pushed her way into the office. The first person she saw was Irving Wolfe. The second was Sheriff Hess. The sheriff looked up in surprise as his eyes met Kate's.

Chapter Fourteen

The sheriff stared at Kate Winchester, the expression of surprise frozen on his face. His eyes shifted back and forth between hers, and finally he said uncertainly, "I'm glad you changed your mind, Mrs. Winchester. Umm, could I ask you to wait outside for just one moment while

I finish with Mr. Wolfe?"

Kate felt her own hate being hurled out toward Irving Wolfe. It was a kind of hatred she had never known, and she had no concept of how to disguise it. She knew it must lie like an ugly, living thing across her features. But before she could say anything, Irving Wolfe spoke, pointing his finger accusingly at her.

"No, Sheriff. You can talk to us both at once. I can guarantee you something. There is your culprit, right there. If she didn't do it, she hired it done."

"Now, just hold on." Sheriff Hess held up his hands as if to pat down Wolfe's anger.

Before he could say anything else, Kathryn was shocked a second time to see three men come walking up from the basement, where the prisoners were housed. One was the sheriff's deputy, Luke Weaver. The other two were none other than Case Deckan and Dunn Yates.

Weaver looked her up and down. He looked over at Deckan and Yates with a glance of apprehension.

Hess's glance jumped toward the three men, then right back to Wolfe. "What in the world makes you blame Mrs. Winchester, of all people?"

"Because she's the— Because she blames me for the attack on her husband, that's why!"

Hess's eyes spun again to Kate, and she could see a gray pallor come over him. "Ah, hell," he said, dropping down onto his desktop, where he sat with one thigh supporting him. "Well, we'd better get to the bottom of this."

It was a tall order they never "got to the bottom of." In fact, Kathryn was far more confused and doubtful by the time she finally left the office, an hour later, than when she went in.

To start things off, she was forced to listen to Wolfe's account of how four hundred and fifty of the beeves he had been fattening up for his drive to the Salmon City meat markets had been killed off—driven to the brink of the Blackfoot river and held by unknown horsemen while someone deliberately shot them all to death or pushed them over the edge. Of course he accused Kate, for she was the one who had come charging onto his property accusing him of kidnapping her son and of trying to kill her husband. And, according to what the clerk at the hardware store had told him, she had recently come in and purchased a rifle. What more proof could Hess ask for than that? It was significant that Kate's refuted accusation, the rifle purchase and the slaughter had occurred so closely together.

Even while the accusations hotly flew, Kathryn had the presence of mind to surmise that this time Irving Wolfe was here on business for certain. This visit, at least, had nothing to do with trying to run Hess's office. With that realization in mind, and considering the current demeanor of the sheriff, she slowly came to see, past her frustration and anger, that Hess might be a man she could trust after all. A vague doubt still lingered, the vestiges of a hatred and distrust so complete she had been able to taste it. But her instincts told her she owed the sheriff an apology.

And then it came time for Kathryn to tell her side of the story. She left nothing out. The sheriff had already heard the beginning. But still she told about the horsemen she had seen running from the ranch, and as she told that part she made sure to give a long, hateful stare to Case Deckan and Dunn Yates. Then she told Hess the things she hadn't yet shared: the barn burning and the kidnapping of her sons. Last, she recounted the gunfight in the Narrows. Trying to recall the details of it made her heart feel ready to burst once more. Her lower lip began to tremble as she held back her emotion.

When the talk was over, Irving Wolfe's face was dark red. He stared hatefully at Kate. He slowly pushed back his chair, his entire body shaking with the effort to stay calm.

"I told you the truth when you came to confront me, Mrs. Winchester. I'm sorry you didn't believe me. And I'm doubly so now, after losing a good share of my herd. You little squatters have been a thorn in my side from the start. I would certainly shed no tears over your being gone from t his country. But your own lawlessness is what will get you killed. If there is someone after you, you had better seek elsewhere to find them. Sheriff? This matter is in your hands. I want to file a formal complaint, so if you wish to have my signature on any paperwork, please make your request within the next hour. I will be at the feed store."

With that, the rancher and his two hired hands walked out. The sheriff didn't even have time to clear his throat when the door swung open again. This time the banker, Ward Brassman, was standing there, hat in his hands.

"I'm sorry to interrupt your proceedings, Sheriff," he said with a nod, ignoring Deputy Luke Weaver completely, "but, Mrs. Winchester?" He turned fully to her. "Is everything all right?"

Kathryn was staring at the banker, feeling her heart suddenly grow warm. Without even knowing it, tears raged up into her eyes and tried to spill over. Ward Brassman wasn't her man, which was perhaps unfortunate, but she could never have told anyone how much it meant to have him show up now. Wiping quickly at her eyes, Kate started to stand up. The look of sympathy in Brassman's eyes was too much for her. As she came to her feet and again met his eyes she started to cry. There was no holding it back.

As if some strange power had drawn her there, Kate found herself in the banker's arms, her tears soaking the shoulder of his coat. Brassman just patted her back softly while he held her and spoke comforting words in her ear. He looked over at Hess, bewildered, and the sheriff just stood there, confused, his hands on his hips. At last, in obvious discomfort at this outburst of feminine emotion, Hess and Weaver looked at each other, then turned and walked into another room, shutting the door behind them. Kathryn and Ward Brassman stood there alone.

Kate's sobbing ebbed, and she looked up at the banker, not wanting to let go of him. His dark eyes searched hers, and the depth of feeling in them was too much for her. He started to speak. "Mrs. Winchester, I—" It was as far as he got.

Almost hungrily, Kathryn's mouth sought his. She pulled herself against him, moved by a sudden passion. She didn't want to let go of him.

The sickening realization of what she was doing hit Kate Winchester like a blow to the pit of her stomach. She pushed away from Ward Brassman as if from a hot iron and drew the back of her hand harshly across her pressure-reddened lips. Brassman's dark skin held a blush few people in Blackfoot had ever seen, and he shoved his hat back on his head, somewhat crookedly.

"Ma'am, I—" It was the first time Kate had known the banker to be at a loss for words. "Mrs. Winchester, I didn't mean for— I apologize for coming here, ma'am. I saw you come in alone, and I saw you earlier with the bodies. I . . . I'm sorry, ma'am. I'll go if you'd like. But if you need my support, just tell me. I can stay."

The door to the other room cracked open tentatively, and Sheriff Hess looked past the void. After a look at Brassman and Kate, he walked back in, glancing oddly back and forth at the two of them. Kathryn reached out and squeezed Brassman's arm, mouthing the words, "Please stay."

Brassman turned to the sheriff. "I know you have a job to do, Arch. Mrs. Winchester would like me to stay here with her, but I promise not to get in the way of your duty."

The sheriff just nodded, releasing a weary sigh. "This is the most complicated situation I've come across since I took this office, Ward. By all means, please do stay. Maybe you can help us sort through this."

They didn't sort through very much, but with the help of Hess and Brassman, Kate was able to pen a detailed account of everything that had taken place since Kate went out to find her barn on fire. She signed her signature at the bottom of the last page and sprinkled it with blotting powder, which she blew away. She held the papers out uncertainly to Hess.

"I appreciate your cooperation, ma'am. I'll give you a day or so, and then I'll probably be out to talk to you again. You deny having anything to do with the killing of those steers, but Wolfe is sure you did it, so of course I'm forced to act on it. I don't imagine anything will come of it.

"And as to the matter of what happened in Wolverine, I'll let you know as soon as the coroner's jury makes its decision. Most people around here know you, ma'am. I wouldn't let the outcome worry you."

Kate nodded quietly. The events of this day—of this month—had drained her beyond anything she had felt since losing Tom Briggs. The sheriff could come out and talk to her tomorrow or the next day. She didn't care right then. All she wanted was to take a hot bath and then to go to bed and try to sleep away the sick feelings she had for the sins she had committed that day. She had taken a human life, and she had been unfaithful to her betrothed. She could never have imagined being guilty of either.

Luke Weaver was sitting on a chair in front of the Gem Saloon at four o'clock in the afternoon. He was drowsy from the pleasant heat of the day and the fumes from his cigarette that found their way deep inside his body and soothed him and made everything around him so calm and serene.

He let his eyes go half shut while he listened to the sounds of the town around him. Glasses were clinking together inside the saloon, not from merrymaking, but from Hal, the barkeep, wiping them dry. Four oxen pulling a freight wagon lifted their heavy legs ponderously and leaned against their huge wooden yokes and seemed ready to fall asleep even as they went forward. The driver sent a glance of longing back toward the El Dorado Saloon. His wagon was jingling its trace chains, and its wheels cranked round and round and spat streaks of sandy dust as it turned west and headed out of town toward Lost River.

Weaver's eyes came open as he heard yelling across the street, and he looked that way. The redheaded shopkeeper at the hardware store came out with a little spotted pup by the scruff of the neck. He threw it out into the dust of the street, grumbling something about a "mangy cur." Luke

Weaver was up out of his chair immediately. When two boys of eight or nine came out of the hardware store and took up the crusade against the poor pup, yelling at it and tossing rocks picked out of the street, Weaver headed their way at a fast walk.

"You stinkin' kids!" he yelled angrily when he was ten yards away. "Leave the dog alone or I'll kick both your butts. You get out of here right now!"

The boys took off running, and Weaver walked over to where the young pup cowered against the hitch rail. Leaning down, he picked it up gently with both hands, cuddling it against his chest and caressing it. The pup was dusty, but when he put his face up near its mouth he smelled that warm milk odor of a new pup and knew the thing couldn't be over seven weeks old—and being treated like a piece of trash.

The little fellow began to lap at Weaver's face, bringing a smile to his lips. With his big hands he caressed it over and over and spoke soothingly to it. "No call to hurt a little feller like you," he said. "Brats." He shot a sullen look toward the hardware store where the redheaded clerk had gone back inside. "And that pencil-pushin' idiot," he spoke quietly to the dog. "He'd better hope he never steps out of line with me, or he won't get an ounce of mercy."

Before Weaver could decide what to do with the dog, he looked up to see Kate Winchester coming out of the Star Restaurant and Bakery carrying a loaf of bread under her arm, with her little daughter at her side. The thought quickly crossed his mind that here was a family who would probably love this little pup like one of their own.

"Hey, Mrs. Winchester!" he called across the street. He hurried toward them when they stopped.

Walking right up to them, he smiled at Kate and crouched down so that his face was level with Cheyenne's. Her eyes began to glow the moment she saw the pup, wriggling and wagging its tail in his arms. "What's your name?" Weaver asked.

"Cheyenne."

"Well, that's a pretty name! Say, I found this little feller a while ago, and I got thinkin' maybe you'd like to have you a pup. If your mama says it's all right, of course." He looked up quickly at the woman to catch her reaction.

Kate was looking down at him in surprise. She had never known what to think of Luke Weaver. She didn't like the way he watched her. But then, plenty of other men watched her that way, too. Kate looked quickly from Weaver to Cheyenne to the little squirming pup.

"Well, it sure looks like they've made up their minds." She smiled at Cheyenne. "I suppose if you don't have any need for the little thing we would love to have it."

Luke Weaver pushed the pup out toward Cheyenne, who took it instantly and gave it a big hug. "There you go, Cheyenne. Make sure you feed him good."

Standing up, he looked at Kate and gave her a smile. She couldn't remember him ever giving her a real smile before, and it surprised her. "I hope it's really okay, ma'am. He was taking some abuse from a couple of boys. Didn't want to see him wandering the streets that way."

"It's perfectly fine," Kate replied. "I'm sure the kids will love him to death."

She turned to Cheyenne. "What do you say now, Chey?"

The little girl looked up shyly at Weaver. "Thank you," she said.

"Well, you're welcome, honey." Weaver gave a smile and turned to amble back up the street toward the courthouse. Kate looked after him. She almost wished she had taken the chance earlier to get to know Arch Hess's deputy. He seemed like a decent man.

Kate Winchester, her family and Clyde Hall returned to the ranch that evening. Vest McShannock remained alone in town, telling Kate he had some business he needed to finish before coming out to the ranch that night.

The first business he took care of was running off three seedy looking gunmen in the El Dorado Saloon who had come to Blackfoot looking to answer Kate's advertisement in the Salt Lake Tribune. After leaving the El Dorado, McShannock visited the handful of other saloons on the same errand, then went over to the sheriff's office and stepped inside.

After talking to Kate upon her return to the Websters' house, he understood her desire to forget any doubts about the sheriff's trustworthiness. But McShannock was still suspicious, perhaps in part because he hadn't had the chance to listen to the sheriff, to read the innocence Kate claimed was in his eyes and in his voice. The sheriff could quite possibly be an honest lawman. McShannock had met a few of those in his time. Yet even though he was a gambler, that wasn't the kind of thing a man wanted to gamble on. And maybe more than anyone else, McShannock knew, as a gambler, how a man with a calm exterior could make people believe a lot of things that weren't true. McShannock had come to Blackfoot, Idaho, to help out a woman from his past who sounded like she needed a friend. Part of his self-appointed job was to make certain who

147

her enemies were.

Sheriff Hess was in the basement feeding prisoners when Vest McShannock first went inside. He spent a few minutes thumbing through some wanted posters before hearing the slow-plodding steps of the lawman coming back up.

Hess was surprised to see someone waiting there. He was doubly surprised when he realized who it was. "Well, Mister . . . McShannon, was it?"

"McShannock."

"McShannock. Sorry. What do I owe this visit to?"

"Well, Sheriff, Mrs. Winchester headed back out to the ranch. She was pretty beat. But she asked me to stop by and let you know her husband's doing well and that she's having him brought back on the train to Pocatello. They'll go there and pick him up in the wagon for the rest of the trip. They want to keep a low profile. He should be back by the day after tomorrow."

Hess grunted quietly. "I hoped she'd wait till we learned a little more about all this before she did that."

"Well, you know. She misses her man," replied McShannock, tossing a shoulder. "But nobody will know. His uncle will escort him to Pocatello as a shotgun guard, and then Kate will pick him up there. She figured that way no one would see him coming back, and he'd be safe out there at the ranch. Of course, he'll still be laid up, in the boys' room at the back of the house. He isn't completely recovered, but he's close enough."

Hess nodded. "Well, all right. Mrs. Winchester's a stubborn woman. It doesn't surprise me that she's doing this, but I'm glad you told me. You'll take care of her, of course."

McShannock cleared his throat. "Well, I'm ashamed to admit it, but I have to ride to Eagle Rock tomorrow, and I won't be back for three days or so."

Hess searched McShannock's eyes. "I see. I . . . So Mrs. Winchester and those kids will be alone out there with Ira?"

"For that long, yes."

"Then maybe I'd better go out and check on them."

"You might," said McShannock. "And I trust Mr. Winchester coming home will be our secret. And my being gone, too."

Sheriff Hess looked at him and frowned. "I hope you're just speaking lightly to me, McShannock. I'm not a fool."

One side of McShannock's mouth tilted up in a half-grin. "I didn't figure you were, Sheriff. I hope you'll prove it by solving this thing so that woman can stay out of any more killing. She's had a hard life."

"Yes, and she seems to trust you with what's left of it. I hope you're the man she thinks you are."

This time McShannock just nodded, his glance cool. "I'm the man who'll keep her alive."

Two evenings later, shadows moved up the Blackfoot Mountains in a fluid violet wash. They extinguished the yellowish light from the sagebrush and juniper and slung themselves in long, deep-colored bouquets from the bottoms of the cottonwood trees around the Winchester ranch house. They all sat on the porch, watching the pink fade from the clouds and the look of burnt dust fog up along the horizon, fading into the soft greenish blue, almost white, of the sky. The one place they could see the river, it was light blue and serene, slithering through the soft green pastureland like a giant serpent going home.

The horses whickered contentedly out in the corral, rubbing against each other to kill an itch now and then. Nighthawks screeched across the sky, and before long the bats replaced them, hunting the mosquitoes and the funnel clouds of gnats that ornamented the air about the yard.

The horses suddenly began to whinny, and it was Clyde Hall who first heard the buggy coming up the dusky lane. Its lantern rocked jauntily on its hook, but most of the light was directed toward the house by its reflector. The light didn't make the buggy much easier to see. Stepping out of his chair, Vest McShannock said to Kate, "No one must know I'm here. If they ask, I've gone to Eagle Rock." With that, he disappeared inside the house.

The others looked after McShannock in confusion as the buggy drew up fifty feet out from the house. Everyone stood up, Clyde Hall leaning over to put a restraining hand on Red Dog's head. Kate Winchester peered into the night, remembering against her will the dark night Kelly and Tracker Brooks rode into the yard and her Tom wound up dead.

"Who's out there?" she asked uncertainly.

"Ward Brassman, ma'am," came the quick reply. "I hope I'm not here at a bad time."

Kate's heart leaped, and she looked quickly over at Vala. Her daughter's eyes had lit up, and she turned to meet her mother's.

"Bring your buggy on in," Kate said, shaking herself free of her surprise. "Please don't sit out there in the dark."

Obligingly, the buggy rattled in, and near the porch it came to a halt. Brassman hopped down from it after extinguishing the lantern and glanced quickly around, drawing off his hat. "I'm sorry I'm unannounced, ma'am. I know you asked me not to come out, but I . . . Well, it just seems wrong to leave you out here alone. I have those investments to protect, you know." He laughed, and Vala laughed with him, probably louder than she would have if she could have heard herself.

Kate's heart was thumping heavily. She had felt her body temperature seem to rise, and it angered her. She was a married woman, but Ward Brassman had a way of making a woman . . . almost wish she weren't. "Please come in, Mr. Brassman. We'll have coffee on right away."

Around the kitchen table they talked for over an hour. Both Brassman and Clyde Hall were fairly well educated, albeit in different disciplines, and they kept each other surprisingly good company. It provided ample time for Vala and Kate to embarrass each other over and over by one and then the other being caught staring at the banker. As for Ellis and Marshal, although they struggled, both fell asleep on the divan, and Cheyenne was not long in following suit.

There was a little lamp Kate kept sitting on top of a pine hutch. It had a white chimney with little rosettes sculpted on it, a delicate brass center, and a base of clear white glass with rosettes to match the chimney. The lamp was one of the many gifts Ira had given Kate in the last several months, and it sat on a dresser scarf of Battenberg lace that was also one of his gifts. It had caught Ward Brassman's eye earlier, and during a lull in the conversation he pointed at it. "My mother used to have a lamp like that," he said. "I've never seen another one like it."

Kate looked at the lamp. "Isn't that pretty? It's called a courting lamp. Back east they use them quite extensively."

"A courting lamp," Brassman repeated. "What's its purpose? It doesn't look like it would light a house for long."

Kate laughed. "No. That's precisely the point. When a suitor would come calling, a young lady's mother or father would fill it up with oil, and when the oil ran out and the lamp died the suitor was to depart gracefully."

"Oh-h-h!" Brassman chuckled. "A courting lamp. Now I see! I'm flattered you didn't light it when I sat down."

"I don't imagine anyone would light it for you," Kate said lightly. She was instantly angry with herself for the comment. It sounded very close to flirtatious.

Clyde Hall saved the day by mentioning the condition of the ranges, and the conversation moved on. Kate looked over and caught Vala staring at Brassman again and thought maybe she *should* light the lamp!

Outside, seated against the rear wall of the shed where they were keeping the horses, Vest McShannock, who had sneaked out the boys' bedroom window, cradled his Winchester and listened into the night for the occasional ring of laughter from the open doorway of the house. Other than a quiet nicker now and then, the horses had settled down. If not for the crickets, there would have been little sound to disturb the night.

And then Tarnish whinnied loudly, and McShannock stiffened. He strained his ears into the night. Several minutes went by. All of the horses had gone to lean their heads over the same side of the corral, staring toward the east. At last, McShannock heard the soft drum of hooves. It came once and faded, came again and faded a second time. Then his keen ears picked it up a third time, and this time it grew and came on slowly. Two horses . . . or more.

The noises stopped suddenly, and McShannock stood up against the wall of the shed and stared into the night. There was no sound but the crickets. Even the horses were still, and there was no more ring of laughter from the house.

And then two man-shadows slunk across the yard toward the back of the house, and McShannock quietly drew back the hammer of his Winchester.

Chapter Fifteen

Vest McShannock swore under his breath. Why couldn't there have been a full moon? He could see the two prowlers one minute, and the next they were gone. But then a full moon would have lit him up, too. At least he had the advantage of knowing the other men were there.

He thought for a brief moment of Sheriff Hess and cursed the man for the dastard he was. Of course neither of these two men would be him. He was too smart for that. He would have passed on to Irving Wolfe that Ira

Winchester was coming home, and Wolfe would send two of his hired dogs to do the dirty work. That wasn't something Hess or Wolfe would take the chance of getting caught up in, not when they had men like Case Deckan and Dunn Yates to do the job. It was too bad Hess didn't come himself. McShannock didn't like to kill, but if anyone needed it, it was a skulker like the sheriff.

McShannock hadn't told Kate Winchester his plan. He knew it would work better without her knowledge. Besides, she had been in a charitable mood for the last two days. She had wanted to believe Sheriff Hess was a good man, and McShannock didn't want to bring the doubt back to her mind. After all, for a time even he had half believed the sheriff might actually be honest. But now, without any further doubt, these two prowlers proved otherwise.

Crickets chirped, and a wedge of moon angled over in the sky, struggling to light the scene but doing little good. McShannock, with his rifle poised, worked carefully along the corral rail, peering toward the house. He passed one window and caught a glimpse of the top of Kate's head. And then he was out of view of the house front, and the darkness closed fully over him.

At the corner post of the corral he stopped. He searched the sagebrush and the side of the house but saw nothing. No sign of any man or of anything that shouldn't be there. A chill ran along his spine. In his head, he ran back over every eventuality he had imagined. He had planned carefully for this very situation. He had managed to talk Mrs. Winchester into letting him stay in her sons' room, so that would keep the boys out of harm's way in the event someone came to kill Ira. He had also told her he didn't want anyone to know he was staying out there with her, and he hoped neither she nor any of the others would slip and tell Brassman he was there. If word returned to the sheriff by any means that McShannock had tried to play him for a fool, the sheriff could become very hard to live with. Hess came across as an extremely proud man. He wouldn't like the thought of being someone's pawn.

But as for tonight, McShannock couldn't come up with anything he had done wrong. In the boys' bedroom, where he was supposed to be staying, he had left a lamp dimly glowing and made one bed look as if someone were asleep in it. But otherwise, the room was empty. Still, some vague thought bothered him.

He began to work his way around the house. When he laid eyes on it, he knew what had been troubling him. There were two bedrooms at the back of the house. One belonged to the boys, and the other belonged to

152

Vala and Cheyenne. Both had lamps glowing in them.

McShannock's heart leaped. He hadn't thought of everything! What if Vala was preparing for bed? What if she got in before the killers identified her? There was a chance they would see that both beds were occupied and decide to shoot into them both, just to be sure!

With a curse, McShannock crouched and started away from the corral. No sooner had he done that than he saw them. He was out in the open, away from any cover or concealment. He dropped instinctively to his knees, bending low to make himself look as much like a clump of sagebrush as he could. Both men had stopped. Had they seen him? He couldn't tell. He couldn't see their faces, couldn't even see which way they were turned. And then Vala's room went dark.

The would-be killers moved again, straight toward the still-lit window. They must have seen Vala in her window.

Even when the two men stopped at the boys' bedroom, McShannock waited. He could have fired now and probably had ample reason. He might even convince most coroner's juries that the killings were justified. But could he convince himself? Had there been immediate danger to anyone, yes. He would have fired before they knew he was there. But so far they hadn't done anything but look shockingly guilty of an intended crime. And even McShannock, whom no one had ever claimed to be an angel, couldn't shoot a man for doing nothing but looking ready to do something wrong.

The crash of a shotgun was shocking in the quiet night. Its white-orange light lit up the windowpane that shattered into a thousand pieces. It fired again. McShannock raised his rifle.

He fired at the fleeting shadow of the man with the shotgun as he whirled away from the window. The man let out a cry of pain, but both of them took off running across the yard. McShannock heard boot steps on the front porch, and from the corner of his eye he saw shapes careen around the side of the house. But all his concentration was centered on the two would-be assassins. He had his sights on one of the men when Ward Brassman's voice crashed against him, breaking his concentration. He tugged the trigger, pulling off and throwing his shot haphazardly into the dark.

The two men ran all out. All he could see was glimpses of shadow, and he fired at those, cursing Ward Brassman's untimely interruption. He ran after the two men, but not too fast. He didn't intend on dying of a shotgun blast from the dark. He fired again, again and again. He pumped fourteen shots into the dark. Then he heard the pounding of hooves, a sound that died with amazing quickness in the cool night air.

He turned around to see Ward Brassman and Clyde Hall near him. Clyde carried a rifle, and the banker had a short-barreled Colt Storekeeper's model pistol in his hand. The banker turned to look at him, and his look of anger turned suddenly to one of bewilderment. "You're the hired man. I thought— What are you doing lurking around out here in the dark? I might have shot you."

"My hobby is lurking," McShannock said dryly.

Kathryn Winchester hurried over, her carbine in her hand. The boys had gone to the back of the house to observe the damage to their window.

Kate gasped. "What happened?"

McShannock shrugged and closed his eyes wearily. "Well, looks like somebody paid you a visit. A shotgun was their calling card."

"But why?" asked Kate, dismayed.

"Who knows?"

Brassman looked back and forth between them. "I don't—" His eyes shifted toward the shattered bedroom window, and he dropped his gun to his side. "I guess I don't understand anything that just happened. Why would someone do this? Is Ira— Is your husband home, ma'am?"

"No. I knew it wasn't safe yet."

McShannock quickly looked away when Kate turned her eyes on him. She started to say something, and he whipped up his hand to silence her. Everyone else must have caught the motion, too, for the yard went quiet. McShannock listened to the night, and the noise that had first cautioned him came again—the quiet grunting of a horse out in the sagebrush.

Looking at Brassman and Hall, McShannock waved them off into the brush. "There's somebody out there," he hissed. And even as he spoke he was clutching at his pocketful of rifle shells and trying to thumb them into the Winchester's magazine as he stalked across the sagebrush flat.

As if out of nowhere, a big clump of brush appeared in his path. McShannock stumbled into it and nearly went down. Over his own noise, he thought he heard someone groan. Cursing his clumsiness, he shoved one last shell into his rifle and started to circle around where he thought he had heard the voice. It came again. He yelled out, "Who's there?" and leaped to the side.

A single shot split the night, and McShannock dropped instinctively to one knee, assuming one of the would-be assassins was shooting at him. A second shot made its booming statement, and McShannock saw its piercing light stab at the ground and aimed his Winchester that way.

"Hall! Brassman! Sing out or I'll shoot!"

"It's me—don't shoot," came back the voice of the banker. "There's a man down."

McShannock started carefully toward the sound of the banker's voice. "Is he dead?"

"I— Yes, I think so. Come and see for yourself."

McShannock heard the crunching of brush, and suddenly a match flared. Moments later, when he was nearly on top of the banker, a branch flared to life, flickering eerily in the night. Brassman held up the hunk of sagebrush he had just broken off, whose branches crackled spitefully. He and McShannock looked down at the huge dark form of a horse. Beneath it, his leg pinned, lay a man. His eyes flickered wetly against the firelight, and he held out a hand toward them. Before McShannock could move toward him, the hand dropped. A long breath issued from the man's mouth.

Vest McShannock stared for a shocked moment at the man on the ground, whose lungs were making their dying gurgle.

When Marshal Briggs obeyed McShannock's request for a lantern, the gambler used the now-dead horse as a seat and sucked in a deep breath. Sitting there with his heart pounding like war drums, feeling the heat of the horse's body beneath him, he tried to piece the fight together while Brassman stood there sighing like he'd killed his own mother.

"I've never killed anyone before," the banker said suddenly. "I thought he had a gun."

McShannock set his lantern nearby and studied the dead man. He saw a nickel-plated pistol with mother-of-pearl grips lying by his right hand. "He did have a gun," he said to Brassman without looking at him.

The dead man had a long face, dark hair, and eyes that slanted up at the outside. His shirt and silk scarf were soaked with blood, and beneath him spread a huge dark stain. After ripping his shirt open McShannock saw two bullet holes, closely spaced. Brassman had hit him solidly with both bullets. There was one more bullet hole in his left sleeve, and that sleeve was also soaked with blood. That had to have been from McShannock's shot at the window.

McShannock straightened up and looked at Brassman. "Well, you killed him, all right. Both of the lethal bullets are yours, but I suppose you already knew that."

Brassman nodded. "I knew I didn't miss. I thought he was going to shoot me."

"He probably would have—if his horse hadn't been crushing him,"

McShannock said with a shrug. "He came here with the intention of shooting someone."

Stooping down to retrieve the lantern, McShannock saw blood all over the back of the horse's neck. That would be from his own rifle shot that had brought the horse down on top of its rider. He was still standing there looking when Clyde Hall and Kate Winchester walked up.

"Ma'am, I know you've had enough of the killing," said McShannock in a sympathetic voice. "But you have to look. Do you know this man?"

Numbly, Kate walked over to the dead horse and peered over its side. "Oh my— Yes, it's one of his men. Wolfe's. One of the men that attacked Ira."

"You should have asked me. I know him," Brassman admitted suddenly. "His name is Dunn Yates. He came into the bank all the time with Irving Wolfe. He was some sort of bodyguard for the rancher."

"He'll need another bodyguard," McShannock said.

"Now, don't be too brash," the banker countered. "I've dealt with Irving Wolfe for years. He seems to be a pretty decent man. What if Yates and some of the other men have been acting on their own?"

Kate was shocked into silently staring up at the banker's shadowed face. "You can't actually believe that," she said finally. "Why would they do that?"

Brassman shrugged. "Why would Wolfe?"

"For our land."

Brassman sighed. "That's too thin for me."

Kate's eyes flickered over at McShannock, surprised at herself that just for a moment a doubt entered her mind. Brassman seemed so knowing and intuitive. If he didn't feel Wolfe was responsible for all of her problems, shouldn't that give her reason to rethink everything? Or did it just mean Brassman was a fool? She knew the last wasn't true.

They returned to the house together, and McShannock went with Kate to survey the damage in her sons' room. The first thing she noticed was the large hump under the blankets on their bed. It looked shockingly like a human form asleep. She stared at it for a moment, then went and pulled back the bedspread, revealing all of the other blankets mounded up. She whirled on McShannock. Looking back at the bed, a weak feeling came over her.

"You knew they were coming," she said quietly.

He nodded, although she was still looking at the bed. "I knew."

"How?"

"I don't trust many people, ma'am. I didn't trust the sheriff. After you came home yesterday I told him we were bringing Ira back to sleep in your sons' room and that I'd be gone to Eagle Rock for a few days. I'm sorry, ma'am. I had to know."

Ward Brassman had come in behind them, and his voice made them both turn quickly. "You can't trust anybody."

McShannock shrugged. "Hess has been too helpless," he said. "From what Mrs. Winchester has told me, it just seemed like he could have done more. So I had to find out if he had reasons for doing nothing. I guess he did. I have all the proof I need that Irving Wolfe is buying him off."

Kate Winchester didn't hear McShannock's last words. Something had struck her suddenly, something she was appalled at herself for never seeing before. It was far better evidence than anything she had thought of yet. Who was the person who had always known where her husband was being kept in town? Who was the one person she had always confided in? Sheriff Hess. He had always known Ira's whereabouts, and someone had always come to kill him there. Yet why had Hess suggested Ira be sent away to Utah? A chill went up her spine. Was it so Ira would be far from home with no protection, so they could kill him?

It was Clyde Hall who summoned Sheriff Hess out to the ranch the next morning. Knowing how deeply Hess was involved, Kate didn't dare send one of the boys and risk their being kidnapped again—or worse. Who knew what such men were capable of?

Hess, Luke Weaver and Thornton O'Toole, the undertaker, arrived with faces grim. The three men climbed down and walked out to where the dead man still lay trapped under his horse. McShannock, Hall and Ward Brassman, who had spent the night on the Winchesters' floor, walked out there with them.

"I left him where he fell," Vest McShannock said.

Hess nodded perfunctorily, for that fact was obvious enough. Kate Winchester stood back and watched the men, not trusting herself to talk to Hess. McShannock had asked her to pretend she had no idea he was involved in the attempted killing, and she was not a very good pretender. She was better off keeping her mouth shut and listening while Hess carried on his farce.

Hess looked over at McShannock suddenly. "Tell me this, McShannock: was Mr. Winchester hurt?"

The gambler gave Hess his best poker face. "Well, a funny thing happened, Sheriff. We decided not to bring him back here. These two were just shooting at an empty bed."

Hess searched McShannock's eyes. "Imagine that," he said finally.

"Dunn Yates," Deputy Luke Weaver said suddenly.

Without comment, Hess turned back to McShannock. "You shot him two times at close range. Wasn't once enough?"

McShannock's eyes shot over to Clyde Hall, then to Brassman. He was about to say something when Brassman spoke. "I was the one who shot him, Arch. I thought Mr. Hall would have told you."

The sheriff gave Hall an irritated glance. "Mr. Hall didn't talk at all. I guess I'll need statements from all of you."

Hess turned suddenly, his eyes seeking out and settling on Kate. "Ma'am, I don't know what to make of all this. I don't know why somebody suddenly decided your husband was home, after all this time. But I'll get to the bottom of it."

Kate just glared, her words of hatred stuck in her throat. Sheriff Hess stared at her until an odd, confused look came over his face, and then he turned away, obviously flustered. He was looking down at the dead man when he spoke again. "I'll get to the bottom of this or I'll give up my badge."

Judith Wolfe sat in front of her dressing table mirror combing her long blond hair. She studied her green eyes in the sparkling beveled glass and remembered them looking much younger just yesterday. Much more vibrant and hopeful. She also remembered her cheeks having more color, and her lips. And her hair . . . it was so dull. What had become of her over the years? Was it Irving? She asked the question of herself, already knowing the answer and sick because of it. Yes, it was Irving. He was the one who had brought her here, taken her away from St. Louis, her home. St. Louis was the only place she had ever felt truly alive, and being away from it had nearly killed her.

Now she lived here, in the middle of nowhere. Not "lived"—existed. There were no niceties here. The house was fine but it was no more than a prison to her. For all its impressive architecture—the balcony, portico, columns, balustrade, and all the windows—it was still only a huge, well furnished, beautiful gray and white prison. She lived here practically alone while Irving was out on his business trips, or gambling, or . . . whatever Irving did. She didn't even care anymore. Even when he was home he slept in his separate bedroom, and the only time they saw each other was at mealtimes.

It didn't matter anyway. She could tell by some of the things Irving said, and by how Harvey Manfred talked, that this ranch was dead. Her husband was so far in debt only a miracle could pull him out, and now his hole card was gone. His cattle, the cattle he had planned to sell at a handsome profit to the Lemhi County miners, were slaughtered. Two nights of killing had destroyed thirty percent of their herd of Herefords. And several nights more had destroyed all but the last three hundred head or so. To Judith Wolfe, it meant the end of an empire, the end of the only thing that had served to keep her remotely satisfied here: wealth. Wealth and the immense satisfaction of walking through town knowing everyone recognized her as the wife of the county's most successful cattleman.

Yet in the last year someone else had come into Judith Wolfe's life. Someone wonderful, caring, gallant. Someone who would take her away from all of this. She wasn't tied to Irving Wolfe anymore, and his downfall did nothing to hurt her. In fact, she was almost glad of it.

Irving didn't even suspect her of having a lover. He was too wrapped up in his own world to notice what she was doing. She didn't even need to do housework anymore. They had a maid. They had a cook. Judith wasn't needed here.

She put down the comb and picked up an ivory-handled brush, running it through the strings of her hair over and over, hoping somehow to bring the life back to the once-luxurious tresses. Yet it didn't matter. Her new man loved her however her hair looked, and that was the way it should be. He loved her, he made love to her, the way she had always dreamed of, since she was old enough to know about men. He made her feel like the world revolved around her, and he was all she could see. He was taking her away from here.

She stared at her eyes in the mirror, finding a new light there she hadn't noticed when she first sat down fifteen minutes before. The life was coming back to them, and it had nothing to do with Irving Wolfe. She was leaving this place—leaving it for good. They would make plans today when they would go, and where. It hadn't mattered to her until now. All that had mattered was that she would see the last of Idaho, the last of Irving Wolfe.

Irving Wolfe was going to die a destitute man. But she didn't care. None of that made any difference to her anymore. He was overbearing, sometimes cruel in the things he said. And if he had ever had any tenderness it had vanished long ago. He deserved no mercy. The only person she regretted hurting was Arthur.

Oh, little Arthur. Their only child. Why had he been made to come into this cruel world with Irving as his father? Oh, Irving doted on him.

He was never mean-spirited toward the boy. What scared her was she could see Arthur becoming more and more like his father every day.

But she had to press her mind on to brighter things. She was going to see her new beau now, the man who made her feel like a young woman once more. Today, that was all that mattered.

Harvey Manfred had the buggy hitched and waiting when Judith Wolfe descended the stairs and stepped out on the front porch to look around. July was nearly over, and August coming on. It would be her birthday soon. August second. Curse that day. She would be officially forty-two years old. Forty-two! It didn't seem possible. But her beau made her feel twenty.

The buggy stood waiting, Harvey Manfred beside it. Its top shone dully under the summer sun. Judith walked to the rig, and Manfred stood staring at her with the habitual stupid little smirk on his face which he had for everyone he felt too comfortable with.

"Where you headed, ma'am? Like me to drive you?"

Judith half ignored him as he helped her into the buggy. "No, thanks, Harvey. I can't think unless I'm by myself. I'll be back in three or four hours."

She said no more. He needed no more. He was a hired hand and as such not worth wasting words on. What business was it of his what she did? He was too slow-witted to ever figure there was anything afoot.

She drove toward Wolverine, Dutchman's curve taking her very close to the high black cliffs above the river. She let the warm wind work against her cheeks, lifting her blonde hair jauntily, only to fall back against her green silk blouse. After a time, she left the river when it turned south, and she continued east. Soon, she could see the beginning of the Narrows ahead. A quarter mile from it, she pulled off to the right and crossed Wolverine Creek, the seat bouncing beneath her as the buggy wheels made their way over the rocks.

The cabin was there, all alone. It had been a squatter's cabin, she remembered, a squatter whose daughter had died after falling into a spring snake den and being bitten to death by rattlesnakes. What a horrible death! Horrible enough that the squatter took his family and moved on, no longer able to bear living with the memories.

The cabin stood much as the squatters had left it. Rats had tried to build a nest in one corner, but she kept them shooed away, for this was her special place. It was here she came to share her life with the man she loved.

Judith Wolfe was untying the bonnet from her head, unable to hold back the smile on her face that seemed to fill every hour she spent with this man, physically or just in her mind. She felt her hair nudge against her cheek and imagined just for a moment it was his hand touching her softly.

And then she saw the note.

It lay on the table in plain sight, obviously meant to be discovered. Judith's smile still lit her face, but she stopped fussing with the bonnet strings momentarily and walked curiously to the piece of paper. She hoped he hadn't been here already and had to leave. She was early herself; what would force him to leave so soon, unfulfilled?

She hadn't made it four steps across the floor when something seized her, made her steps slow. Did she really want to read this piece of paper? Was it good news? She couldn't stand bad news. What might have happened?

Her heart beating dully, Judith picked up the note and started to read. She knew almost instantly. She knew by instinct more than by the words, that her world was suddenly coming to an end.

My dear Judith:

I am writing to you on this bright July day that for me becomes gray as I pen these words. For all the world I do not wish to hurt you, yet I have come to realize that we are wrong for each other. I hate to dash your dreams, but I could never love you or be married to you. I have found another woman. We plan to marry soon, and I hope you can be at the wedding in town. I have enjoyed the time I have dallied with you and trust you will return to your man in renewed faithfulness but keep my memories dear to heart, as I will yours. Stay happy.

He didn't sign it.

By the time Judith Wolfe finished reading the letter, she was on her knees. She almost couldn't make out the last words through her tears. Stay happy? Stay happy! What kind of evil man could say something like that? Stay happy? He had taken her heart and played with it like a toy. Oh, God, she thought, please help me. Help me die.

Numbly, Judith pushed to her feet and stumbled outside, feeling suddenly claustrophobic inside the house. She found herself gasping for air, holding onto the doorframe. Tears streamed down her cheeks. She almost fell, stepping off the porch, and let her weight land against the side of the horse. "God," she cried out loud, "please don't let this happen. Please, God. Please!"

Somehow she managed to pull herself onto the buggy seat, and numbly she started the horse moving back the way she had come. She drove and drove, her mind delirious. She kept thinking of going back to the big old lonely house. To the house that soon would not even be theirs, if certain mortgages could not be covered. To a husband who didn't know she existed. To a twelve-year-old son who grew more like his father every day. Judith Wolfe wept bitterly, yet all of the tears that flowed washed none of the despair from inside her chest.

Almost without Judith's noticing it, the buggy was rolling along Dutchman's curve. She suddenly turned the horse off the main road onto a little dirt trail the cattle had worn down. The confused horse balked, habituated to traveling the same route every time they came here. But then he turned dutifully and started off through the sagebrush toward the river cliffs.

The canyon suddenly opened up before them out of the sagebrush itself. The Blackfoot River flowed below, and on the opposite side the banks were gentle, curving up into rolling hills of sagebrush and juniper. But on this side the walls of black lava dropped down seventy or eighty feet to great dark piles of angular stone that piled in tortured heaps right up to the banks of the river in some places. The water, no more than sixty feet wide, flowed a deep green. It trickled quietly in this particular place. She looked at it and watched the swallows darting to and fro across it, flying from their homes in the lava cliffs that swept away below her. The birds sought food, perhaps, or maybe just the thrill of unrestrained flight.

Judith Wolfe pictured herself as a swallow. Yes, of all birds that was what she would choose to be. She had no illusions of being a bird of prey. She didn't have the strong heart for that. Yet she was too graceful to be a sparrow or meadowlark. She was a swallow, sleek in her contours, daring in her flight.

Pulling back the top of the buggy, she coaxed the horse as near the edge of the lava cliff as she could before he shied. She stood up on the seat and surveyed the tangled mass of black rock below her, the river that flowed gently and soothed all who gazed upon it, massaging the slender trunks of willows as it moved eternally past.

Judith Wolfe was a swallow with untried wings. Now, for the first time, she used them.

Chapter Sixteen

It was Marshal and Ellis Briggs who found the battered body of Judith Wolfe, crushed to death on the lava rocks along the Blackfoot River. Taking their first opportunity since before their trip to Utah, the boys had saddled Bob and Tarnish and ridden out from the ranch early that morning, cane poles and a can of worms their main cargo. Their mother hadn't liked the idea of their being out alone, especially riding right past the Wolfe ranch, but being boys they made their own rules.

They had yet to bait a hook, or even find a place to make their way down through the treacherous rocks to the river, when they saw the black buggy sitting there in the sagebrush, a bay horse waiting patiently in its harness. The brake was set, and the wheels of the buggy had become caught up in rocks, which were the only reasons, they surmised, that the horse stood there at all. The ribbons were wrapped around the brake handle.

On the seat of the buggy, Ellis found the carefully folded note and slowly read it out loud to Marshal. When he was done, the boys could only stare at each other, bewildered. It was so obviously a distressing letter for this woman named Judith that even two boys who didn't know the ways of the world knew it meant trouble. And the only woman they knew of named Judith was the wife of Irving Wolfe.

Being not only curious boys but eager to help anyone in a jam, Marshal and Ellis set out immediately to discover the reason for the buggy's being there. They studied the tracks and found that the horse appeared to have dragged the buggy for a ways on its locked wheels before getting them caught up in the rocks. They followed the tracks back through the sage, using tracking skills gleaned from years of being boys with little to occupy their time besides crafts of nature.

It wasn't long until they came upon a spot where the buggy had gone right up to the edge of the rocks—dangerously near. The tracks from that point made a beeline back to the road, and it was obvious by the easy rolling tracks that the brake had not been set.

Curiously, Marshal and Ellis scanned the ground, and Ellis found a buggy whip lying there in the brush. He picked it up and looked over with concern at his older brother.

Marshal tugged off his hat and ran a hand back through his blond hair and glanced over where they had left the horse, now a hundred yards away. He met Ellis's eyes with a serious gaze, then at last looked down toward the river. The two of them had been together since Ellis's birth . Each knew without asking what the other was thinking.

Feeling uneasy, they moved carefully toward the edge of the rocks and looked down. Ellis's face turned white. He stumbled back from the edge, staring with shocked eyes at his brother. Marshal couldn't take his eyes off the limp-looking form below. He gazed with morbid curiosity until at last he heard his brother's voice.

"Is that her?"

Marshal turned slowly. "Yeah, Judith Wolfe."

Ellis slowly nodded his head. "They're gonna think we pushed her off."

Marshal started to scowl at that, but the full import of what his brother had said struck him, and his mouth clamped shut. "We better get out of here."

Ellis eagerly agreed, and they jumped on their horses and spurred them into a lope back to the road. Once there, they kicked them up to a gallop and raced back to the house. They had to drop back to a trot long before they reached the ranch, but they had made good time. They found Kate Winchester and Vest McShannock shooting targets in the yard. Clyde Hall and Red Dog had returned home the day before.

Half out of breath, Marshal managed to gush out the news of what they had found. At the end of the tragic tale, Kate looked over at McShannock, her eyes large and worried. "What in the world— What are we going to do?"

McShannock gave her a queer look. "Well, there's only one thing we can do. We can't trust Hess, but we have to turn this in to him anyway."

"But what if— What if he blames the boys? What if he tries to accuse them of pushing her off the edge?"

McShannock shook his head, putting a hand comfortingly on her shoulder. "Don't get all worked up, Mrs. Winchester. I'm sure that won't be the case."

"Ma . . . we found this, too," Marshal said suddenly and held out the folded piece of paper.

Kate slowly unfolded the paper and read silently. Tears welled up in her eyes before she was finished. She looked up at McShannock, and to answer his questioning look she just handed him the note.

When McShannock finished the note, his sober face had taken on a sad cast, and he handed the note back to Kate. She squeezed it in her hand and thought how Wolfe would react when he saw those words.

"Do we have to tell 'em we found her?" Ellis asked suddenly.

Marshal was staring off toward Pocatello, and his voice quieted them all. "That's the sheriff," he said, almost as if to himself.

The others whirled to see Sheriff Arch Hess and four riders coming toward them at a long trot, the dust sifting off behind them to fall languidly back to earth. In spite of the day's growing heat, Hess wore a dark gray wool suit, and his narrow-brimmed hat barely shaded his wide-cheeked face against the sun.

The riders stopped in front of Kate and the others, and the sheriff nodded. Beside him sat Irving Wolfe, Harvey Manfred, Case Deckan and Deputy Luke Weaver.

"Ma'am, McShannock," said Hess with a nod. Wolfe started to say something, and Hess cut him short. "I'll do the talking. We don't need any undue problems here. Ma'am, we're sorry to disturb your day, but it seems Mr. Wolfe's wife went for a buggy ride yesterday afternoon and hasn't been heard from since. We're stopping at every neighbor's place to ask if someone might have seen her."

Kathryn looked over at Irving Wolfe, who glared at her openly. Yet through the look of despite, she saw something else—despair, perhaps, or anxiety. At that moment, she pitied him.

"Mr. Wolfe," she said, deciding it best to speak directly to him, since it was his wife they sought. "I— This isn't easy." She glanced at Ellis and Marshal, then looked back at the rancher, who stared silently, a look of dread creeping past his façade of anger. "My boys rode to the river to go fishing this morning, and they found a buggy. There was a body below it in the rocks. A woman's body."

The posse was silent, and Hess's eyes ticked toward Wolfe and away. He cleared his throat. "She was . . . dead?" he asked Marshal.

Marshal first shrugged, but then nodded. "I'm pretty sure. We didn't try to get down to her."

Irving Wolfe just stared at them, his face gone even more pale than normal. His reins took on a tremble from the hand that clutched them.

"Can you boys take us there?" asked Hess.

"We'll all go," said Kathryn.

Half an hour later, they came to Dutchman's Curve, within sight of the buggy, and the bay horse whinnied a lonesome greeting. They rode grimly past the horse and back to the edge of the rocks, everyone climbing down. Irving Wolfe walked tentatively to the cliff rim and looked over. A pained gust of breath huffed from his lungs. Avoiding everyone's eyes, he turned and walked away through the sage, then stood staring off at the juniper-covered horizon. At last, Kate saw his face drop, and his entire body began to shake. A hand came up to shelter his eyes.

It took another hour before the searchers were able to find a way down through the rocks and reach the body, then bring it back up to the top. Wolfe stood over his wife's stiff form and simply stared down at her, not saying a word. Harvey Manfred had removed his coat and laid it over her face and torso, and he stood there with dull eyes.

Kate looked at Irving Wolfe. She had hated this man with all of her heart, yet now all she could feel for him was an overwhelming pity. It was plain that he was grief-stricken and trying to hide his face from the rest of them. He must have dearly loved his wife. The thought shocked Kate. Love was an emotion she hadn't imagined the rancher's heart to hold.

There was one question in Kate's mind. She knew the answer could destroy Irving Wolfe completely, and there had been a time she would have been glad to do that. But now . . . should she tell him about the note? It was his right to know that his wife had been unfaithful. But why spoil the man's image of her now? Why destroy his memories? Kate was almost shocked at herself. This man had been trying to kill her husband, to destroy her entire life. Now his wife had taken her own life, and Kate was too gentle to even tell him why.

The day after Judith Wolfe's funeral, Ward Brassman rode out to the Wolfe ranch and knocked on the door. It was quiet that day, the leaves of the cottonwoods and fruit trees hanging lackluster in the dead summer air. Grasshoppers rattled their wings out in the dry yellow grass, and a red-tailed hawk made voluminous circles in the sky, its shadow changing form and magnitude in relation to the earth and rocks and vegetation over which it glided. Flies flitted about the door and bounced off the windowpanes.

Soon the door cracked open, and Irving Wolfe's large dark eyes peered out, his face unnaturally gray in the shadows of the house. A smattering of black whiskers gave his face a dirty appearance Ward Brassman had never seen in the rancher.

"Brassman!" Wolfe said with surprise. "Uh, come on in. Come in." He opened the door wider and stood aside from it, and the banker walked past him and shot his glance about the room. He had never been to the ranch before, but he had heard it was grand. The real thing was no less spectacular than the rumors. But it wasn't as tidy as he had expected it to be.

"Excuse the clutter," Wolfe said, waving a hand. He was still in his robe and slippers, although it was eleven o'clock in the morning. His eyes were red, his tongue and lips caked and chalky.

"A little bit of clutter makes a house a home," said Brassman, forcing a tight smile.

"Yes, well . . . My maid quit me. My cook, too, the worthless trash. Quit me the minute they found out about Judith. Sit down! Excuse my manners."

Brassman cleared his throat, his eyes meeting the rancher's. "I didn't have a chance to speak with you at the funeral. It was a nice service. Reverend Malthese was in top form. I give you my condolences, Mr. Wolfe. Your wife was a gentle woman."

"She was a lazy good-for-nothing—" Irving Wolfe's voice broke. To Brassman it appeared the man caught himself on the verge of bursting into tears. "Always dreaming," he said. "Always wishing things were a different way. How about a drink?" asked the rancher suddenly, forced levity coming into his voice. "Anything you like."

Irving Wolfe had started toward his liquor cabinet without awaiting a response, but Brassman stopped him. "Actually—" The tone of his voice made Wolfe turn back around. "I'm honored to pay my respects, Mr. Wolfe. But to be honest with you I came mainly on bank business."

Turning fully to face the banker, Wolfe folded his arms, his fingers looking pathetically small and soft and pale against the red silk of his robe. "Business, Brassman? What business?"

"Wouldn't you like to sit down?" asked Brassman. "Please do."

A look of suspicion leaped into the rancher's eyes. "What business?"

"I'm afraid we have to call you due on your mortgages, Mr. Wolfe. I'm sorry about your wife, but—"

"You're sorry about my wife!" Wolfe barked. "Sorry about my wife! She's barely cold, and already you're coming here to do your dirty work. I'm not late on any payments. I have paid in full, and I can show proof of every payment. You have no cause to foreclose on me now."

It didn't go unnoticed to Ward Brassman that for the first time in their relationship the rancher had used the title "mister" on him. Yet now it was used only with a tone of contempt. Controlling his voice, he said, "The fact is, it has come to my attention that you're late paying two of your mortgages, Mr. Wolfe. And considering the recent slaughter of your cattle, frankly I'm concerned as to your ability to cover them."

"I'm late on nothing!" Wolfe boomed. "Just what do your so-called records show?"

"The first delinquency is on five hundred acres of river acreage—near where . . . where Mrs. Wolfe passed on. Dutchman's Curve. The second covers the five hundred acres bordering the Winchester property."

"You just stay right here!" said Wolfe, his voice rising almost to a yell. "I'll bring you your blasted receipts—that you yourself signed."

Keeping the pleasant calm about his face, Brassman nodded. "If you have those it would quickly clear up the whole problem. Please do bring them, if you don't mind. I'm sure we'll find it all to be a big misunderstanding."

Wolfe stalked out of the room, going into an adjacent chamber where Brassman could see a steer head and several big game mounts gazing out regally upon the shadowy interior of the oak-floored space. He heard a door creak open after half a minute, and then a metal box slide across a wooden surface. Patiently, he waited. Soon, there was a violent shuffling of papers, a few curses under breath, and last the sound of the metal box flying to the floor, the lighter sound of falling papers muffling its clatter.

A long minute passed in which there came no sound at all but the tock, tock of the grandfather clock in the corner. The clock stood two feet taller than Brassman's eyes. The next sound was of footsteps, slow and measured, approaching from the other room. Irving Wolfe's leather slippers made scuffing sounds along the floor, and he appeared suddenly in the doorway, not initially meeting Brassman's eyes. The banker watched him, and it was immediately apparent the rancher carried nothing that would substantiate his claims. Brassman waited for Wolfe to speak as the older man stopped in front of him.

"I can prove those loans have been paid," said Wolfe. "My paperwork was . . . simply misplaced. Give me a day to sort it out, Brassman. Just one day. That's all I ask. I made those payments, and you'll have your proof."

Brassman looked at the rancher searchingly, taking in the lines of fatigue spun around his eyes and mouth, the dirty-looking red veins grown large in his eyes, making them appear pink, and the black whiskers and thin, ragged hair. He didn't have the heart right then to inform Wolfe that the bank could foreclose on him whether he was making his payments on time or not. There were no laws governing such things, other than that of common courtesy.

The banker sighed, giving a little shake of his head. "I . . . I hope for your sake you find those receipts, Mr. Wolfe. You really do have a nice ranch here. It would be hard to lose. Something you should be able to pass on to your son someday. Good luck. And remember, I'll do what I can for you, but when the stockholders come demanding to know why mortgage payments haven't been made, there is only so much we can do."

Irving Wolfe just nodded tiredly and waved Brassman out of the house.

Ward Brassman drove his buggy away, and Irving Wolfe stood on the porch and watched its dusty back, watched the churning wheels pick up and throw away clots of dust that sifted back to earth like flour on a giant bread board. Numb to his very heart, he turned and shuffled to his liquor cabinet. He pulled out a black bottle of brandy and poured it, not into a shot glass, but into a goblet. He filled that goblet to the brim.

Like a desert traveler with a glass of cool water, Irving Wolfe gulped at the brandy until only a fine purple film remained in the bottom of the goblet. It burned his throat, made him lose his breath for a moment. He leaned over and rammed his eyes shut, clutching at his chest until the burning passed. Finally, he rolled his eyes open and shook his head gingerly. He looked down at the bottle, then threw it against the wall, sending a shower of glass and brandy all about that side of the room. He looked at the mess he had made and swore violently, then started taking other bottles of liquor and tossing them after the first until the floor there was a battlefield of dark and blood-red liquids, punctuated by bottle bottoms and shards of glass.

Whirling suddenly, a grogginess coming over him, he stalked to the wall where the family portrait hung. There was his son, Arthur. A good-looking boy, if too round in the cheeks, too big in the eyes. But Irving Wolfe only had himself to blame for that. Those were his traits, and the boy looked a lot like him. Arthur was in town, staying with friends. He hadn't been able to bear the thought of coming back yet to the big house with all the memories of his mother. Wolfe was glad of it. He couldn't stand his boy seeing him this way.

And there . . . there was Judith, standing behind her man like a dutiful wife should. Arthur—through no fault of his own, of course—had nearly destroyed his mother's insides in coming to the earth. He had taken away any matter of choice in their having more children. So it was just the three of them.

Wolfe stared at his wife, stared at her hatefully, wanting to punish her for leaving him to raise their boy alone. But that was like Judith: take the easy way out. And why? What had brought it on? He had always treated her well, given her everything a woman could want. Granted, the social life was not what she had been accustomed to in St. Louis. But a married woman didn't need that kind of life. No, she was just worthless. She always had been.

In a fit of rage, Wolfe tore the picture from the wall and threw it as hard as he could against the fireplace. Glass shattered and flew everywhere, and the photograph ended up floating in the pool of alcohol. For several minutes, Wolfe just stared at it. Then suddenly he ran to it and picked it up out of the mess on the floor. He stared at his wife, at her pretty eyes—too close together; at her half-smiling lips—too thin; at her slim, gracious neck—too long. "Why, Judith? Why?" he said out loud. "How could you do this, after all we've worked for together?"

His face contorted, and he began to cry. He was so overcome with emotion that he sank to the floor among the liquor and chunks of glass. He didn't even feel the broken ends that pressed threateningly and fiercely against his legs through the robe. He slouched over with the photograph cradled in his arms and wept bitterly.

Chapter Seventeen

Kate Winchester sat at the kitchen table, absently passing the cameo broach back and forth between her hands as she tried to decide how she was going to pay her loan. She hadn't told her children of the dilemma she was in. It wasn't fair to them. Ellis sat blissfully reading a copy of *Hamlet* on the divan. Marshal was cleaning the Colt shotgun which seemed to have become his constant companion. Vala was sewing lace across the bodice of her favorite dress. And Cheyenne was fighting her new spotted puppy, which the children had given the name "Trouble," and drawing—

Kate stopped what she was doing, and her thinking also came to a halt. She leaned closer to peer at what Cheyenne was drawing on. It looked like . . . Kate stood up, almost upsetting her chair, and hurried across the room, startling Cheyenne. The girl looked up, her blue-gray eyes wide with surprise, her mouth open.

Kate couldn't believe what she was seeing. Cheyenne had paused with a crayon poised in her little fist. "Is it all right, Mama? I'm drawing?"

"Yes, yes, sweetie, it's all right. But—where did you get this?" She reached down and picked up a handful of what Cheyenne had been using for drawing paper, pushing Trouble gently out of her way with the back of her hand. It was cash—hundred dollar bills!

Cheyenne just stared at her mother, waiting for the scolding she knew was to come. She looked down at her crayons, probably hoping that by ignoring the problem it would just go away.

"Cheyenne," Kate said sternly. "Where did you get it? It's okay. I'm not mad. I just need to know." Her trembling hand held what she guessed to be over a thousand dollars, if all of them were hundred dollar bills.

"With the chickens," Cheyenne said innocently. "Just in the chicken's house."

By now the whole family had gathered around, and shocked, confused delight filled their faces. Kate picked Cheyenne up and said, "Come with me, Chey. We'll go out to the hen house. Show me where you got the paper."

They hurried out to the hen house, Trouble running along behind. Vest McShannock, walking from the horse shed, met their obvious concern with a puzzled glance. In answer to the question in his eyes, Kate just held up the handful of bills so he could see them as she hurried through the hen house door.

"Where was it, Cheyenne?" Kate asked again.

Proud to be the center of attention, Cheyenne led them over to the pile of straw that lined the wall beneath the laying boxes. "Under there," she said. "I was playin'."

Kate knelt down and parted the straw. There, in a place only a child would ever have discovered until it came time to change the straw, was a wooden case. Kate picked up the case and looked at it. It was ornately carved with a floral design all the way around, with a sort of medallion made out of what appeared to be pieces of bone inlaid in the lid. She turned and handed it to McShannock, who opened it.

"Looks like it used to be a gun case, with all the partitions knocked out now to put the money in it." He turned it curiously around, then flipped it over. There, on the bottom of it were the deeply engraved initials, "I.W."

Kate recognized the initials, and her eyes jumped to McShannock's. "Irving Wolfe!" she said with conviction. "That ought to be some kind of proof of Ira's dealings right there. He must have stolen that from Wolfe or something. First there was the beaded purse and now this."

McShannock just stared at Kate blankly. "Uh, ma'am . . . you told me about the coin purse before, but . . . you know, your husband's initials are I.W."

Kate didn't speak. All she could do was look at McShannock for the longest time. Finally, her lips moved. "I . . . oh no," she finished in almost a whisper.

She felt so stupid! She wanted to just run away and hide her embarrassment. Here all along she had been so sure that if she had hung onto the coin purse she would have solid evidence that might be used against Irving Wolfe later. Now, with one simple sentence, an observation of something so obvious she should have thought of it herself from the very first moment, her evidence was gone. Sure, she didn't recognize the case, and she hadn't recognized the purse. But Ira had been secretive about many things. What was so strange about his not mentioning the purse or the case? She herself had belongings that Ira had never seen.

Vest McShannock looked silently from the case in his hand to the handful of bills in Kate's, and then to her face. All the woman could do was look back and forth from the money to her children.

It was obvious to Kate, once she got over being embarrassed about the case and the beaded purse and her mind had calmed down enough to actually sort things out, that this money would have a big part to play in the puzzle of why they had tried to take her husband's life. Sure, the case could belong to Ira and probably did. But the money certainly couldn't be his, not unless he had been hiding it from her all these years. And she didn't believe that for a moment. It made her sick to see this money lying here, this proof that her husband had cheated someone, or robbed someone, or . . . She couldn't guess where it had come from, but it was certain it wasn't from the meager operations of this ranch. Perhaps they would never learn where it came from if Ira . . . if Ira died.

Kate shook herself free from that horrible contemplation. She walked slowly back to the house, and the children followed her. McShannock went back mechanically to brushing his horse.

The following day, Kate struggled mentally with herself. Through all her household chores; through gathering scattered eggs with Vala; going to the river in the wagon to draw barrels of water for washing; and cleaning fly-specked windows, Kathryn sweated over the dilemma of what to do with the money. True, she didn't know where Ira had come by it. Undoubtedly, it had been gained by some dishonest means, or he would have told her about it. Yet it was money, and at least for the moment it was hers. So why not use it? She had never liked owing anyone, especially not a financial institution. This unexpected find gave her an escape from the loan she had taken out at the bank. After fighting with her conscience all day, she decided to pay it off.

If she were to make it to the bank on time, she had to leave that very minute. Telling the boys to watch after the place with McShannock, she hitched the wagon, and with her two daughters on the seat beside her she drove off toward Blackfoot, keeping the horses to a long trot.

As they pulled into the street, Kate saw two men stepping out of the bank. By the time they reached it and pulled to a stop, Ward Brassman was straightening up from locking the door, and his colleague, Robert Lynch, had started off down the boardwalk, his white hair glistening in the sun beneath the narrow brim of his hat. Brassman heard the wagon and glanced over. His face broke into a wide grin when he saw who was on the seat.

"Mrs. Winchester! How nice to see you! Are you just getting in?"

Kate sighed, smiling. "Yes, yes. I was coming to see you."

Brassman's smile didn't lessen, but his confused eyes darted back and forth between Vala and her mother. "To see me? My. I'm honored."

Kate laughed, standing up to climb down from the wagon. "No, wait!" Brassman ordered, hurrying over to give her a hand down. Although knowing better, Kate allowed the banker's hands to rest over-long on her waist. After several seconds, he dropped his hands and raised them again to Cheyenne. "Young lady?"

Cheyenne looked at her mother for approval, then jumped into the banker's strong hands. He hefted her and then set her gently on the street. "My, you're getting big!" He straightened up and looked at Vala, cocking his head teasingly to one side. "And the beautiful young woman?" he said. "Would she like a hand down, too?"

Vala blushed fiercely but stood and leaned down to let Brassman's strong hands lift her off the seat and down to the ground. Finally, Brass-man turned back to Kate, who waited patiently. "Now. You came to see me?"

Kate laughed again. "Well, the bank, actually. I wanted to pay my loan."

"Ah-h-h," said Brassman, pretending to flinch. "I'm sorry I can't help you there. It's all locked up, as you can see. I hope you didn't make a special trip."

"Well, uh . . . no, of course not. I—"

"You did!" the banker said perceptively. "Well, you said you came in to make a payment? Maybe we can work it out to both of our benefits. In fact . . . You know, I was planning on walking over to the restaurant for some supper. I can't tell you how honored I would be to have three such beautiful ladies accompany me. Could I hope to have your acceptance? My treat."

Kate looked at Vala, who was watching her hopefully. Cheyenne, too, looked at her with big eyes, waiting for her decision. It wasn't very often the Winchesters ate food cooked in a restaurant.

"We accept, Mr. Brassman. But really, we can pay for our own."

Brassman shook his head. "Oh, no you won't. I can never go back on an offer once it's made."

Kathryn just laughed, and when Brassman offered her his elbow she threw caution to the wind and took it. Together they walked down to the Star Restaurant, which besides its bakery boasted fresh ice cream every noon and evening.

After treating Kate and the children to Kate's favorite meal of chicken noodle soup and fresh wheat bread topped with oleo margarine, Ward Brassman pushed his plate away and patted his stomach appreciatively. With his hat off, his head of dark, thinning hair was revealed, a widow's peak pointing like an arrow down the exact center of his forehead. Every time Kate looked over at Vala, she caught her staring at Brassman like he was the most beautiful creature in the world. And, in truth, her daughter had good taste.

They talked of Blackfoot, of the latest entertainment at the Isis Opera House, of the insane asylum, and of how the new poplar trees around the courthouse were coming along. People came from miles around to see those trees. They spoke of Cleveland Bay horses, especially the eight fine stallions A.T. Stout, of the firm of High and Stout, had imported from Europe the February before. They also spoke of St. Mary's and the Sacred Heart Academy, both run by the Sisters of the Holy Cross, the first in Salt Lake City, and the second in Ogden. A young lady could learn many fine things in either of them, but most importantly, how to be a lady. As a Quaker, the importance of education had been drilled into Kate, and she hoped Vala would go there some day. But at the moment Vala had no ideas of leaving Blackfoot. It made Kate ache to know part of the reason was Ward Brassman.

After dinner had had time to settle, Brassman insisted on dessert. Doughnuts were Kate's favorite sweet, but when she ordered one she was the black sheep at the table. The others all ordered fresh vanilla ice cream. When they were finished, Brassman's deep brown eyes met Kate's, and he cocked an eyebrow. "Now. You came to see me on banking business. I suppose we've put off the unpleasantries long enough."

"I suppose," replied Kate. "I want to pay off the loan you made me."

"Pay it off? The recent one?" Brassman said in surprise. "You've done well for yourself. Good!"

"But I'd rather not have to come back tomorrow," Kate admitted, hoping he would take the hint and either take the payment himself or open the bank back up on the sly, long enough to make the quick payment. The banker didn't disappoint her.

"Mrs. Winchester, I'll make you an offer, if you promise not to let anyone else in on the secret. If you'd like, I'll take your payment and just make it in the morning. Of course, you'd have to trust me."

She searched his eyes, feeling herself sink into the depths of them. How could she not trust a man with eyes like those?

Brassman suddenly laughed. "I'll also write you out a receipt. In my dealings I've found they can go a long way toward building trust."

Kate reached into her reticule, drawing out the six one hundred-dollar bills that would cover her loan. She folded them into her hand and held them to her chest for a moment before handing them to him. "I'm completely embarrassed to give these to you, the way they look. Cheyenne decided to do some artwork last night . . ." With only those words as explanation, she passed the bills to Brassman. Puzzled, he took them from her and then began to laugh at the pretty crayon colors on the bills.

"Now, who would complain about that?" he said, giving Cheyenne a fond look. "It only enhances a piece of paper that otherwise is not so very pretty."

Kathryn shrugged. "Well, as long as you feel that way." She waited while he took an envelope from his pocket and began to scratch on it with a pencil. She took the makeshift receipt he handed her and smiled, slipping it into her reticule.

"Thank you for the meal, Mr. Brassman. It was delicious."

"You're always welcome, Mrs. Winchester. I only wish I could do more."

Kathryn blushed, but her eyes held his. She was remembering the pressure of his lips, hot against her mouth. She believed him. She was sure he wished he could do more. It showed in his eyes as it had shown in his kiss.

She stood up abruptly, and Brassman followed suit. They walked out to the porch together, and Brassman looked fondly at Kathryn and held out his hand. Kathryn took it and let him hold hers for a long moment. Her heart thudded dully, and she felt a sudden ache to see Ira come home. She couldn't bear having him gone any longer.

Kathryn Winchester sat on a chair out on the porch as stars salted the sky, dimmed as if by the sultry summer air. Her children were in bed. Kate stared across the yard at the blackened remains of her barn. Her mind drifted to the day she heard the shots that began this entire nightmare. She wondered if she would ever learn from Ira what had brought this wrath upon them. If he didn't tell her, she would leave him. She couldn't abide a man who kept that kind of secret from her, even if it did mean she was losing her fourth husband. It wasn't like she couldn't find another. As much as she didn't want to, she could. Ward Brassman was the obvious first choice, for in spite of herself he had gotten under her skin and into her heart. And she had no doubt he would have greatly interested her in her younger days. As if he no longer did! And if not Brassman, then what about Vest McShannock? He never talked of such things with her, but she knew from looks he sometimes gave her that he had stayed here for more than just the money, and even more than the thought of helping out a "damsel in distress." Vest McShannock wanted her. She had seen that in the eyes of enough men to know. But at the same time she knew he would never tell her. That was what she liked about the man—his self-control. Perhaps that was the gambler in him. He didn't have enough self-control not to join in a foolish game of chance, but enough not to rashly give himself away. It was the mark perhaps not just of a gambler, but of a successful gambler.

Ward Brassman, on the other hand, had his own way of making a living, and a very comfortable one at that. He might not ever be a millionaire, but he would never hurt for anything. Sometimes Kate thought she would like nothing more. And after feeling Brassman's lips against hers she was certain he was full of passion, too. Not that it mattered, at her age. She laughed deep inside. Her age! If she were honest with herself, she would admit what everyone else seemed to think when they looked at her: she wasn't really very old, although she would officially gain another year in two months, on the thirtieth of September. Still, she was young enough to be a woman of beauty, a woman of romance. A woman of passion that lately had gone far too often unfulfilled.

Kathryn Winchester shook herself free of these musings. They could only lead to no good. Ira Winchester, no matter how gallant other men might seem, was the man she had married, the man she loved. Or at least the man she *had* loved . . . They were going to have to work together to bring that back. And speaking for herself, she would. She was willing to do whatever it took to bring their love back, if only he would again become the man she had married.

Kate sat and thought of what the last month had been like for her. Things had seemed so desperate. She attributed her weak moments to the feelings of despair and utter helplessness she had felt. It would be easy for other people to look at Kate and the feelings she had experienced lately for Brassman and McShannock and say she was a loose woman. But it was always easy for someone to judge everyone else, wasn't it? No one who hadn't ever been in her situation could ever understand what had driven her to do the things, to think the things she had. She only wished someone else *could* understand. She wanted so badly to talk to someone. The only person she thought might actually know what she felt was, oddly enough, Vest McShannock . . .

As if called up by her thoughts, the shadow of Vest McShannock appeared in the horse corral. He moved gracefully, brushing his horse, which he had been out riding until just after dark. Often, he brushed them all. He was only a gambler, but he cared deeply for horses. Kate liked that in him. A man who liked animals came a long way toward winning her respect.

With her steel cleaning rod, Kate ran a snip of rag through the barrel of her carbine and thought of what this weapon had accomplished since its purchase. What had it accomplished? It had made Kate Winchester, the Quakers' daughter, a murderer. A thought so simple made her mind roll back to the events of that black day. It made her think of what she might have done differently. It made her think of what the man she killed might have been like, and what had caused him to do what he did.

The sickness welled up in her stomach, and tears started to roll down her cheeks, past her quivering lips. It was like this every night once the children had gone to bed. The waves of guilt and sadness caught her, and she had no recourse but the tears. She couldn't talk to anyone. It seemed like she only had that useless cameo broach at her throat for comfort anymore, and that was no comfort at all—just a constant reminder of her troubles.

Suddenly, Vest McShannock was walking toward her, a dim blur through her tears. Kate hastened to dry her eyes, but he moved too quickly. Before she could drop her hands he stood before her. He looked from her glistening fingers to her face.

"It sure is a calm night, ma'am," he said, glancing up at the stars. She followed his gaze, and when she looked back at him he was watching her. His eyes didn't fall away.

"It's been a hard time for you."

"Yes," she agreed, almost whispering past the stiffness in her throat.

"Killing and bloodshed isn't easy for anyone—at least not anyone with a conscience," said McShannock, a match's light flaring against his face as it raised to ignite his hand-rolled cigarette. "Even seeing a criminal dead isn't the relief some people believe it would be. It's still a life God put on the earth. A life that used to be someone's helpless little baby."

Kate watched him, feeling the tears well up inside her again. Had he pinpointed the reason for her grief? The hidden reason even she hadn't been able to find? That man she had killed . . . he had once been a little boy, with a mother watching over him. A mother perhaps not unlike herself.

With little warning, the tears spilled over onto her cheeks. She tried to stop them. She turned her head so McShannock couldn't see. But he knew. He knew before the tears came out. She felt his hand touch her shoulder softly. She tried to stop herself, but she needed someone, and she stood up and let the carbine fall up against the side of the chair.

With her heart aching, and the first signs of real relief coming up from the depths of her, Kate fell against McShannock, and he held her. He held her tightly, the way she needed to be held. He acted like she wasn't hurting him, but then she noticed how hard she was hanging on. She sobbed uncontrollably, her tears soaking McShannock's neck and shoulder. She couldn't help it, even if she had wanted to. For so long she had needed to let out her grief, and now here was the one man, even above Ward Brassman, that she thought would understand. Ira couldn't. He had never killed anyone himself.

Kate cried and cried, and every time she thought the tears were gone they came back. Killing another human, even one who had hurt her son and would gladly have killed him, was the most painful thing Kate Winchester had ever done. She hated Star, hated him for making her do it. A human being had no right to do that to another, to force them to the point that they had to take another human life!

Kate thought the tears would never go away, but they did. They went away slowly, leaving her spent, leaving her sobbing. She would just start to relax against Vest McShannock, and then a great heaving sob would shake her, shake them both, because she held him so tight that right now they seemed like one body. Vest McShannock had to take the cigarette out of his mouth once and knock the ashes off to keep her from shaking them loose onto herself. The brief memory crossed Kate's mind of kissing Ward Brassman, and she thought how easy it would be to kiss Vest McShannock. But she had no desire. Holding her and letting her cry against him was more meaningful than any kiss could ever be. And it was just what she had needed for so long.

He reached up and took the cigarette from his mouth. "You're going to be all right, Mrs. Winchester. You're safe now. I'm here."

"I know you are." Kate's voice was a whisper. "Mr. McShannock... you can call me Kathryn, if you'd like. Or Kate."

There was a long moment of silence. He made no reply until she moved her head and started to look up at him. Then he took her by the shoulders and held her a little ways away, his cigarette held expertly between the fingers of his right hand so that no part of it touched her. He studied her with a kind light in his eyes. "Ma'am, I'm gratified by the offer. But you should be a Kate or a Kathryn only to the man who married you. Giving a man any more leeway than that is a danger a lady like you can't afford."

Kate knew that by "a man" he meant himself. "What is a 'lady' anyway?" Kate asked, her voice coming out more gruffly than she meant it to.

McShannock put the cigarette back between his lips and drew deeply on it and took it again between his middle and forefingers to remove it, thoughtfully massaging his lip with his thumb. "I've known one true lady, ma'am. The places I frequent aren't known for the ladies they draw. And my mother was a stranger to me. Gone and left me to my father when I was . . . well, I wasn't any older than little Cheyenne. Just a nub, a nub of a boy that an old gray-haired daddy didn't know how to raise. But he did his best."

"He did well, Mr. McShannock. He raised a gentleman, even if his gentleman doesn't know it." She paused and searched his smiling, embarrassed eyes. "Tell me about this one true lady? What was she like?"

McShannock grinned and looked down, tossing his cigarette between his boots and crushing it with a heel. "Why, you know all about her, ma'am. She's you. Lady Winchester."

Kate stared at him for a long moment, lost in the depths and lamp-lit greenness of his eyes. "Lady Winchester?" she said finally. "Where did that come from?"

McShannock laughed. "Well, you kind of remind me of some royalty over in Europe or somewhere, a woman who is beautiful yet very wise and brave. The title fits you."

Kathryn sighed. "I'm not brave."

"Some things are scarier than others. We're all scared of something."

"Not you," Kate said after a moment.

He looked at her for several seconds, opened his lips to speak, then stopped and looked away. Kate waited, and when she realized he wasn't going to say anything, she pressed him. "Are you scared of something, Mr. McShannock?"

"It's no matter." He watched her for a moment, his eyes thoughtful. "I don't mean to embarrass you, but you look very beautiful in that red dress . . . Lady Winchester."

Kate felt herself blush fiercely. "Thank you, Mr. McShannock. Red's my favorite color." She suddenly sighed again and looked down at her carbine. She changed the subject abruptly. "I'm going to ask my husband to come home, Mr. McShannock."

"I thought you weren't going to attempt any contact until this whole thing was resolved."

"We weren't. But I need Ira back here, if he's able."

"Well . . . at least allow me to send the message."

Kate smiled. "I was going to ask you if you would. I don't trust that telegraph operator. And besides, he always seems too busy for me. He doesn't seem to like women much."

"Sounds like a strange man. He should bow to Lady Winchester."

Kate laughed, and McShannock suddenly stood back from her. "Wait here for a moment, would you?"

Puzzled, she just nodded. McShannock stepped off the porch and went around the side of the house. When he returned, he had his left hand behind his back. He climbed the steps and stopped in front of her. She cocked her head to one side, curious. With a warm look, he brought his arm around in front of him. He held a red rose and a white one.

"What's this?" Kate asked.

He took the red rose with the fingers of his right hand and held it up. "This is your husband Ira," he said. Then taking the white rose, he pushed it toward her. "And this is you. You have the dead roses to remember your first three husbands by, ma'am. Seems to me you're remembering the wrong people."

The next morning, R.M. and Susan Sievers came to the house early to pay their respects. Sievers stood back in silence while his wife threw her arms around Kate and squeezed with all of her might.

"Susan, I'm so glad you came. I've missed you," said Kathryn.

"Bringing in the hay has been so busy," said Susan. "We've come before, but you were never here. We tried to feed your stock here for a while, but it was easier to throw them in with ours. And your chickens seem to scavenge well enough to live alone in the desert."

Kate laughed. "They've had a lot of practice lately."

The Sievers stayed for breakfast, and everyone sat wherever they could find a place. Clyde Hall came back in time to eat, and the house was filled with people. During the meal, R.M. Sievers looked up at Kate over a poised fork of potatoes. "I don't know if you're ready, but I think it's time someone checked on Ira," he said.

Kate's eyes swung to McShannock, who was watching her. She looked back at Sievers. "You read my mind. I already asked Mr. McShannock to send word for him to come home."

"Well, I don't know if— Have you thought of everything?" Sievers asked.

Kate studied his eyes. "Everything?"

"Yeah. They'll be back to try and kill him if he comes now."

Kate's jaw hardened. "They aren't the only ones who know how to kill."

Long after the Sievers had left, Kate pondered on their words. She wanted Ira back, yes. She didn't *need* him back, not like she once had, for she had become self-sufficient, to a certain extent. And what she couldn't do, Clyde or McShannock could. But even though Ward Brassman had temporarily weakened her—and McShannock, too, when she admitted it to herself—she couldn't lie to herself about her love for Ira. Ward Brassman was a nice friend, but that was all he could ever be. She couldn't see herself fitting into his kind of life. And as for Vest McShannock, unless he brought himself to change careers she would never go with him, either. Both McShannock and Brassman, she guessed, were a way for her to escape reality, but in the end life came back to the father of little Cheyenne, to her betrothed . . . Ira Winchester. The only way she could ever bring herself to break the vows she had made was . . . through the way she had been forced to break them three times before.

She sat on the porch, her boys gone off to hunt jackrabbits, Vala doing housework, and Cheyenne using her crayons to draw pretty little pictures on some pieces of paper Ward Brassman had bought for her in town. Trouble, the little spotted pup, was running around the yard chasing bees. Kate watched Cheyenne and wished she could be with her all the time. She had neglected her so often since Ira's shooting. It just wasn't right for her to leave the girl alone so much, but she didn't know what else she could do. She would make it up to her when their lives returned to normal.

As she sat thinking, Vest McShannock came riding in without Clyde Hall and Red Dog, who had ridden out with him earlier. He turned his palomino loose in the corral and walked over to Kate on the porch.

"That Indian could ride all day," he said. "Between him and that dog, they about wore me out."

Kate laughed lightly. "Clyde is quite a friend," she said.

"I can see that."

Kate invited McShannock to have coffee with her, and he accepted. He sat down in one of the handmade chairs on the porch while she went in to bring the coffee. When Kate came back, she was loaded down. Since McShannock was never consistent in how he took his coffee, she had brought the little crock of cream and the sugar bowl, trying to balance them along with two cups of steaming coffee as she came through the door.

Somehow, when she walked past McShannock to the house the first time, she hadn't noticed the hunk of bone Trouble had left lying there. Now, on walking back, her foot managed to catch it just right. Her ankle turned, and between the bone and Vest McShannock and the steaming coffee, everything was in the wrong place.

To Kathryn's horror, as she lost her balance, both cups of coffee tumbled from her hands, and before she knew it Vest McShannock was lurching up out of his chair with a yelp. Both cups had dumped their entire contents down the front of his chest.

"I'm so sorry, Mr. McShannock! Hurry—undo your shirt. That's going to scald you." Kate could feel the blood rush into her face. Without thinking, she fumbled helping McShannock unbutton his vest and shirt, tugging them away from his chest. His skin had already reddened where the hot liquid had poured down it, and his shirtfront was soaked clear down to his navel.

"Oh, Mr. McShannock. I can't believe—"

The gambler's fingers went to Kate's lips, hushing her next words. Their eyes met and held. He cleared his throat. "It just happened, ma'am. It's all right. Don't fret about it."

Kate drew in a deep breath and blew it out, feeling so bad about the accident she didn't even know what to do. "At least come in and change," she said. "Ira has some shirts in the closet. The sleeves may be too short for you, but it's better than what you have on."

McShannock laughed. "That I'll grant you."

He followed her to the bedroom, walking past Cheyenne and then Vala, who was scrubbing scalded potatoes from the bottom of a huge pot. As they passed the corner shelf, the man paused. His attention often seemed drawn by the dried roses tied together there on the shelf. Since he had brought her the live red and white ones she had temporarily slipped off her wide gold band and was using it to hold the two of them together in a vase of water. Kate turned and looked at the man, who seemed mesmerized for a moment. Then he gave a little shake of his head and came on in the room. He glanced about the room nervously as Kathryn led him to the closet.

"Pick out whatever suits you," Kate said, looking at the shirts. As she turned, she nearly ran right into McShannock, and his hands came out instinctively to catch her arms at the elbows.

She looked up at him and felt a strange rush of feeling come over her. She had never allowed any man but Ira into her bedroom. Now here she was with this man she hardly knew who stood here half-dressed, his strong slender hands holding onto her. There was very little hair on his torso, allowing her to see clearly the well-defined and lithe grace of him. His chest was square and flat and wide, giving way to ridges of muscle along the length of his abdomen. She thought of Ira and the red and white roses and thought to pull away, but she didn't. With Vest McShannock, she felt so . . . safe.

McShannock must have seen something in her eyes, for he dropped his hands abruptly. There was a key in the door lock, and he turned and locked the door. A twinge of fear came to Kate just for a moment and went away just as suddenly.

When McShannock turned back to her she searched his eyes, finding in them something lost, something almost scared. She had never seen that look in his face—nor ever imagined seeing it. "Ma'am . . . I have to tell you something." He spoke abruptly, his words spilling out as if he had to force them out or keep them locked inside.

"Please don't, Mr. McShannock. You don't have to say anything." She had the sickening yet somehow thrilling feeling he was going to tell her he loved her. In one way she wanted to hear those words. It had been so long. But in another way she knew she didn't ever want to hear them coming from anyone but Ira. Certainly never from Vest McShannock. She had no idea how she would handle it.

"No, ma'am. You have no idea. I do have to tell you something."

The look in McShannock's eyes began to register on Kate. It wasn't the look of a man in love and trying to think of how to say it. It was something else, something that was scaring him more than she thought that revelation would have. "What is it?" she asked quietly. She wasn't sure she wanted to know. A cold feeling welled up inside her chest.

"Ma'am. I don't have any good way of saying this, but . . . I . . . Ah, for the love of— Ma'am . . ." He stared at her helplessly, finally putting his hand to his forehead to push back his hat. "Mrs. Winchester . . . It was me that killed your husband."

Chapter Eighteen

Kathryn Winchester, in spite of everything changing and raging around her, had started to feel safe in her life once again. She had Clyde Hall as a friend. She had her family—all except Ira—back with her. And she had Vest McShannock. He was the man who held it all together. The man who seemed to know the answers that made everything all right. The man who made her feel like she could close her eyes and rest at night and not worry about being killed while she slept.

But with one short sentence he had brought her world crashing down around her irreparably. She stared at him, unable to speak. She had raised her fingers to her mouth without knowing it. Her eyes were fixed on Vest McShannock's face until it began to blur.

"Ma'am, I . . ."

Her right fist caught McShannock hard on the jaw, knocking him back into the door. Surprised, he brought up his hands to protect himself. There was nowhere for him to go. Kate's fists battered his arms, his hands, two or three times slipped through to strike his face again.

His belly was open to attack, but Kate never even gave that a thought. It was her instincts fighting this fight. Her instincts said she had to hit him in the face to damage him, to make him pay for the wrong he had done. Ira—dead?! There was no other thought in her head. No thought of the children, or Clyde Hall or the sheriff. Nothing. Only the driving desire to attack, to inflict pain on a man who had so completely taken her in after destroying her world.

Suddenly, Vest McShannock's arms came open, and he threw them around Kate, pinning her. She kicked at his shins, stomped down on his boot tops. With a growl of pain, the man threw himself forward, taking Kate with him. They went to the floor and lit hard. Kate lay there, the wind knocked from her. Vest McShannock lying on top of her made certain she wouldn't gain it back right away.

Kate's mouth opened and shut, trying to suck air like a helpless fish thrown mercilessly on the bank to die. Her face reddened, and she felt the hot tears coursing out of her eye corners and back into her hairline. Even without breath she tried to struggle, to push McShannock away, to buck him off of her.

The man was bleeding from his nose and mouth. He was speaking gruffly to her, his eyes angry. But she couldn't grasp a word he said. A drop of his blood landed on her cheek, and then another.

Kate's breath came back in a rush, raising McShannock up a little with the force of it entering her lungs. She sucked more air in, sucked so hard it hurt her throat. She struggled to push the weight of the man off her. When that didn't work, she screamed out in frustration and tried to roll out from under him.

At last, Kate lay there exhausted, the sides of her face streaked with tears and stained with McShannock's blood. She could hear Cheyenne crying and Vala beating frantically on the door and screaming at her, but she didn't even make an attempt to call out to them.

McShannock hadn't tried to speak for some time. He just watched her quietly, making no more than a grunt each time she tried to get away from him. At last, her struggling ceased, and she turned her head away and closed her eyes.

"Are you finished?"

Kate forced herself to turn her head and look up at him. His face was so close to hers now, so close she could feel his breath. She stared at him for ten or fifteen seconds, searching his eyes with hate and desperation swimming through her head. In the back of her mind she could still hear Vala beating the door. Cheyenne continued to cry, and now tears tried to force their way into Kate's eyes too.

"I'm all right, Vala," she said in her strongest voice. "Everything's all right. I'll be out in a minute, Chey honey. Don't cry." She was answered by sobs, and she turned her eyes back to McShannock. "Ira's dead?" she finally asked.

Vest McShannock sighed. "No, ma'am. I tried to tell you."

"Tell me what?" she said through clenched teeth.

"Can we get up and be civilized?"

Kate sucked in another breath, made difficult by the weight that still crushed her against the floor. "Please," she said.

Looking at the woman dubiously, McShannock released his hold and pressed himself up, getting to his feet. He held his hand down for the woman, but she just looked at it hatefully and rolled over, standing up on her own strength.

McShannock ran a hand along his mouth. He sniffled against the blood from his nose, which had stopped flowing now. He pulled out a handkerchief from his hip pocket, but instead of using it for himself, he held it out to Kate. She angrily looked at it and wiped the back of her hand across her face, smearing the blood rather than removing it.

McShannock calmly wiped blood off his nose and mouth and returned the handkerchief to his pocket. "Mrs. Winchester, when I came here I tried to tell you about myself. I thought you'd know my name. I came from Abilene, Kansas, ma'am. Didn't that mean anything to you? I don't know Ira Winchester. I was trying to tell you about Conn Scarbrough."

Conn Scarbrough! Kate stood shocked. Conn Scarbrough . . . Now there was a name that seldom even entered her thoughts anymore. Conn, her second husband. She remembered the night they brought his body back to her on a plank.

"You . . ."

McShannock watched her, waiting for more. Kate was silent.

"It was me," he said. "I tried to come and talk to you. They wouldn't let me. They said you didn't want to see me."

"Why would I?" she asked him unbelievingly. "Why would I? You left me a widow!"

McShannock dropped his eyes. "Yes, ma'am. And I'm sorry. I've always been sorry." He looked back up at her, searching for something in her eyes. "Do you remember my name now, at least?"

"I never knew your name. They tried to tell me who killed my husband, but I wouldn't let them. I sent them all away."

"He drew a gun on me, Mrs. Winchester," he said suddenly.

"Conn had a very bad temper."

McShannock nodded his agreement. "He lost a lot of money to me that night, and he was drinking enough for two men. He went crazy. He tried to kill me. There's nothing I can say that could bring him back, ma'am, but I didn't want to kill him. I've never wanted to kill anybody."

Raising both hands, Kate placed her fingers at the outer corners of her eyes, drawing the tears off her skin. She sniffed and looked back up at him. "You don't have to try and explain it to me. I didn't love Conn Scarbrough. He was a violent man, and there was only one thing he wanted from me. If he didn't get it, he beat me. But he was my husband."

McShannock's eyes narrowed. "Is that so important? Why would you stay with him?"

"I was young!" she said angrily. "A woman doesn't want to be known as a widow. And she doesn't want to be known as a divorcée. I'd already been one. I couldn't stand the thought of becoming the other."

"Ma'am, I—"

"You'll have to leave, Mr. McShannock. I couldn't have you stay here now."

McShannock looked at her and sighed resignedly. "I'm sorry about your husband, ma'am. I'm sorry about everything."

He walked to the door, leaving Kathryn standing there in silence. He unlocked and opened the door and stepped out into the main room, moving quietly past Vala and Cheyenne and looking straight ahead.

The moment McShannock was out of the way, both girls ran into the bedroom with Kate. They threw their arms around her, and the three of them stood and cried.

The apple pie was almost done. Its waves of tantalizing aroma wafted throughout the house, making Kathryn's stomach alternately purr and growl with anticipation. She set the last biscuit on the baking sheet and put the flour and salt and the Royal baking powder back up in the cupboard. With a cured goose wing, she dusted the flour off her board, then checked the potatoes simmering on top of the stove. All the heat from oven and stove top had soaked her with sweat. Strands of her hair were sticking to her forehead and temples, and to the back of her neck. Her dress at the small of her back was glued to her, the front of her dress under her breasts was dark, and what was visible at the top of her chest glistened wetly. Her cheeks, too, were flushed bright red. Oh, how she had often wished there were another way to cook in the summertime!

Now that everything was either in the oven or waiting its turn to go in, she took the opportunity and started for the door. Even as she opened it, she heard the horses coming. She knew the boys must be returning, and just in time to wash up and eat.

When she recognized the riders, her heart leaped. It wasn't the boys. It was Sheriff Hess and Irving Wolfe! They came to a stop at the front of the house.

"Afternoon, Mrs. Winchester," said the sheriff. Wolfe just scowled at her.

"What's your business here?" asked Kate coolly.

"Mind if we step down and stretch?"

Kate shrugged. "Do as you please."

Hess and Wolfe climbed down. Wolfe wouldn't take his big, hateful eyes off her face. He didn't bother to remove his wide-brimmed, rakish white hat the way the sheriff did.

"It's about your boys, Mrs. Winchester," Hess said.

Kate's heart leaped. "What's happened?"

Hess raised his hands reassuringly. "Calm down, ma'am. Nothing's happened. I just need to talk to them. Some serious charges have come up, and I'll need their cooperation."

"Charges?" Kate's eyes flickered suspiciously toward Wolfe. "What kind of charges?"

"Your boys killed my wife!" Irving Wolfe shot out before Hess could stop him.

"Wolfe!" Arch Hess's voice was deep and angry, and it stopped the smaller man short. But he had said what he wanted to.

The sheriff turned back to Kate. "That's it, ma'am. Mr. Wolfe thinks your boys had something to do with his wife's death. That's—"

"Something to do with it?" Wolfe cut in. "They pushed her off those rocks!"

Hess whirled on the other man again. "You either button it up or I'll send you packing. I told you I'd do the talking here."

Kathryn was surprised the sheriff would talk to Wolfe like that. She had pretty much decided the sheriff catered to the rancher's every desire. But she didn't contemplate that for long. She was thinking about her boys, and her thoughts were frantic.

"Sheriff, you know what Marshal and Ellis found. You saw what happened."

"That doesn't prove—" Wolfe cut himself short and glanced over at Hess, who was glaring at him again.

The sheriff returned his eyes to her. "Ma'am, I know. And I'm sorry about this." By his voice, he genuinely seemed to be as sorry as he said. "But can I have a talk with your boys?"

Kate stared at him for a long moment. "You send that man away and I'll talk to you."

"I won't go!" shouted Wolfe. "Your boys killed my wife. They're going to have to pay. I have every right to be here while they try to refute the evidence."

Evidence! Kate just stared at him, the venom rising up inside her. She thought of how she had felt sorry for him when they found his wife, how she had hidden the note from him to save his feelings. But now she didn't care. He was after her boys, and her boys had been through enough.

"Wait here," Kathryn told the sheriff. "I have something you need to see."

She went inside the house and to her knickknack shelf. Opening the glass door, she pulled out the little folded piece of paper. She looked at it contemplatively for a moment, then returned to the porch with it closed tightly in her fist.

"My boys found this on the buggy seat that morning, Sheriff. Maybe you ought to read it."

She walked to the edge of the porch, and he stepped closer and took the piece of paper from her, unfolding it carefully. Irving Wolfe just glared from the woman to Hess. He tried to hide the curiosity fairly boiling out of his eyes.

Kate stared at Wolfe as the lawman read the note quietly. Even Wolfe, as self-important as he was, couldn't hold her gaze for long.

At last, Arch Hess cleared his throat. Kate looked over at him, and his face had saddened. "Why didn't you show me this before? You were withholding evidence, you know."

Kate raised her chin and turned her head to meet Wolfe's gaze squarely. "I didn't show it to you because I thought Irving Wolfe had been hurt enough for one day."

A brief look of incredulity struck through Wolfe's eyes, turning to a look of confusion. He turned his eyes to Hess, and the lawman was studying him sadly as he held out the piece of paper. "Mr. Wolfe, I wish it never had to be this way."

With a trembling hand, Wolfe took the note. His eyes were confused for a moment when he first began to read. He had probably thought it was a suicide note from Judith. By the time he had finished the note, the shake had gone from his hands, but his face was twisted in pain. He raised his glance to Kate, and a shocked look came over his features. Without seeming to think about it, he handed the note back to Hess, almost letting it fall before the bigger man's fingers closed on it. Then he turned and went down the steps and shuffled to his gray horse, his shoulders hanging. He climbed on board the tired gray and turned it out of the yard without another look Kate's way.

Sheriff Arch Hess watched Irving Wolfe go, a defeated man. Absently, he crumpled the note in his hand and put it in his pocket. Then he turned to Kate. But he said nothing of Irving or Judith Wolfe. "There's something we need to settle, too, Mrs. Winchester."

Kate looked at him levelly. "I don't think so."

"I do. I won't have you hating me for something I didn't do."

"I don't. I hate you for things you did."

"You're wrong," he said flatly. "Whatever it is, you're wrong."

"You are working for Irving Wolfe. And I can't be wrong."

"That's what you think?" His eyes were full of disappointment. "How could you think that? I thought we were friends."

"So did I."

"I don't work for anybody, Mrs. Winchester. No one but Bingham County. Everyone in it. No one buys off a Hess."

"Then why is it that every time we moved Ira they always knew where to look?"

"I don't know that, ma'am. I know how it looks, but you and I were the only ones who ever knew about that. And the people we put Ira up with."

Kate's mind skipped from the Websters to the Selders. She couldn't believe that any of those kind people would have had anything to do with the attempts on her husband's life. But then, like Ward Brassman had said, you couldn't trust anyone . . .

"What about the other night when Mr. McShannock told you we were bringing Ira back?" Kate asked. "You were the only person he told. He didn't even tell me."

Hess was silent for a few moments. "I can't answer that, ma'am. I didn't tell anyone."

"And what about the time I saw you and Mr. Wolfe talking in town? As soon as you saw me you both practically ran away in shame. And what was the money he gave you?"

A great sadness returned to Sheriff Hess's eyes. "You want to know what that money was for? Do you really want to know? That, I can tell you. It was for you. You and your family."

Kate stared at him. "What are you talking about?"

"Mrs. Winchester, Irving Wolfe can be a hard-boiled man. I know a little of his past, and he's dealt harshly with some people in business. But he has soft places, too. He knew you were struggling out here. He felt sorry for you, being here without a man."

"Irving Wolfe would never give me money," Kate said flatly.

"That's what he would want you to think," Hess said softly. "The fact is, he told me not to ever tell you where the money came from. It was to be given you as if by an anonymous benefactor. It would have been yours, too, except his cows came up dead shortly after that, and he came screaming to me to give back the money."

Kate couldn't believe what she was hearing. All the hatred she had thrown at Wolfe, and all the despite she had learned for Arch Hess—what had it all been for? Could Wolfe really be trying to kill her husband, yet on the other hand giving her money to survive? What kind of an unstable man would do that? Maybe that was exactly what Wolfe was—unstable. Or maybe it was part of his insidious plan. What better way to look innocent to the sheriff than to make such a benevolent, anonymous gift of money to a woman who considered him her enemy?

But as for Sheriff Hess, Kathryn Winchester was filled with shame. Once again, she had allowed her emotions to carry her away. She should have gone to him from the first, but she didn't know what she could reveal to him. This time it was partly Vest McShannock's fault, but still she had had the final choice to believe him guilty or not. She had been too quick to assume his guilt. What did a woman say to apologize for something like that?

Kate pressed her hands together. "What can I say to you, Sheriff? I believed the worst of you. There were just so many things . . ."

"I know that, ma'am. I know. Some things still look bad, and I can't answer for everything. But . . . Emotions as strong as what you've gone through can run your mind however they see fit, Mrs. Winchester. I don't blame you for anything."

He reached out and squeezed her shoulder. She patted his hand, and tears came into her eyes. "I'm sorry about keeping the note," she said, sniffling. "I couldn't let him have it that day, when he was in such obvious pain. And later . . . it just didn't seem important anymore. But I had to keep my boys from harm. They're good boys."

"They are good boys. My son Berdett has a lot of respect for both of them. And my daughter Cherie has an eye for young Ellis, too. My children have nothing but good to say about yours. I'm glad for that."

The sheriff looked down at Kate's hands all of a sudden and noticed the torn skin on her knuckles. "Are you getting ready for a prizefight?"

Kate's eyes fell to her hands, and she laughed sadly. "I've been in too many fights already, Sheriff. Far too many."

Her eyes filled with tears again, and Sheriff Hess stepped closer to her and put his arms around her. His move of support and forgiveness was all she needed. It released her emotions, and she held onto him and cried herself out.

Arthur Wolfe was a small boy for his age. When his father wasn't around the other children teased him. They called him "Nancy boy," "weakling" or "worm." Twelve-year-old Arthur had white skin like pie dumplings, and his big dark eyes shone wetly in his face, making them stand out even more.

But his mother had always made him feel better. She had said all the right words, as she said mothers were supposed to. She would soothe him with a kiss, or maybe a cookie or a peppermint stick. She would take him to eat with her in town like the grownups did. They would eat steak, sometimes, or smoked oysters or clams or pork ribs. Sometimes they treated themselves to a big piece of cherry pie. That was his favorite.

He didn't go outside as much as other boys. His mother said the sun would hurt his skin. But sometimes they would go walking, on a mild spring day. They would stroll together among the fruit trees, smelling their beautiful blossoms. They would sit and watch the bees hum over the flowers, busy at their work. His mother always cautioned him not to go too near them. They might sting him. When she was only a child her brother had died from the sting of just one honeybee.

In the autumn, they would watch as a light breeze rolled yellow cottonwood leaves across the rutted lane and made many others flutter down like butterflies. They would study the many colorful songbirds that flitted through the thinning treetops, making so many different songs they couldn't count them all. They would sit and talk about St. Louis. About Chicago. All the places that were so fine and elegant and full of life. Not like Idaho. Places where nice-looking, educated, refined people gathered for elegant soirées or for the opera. One day she said she would take him there. She would show him what life should be like.

But now his mother was gone.

His mother would take him nowhere. His mother had taken her life.

For a time, little Arthur had blamed himself. But that had passed. Just that afternoon his father had told him it wasn't his fault. His mother had died because someone had come into her life and hurt her badly. Some man they didn't know. Some man cruel and uncaring and cold as ice.

Arthur Wolfe stared at the pasty white face looking back from the mirror, at the big, dark, wet eyes so full of pain. One day he would grow up, and then he would kill the man who had hurt his mother. He would follow him wherever he went, and he would shoot him or throw him off a cliff, like his mother. But who was that man? How would he find him?

God would show him the way.

Chapter Nineteen

Vest McShannock couldn't ride away. He sat in the Gem Saloon and sipped his whisky and stared at his handful of cards and cursed himself for answering the advertisement in the Salt Lake Tribune. But now he was stuck in Blackfoot, Idaho. He couldn't leave.

Kathryn Winchester was in a spot. She was in a dark place she couldn't get out of alone. She needed a man, and hers was gone. Of course there was True Shot—Clyde Hall. He was a capable man. But he was an Indian, and there was only so much an Indian could do in that day and age without getting himself into more trouble than he could ever get out of. Especially against an influential white citizen of the community like Irving Wolfe. Hall would do what he had to. McShannock had no doubt of that. But he hated to see the big Indian throw away his life and end up dead or in prison. He was too good a man for that.

No, Vest McShannock couldn't leave Blackfoot, and he had no intention of it. But he was no longer welcome at the Winchester ranch. For the moment it was in town where he must make his stand.

McShannock had told Kate Winchester he would go to the telegraph office and send Ira a message that it was time to return. Of course she wouldn't still expect him to do that. She wouldn't even want him to. But he intended to, anyway. He had sat there in the saloon for hours, trying to think of how to word the message. That wasn't, however, the only thing holding him up. He had a gut feeling—a bad gut feeling—that this telegraph wouldn't go the way it was intended. He didn't know why. Maybe something he had inherited through years of gambling, and observing other men? It wasn't that, though, for he had never even met the telegrapher at Blackfoot's train station, much less sent anything through him. Still, something kept giving him that strange warning. He decided to trust his instincts and go into the telegraph office with mistrust riding his shoulders all the way.

McShannock sat at a lonely corner table in the saloon and on a pad of paper scribbled out the rough wording of the message he would send asking Ira Winchester to come home. It had to be something sweet, something loving. It must be something Ira couldn't resist, if he was in good enough condition to travel. It had to at least be something he would reply to. When he had come up with what he thought was the perfect wording, he walked down to the train station, where the telegraph was housed.

Tryon Holt was Blackfoot's telegrapher. He was a short man of perhaps thirty-five years with teeth that were much too big for his mouth and a black mole on his upper lip that his thin little brown mustache couldn't hide. He paid little attention to McShannock when he first came in, but when he mentioned that he had a telegram from Kate Winchester to her husband, he gained the little man's full attention. That was McShannock's first actual danger signal, beyond any intuitive feeling.

Holt suddenly became very accommodating, dropping anything else he had to do and going straight to work. He was all smiles, flashing those large white teeth over and over as if it overjoyed him to be able to help McShannock out.

McShannock paid the little man with a half eagle, took his change, and returned to the Gem Saloon to wait as long as he must. He chose the Gem Saloon because from there he had a perfect view of the train station.

Ira Winchester spent most of his time in bed. But his strength was returning quickly. His shoulders and chest were fleshing out, and in spite of the scar on his side and the thin spot of hair on his head where his stitches had been, he looked like a whole, healthy man again. His once clean-shaven face was covered with four weeks' growth of beard.

Ira stared out at the world that passed back and forth in front of his thinly curtained window. There were people living out there. People loving, sharing their hopes and wishes and fears. Why was he here so far away from his home? Why had he done the things he had to put him in this bed?

Ira had been awake for two weeks. But two weeks weren't enough to convince him to come clean about his activities in Blackfoot. After all, his main concern when all was said and done was Katie and the kids. Before the attack, he had tried to tell his wife that, but she didn't believe him. He had to admit that to anyone watching him he hadn't seemed to care about anyone but himself for perhaps the last six months. He had kept an awful lot from Katie and the kids. But it was for their own good. The things he had become involved in were better kept to as few people as possible. Keeping Katie and the kids in the dark was the only way he knew to protect them. Of course, as it turned out, even that had been little protection.

But what else could he have done? He loved Katie with all of his heart. He had become sullen with her, but only because of the stress he was under, the stress from what he was hiding. It slowly ate him away inside. But that didn't change how he felt deep down about Katie and the kids. He wanted only the best for them. But he had been horribly wrong in how he went about getting it.

And now, what did a man do to right a wrong like his? What could he possibly do? He could land in prison for his involvement in what was going on in Blackfoot. That would leave Katie and the kids alone. Ira couldn't stomach that.

So he spent his hours lying in bed, aching for some way to make things all right, to see that justice was done. Most importantly, he just wanted to know that Katie had someone to watch out for her when all the cards were on the table. If that couldn't be him, then so be it. But it had to be someone she could trust.

He had been wrong in what he had done. He cursed himself for it. He had been wrong for getting involved. He should have gone to the authorities from the very beginning. And he had been even more wrong asking for the extra money. But he and Katie had had nothing for too long. He wanted so much to provide his wife with some of the nicer things in life. It was that drive which nearly destroyed them. And if he lost his wife over it now, then it had, indeed, destroyed him.

It was early afternoon when his Aunt Betsy brought him a bowl of soup and a handful of crackers. Aunt Betsy was almost five feet tall, with hips and chest as big around as she was tall from her knees to the top of her head. She had her thinning hair on top of her head, and a couple yards of red, flowered fabric in a loose wrap around her. Ira could see by the beginnings of a grin on Betsy's face that something had happened. She hadn't seemed in such high spirits since he awoke the first day to find her hovering over his bed.

"A man from the telegraph office came by today," she said suddenly, still hiding her smile.

Ira pushed himself up quickly in his bed. "Something from Kate?"

A grin broke over the heavy woman's face, and she said in her gravelly voice, "It sure is." She pulled a slip of folded paper from behind her apron and handed it to him, watching him with quiet expectance.

Ira fumbled open the piece of paper and hurriedly read the words scrawled there.

Ira stop
Know I am not to write but am weak stop *World is not the same without you* stop *Still in danger but need you here* stop *Without you it is not worth fighting* stop *Come home* stop *Let us know when* stop
Kate full stop

Ira looked up at Betsy. "I think she wants me back."

Betsy smiled, her blue eyes twinkling and becoming lost in a field of crow's feet. "I think you could safely guess that. I'll send Katie a reply, if you'd like. It's time you went home to your family."

Ira smiled. "Way past time."

Aunt Betsy went down to the train station and checked the schedules, bringing home a copy with her. After studying out the various runs, Ira sat down and put a pen to paper. His message was simple and direct:

Kate stop
Coming home Tuesday evening train nine fifteen stop *Want to tell you everything* stop *Stay home don't talk to anyone* stop *There is a madman there who will not rest* stop *Cannot tell you more* stop *Knows everything and owns everybody in town* stop
Ira full stop

Betsy took the piece of paper her nephew handed her and folded it into her chubby hand. With a smile, she hurried off to the telegraph office.

In Blackfoot, Tryon Holt, the telegrapher, wrote the return message in his awful hand, no plainer to an onlooker than badger scratchings. He wrote it, waited to make certain the telegraph had stopped, then clicked away to let them know on the other end that he had received the message. Then he traded his eyeshade for a narrow-brimmed gray hat, pulled his suit jacket over his shirtsleeves, and hurried out the door. Ira Winchester was coming home, and Tryon Holt knew someone who had waited anxiously to hear that news. Kathryn Winchester was probably anxious as well.

But it wasn't Kathryn Winchester to whom he ran. It was down the road to the courthouse.

"This is your last chance," said the speaker to Case Deckan and the big New Yorker named Stewart Lords, the man Kate Winchester had thought of as "Calico." "He's in Brigham, Utah. He'll be coming back on Tuesday, and he's scheduled to arrive at dusk, on the nine-fifteen. He had better not arrive. I'll let you have the particulars tonight. But I'll tell you right now: if he arrives here and has a chance to talk to Kathryn Winchester, we're all finished. Do you understand me? All of us. I won't go down alone."

Lords twisted his blue calico scarf up in his fist. It was an action that might imply nervousness, but the man didn't otherwise appear nervous. He stared at the man who paid him, and he made no pretense of hiding the disdain in his eyes. In his New York accent, he said, "Figured you for a man like that."

The other man leveled a gaze at him. "Then why weren't you smart enough to leave me sooner?"

"Money. But how does it feel to have people trust you and look up to you and to betray them?"

The man laughed. "It doesn't feel any way at all. Fools are not worth my consideration."

Lords picked up a napkin and wiped mustard off the corner of his mouth, casting Deckan a disgusted look. He looked back up at his employer, and when he stood up he was the much bigger of the two. But the other man showed no sign of fear. He never had.

"One day I may kill you," Lords said.

His employer just smiled thinly. "I would invite you to try. Until then, you just stay out of trouble. I want no mistakes this time. You've been thrashed often enough by a woman and some boys. It's time to show me you aren't completely worthless."

The New York man grunted. "Five hundred dollars. Five hundred dollars, mister. And it had better be there tomorrow night."

197

Case Deckan spoke for the first time. "What about the Winchester woman? She knows Stewart. She's bound t' see 'im before too long an' point 'im out to the sheriff. What then? We kill her?"

The man stared at Case Deckan, his lips making a thin, straight line. "You keep your filthy hands off the woman. I have plans for her."

It was quiet in the Gem Saloon, and Vest McShannock sat and smoked a cigar, idly studying the street outside. The telegrapher had gone to the sheriff's office within an hour after he had him send the message to Ira. Then he had quickly returned. It might not mean anything. Holt could have been delivering any number of different messages. But it was a move McShannock's guts had told him the little man would make. He hadn't felt good about the telegraph, and something told him any answer to it would go to someone besides himself or Kate. The first person that came to his suspicious mind, of course, was Sheriff Hess. Kate Winchester couldn't seem to make up her mind about Hess. She was easily swayed. But Vest McShannock had dedicated his life to reading men. Arch Hess was just a good actor—a typical politician.

Now the question remained: had a message indeed come back from Brigham? There had been ample time. And if one had, would the telegrapher give it to him? Or only to Hess?

McShannock smoked the cigar down to a stub and snuffed it on the glass dish in front of him. He looked around the room one last time and left a dollar sitting on the table to pay for his drinks. Then he stepped outside and crossed the street to the train station.

Tryon Holt was behind his desk when Vest McShannock walked in. The little man looked up at him and squinted through thick glasses, nudging them back up in place with a knuckle. "Can I help you?"

"I sent a message earlier. Just checking to see if there's a reply."

The little man's eyes flickered, and for just a moment he looked away, steadying his voice. "Well . . . No, I don't think there has been. Maybe you could check back tomorrow."

"I don't mean to bother you, but did you get any other messages since then?" asked Vest McShannock casually.

Tryon Holt seemed to be made bolder by the soft words, and his own voice became gruff. "I'm not sure that's any business of yours. Listen, I'm a little busy right now. If you could check back tomorrow I'll let you know if anything has come in."

McShannock smiled amiably. "Well, all right. But I do have another message from the lady. She forgot this earlier and wanted to make sure her husband knew about it."

Holt cocked his head. "Yes? What is it?"

"Well, she didn't write it down, but I have it in my head. Give me a piece of paper, and I'll write it out for you."

Holt complied courteously this time, and McShannock scratched the quick note on Holt's pad. It read,

Ira stop
Before you leave send word who tried to kill you stop *Need to know if my suspicions are correct* stop
Kate full stop

McShannock was under no illusion of having the message answered. He didn't need to have it answered. The only answer he needed was to watch what move the telegrapher made after taking it from him.

Tryon Holt took the slip of paper with a glance of indifference at it and said, "Just a moment." He started up the telegraph and clicked away, acting as if he thought nothing of the strange message. When he was through, he charged McShannock one dollar and fifty cents, and McShannock thanked him politely and left, returning to the saloon.

Tryon Holt was a fool. He didn't even wait long enough to look like he had a valid reason this time. Not two minutes after McShannock's departure, he left the telegraph office and went toward the courthouse, this time almost running in his haste. With no need to wait any longer, McShannock immediately went outside, climbed onto his palomino, and rode at a hard trot toward Pocatello Junction.

Without trying to win any races, it took nearly three hours to ride to Pocatello. There, McShannock went into the telegraph office at the train station and paid to have a message sent to Brigham. It stated that the Blackfoot telegraph had experienced a problem receiving his message and asked him to send it again.

"I'll wait for a reply in the lobby of the Pacific Hotel," he told the telegrapher.

An hour didn't pass before the old man who ran the telegraph came looking for him. He found him seated on the long red wool sofa in the Pacific Hotel's big lobby and handed him a folded card. McShannock thanked him and gave him two bits as a tip. He read the message from Ira and smiled grimly. It simply said that Ira wasn't able to tell them anything yet. So little Tryon Holt would be another tree that came down in the forest fire that would sweep Blackfoot before this was all over!

Actually receiving this message, and so promptly, was enough proof for McShannock that the little telegrapher was another of Hess's pawns.

Clyde Hall and R.M. Sievers met Vest McShannock in the lobby of the Commercial Hotel the next morning at five thirty. The world lay in shades of dim gray, with a pale light hanging in the east and a few stubborn stars still glittering. Other than at the train station, there was little movement along the street. The only sound was of a jackass braying loudly in the distance.

The big Indian was the first one through the hotel door, his frame hiding Sievers until the smaller man walked around him to lean up beside the door. Sievers's only acknowledgment was a nod, and he watched McShannock with what McShannock took as a hint of mistrust.

Clyde Hall's eyes were puffy with missed sleep. He didn't like to rise so early. Yawning, he hooked his thumbs behind his waistband and looked McShannock over. "It looks like the woman give you a whoopin', I'll say."

McShannock gave a half-grin, digging sleep out of the corner of his eye. "She packs a wallop, True Shot. And I never even saw it coming."

"So what's happenin'?" asked Hall.

"Well, I needed somebody that would help Mrs. Winchester out. You were the two that came to mind. I thought of bringing that banker in, too. He seems pretty willing to look after the woman. But after a little experience with the telegraph office yesterday I have no idea who I can really trust in this town. You didn't tell Mrs. Winchester anything, did you?"

Clyde Hall just shook his head.

R.M. Sievers stepped away from the wall, a sign that he intended to say something. McShannock and Hall looked at him as he spoke, "You ain't told us much. Why're we here?"

McShannock smiled. "No, I guess I haven't told you much. I'm half afraid to."

"Why?" asked Hall.

"Because the three of us could wind up dead."

Chapter Twenty

The train station in Brigham, Utah Territory, was abustle with activity the next morning, when Clyde Hall, R.M. Sievers and Vest McShannock watched Ira Winchester climb on the northbound ten-forty-five. People stood all around the platform, saying their goodbyes and hellos. Some people cried, some laughed. One boy hugged his father's legs. Another shyly shook the man's hand. Life was peaceful for these people. There didn't seem to be any threat of death hanging over them. That was the way it should be.

The air around the station was clogged with the smell of coal smoke and cinders, and some of the women who stood by waiting to board had handkerchiefs pressed daintily to their mouths. Some of them wore linen coverings to protect their dresses. The fireman stood beside the train with a lit pipe in his mouth, trying to suck even more soot between his teeth and down into his lungs. His forehead and cheeks were nearly black.

With a good breakfast inside them, Hall, Sievers and McShannock climbed into the same car Ira had boarded. They seated themselves back in a corner, as inconspicuously as they could. For Clyde Hall that meant as inconspicuous as a horseshoe in a basket of eggs. He was too big to hide in the first place, and being an Indian to boot made everyone there look at him at least twice. Indians were not generally allowed to ride inside the cars (around Blackfoot and Pocatello they could ride free, as part of their treaty agreement—as long as they rode on the roof) and the trio was pushing its luck having Hall try it now.

Even though Ira knew R.M. Sievers, Sievers kept his hat down low, and Ira didn't notice him. He was busy looking out the window at a short, fat older woman in a blue dress who kept raising her hand to wave at him. A bright smile adorned her face.

Vest McShannock slowly scanned the rest of the car. There was no sign of anyone he recognized from Blackfoot. But the fact was he didn't expect anyone to make an attempt at pulling Ira off the train until much farther down the track. Because of that, he had hated the idea of having to come clear to Brigham to accompany Ira back. It was eight dollars and twenty cents, just for a one-way ticket! But he couldn't risk not being there when the assassins appeared, as he had the strongest of feelings they would before the ride was over.

McShannock couldn't bring himself to like Ira Winchester. He had gotten himself involved in something illegal, leaving his wife to hold the bag and try to keep the family together. He didn't deserve the woman's loyalty and affection. But he had it, all the same. And because he did, and McShannock owed Kathryn Winchester, McShannock would defend Ira even at peril to his own life. He had never thought about doing anything else.

After ten minutes, they heard the long, mournful howl of the whistle. A cloud of steam gushed by the windows, and loose pieces of ash began to tumble past and to the rail bed. The car lurched forward, and then, after a number of lesser lurches, it began to roll smoothly, clacking along the rails, picking up speed. It took them several minutes to reach their rolling speed of a little over thirty miles an hour.

McShannock sat and watched the back of Ira Winchester's head, wondering how a man could be as lucky as he was. Kathryn Winchester was the most handsome woman he ever remembered seeing, and a lady on top of that. He knew something had gone wrong between Ira and the woman. But she had never told him what. She wasn't that kind. For Ira's sake, McShannock hoped he came to his senses soon. There were plenty of other men around who would welcome the chance to court a woman like Mrs. Winchester, even if she was a divorcée—or a widow. Vest McShannock knew one of them personally. In fact, if he counted the banker in Blackfoot, he figured he knew two.

The train ride wasn't something a body would look forward to every day. It was rough at times, and the car tended to sway back and forth. It could get stiflingly hot, at other times almost unbearably cold. Yet everything bad about trains was magnified ten times by the old stagecoaches, and in that light the ride didn't seem bad.

The rails stretched on and on, and the three of them took turns sleeping. McShannock didn't remember sleeping much, however. His mind was too occupied with Kate Winchester to sleep. What he felt inside was an ache, he decided at last. He ached with the knowledge that he should have told the woman who he really was when they first met. He should have told her he came there because he felt he owed her a debt for leaving her widowed.

He couldn't tell her the other reason he had come there, that his heart had been with her since the first day he saw her. He couldn't tell her about all the lonely nights he had spent wondering where she had gone after leaving Kansas. He couldn't tell her about the women he'd held and wished somehow they could have been Lady Winchester. He couldn't and never would tell her any of that. And he would never tell her that he loved her.

Ira Winchester was a decent-looking man. McShannock had to admit that to himself, even while he hated him for owning what he loved. He had seen Ira smile at the woman at the train station, which must have been his Aunt Betsy. The man had a kind smile. He had kind eyes, too. Whatever it was he had done to get him and his family in the spot they were in now, McShannock hoped he could repair it. McShannock had never had any part of Kate Winchester, and he never could. But Ira had. He had had all of her—her mind, heart and body. It would kill a man to know that and then to lose it.

The train stopped at Honeyville, Dewey, Collinston, Cachill and Mendon. It stopped in Logan at twelve-fifty, where they had to wait twenty minutes to register the train. Not in any of the stops was there any sign of trouble. They crossed the Idaho border just after two-twenty in the afternoon, passed through Franklin and Preston and took on wood and water at the Battle Creek station, where they had to register once more.

Clyde Hall was very sober and quiet at Battle Creek, and he stared across the sage. McShannock watched him in silent contemplation for a minute or more before he realized there was a tear rolling down the big Indian's cheek. Even as he was turning to look at R.M. Sievers, the smaller man spoke quietly.

"That's where they rubbed out a good bunch of the Shoshone nation."

McShannock shot him the question with his eyes.

"The Battle of Bear River, they call it," Sievers went on. "Back in sixty-three. It ended up a massacre—for the Injuns. Patrick Connor killed three hundred or so Injuns in a village over there on the crick. The soldiers lost less than twenty men. But they destroyed a nation."

McShannock looked back over at Clyde Hall. The big Indian was rock still, and the tears ran unabashedly down his cheeks. So the big Indian had lost people here. Hallowed ground . . .

On leaving the Battle Creek stop, a helper engine had to be added to the front of the train to help it up over the grade away from the Bear River bottoms. McShannock, Hall and Sievers hadn't said much the entire trip. Their personalities seemed much the same when it came to impending danger. Rather than make them jabber aimlessly, danger turned them silent. But Hall was especially silent now. McShannock didn't expect much from him the rest of the trip.

Between Battle Creek and McCammon Junction were seven stops, and with each one McShannock felt his heart rate quicken. But he saw nothing suspicious at any of them. They passed Morrell and Oxford, Swan Lake and Calvin, Downey and Thatcher and Arimo.

Just after six o'clock in the evening, they neared the little station at McCammon Junction. Here, the broad gauge track of the Oregon Short Line Railroad, coming in from Wyoming Territory, would join the narrow gauge of the Utah and Northern. The tracks would parallel each other the rest of the way on into Pocatello Junction. This arrangement had allowed the new Oregon Short Line company, bringing their line through in eighty-two, to simply lay down one rail to the outside of one of the Utah and Northern tracks, to accommodate their wider cars. Both trains used one common outside rail. The odd-looking three-rail track ran all the rest of the way into Pocatello before the lines split again and the Oregon Short Line headed west toward Snake River. Across the valley to their left rambled Old Tom Mountain with its bald, windswept ridges and long dark pockets of spired fir trees.

Vest McShannock found himself starting to wonder if anyone would come after Ira Winchester at all. Maybe they were safe. Maybe the sheriff and Irving Wolfe and all of their cohorts had been afraid Ira had already decided to turn them in, in Utah, and that the authorities would be coming for them today. Maybe all of them had run for it.

That contemplation made McShannock's heart lighten a touch. Maybe there would be no more killing. But when would they know? One thing was certain. If something were to happen, it had to be somewhere between McCammon and Blackfoot. Once Ira Winchester made it to Blackfoot, the town was going to blow wide open. Whoever was after Ira might still kill him, but they would catch their tail in a crack in the process.

The train's shrill whistle blew, and it started its mile and a quarter slow-down to the McCammon station. Past the farms and ranches they went, past farm boys in coveralls and girls in calico with bonnets tied at the chin. A pair of Percherons was pulling a load of hay down a side road. The driver of the wagon couldn't have been much more than fourteen. He waved at them with a big grin.

McShannock watched the green fields, faded beneath summer's onslaught. His vivid imagination carried to him the smells of the burned grass, the aroma of the new-mown and the dried hay. But the only air he could really smell was dominated by waves of blue tobacco smoke, tainted now and then by the odors of stale sweat and toilet water and the occasional waft from a tin of ham or sardines opened by some traveler.

The train slowly came to a halt, burping steam from underneath and letting out one long last whistle to let the world know it had arrived. This time the general exodus included McShannock and Sievers. They had had enough of the cramped seats and had to have a breath of fresh air, to at least feel a breeze drift lazily around them after sitting and sweating for the past seven hours. As for Hall, he knew what kind of reception he would receive inside the hotel, so his only respite from the long ride was to step out the back of the car and breathe in the cinder-tainted air. The good thing was that kept him near Ira Winchester so he was able to keep an eye on him in case assassins made any move.

McShannock left the others and wandered over to the magnificent Harkness House, going inside its shaded and elegant interior to sit down and order himself a cup of coffee and a piece of pie. After a few minutes, R.M. Sievers found him and came over to sit down across from him, casting his sober glance around at the crowd.

"You ain't spoke much the whole trip," Sievers said.

McShannock sipped his coffee. "What's to say? I was waiting for you and the Indian."

Sievers ran a hand across a forehead whose wrinkles looked like they were carved with a knife. He scratched his whiskered jaw and studied McShannock, making no attempt to hide the fact that he was reading him.

"Why'd you come to Blackfoot in the first place?"

"I read the ad in the Salt Lake Tribune," McShannock said. "Sounded intriguing."

Sievers frowned and looked down at the table. "Kate told us who you are, so . . ." He looked back up. "Really. Why'd you come?"

"Hell, Sievers, why does dust stick to a polished chandelier? Why does a honeybee keep seeking out that prettiest flower? Why—" McShannock stopped and stared at Sievers for a moment, then finally looked away. "I came here because I'm a fool, I suppose. I've never been able to forget Kathryn Winchester. I went to her husband's funeral. Watched it from a distance. I saw her there and saw something I've never seen since. A genuine lady. She doesn't remember me, but she smiled at me that day when she was leaving the cemetery. It was the smile of what I judged to be the closest to a perfect person God ever put down on this miserable earth. I came to Idaho partly because I felt I owed Kathryn Winchester a debt. And partly because I hoped to see that smile again."

Sievers kept looking away as McShannock talked, but finally he met his eyes as he spoke those last words. "Was it worth it?"

McShannock smiled sadly. "That smile would never be for me like it would for Ira Winchester. It's made me a miserable man. But so does whisky, and we keep coming back for it. Don't we?"

When they climbed back into the stiflingly hot train car, Clyde Hall was sitting back in the corner again, watching them expectantly. He answered their questioning looks with a shrug. They sat back down across from him, and McShannock looked over.

"Maybe we took this peach of a trip for nothing," he said.

Hall just grunted.

The long whistle shrilled and five minutes went by. The whistle sounded again, and a shudder went through the train. A few last people climbed on board, and McShannock heard the conductor yell his final warnings. Then the car lurched forward and slowly pulled away.

McShannock's heart began to pound inexplicably hard. He had begun to think his instincts wrong. Had they come for nothing? They had just crossed the bridge over the Portneuf River and were crawling along beneath the Portneuf range, with Haystack Mountain and Snow and Bonneville Peaks on their right and Scab Mountain* across the valley to their left. They were getting very near their final destination, and as of yet there had been no trouble at all. Why would the assassins wait so long?

Outside the left window now loomed a sometimes vertical wall of purple-black lava rock, some of it lying in gigantic chunks at the base. Some of them had rolled nearly to the edge of the Portneuf River, which picked its course through the rank yellow grass of summer.

Outside Clyde's window, Haystack Mountain ran long and flat against the dull blue summer sky, nearly as straight up and down on its west face as it was horizontal across its top. Most of the west face was too steep to grow much timber, and only scrub brush colored its flanks, growing thick toward its base. But on its north end jagged, rocky cliffs pierced through the forest. On its southern end, the white cliffs at the head of Harkness Canyon seemed to flank Haystack, and only down lower was the terrain gentle, its rolling hills blanketed with maple and juniper and sagebrush.

McShannock was watching diamonds dance on the river when he heard the rear door of the car open, letting in the clatter and hiss of the

*See Author's note

206

train outside. His first instinct was to whirl around, but he forced himself to do exactly the opposite. He held perfectly still.

His hand crept slowly up to the butt of his revolver, and from the corner of his eye he saw R.M. Sievers's hand slide inside his coat. As for Clyde Hall, he didn't move. McShannock wasn't sure exactly where he had a weapon, if he had any at all. Chances were, being an Indian in that era, he hadn't dared bring a weapon with him. McShannock couldn't blame him.

Vest McShannock slowly tried to bring his head around to see who had come in. The door had shut, and he had yet to see anyone. Maybe they had turned around and left. Lost their nerve, perhaps, after seeing the packed car? Or perhaps it was just a Utah and Northern Railroad employee.

A dark-coated man started by, and McShannock turned his head just enough to see. With an imperceptible sigh of relief, he realized it was only the conductor. He had forgotten they had to come through and check boarding passes again. He should have been used to it by now.

But this time they weren't checking boarding passes.

This time they were off-loading a man—to be killed.

Two steps behind the conductor came a big man with a blue bandanna over his face.

He held a pistol to the conductor's back.

To Vest McShannock, the rest of the passengers seemed unreasonably calm as the conductor's and the big masked man's footsteps thudded down the aisle.

It was almost as if nobody else knew someone was about to die.

Chapter Twenty-One

"Nobody move!"

The order rang loud and clear through the narrow passenger car. Vest McShannock jerked in surprise. He had been watching the conductor and the big man with the bandanna over his face. He hadn't been thinking of anyone being behind him. But the yell had come from another man he couldn't see!

From the corner of his eye he looked at R.M. Sievers. The smaller man was watching him, his face set in hard lines. He now held a little Colt Navy Conversion pistol along the side of his leg, and his thumb began to turn white on its hammer.

McShannock looked across the aisle at Clyde Hall. The big Indian was expressionless. But McShannock understood Hall. Hall was like a loaded spring. He wasn't thinking about his own life. He was planning his next move.

The man at the rear of the train spoke again. "Folks, keep your hands where we can see 'em. Keep your eyes to the front of the car. We ain't here to hurt anybody. We're just here to escort one of the passengers off the train. Ladies, you can keep your purses, and gents . . . please keep your heads."

Ira Winchester wasn't moving. He had done exactly as the man said, but it was plain when the conductor and the big masked man stopped beside him that Ira knew he was the passenger they had spoken of. He looked over at the big man with a fatalistic look in his eyes.

The big man motioned the conductor to keep going toward the front of the car, and he soon disappeared from sight.

Ira studied the big man beside him for a moment, then started to stand up. The big man allowed him to. He backed up a little ways and motioned with the barrel of his gun for Ira to step out from the seats.

McShannock heard the brake squeak as it was lightly applied. Ira and the big man held onto the nearest seat with one hand as the train came to a slow stop, taking over a mile.

When the train had stopped, the man at the rear of the car barked out, "Now, everyone stay put. Bring 'im back here!" he ordered his partner.

The big man nudged Ira along the car. Ira's steps faltered a touch when he saw R.M. Sievers sitting there, but he continued on past without any other sign of recognition. The rear door opened again and shut several seconds later. Clyde Hall turned to look. The second he started out of his chair, Vest McShannock also came up. R.M. Sievers was right behind them.

The trio bailed out the rear of the train car just in time to see a third man with a veiled face come galloping up with three horses in tow. Ira and the other two men were standing on the ground below the grade of the rail bed, waiting for the rider to bring up their horses.

"I'll take the big one." Even as Vest McShannock spoke, the man on horseback yelled something at his cohorts and waved toward him, Hall and Sievers.

McShannock's pistol was already in his hand, coming level with his eye. The big man heard the rider's warning. He whirled and dropped into a crouch. The man next to him was almost as fast. As McShannock's pistol cracked, he heard the big man's bullet hit the side of the train. The big man staggered back under McShannock's shot as R.M. Sievers fired at the second man, who matched his speed. Through the thick blue smoke fogging around them, held in place by the stagnant August air, McShannock saw R.M. Sievers do a quarter turn and slam back against the train car. At the same moment, McShannock was surprised to see the second would-be kidnapper pitch backward into the grass.

Ira Winchester saw his chance and whirled away. Even as he did, the big man on the ground sat up and turned his gun on him. McShannock fired again at the big man, but the big man's shot, aimed at Ira, matched McShannock's.

Through his peripheral vision, McShannock was aware of Ira going down. He yelled out a curse and drew back his hammer, swinging his gun again toward the big man. Before he could fire, the big man dove for the underside of the train. McShannock fired at his legs as they disappeared beneath him. He knew instantly he had missed.

A bullet struck the iron railing at McShannock's hand. He whirled to catch sight of the man who had stood guard at the back of the train, the one Sievers had shot. He was on his knees now, gun leveled. Before McShannock had time to act, the man dropped his pistol unexpectedly and clutched at his chest. His eyes went wide with shock and pain.

Not understanding what had happened, and not having time to try, Vest McShannock started down the steps. He stumbled and almost fell headlong but caught the railing and pulled himself up. By the time he made it to the ground, the man kneeling there had clawed the bandanna away from his mouth and was struggling to pull out a knife planted hilt-deep in his chest. McShannock recalled the whiskered face the moment the bandanna cleared it.

The man was Irving Wolfe's hired hand, Case Deckan.

Deckan couldn't pull the knife out. He looked up at McShannock with pleading eyes, eyes full of hurt that he should die this way. Knowing they had more to worry about than a dying man, McShannock whirled from Deckan toward the train and threw himself to his belly. He looked under the train just in time to see the legs of the big would-be assassin clambering onto a horse on the other side.

He dove under the train, crawling across the sharp rocks, and shoved to his feet even as he cleared the farthest rail. As the two horsemen laid spurs to their animals, McShannock threw one last desperate shot. He was fifty yards away from the horses and didn't trust himself with a pistol at that range. He didn't think his shot could be responsible for what came next. Yet the mount beneath the man who had brought up the escape horses stumbled and flew headlong. Its rider went down in a roil of dust. The horse's feet flailed in the air as it rolled right over the top of him. The big man pulled his mount in. He took a backward look, but he must have thought better of going back. He spurred his horse, and within a matter of seconds he was nearly past the front of the train. McShannock wasted two shots after him and hurriedly unloaded his shell casings to thumb more cartridges into the Colt.

Already out of breath, but desperate, McShannock ran along the train to where the fallen man's horse was coming shakily to its feet. The man just lay there in the dust. McShannock walked up with his gun trained on him and watched for a moment to see if he was breathing. He wasn't.

Just when McShannock was sure the man was dead, he took in a massive breath and started coughing violently. He came to his hands and knees, head hanging down and saliva stringing from his mouth. Sucking in breath through burning lungs, McShannock watched the man until the train engineer and a man who was so dirtied with soot he could only be the fireman came up and looked at the two of them. Their expressions were bewildered.

McShannock started to say something to the two men, but as he was turning to look at them something about the man on the ground struck him, and he spun back. The moment the man started to turn his head to look up at the three of them, McShannock grunted and spat to one side.

"So you boys actually get your hands right in it."

The man struggled to his knees, then sank back so his weight rested on his lower legs. His face was covered with dust and blood from the fall, and his hair stuck in every direction, plastered with sweat and dirt and blood. He glanced back and forth between McShannock and the two trainmen but never said a word. At last, his chin fell to his chest.

"Boys," said McShannock. "I want you to meet one of Blackfoot's fine lawmen. This is Deputy Luke Weaver."

McShannock reached down and took the pistol out of Luke Weaver's holster without any argument from the dazed lawman. He handed it to the engineer. "Keep an eye on him, would you? Make sure he doesn't run off. We've killed enough men for one day."

McShannock walked back over to the train. Climbing up on the platform, he was distantly aware of the hum of voices from inside the car.

Some brave passengers had ventured to the door, and they looked around excitedly.

McShannock pushed past the babbling voices and descended the steps to the other side of the train. He saw Clyde Hall standing over Case Deckan—the late Case Deckan, he had become since McShannock's abrupt departure. Ira Winchester stood by the train, to McShannock's left, brushing dirt and weeds off his suit.

Surprised, McShannock gave him a quick scan. "I thought they shot you."

"Not me," said Ira with a half smile. "I may not be a rock, but I can drop like one—when I have a reason."

McShannock thought of introducing himself to Ira, but he wasn't in the mood. Instead, he turned and limped over to Clyde Hall, just then becoming aware of how badly he had bruised his knees in scrambling across the rocks of the rail bed. He looked down at Case Deckan, the knife still stuck firmly in his chest beside his breastbone. His eyes met Hall's.

"Better not forget your knife," said the big métis.

"My knife?" McShannock gave him a queer look. "My knife never left the sheath."

Hall continued to look at him expressionlessly. "I know it. But I'm a Injun. You can bet I didn't kill no white man. That's your knife today. You feel like it, you make me a present of it some other day. But—" He looked down distastefully at the dead man. "Make sure you clean off the blood first. I don't want no dirty knife."

McShannock chuckled his understanding, and then on a sudden thought, he looked quickly around. "Where's Sievers?"

Clyde motioned toward the train. "He got shot. They pulled him inside."

McShannock turned without a word and went to the train, hurrying up the steps. He pushed on inside, past the people in the doorway. His presence seemed to be the drop that spilled the cup over. The other passengers started crowding outside with faces hungry to get a glimpse at the aftermath of the violence.

McShannock found R.M. Sievers sitting on one of the seats with a woman and three men hovering like nursemaids over him. The sleeve of Sievers's left arm was bloody where a bullet had cut through his shirt midway up his arm. Sievers looked up at McShannock with his typical bland face.

"I guess I'm allergic to lead. Makes me bleed."

McShannock had to laugh, relief washing through him. R.M. Sievers was a reserved fellow, and not easy to get to know. But there was a dry humor in him that McShannock found irresistible. And more importantly, he came across as a man who would risk his life to save a friend. McShannock wouldn't have wanted to see him hurt over the likes of Ira Winchester. From what he knew of Winchester and the way he had done his wife, he wasn't so sure why he was risking his own life over him.

"You didn't know the big man that rode away, did you?" McShannock asked Sievers. "I don't suppose that could have been Hess."

Sievers looked up as if he hadn't heard quite right. "Hess? What would make you say that?"

"Oh, never mind. I figured Mrs. Winchester might have talked to you. It's too long to explain," McShannock said, and he turned and left the train.

A crowd was gathered around Case Deckan's body, and Clyde Hall stood off to the side with Ira Winchester. McShannock climbed down the steps and walked over to them. He looked at the two of them for a long moment, glad for the silence between them. There was plenty of noise being made by the crowd gathered around Deckan.

Finally, Ira Winchester cleared his throat. "Mr. Hall told me you all came here to escort me back. It's pretty plain I owe you three my life."

"Pretty plain," replied McShannock, not smiling. "You've made yourself some important enemies."

Ira looked at him questioningly.

"I'd like some answers before we get back to Blackfoot," McShannock said. "It's obvious who the big bad man in this whole mess is. My question is, is the sheriff in on it or not?"

"The sheriff?" Ira was obviously surprised. "Hess? I—" He looked down, obviously pondering that thought. "I can't believe that," he said finally, looking back up at McShannock. "Why would you think that?"

McShannock tried to explain as briefly as possible the events in Blackfoot. When he was through, he and Ira just stared at each other for several seconds. "I guess I don't know about the sheriff," Ira admitted at last. "But . . . who's over it all?"

McShannock peered at the shorter man queerly. "Irving Wolfe," he finally replied.

Ira shook his head emphatically. "Oh, hell! I hope that isn't what they believe. Does Kate think Wolfe tried to kill me?"

Again McShannock just had to stare for several long seconds. "It seemed pretty plain."

"It isn't," replied Ira. "I can't tell you who's over all this. The only man I know about is Hess's deputy—his name's Luke Weaver."

"I know about Weaver," said McShannock. "He's on the other side of the train waiting for us."

Ira's eyes shot that way, and then he looked back at McShannock. "That's good. Like I said, he's the one that came to me when this all started. But his boss isn't Irving Wolfe. Irving Wolfe's their main target!"

To McShannock, the train seemed excrutiatingly slow in departing the scene of the battle. But at last they loaded the dead man and the prisoner and set out down the tracks. Throughout the journey, they tried to get names out of Luke Weaver, but he had clamped his mouth stubbornly shut. He didn't say a single word to them all the way to Pocatello Junction, just stared at them balefully.

With the faded green of the western sky washed in brilliant orange and pink and red clouds, and a beautiful scarlet sun slipping behind the mountainous horizon, the train pulled up and gushed off its steam at the massive Pacific Hotel. There they unloaded passengers and whatever freight had reached its destination. It was then the conductor decided to make it known the train would be delayed indefinitely while they sorted out what had happened down the line.

McShannock tried to be patient. He talked to the conductor for a while, told them his side of what had happened. He sat on the long sofa in the lobby and leafed through a copy of *Harper's Weekly* and then *Godey's Ladies Book,* out of pure boredom.

Finally, he could take the wait no longer. He stomped angrily into the office of the superintendent and for the first time in many weeks lost his temper. He told them curtly what he knew about what was happening around Blackfoot. He tried to drive home his argument that they had to get to Blackfoot before the third kidnapper did. But the conductor and the other officials made it obvious he wasn't going to have his way. And to make matters worse, they wanted to detain him and Clyde Hall to help them fill out reports before they could even go.

Fortunately, there was no representative of the law in Pocatello Junction. When McShannock realized how the situation stood, he looked at the railroad superintendent and hooked his thumbs in his gun belt. "If you want anything out of me or Clyde Hall, you'll have to get it in Blackfoot. We're through here—and Weaver's going with us." He turned to R.M. Sievers, who had been watching with a slight smile on his lips as

McShannock tried to raise the roof. He stared at Sievers, then glanced down at his bandaged wound. At last, he looked back up and met his eyes. Sievers just nodded, as if giving his permission to leave him.

"Thanks, Sievers. It was an honor to have you along."

With that, McShannock grabbed Luke Weaver by the arm and shoved him out the door. Hall was right on their heels, and he waved a sheepish goodbye to R.M. Sievers as they went out. McShannock went down to the livery stable and rented the three best-looking Thoroughbred horses he could find, and he, Clyde Hall and Luke Weaver made their run for Blackfoot in the saddle.

The miles seemed endless. The dusk and then the darkness swept down upon them. It was more than twenty miles to Blackfoot, and they weren't easy miles, particularly for the bruised up deputy. McShannock's eyes were set grimly ahead, hoping the man who had run had done just that—run. He hoped he hadn't gone back to Hess to tell him what happened. If he had, they might be gone before McShannock and Hall ever reached town.

McShannock couldn't explain his feelings about the revelation of Wolfe's innocence. He had gained his knowledge of the entire convoluted affair from Kathryn Winchester, who was convinced beyond any doubt that Wolfe was the man in charge. It would have been next to impossible not to become sure of that fact himself, as indeed he had. It was hard coming to grips with the idea that Wolfe had nothing to do with it. He had seemed the perfect culprit. So perfect that McShannock was almost disappointed to see him vindicated. And even more baffling than the rancher's innocence was the thought of him as a victim. The entire scenario was a perfect argument for the adage that nothing was ever as it seemed.

Stewart Lords, the big man from New York, let the big chestnut horse carry him through the silent, dusty darkness of Blackfoot's East Main Street. In Pocatello, he had traded his strawberry roan for this horse, for the roan was nearly played out.

Lords was bleeding from a bullet hole inside his left shoulder. The fancy-looking gent in the planter's hat had hit him there. The same man had put the first hole in him, too—the one that was slowly bleeding him to death. It was in his abdomen, just under his ribcage.

There was blood all over Lords's shirt. It had dripped down and soaked his pants, too. The pounding five hour horse ride had made certain of that, and had shaken his guts up beyond repair. But he held his suit coat around him in such a way that it covered up most of the blood. He had tears in both knees of his trousers, and his skin was ripped there, but what did it matter now? The looks of a vagrant and the mild pain in his knees were nothing compared to the hate that burned in his guts. In the darkness, no one could have noticed what he looked like anyway. Besides, the town was dead and cold at that late hour. Other than the saloon crowds, there was no sound.

Stewart Lords might have been saved by a doctor. He had seen worse-looking wounds treated with success. But the most important thing was time. Immediacy of care. And Stewart Lords had no time. Had there been a doctor in town, he might have saved him, but Stewart Lords knew for a fact there was no doctor in this town. There once was, yes. Dr. Sims. But Dr. Sims was dead. Stewart Lords, in trying to kill Ira Winchester, had made sure of that.

There was only one thing that would make Stewart Lords happy now. There was only one man he wanted to see. That was the man whose hate ate him up inside and destroyed everything around him. That was the man who had sent him after Ira Winchester alongside Sid and Dub and Deckan and Yates. That was the man who had paid him to shoot through the doctor's window the minute Ira Winchester regained consciousness. The man who had made him burn a barn, kidnap two helpless boys and bedevil one of the handsomest women he had ever seen. The man who had made him and the others surround helpless herds of cattle and slaughter them like so many flies. Who had sent him after Ira Winchester a second time and got him peppered by Curtis Selders's shotgun—and this third time got him killed.

Yes, there was only one thing that would make Stewart Lords happy. There was only one man he wanted to see.

And he would take that man to hell.

Chapter Twenty-Two

In the darkness, Stewart Lords drew in his horse at the rear of the big house.

The street was deserted. Lords climbed down and walked around the side of the house, leaving drops of crimson on the weeds and in the dust. He stepped up onto the porch, clutching his coat tightly to his body with one hand. At the door, he paused and took one last look about the street, and then he pushed down on the door handle and stepped inside.

For several seconds it seemed very dim even though a lamp was lit there in the parlor. Lords was afraid it was his loss of blood affecting his sight. Terrifyingly, it seemed to be affecting everything—his perfect vision, his impeccable balance, his vast strength.

He was surprised there was a light at all, for at that late hour he had expected the house to be asleep. As his eyes became adjusted to the light, Lords started softly across the floor toward a more brightly lit room farther into the house. There he could see a fine rug on the floor and the end of a sofa that told him it was some type of sitting room. As he stepped through the doorway and into the room, he spied Ward Brassman sitting in an armchair, an open book in his lap. There was another book lying on its back on a shelf beside the door, and Stewart Lords reached over and swept it across the room to land with a crash against the far wall.

The book Brassman was reading flew to the floor as he started to his feet. "What the—" His perturbed words ceased the moment he recognized Stewart Lords, and he eased back into the chair.

Still angered by his weak condition, Stewart Lords brought his gun up level with Ward Brassman's face. A gush of blood ran down into his trousers as the coat he had used as a compress fell to the side.

"All right, banker man," Lords growled. "I want to make a withdrawal."

Ward Brassman's face had become surprisingly cool. The sides of his mouth even started to lift in a faint smile. "Why, Mr. Lords. It looks like you've had a brush with death."

"You son of a—" Lords's face formed into an ugly grimace. "A brush with death is right. Doing your dirty work! And now I've come for you. An eye for an eye and a tooth for a tooth."

Brassman leaned back in his chair. "I didn't realize you were a student of Holy Scripture, Mr. Lords. But considering your name I suppose it's only natural. Is there something I can get you? Someone I can call for you? A doctor might be in line, I would think." His eyes glittered mischievously as he spoke.

"Why you—" Lords cocked his gun and took a step closer. His mind flashed again to Doctor Sims, to the awful shock he felt when the news came that instead of killing Ira Winchester he had shot an innocent man. Brassman hadn't let him forget it, either.

"Are you going to shoot me, Mr. Lords?" Brassman asked suddenly, tilting slightly forward in his seat. "Right here in town where everyone can hear?"

Stewart Lords laughed. "What's the difference?" He lifted the side of his coat so Brassman could see his glistening, blood-soaked shirt. "Why should I care who hears? I only care what happens to you."

"Perhaps I should be flattered," said Brassman.

"You shouldn't."

Lords suddenly heard a door close in the other room. His eyes grew large and full of warning, and he cocked his pistol. "Who's that?" he whispered.

"Just my housekeeper. You must have disturbed her."

"You get her in here," Lords rasped.

Brassman called out the name "Mary," and presently a woman in her sixties, with her hair all disheveled, stepped through the doorway wearing a robe and stopped abruptly at sight of Lords's pistol. Her shocked eyes bounced back and forth between the two of them.

Lords cursed and glanced over at the transparent, spring blue curtains drawn over the blinds. "Rip down those curtains," he ordered. "Tie her up."

"Why?" asked Brassman, his voice soft.

"To protect 'er. I don't want 'er in the way when I kill you."

The woman staggered to one side, nearly losing her balance in her attempt to get far away from the big killer. Ward Brassman lifted his hands carefully to the sides. "It's all right, Mary. He won't hurt you."

Standing up from his chair, he turned to the curtains and carefully unfastened them. The binding that held them consisted of a gilded chain with a large ring on one end through which a brass fastener passed to hold the curtain in place. The fastener was seven inches long, shaped like an ice pick with the round end inset with pearls.

As Brassman unfastened the curtains, he managed to slide this fastener up inside his coat sleeve, cupping the chain in his hand. He let the second side loose also, then slipped the curtain rod and pulled the curtains off. Going to the woman, he tied her hands securely—perhaps more securely than he had to.

As he was putting the last touches on his knot, Stewart Lords started to cough, a very wet cough. Lords finished his coughing spell, and as if trying to show he still had a voice, he growled, "Your scheme didn't play out quite the way you had it planned, did it, banker man? Ira Winchester's still alive. And they got Weaver and Deckan. I'm sure one of 'em's spilled their guts by now. So I guess it wouldn't matter whether it was me that got you or one of them. You're a doomed man either way. And best of all, you ain't layin' one stinking hand on that Winchester woman. She's too good for the belly-slithering likes of you."

"But my scheme, as you call it, did work," said Brassman as he drew the knot in the curtain up horribly tight on the woman's wrists. "Irving Wolfe's life is ruined. Just like he ruined my father's."

Even as he was speaking, Ward Brassman whirled. The curtain chain flashed in his hand, and before Stewart Lords could even blink, the sharp end of the fastener, almost up to the pearls, was buried in his breastbone. At the same time, Brassman's strong left hand came up and went around the cylinder of Lords's pistol. His thumb settled between the frame and the hammer, and when Lords pulled the trigger it came down on Brassman's thumb and didn't fire. With a curl of his lip, he gave one more spiteful thrust against the curtain fastener.

Lords gasped for breath, letting go of his gun and clutching at his chest and the makeshift knife with both hands. He stared at Brassman with a pleading look in his eyes. He tried to speak, but no words would come. His mouth opened and closed like that of a fish on a dusty bank. Then he pitched over sideways, still struggling for a last breath that wouldn't come.

Brassman looked down at Lords and smiled grimly. "I guess I am laying a hand on the Winchester woman," he said.

Mary stared at the bloody scene, shocked beyond words. She looked from her employer to the dead man, and finally she stuttered, "Please let me loose, Mr. Brassman. I feel faint, and you've tied my hands very tight."

Brassman turned on her. "Not just this minute, Mary. There is some tidying up to be done."

The woman stared at him, mouth agape. "I— I'm not sure what you mean," she finally stammered. "You— Shouldn't you call Sheriff Hess?"

Brassman walked wordlessly to a big hutch on the far end of the room and opened a drawer, tossing a few small items into a carpetbag that was lying beside it. He opened another drawer and started to do the same, and then the futility of it settled over him.

With a sigh, the banker walked back over and sank into his big soft chair and stared at the desk. He steepled his fingers and settled his chin onto them, letting the quiet of the sitting room fold over him.

Had he accomplished what he wanted here? Had he made Irving Wolfe pay sufficiently for his sins? Had he assured that the rest of Wolfe's life would be nothing but an endless stretch of suffering for the evils he had perpetrated on a little boy?

Brassman sucked in a deep breath. He thought of his little "Tiger." Tiger . . . Lonely Judith Wolfe. She had loved him so. And that, after all, was what he had wanted. Yet it had hurt him to see her that way, the life crushed out of her. He had never loved her. He never could have loved her, not a woman who had shared a bed with Irving Wolfe. Yet he pitied her. He pitied her life, and he wished there had been some other way to make Wolfe lose her without making her die. There was one other way, but that would have meant taking her with him when he left. He couldn't do that. There was only one woman he wanted with him.

Kathryn Winchester . . .

According to Stewart Lords, Ira Winchester was still alive. If that was true, what did it mean? It meant little, really. Not to Ward Brassman. He had seen the way Kathryn watched him. He had felt the electricity when her hand touched his. And he had seen the breathless way she stepped away from him when he kissed her. Or rather, *she* kissed *him*. She couldn't deny that was how it happened.

Kathryn Winchester wanted him. He had no doubt of it. And he wanted her. He was through here in Blackfoot. His most high-reaching aim had been accomplished, after years of careful planning. Irving Wolfe had been destroyed. And now he must leave here. He must make his final voyage, this one to Spain, the home of his mother's parents. He had bank accounts waiting there for him. He had invested well over the years. He had people who expected him there, business people and his mother's relatives. There would be only one thing they didn't expect. He would come with a bride.

Walking over to Mary, Brassman took a pair of scissors out of his middle desk drawer and cut a long strip from the two ends of the curtain that held her hands. As she gaped at him, aghast, he stuffed a wad of that into her mouth and lashed a piece around her head to keep her quiet. "You might as well sit and keep quiet, Mary," he said at last. "They'll find you soon enough."

With that, he picked up his carpetbag and walked out into the main room. With deft fingers, he opened a wall safe behind a painting of Abraham Lincoln. Inside were bundles of bills and three sacks of coins, and he tossed them all into his bag until the safe was empty. Bank money, it was, set aside in case of just such an emergency. Irving Wolfe's mortgage payments, to be exact. None of it had ever been entered in the books; Brassman had done everything necessary to make it look like Irving Wolfe had never made any . . . He took one last look around the room and went out the front door.

He went down to the livery stable and rented his usual horse and buggy. Then he started up the street in the darkness and finally turned off . . . toward the Blackfoot Mountains.

Kathryn Winchester sighed as she awoke from some disturbing dream and looked out the open window at the moonlight on the mountains. A beautiful evening had turned into a beautiful night. The cool air filtered down out of the canyons and fluttered the kitchen curtains, mixing in with the stale air the day's heat had left inside the house. It huffed against the dampness on her brow, cooling it, making her close her eyes and draw deeply of the fragrances of the night.

Standing up, she tied a red robe over her flowing cotton nightgown. As she was walking out of the room, she absently reached over and picked up her broach, taking it with her. It wasn't something she thought of anymore. It was her security blanket, and it went everywhere she did. She went to the main room and lighted a coal oil lamp, then carried a chair out onto the porch, where she sat down. She was fondling the broach, thinking about the boys, and the dream she had just had about them being gone. In the dream she had wondered if they were gone forever.

But the boys had returned home just after dark, and after eating the hearty meal she had waiting for them they went right to bed. It had been a long day for them. They had gone hunting with their friends, Michael Perkins and Chris Dederscheck. The boys had been enjoying each other's company immensely since their reunion, perhaps realizing how close they had come to being forever separated by death. Kate was glad. She was happy with the world. Well, most of it.

She found herself thinking about Ira. Aching for him. What had become of him? He couldn't have died. Betsy and Nat would have told her. They weren't the kind to just ignore her and bury him without her. She had to admit she had only met them one time, but it wasn't in her to believe they would do something so cruel.

She hoped they had understood why she had to send Ira away. She had tried to explain it all in the letter she had had R.M. Sievers deliver to them. She had hoped to make them understand how desperate their situation here was, how every day was a waking nightmare while they waited for someone to come again, and perhaps the next time to succeed in their scheme of assassination.

Kate sighed, thinking of Vala and Cheyenne, lying asleep on the bed, in each other's arms. What a pair of lovely daughters she had brought into the world, with the help of Tom and Ira! Who could ask for anything more? Four children and a husband who loved her.

Kate had thought about that and knew it was true. Ira loved her. He loved all of them. He had made some grave mistake, perhaps several of them, but she had no doubt he loved his family. He would come back, and things would be straightened out. If he was still alive. Tomorrow she would send him a wire and tell him to come home.

While the emotion built inside her, from out of the deep reaches of her mind came a picture of a tall man dressed in a gaudy vest and a gambler's attire, a man wearing a white planter's hat, with the butt of a gun pushing out the right side of his coat.

Vest McShannock was gone. Of that, she had no doubt. He had no further reason to stay after she had thrown him out the way she had. But so many times since then she had fervently wished he were still there. Things had seemed so safe while he was around. She had felt protected . . . and desired. The last wasn't so important, she guessed. But to feel safe . . . that was a necessity of life.

Why had she been so harsh with him? Surprise, she guessed. She just hadn't known how to deal with the shock of knowing she had hired a man who had once made her a widow. But the fact remained in her head and in her heart that Vest McShannock had saved her life more than once, for Conn Scarbrough would one day have killed her . . .

He was a harshly handsome man, Conn Scarbrough. His eyes were sky blue, shaded by dark eyebrows that contrasted the cornsilk blond of his hair. He wore a thick mustache that in the beginning had expertly hidden the cruel set of his mouth. And he wore a false smile whenever he had courted Kate Winchester that she found irresistable.

Kate was only nineteen years old when she met Conn Scarbrough. Nineteen and running from her past and from the dark side of life. Conn was like a shining knight that just came stalking out of the darkness in all his magnificence. Dan Lauder had been a good looking boy, but Conn Scarbrough was, at the time, the most handsome and smooth man she had ever met.

They were married in a Protestant chapel, only because it was the first chapel they found. They were married, and within a day Kate feared she had made a grave mistake. She only had Dan Lauder to compare to, but Conn Scarbrough made love to her on their wedding night like some kind of animal trying only to satisfy his own lustful needs. There was no softness about him. She was like something he owned, just a possession without a heart or a mind or a spirit.

And from there it only grew worse by the day. Conn was seldom home. He was usually gone gambling—that was how he made his living. But it wasn't much of a living, for most of his profits went for liquor. And it was rumored about town that some of his money found its way mysteriously into the purses of the women who worked the brothels on the other side of the tracks. Kate had always forced herself not to listen to those rumors. It was easier to ignore them than to contemplate their truth.

The days when Conn stayed away were the good days. The days when he came home, he came home drunk. And after forcing himself on Kate, which was the first thing he always did, he generally passed out. But not always. Sometimes he took the time to beat his young wife if something in the house was out of place, or if his boots weren't polished just right, or if she hadn't prepared exactly what he wanted for supper. Once, because he couldn't find his mustache wax, he had beat Kate into near unconsciousness before finding it in the pocket of his suit coat. He had laughed about that later and tried to make her laugh, too. That time he was sober, and instead of beating her when she wouldn't respond he just left the house, angered by what he termed her lack of good humor.

And then came the night, that deep dark night in the middle of summer, with the crickets screeching in full force and the moon hanging white and stark like a scythe blade over the prairie. Kate was writing in her journal, writing numbly, waiting because she knew her husband would soon be home. Her eyes were tired, and there was an ache down low in her back, where Conn had kicked her in a fit of rage the night before.

The knock on the door surprised her. She answered it and stared at the little lawman with the narrow-brimmed hat and the too-small suit coat and the big boots pulled up over his pant legs. He took off his hat and swiped nervously at his mustache, and instead of saying a word just turned as the four men walked up behind him grunting with the exertion of carrying something. Like a mute, the lawman stepped out of the way, and his eyes flickered from Kate to the body hanging limp and bloody over the plank the other men carried.

"Ma'am," the lawman said. "The city of Abilene regrets to inform you . . . your husband has been killed . . ."

It was all so many years ago. The silent vigil she had kept that night, staring emotionless at the body laid out on her table. The thoughts of where she would go from there, and how she would live. The funeral which she felt obligated to attend. The attempts by people she knew to tell her what happened and who the man was who killed her husband. It was so long ago, yet some parts of it were so vivid. And now she knew that Vest McShannock had sat there in the same town with some of the same sick feelings inside his heart. And she knew that had she met McShannock instead of Conn Scarbrough when she was nineteen her whole life would have been different . . .

Feeling a sudden urge to cry, Kate stood up and stepped down off the porch, crushing the broach against the palm of her hand. She was walking toward the horse corral, feeling the pent-up emotions well inside her, when she heard the rattle of wheels coming down the lane from the main road. Hurriedly, she composed herself and forced away her thoughts. She willed herself to smile and change her mood. She pinned the broach to the belt of her robe, just to keep it out of the way.

Who in the world could be out here that time of night? Ira? No, of course not. She hadn't told him to come yet. Could it be . . . Vest McShannock? No. She had sent him away with harsh words. He was gone forever. He wouldn't come back . . . would he?

She gazed in the direction of the dust. What if it was McShannock? What would she say to him? What could she say to him? She owed him an apology. She owed him her life. He had done nothing to be malicious. He had killed Conn Scarbrough in self-defense, the same way she had killed Star. And McShannock's putting her second husband in the grave had only improved her life, anyway. She had had three days to think it over, and she had realized Vest McShannock had saved her life not just once, but twice. Once from a brutal husband, and once from Lang Gutterage. He had also saved the life of her son. Yet she had sent him away like a mangy cur.

The shape of a buggy finally materialized from the dark. Her heart fell with the sudden realization that McShannock would have ridden his horse. Then, in a few moments more, she recognized Ward Brassman as the dim light coming from the house touched his smooth cheeks! Her heart took an unexplainable little jump. She hated that feeling. She hated this power the banker held over her, making her heart start beating faster, and her body temperature rise every time she saw him, even though he meant nothing to her. He couldn't mean anything to her. She already had a life, and he wasn't part of it. And she loved Ira. She loved him with all of her heart. That, at least, was what she kept telling herself.

Brassman's buggy rolled into the yard, and Kate smiled with concern. She raised a hand and waved at him.

"Why hello, Mr. Brassman! What on earth brings you out here at this hour? It must be one o'clock! Were you worried about us?"

Brassman smiled broadly. "Yes, I was, Mrs. Winchester."

He hopped down from the buggy, and when he turned to face her his eyes had become serious.

Kathryn searched them. "Is something wrong?"

"Nothing," he said, a little too quickly. "Nothing at all. But I have something to tell you, Mrs. Winchester. And something to ask you. I'm going to Spain. My maternal family is from there, you know. Anyway, I've had an important opportunity come up over in Valencia that I couldn't turn down."

Kathryn's heart fell a little, and she frowned at herself. She forced a smile. She should have been glad the banker would be out of their lives. "Do you mean . . . permanently?"

Brassman nodded. "Yes, ma'am. Permanently. I have only to take a train to San Francisco, to board the nicest vessel I can find, and I shall be on my way. Goodbye to the Wild West!" He spoke with a broad smile that made her wonder if he wasn't forcing it. Maybe it was vanity, but she had felt something in Brassman's demeanor that was more than mere cordiality. Was he that ready to leave her forever? If so, that was good, she told herself. It was the best thing for both of them.

"That sounds wonderful for you," Kate said. "Maybe that's where you'll make your fortune. But . . . you said you had something to ask me?"

Brassman cleared his throat, looking momentarily uncomfortable. "Well, yes, ma'am. And I wouldn't do this to you so suddenly, but . . . well, this has been sudden for us all. I . . . I would like you to go with me."

Chapter Twenty-Three

Kathryn Winchester was stunned. She stared at Ward Brassman, her hand gone automatically to her throat. She started to smile, uncertain what to say, but Brassman wasn't smiling. He gazed at her with complete seriousness.

Suddenly, the banker took a step forward, and before Kate knew what he was doing his strong arms closed around her back. Taken completely by surprise, she didn't fight when he leaned into her and his lips touched hers. Her first reaction was to meet his embrace, but even as her hands touched his back she recoiled and tried to push away from him. He was too powerful. He held her to him and kissed her with more passion than she had felt in months. But it wasn't the same as the first time. She didn't feel helpless, like she had before. She knew what she wanted out of life, and who.

Moving her arms, Kate pushed against Brassman forcefully until he let go and backed away, searching her eyes.

"Kathryn, I—"

Kate drew the back of her hand quickly across her lips, blinking her eyes to clear her vision. "I have to apologize, Mr. Brassman. Please. I . . . I . . ." She searched for the right words. "I've led you to believe I felt . . . Mr. Brassman, I'm truly sorry."

She stopped and looked at him, helpless to say what she wanted. He had been a kind friend, so dear to her when she needed someone. And he was, indeed, very attractive. But he was not Ira.

"Kathryn, I'm not sure you know what's best for yourself."

Kate started to speak but stopped. She stared at the banker, trying to comprehend what he had said. "You're not sure . . . Mr. Brassman, please believe me. I know I kissed you, and I was wrong to do it. You know I belong to another man. I had my weak moments. And I'm sorry. I'm so sorry you misunderstood. I never meant for anything like this to happen. But I must tell you now—I'm happy with my life. I can't change now. I *won't* change."

Brassman listened to her, his eyes going back and forth between hers. "Kathryn, like I said, I'm not sure you know what's best for you. You know, if Ira were still alive he would have sent you word. I think he's passed away. There's nothing left for you here."

Kate felt anger born of frustration start to rise up in her chest. She would listen to advice from many different people on varied topics, but this time she knew what she was doing. And yes, she did know what was best for her. And she knew it was not Ward Brassman, no matter how brilliant and handsome and dashing and wealthy he might be. He was not her man and was never meant to be.

"I could never go with you, Mr. Brassman," she said flatly. "And I think I do know what's best for me. I'm a grown woman. I admit I'm not the strongest person in the world, but I know where my place is, and it isn't with you. I'm sorry if I led you to believe I felt something for you. I was frightened and confused. I didn't know what was happening to my world. But I do now. Mr. Brassman, I'm afraid I'll have to ask you to leave. Tomorrow, if you'd like, I'll drive into town and we can talk more. But for now I'd like to be alone. Please. It's late."

There was no foreseeing the anger that took hold of Ward Brassman. It came up from deep inside him, from some bottomless, carefully guarded well. Even Kathryn, watching him, saw no hint of it until it was too late.

As if out of nowhere, his right fist came up, and it struck Kate on the bottom of the chin. Her head snapped back, and she dropped in the yard like a sack of feathers. Without hesitation, Brassman bent and scooped the woman into his arms, carrying her to his buggy. He hefted her up onto the seat, then climbed on beside her and let off the brake, striking the horse with the ribbons to make it bolt into a canter across the yard and around the house, back to the lane.

Ward Brassman's face was set hard, his eyes blurred with anger. For a few minutes he let the horse carry him back toward Blackfoot. But suddenly the cold calculation returned to him, and he realized what would await him there. He couldn't go to town. He would have to find another way around to the coast. He would have to go carefully along, bribing people to silence as he went. No way could he take the normal routes. They would have his name and his description and his picture everywhere. He would be a wanted man.

He jerked the horse to a halt and just sat there in the road, staring toward Blackfoot. He was going to escape. That was the only way it could be. But . . . what if he didn't? What if they found him and brought him to trial? What if even the best lawyer he found couldn't defend him? Would he go to prison? Would he hang?

There was that chance.

And all because of Irving Wolfe. All because a careless and hateful philanderer who cared nothing about a certain lady as a person had courted her behind her husband's back. He had sparked her with the specific intention of making her fall in love with him. He had wooed her not for her love but for her money—or rather, her husband's money. The money of Walter Wellington. Ward Wellington's father. Ward Wellington, alias, Ward Brassman.

Tears of hate welled up in Ward Brassman's eyes as he thought of the day he had accidentally caught them in the old deserted farm house where he and the other boys used to go to play. His own mother, Armilla Wellington, unclothed and completely vulnerable before the shirtless, young, dark-haired entrepreneur his father had done business with in town. The man he learned was Irving Wolfe.

Brassman had almost forgotten Kathryn Winchester, unconscious beside him. He cringed at his memories and slammed his fist against his knee. Why should a boy of fourteen ever have to see what he had that day? What God of any mercy could have allowed that to happen?

He remembered watching in breathless horror as his mother and the stranger touched each other, fondling, groping, their mouths pressing against each other breathlessly. He remembered running away and crying for days, and never telling his father. It would have broken the old man's heart.

And then came the day he arrived home from school, a fourte-year-old boy with an already heavy heart, to find his mother hanging by her neck from the chandelier. His father was gone on business, not due home for seven days. He had been forced to cut her down by himself, to clean her up and remove the clothing she had soiled. To dress her in her prettiest dress, and then to summon the undertaker. He had been forced to handle her funeral and observe it stoically, her only relative present.

The next seven days he had spent staring out the window, waiting for Walter Wellington to come home. Why? Why had God done that to him? He was just a little boy. Just a little boy . . .

Ward Brassman suddenly let out a roar and struck the horse with his buggy whip. He steered it around so that it made a complete turn in the road and headed toward the Twin Wolfe. Irving Wolfe's life might have been destroyed, but he was still alive. Why should Armilla Wellington have had to die, and Judith Wolfe, and everyone else involved, and yet Irving Wolfe still lived? That was not justice. Justice was what he should have sought from the beginning. He should have sought only to see Irving Wolfe dead.

When Kate came to, she looked around groggily to find herself in the seat of a buggy that was rattling down the cottonwood-lined lane of the Twin Wolfe ranch. Weakly, she tried to sit up straighter, and a wave of dizziness swept over her, nearly spilling her over the side. A strong hand caught her and held her in place. She blinked her eyes to clear them and looked over to see Ward Brassman holding onto her arm but staring fixedly ahead at the big white and gray house of the Wolfes. The windows were all black.

Without thinking, Kate reached for the broach at her throat. Then she remembered she was in her nightdress and robe. The broach wasn't there.

Slowly, her mind became lucid, and she remembered pinning the broach to the sash of her robe. A memory of pricking her finger once on its pin fastener came swooping into her mind, and her hand froze. She very carefully looked at Brassman from the corner of her eye, and his gaze was fixed straight forward, toward the house.

With sudden resolve, Kate reached up with her other hand and undid the broach from her sash. She was amazed that Brassman still hadn't looked at her. He didn't seem aware of anything but the Twin Wolfe Ranch.

Kate's heart pounded mercilessly against her chest. She glanced down at the pin of the broach and took a deep breath. Then, placing the face of the cameo against the palm of her hand, she turned to look again at Brassman. Before he could even bring the buggy to a stop, Kate spoke his name. As he seemed to come out of his trance and turn to look at her, she drove forward with the broach in her fist, aiming the pin for the banker's eye.

The man rammed his eyes shut at the last second, his hands coming up as he instinctively shoved backward with his boot heels. The pin struck his face, but Kate didn't know where.

Brassman started to go over the side of the buggy, somehow managing to grab Kate's wrist as he did so. They seemed to float in midair for several seconds, Kate feeling the rush of cool night wind past her face. She landed on top of Brassman. She felt the air knocked out of her. She could hear the horse leave the road, the buggy's wheels banging against stones as the animal made its way back toward the road.

Brassman seemed as stunned as Kate. For several seconds they both lay there, their mouths open like two fish on a bank, struggling for air. Kate regained her wind first. Dropping her hands to Brassman's chest, she started to push off of him. She had come to her knees when his hand caught her wrist once more.

There was the look of a killer shining bright in Ward Brassman's open eye as he started up. His rising knocked Kate backward. She would have landed on her back, but he still had hold of her wrist.

Kate looked up at the bright blood that poured down the side of the banker's face. He had that eye shut, but she couldn't tell where the blood was coming from. Before she could try to pull away from him, his hand came out of nowhere, his knuckles striking her across the cheek. She started to go down, but he jerked her back to her feet.

Brassman swore at her, blinking against the blood in his eye. Both of his eyes were open now, and Kate could discern no damage to his sight. He took a swipe at the blood, smearing it all over his sleeve, then struck her again. This time he let go of her wrist. She went to her side, then rolled. Her instincts immediately drove her forward, struggling to escape his grasp.

She wanted to scream, but she didn't. She didn't know why. It seemed no sound would form in her throat. It was like some nightmare, where the monster from the dark was nearly upon her and yet she could make no noise and could hardly even move to escape.

She felt Brassman catch her by the nape of the neck, then shove her face into the dirt at the same time he drove a knee into the small of her back, knocking the breath from her just as the scream was finally forming in her throat. He slammed her face against the ground two times, then took his knee off her back. Grabbing her arm, he threw her harshly over onto her back and stood up. His hand went to his gun, and it came out of his holster with a whisking sound. The dark barrel came to bear on her chest. She waited, sucking for wind—waited for the bullet that would pierce her heart.

But the bullet never came.

Heaving for air, Brassman reached down and grabbed Kate by the dress, muscling her, with her help, to her feet. He wiped at the blood seeping slowly down the side of his face from the hole she could now see beside his eye.

"You could have blinded me," he snapped.

He shoved his pistol back in its holster and caught her arms. He stared into her eyes. His own were red-rimmed and sore-looking.

"Why would you do that to me? I love you," he said brusquely.

For a moment, all she could do was stare at him. Finally, she found her voice. "Love me? Mr. Brassman, you're insane!" she said, trying to pull away.

The observation brought a sharp rap across her cheek from the back of his hand, and he turned and dragged her toward the house. She stumbled up the porch with him, and at the door he didn't even pause to knock. He just gave the handle a hard kick, and the big door flew inward. With a growl, he flung her inside and drew his gun again.

As Kate caught herself against a console table to keep from falling, she glimpsed Irving Wolfe carrying a lighted lantern. He stepped across the room in a long blue nightshirt, with shock and confusion all over his face. Before he had time to realize what was happening, Ward Brassman fired. The explosion was shattering to the eardrums in that close space, and Kate cringed. She opened her eyes, expecting to see Wolfe dead on the floor.

Instead, the rancher was standing with his hands raised in the air, his large eyes wider than normal. A little trickle of plaster still filtered down out of the ceiling where Brassman's bullet had gone. "What the devil are you doing, Brassman!? Why is Mrs. Winchester—" He paused suddenly and looked from one to the other of them. "Why, the two of you are—"

"Are what?" Brassman asked. "Together? Yes, she's with me for the moment, but not the way you think. Not the way I was with Judith."

"Jud—" Wolfe stopped again, staring. His hand that held the lantern slowly came down, and his face went pale. "Judith . . . you . . . It was you?" Wolfe seemed ready to fall over. He had to catch himself by putting his free hand up against a column of black walnut.

"Yes, it was me," said Brassman. He said it with a measure of pride in his voice, a gleam in his eyes. "I had her probably more than you did. A few dozen times, perhaps. You fool. Didn't you think it odd she suddenly made it a point to go for all those afternoon buggy rides?"

"I— I don't understand," said Wolfe. "Then why is Mrs. W— Why are you here?" He looked Kate's face over as if he had just noticed the battered look about her. "What did he do to you?"

"You don't talk to the woman!" Brassman barked. "I'm the one you talk to. Where's Manfred?"

"Harvey? He's— He went to town on errands, and I guess he decided to spend the night there," Wolfe replied. But it was obvious by his eyes and by his long pause that he was lying.

"Where is he?" Brassman said again, through gritted teeth. "Call him in now or I'll kill you both."

Wolfe started toward the door and stumbled over a throw rug in his haste to obey. At the door, he hollered out into the yard. He had to yell five times, each time progressively louder, but after a minute the voice of Harvey Manfred came back. Wolfe called him in, and in a while the hired hand came sauntering with sleep-filled eyes through the door.

"What's happened, Mister—" Manfred stopped dead in his tracks, his eyes glued to Brassman's gun barrel.

"Step over here, Mr. Manfred." Manfred did as ordered. "Now tie these two up, and tie them up tight. If they work loose, you'll be the first one I kill."

Kate waited, and after tying Wolfe the skinny ranch hand came up behind her. By the way he drew the knots up, she knew he had done his best to obey Brassman. Her hands started instantly to go numb.

"Now come over here," Brassman ordered Manfred.

When the skinny ranch hand obeyed, Brassman told him to turn around. Then, with no mercy, he smashed him alongside the head with the barrel of his pistol, sending him to his hands and knees, cringing. For good measure, he kicked him in the stomach. Manfred rolled over and, with a long, low groan, lay still.

"What is the meaning of all this?" yelled Wolfe suddenly. "I don't understand any of it."

"Then you're a fool," Brassman said bitterly. "You've told me I look familiar to you. Well, perhaps I can help you recall. What does the name Armilla Wellington mean to you—Wolfe?"

Irving Wolfe stared at Brassman, his face blank. Then, as if a sheet had been lifted from before his eyes, his mouth dropped open and a sick look washed over his face. "Armilla . . . You . . . Oh my— You're the boy. You're her son!"

"They tell me I'm the spitting image of my father." Irving Wolfe just stared, so Brassman went on. "Don't you want to know what happened to my father, Wolfe? He died. He died two years after you left St. Louis. He willed himself into the grave when my mother died."

"Your mother . . . How did she die?" Wolfe asked quietly.

Brassman gave him a queer look. "You expect me to believe you don't know?" When Wolfe just shook his head, Brassman's eyes went colder than ever. "She hanged herself from the chandelier in the parlor. She hanged herself for me to come home and find her."

Wolfe swallowed hard and grimaced, closing his eyes. "I didn't mean for that to happen. I really didn't intend . . ."

Brassman turned to Kate. He spoke, but Kate didn't have the feeling he was talking to her. He was talking to place the facts of Wolfe's guilt out there before him at last.

"You're curious, I'm sure. Let me tell you, then, so everyone can know. He courted my mother while my father was away. He was young, and my father was an old man. He wooed her with his words of love and with promises of adventure. He talked her into withdrawing fifteen thousand dollars in savings out of the bank so they could run away together. You see, my father was a wealthy man. He owned a steel mill in St. Louis and a textile mill in Houston. But he wasn't wealthy enough to satisfy his young wife.

"Neither was Wolfe, but to her he must have seemed to be a dashing kind of man. She drew out the money, and then he took it and ran. He ran away with Judith, incidentally. She was already his wife."

Everyone in the room stared at Brassman as he spoke. Everyone but Wolfe. He couldn't raise his eyes from the floor. "I didn't mean her any harm," he said finally. "Your father had so much money. I didn't think . . . I thought she would forget me."

"She did," said Brassman, his face filled with bitterness. "Dead people have no memories."

"I'm sorry, Brassman."

Those words were a trigger. Brassman took four long strides across the floor and smashed Wolfe brutally across the cheek with his gun barrel, knocking him down.

He wiped at the blood by his eye and on his cheek, and this time no blood came back to replace it. "There's a long, long story I'd like you to hear before I kill you, Wolfe," said Brassman. "It's a story about your ranch. About your cattle. About your hired hands."

Brassman reached down and grabbed Wolfe by the collar with one hand. "Get up!" He jerked on the collar, and Wolfe struggled up. Brassman delivered a brutal kick to his kneecap as he was coming erect, and Wolfe strangled on a yelp of pain.

"You weren't losing your ranch," Brassman said. "At least you wouldn't have been had you chosen a different bank." He laughed then, but there was no humor in it. "Your hired hands worked for me, Wolfe. All along, you thought they were taking your orders, but they weren't. They were taking mine. Deckan, Yates—all of them. They killed your cattle. Shot them. Poisoned them. They made sure you had nothing to sell at market to pay off your debts.

"The only one I didn't hire was Manfred, there. He was too much of a fool to waste my time on." Brassman laughed. "Anyone who would be loyal to you is a fool. And another thing. You were right about your payments. You knew it but couldn't prove it. I knew it, too. But Case Deckan was a handy man with a safe. He kept me supplied monthly with all of your payment receipts. I used them to start my fires."

Irving Wolfe stared at Brassman, and for half a minute there was silence in the room. Finally, Wolfe quietly cleared his voice. "So after all those years you found me here? You came here and started this bank just . . . just for me?"

"Is that so strange?" Brassman asked, one of his old, suave smiles coming to his lips. "I gained my hate from my Spanish heritage and my cold, calculating patience from my English side. I wanted it to happen to you slowly, and it did."

"So now that you've destroyed me . . . What?"

Ward Brassman laughed. "You aren't destroyed, Wolfe. I know you too well. I was foolish to think this would set you back forever. I thought Judith's death would send you to the depths of misery, but . . . it couldn't. It couldn't because you don't have a heart. You'll just keep going, and you'll get the bank to embrace you, now that I've been found out. You'll get more backing, buy more cattle, and you'll be right back on top of the world. You didn't care about Judith anyway. I was a fool to think I could destroy you the way you destroyed Walter Wellington. He had a heart."

Kate and Irving Wolfe stared, afraid if they moved or even breathed they were going to find out what Brassman's next move would be. Kate, at least, didn't want to know.

Brassman suddenly shook his head as he reached over to pick up a coal oil lamp off the console table. He clicked his tongue and looked up at Kate Winchester. "I would have liked to take you to Spain with me, Kathryn. There was nothing I would have liked better. We were meant for each other. But I can't put up with the trouble of fighting you all the way."

Kate just stared at the banker, knowing he was a lunatic and must have been since long before she had met him. What does one say to a madman?

"Oh, don't worry," he told her. "You'll die faster than the others. I couldn't stand to see you suffer, even if you are foolish. I wouldn't hurt you at all, but now that you know what's happened . . . Well, it's obvious I can't leave you here alive. You understand that, of course."

Still, Kate just watched him. Her mind was churning with a dozen thoughts at once, yet she was too numb to speak.

"As for you others, I hope heat doesn't affect you adversely." He laughed, looking down at the lamp, and at Manfred, who was stirring on the floor. Picking up the chimney, he threw it across the room. It shattered against the bookshelf and showered the floor with glass.

He turned back to Wolfe. "Don't worry. That's one problem you won't have to clean up. I'm going to burn this house down around your ears."

With that, he opened the lamp and started pouring a trail of coal oil across the floor, splashing a generous amount over the books in the shelf. With a grim smile, he splashed some down the front of Irving Wolfe's nightshirt, then poured the last of it over Harvey Manfred's legs. When he had done that, he threw the lamp down and shattered it, then walked over to stand six feet away in front of Kate.

There was a look of genuine apology in the banker's eyes as he glanced down at his pistol, then back up at Kate. "Kathryn, if I thought there was any other way, I hope you know I would never have things end like this. But I know you too well. You've made up your mind. I just can't leave you to tell them about me. You do understand, don't you?"

A strange streak of iron welled up inside Kate Winchester as she stared into Brassman's eyes. She knew she was about to die, and somehow she knew she couldn't do a thing about it. "Ira will find you, Mr. Brassman. And if he doesn't, my boys or Vest McShannock will. You'll never see Spain."

Brassman gave a sad little smile and raised the pistol.

Chapter Twenty-Four

A mile and a half after crossing the bridge, still at a hard trot, McShannock, Hall and Weaver slowed down their heavy-blowing horses and rode quietly into the outskirts of Blackfoot. After the ride of more than twenty miles, sweat streamed down their horses' sides. It made dark trails onto their bellies, where it matted the hair in clumps. The animals blew, and their muscles quivered, and the loose dust of the road shifted toward the black sky in little clouds with each fall of a hoof. Ahead, lights gleamed on the streets from the El Dorado and the Gem and Hard Luck Saloons, but most of the town was dark.

McShannock's horse shook violently, rattling the saddle beneath him and sending a jarring pain through his raw backside. He was a man of the saddle. He had always preferred riding horseback to traveling on a coach or train. But he didn't remember ever having cause to ride so far so fast, and his rump would pay for it in the days to come.

Looking over at Hall, the big Indian appeared as drawn and weary as the long-legged bay under him. As for Weaver, his face was white, his jaws clamped. His eyes were fixed straight ahead.

They pulled up at the big brick courthouse. A light was glowing dimly inside. McShannock loosened his Colt in its holster before climbing down. They were hoping the sheriff would be working the nightshift again tonight, as he had all week. If so, he would be sleeping at the courthouse.

Hall nearly dropped from his own horse and glanced over to see if McShannock had noticed. "That's what happens to us progressive Injuns," he said, half mocking himself. "We can't take the ridin' like we used to."

McShannock didn't reply. He just looked up at Weaver. "You getting down, or do I have to de-saddle you?"

His face settling, Weaver threw a leg over the saddle. His knees sagged a little as his feet hit the ground, and McShannock threw a shoulder into his back and shoved him up against his horse to keep him from falling.

"Looks like you need to get out and ride more," McShannock said dryly. "Let's go see your boss."

They walked up the steps of the courthouse, and Clyde opened the door, throwing the dim yellow light out onto the steps. The Indian walked in first. McShannock shoved the deputy in before him. He considered drawing his pistol but thought better of it at the last moment. He had no doubt he could beat Sheriff Arch Hess to the gun if the need arose.

Stepping around Weaver, McShannock was in time to catch sight of Hess sitting up on a cot, reaching for his pistol that lay on the floor beside him. The sheriff, caught completely by surprise, just looked at them for a moment when he realized who it was. His eyes darted back and forth between them. Clyde turned up the lamp, throwing a stronger light across the room.

"What are you doing out, Luke?" Hess asked finally.

McShannock eyed the lawman carefully, trying to gauge him. When Weaver didn't reply, Hess turned to McShannock. His eyes were made near-comical by being swelled half shut with sleep. McShannock stepped forward, and the look on his face stopped any words the sheriff had in mind.

"Is there anything you want to come clean about, Hess?" McShannock asked quietly. The side of his coat was drawn back to rest behind the butt of his gun.

Hess's eyes dropped to the gun butt, and when they came back up he was very still. "It's pretty obvious there's something on your mind, McShannock. What can I do for you?" His eyes flickered to Luke Weaver as he spoke, and to the empty holster on his deputy's hip.

"We brought Ira Winchester back safely." Vest McShannock's voice was quiet, and he watched Hess's face for a reaction.

"Okay," said Hess. "I suppose that was your choice."

McShannock suddenly exploded, stepping toward Hess with his hand dangerously near his gun. "What's your part in all this? Tell me before I wrap my gun barrel around your head!"

Sheriff Hess was a big man with a face that could appear kindly. And as McShannock had seen in the past it did so in most situations. But this time his eyes went flat and deadly.

"I don't have a clue what you're talking about, mister. I'll tell you that much. But if you plan to wrap your gun barrel around my head you may have a hard time getting it done."

"He wasn't in on it."

The voice of Luke Weaver surprised McShannock; he had remained silent for so long. McShannock paused and looked over at him, then glanced at Clyde Hall, who watched with a bland expression.

"I wasn't in on what?" asked Hess. "What's going on here?"

One moment McShannock was ready to pull his gun, ready to gamble that he could reach the sheriff and knock him out with a blow to the head before the heavier man could reach his gun on the floor. The next moment a great flood of discouragement washed over him, and his shoulders sagged. His hand dropped away from his gun. He was watching Sheriff Hess, and he made his living reading other men's minds. This time it didn't seem like much of a gamble. Hess was telling the truth.

Taking a deep, lung-filling breath, McShannock studied Hess's eyes and watched the big lawman relax, too. "You really don't have any idea what's been happening here, do you?"

Irritated, Hess shook his head. "I wish you'd tell me."

And so McShannock did. The look of sickness that washed over Hess's face as the truth about his deputy unfolded clenched in McShannock's mind the innocence of the big lawman.

When the story was finished, Hess sat on his desk watching Weaver quietly as if trying to make himself believe it all. He didn't say a word. He just stood and walked over to the deputy with heavy steps and started to take his belongings from him. His empty gun belt he laid on the desk, along with his coin pouch. He pulled out his tobacco sack and jackknife and watch and a rabbit's foot, laying them all beside the gun belt. Then he dumped the coin pouch out and counted each coin carefully, writing the number down in a notebook.

Last, he went again to the gun belt. Gun belts were often constructed to double as money belts, and Hess picked up Weaver's with the obvious prior knowledge that his was such a belt. He opened the space and pulled out a handful of bills, counting them out one by one on the desk for all to see.

As the fourth, fifth and sixth bills were laid out, McShannock, who had been watching, jumped forward. He picked the last one up, staring at it in disbelief for a moment.

Sheriff Hess watched him. "What?" he asked at last.

"This bill!" McShannock said. "Cheyenne Winchester did this drawing on it."

"Hmmm. So?"

"So Mrs. Winchester took them to town that afternoon to pay on her

237

loan. She was too late to get to the bank, so she paid them directly to Ward Brassman, and he said he'd deposit the money the next day."

Hess's eyes turned to his ex-deputy. "Where'd you get this money?" he asked sharply.

Weaver's eyes flickered away, but they returned quickly to Hess. He shrugged. "I guess I must have pulled it out of the bank."

The sheriff's eyes narrowed. "There hasn't been a payday. And I'm good and certain you didn't have a hundred dollars in the bank. He turned to McShannock. "It looks like we need to go down the street and wake up Ward Brassman."

The Utah and Northern was finally chugging up across from the courthouse when Sheriff Hess, Vest McShannock and Clyde Hall found Mary tied up in Brassman's house and Stewart Lords dead on the floor. After they untied her, the woman told them breathlessly what had happened and what Brassman had said about Kate Winchester. She told them which livery stable Brassman patronized when he intended on taking a ride, and the three of them went to the stable at a run. Once they had awakened the hostler, the answer to their queries was predictable. Ward Brassman had rented his usual horse and buggy and headed north on the highway. He was carrying a carpetbag.

They were leading their horses out of the stable when the shape of a man appeared in the door, lit by the dim lanterns of the barn and breathing heavily like he had just made a hard run. It was Ira Winchester.

Hess looked at him, his face drawn. "Hello, Ira."

"Sheriff," Ira said grimly, sucking wind. "I guess—we have some—talking to do."

"We do," said Hess. "But I'm afraid we have to take a ride first."

"A ride?" Ira huffed out. "Where?"

Hess's eyes flickered over to McShannock and back. He cleared his throat. "Ira, I have a feeling you're involved in something illegal." Ira started to speak, and Hess stopped him by raising his hands. "There'll be time for it later. For now, there's a killer on the loose. I have a feeling you know all about him."

Ira's eyes jumped from one to the other of them. "I'm afraid I don't . . ." Alarm arose suddenly in Ira's face as he looked from the sheriff to the others. "What's wrong?"

"Ward Brassman just killed a man and headed out of town with a sack full of money. McShannock thinks he's after Kathryn."

Ira's face was white. "Ward Brassman! He's the one?!"

Now it was Hess's turn to be baffled. "You mean you didn't—"

"Later, Arch," said Ira quickly. "I don't think he's after Kate. It's Irving Wolfe he wants to destroy."

Hess swore. "I'm going to quit my job if I live through all this. Wolfe? Why?"

"I'll tell you on the way."

"On the way?" said Hess. "You can't go in your shape."

"It's been a month, Arch," countered Ira. "And I have a score to settle. I'm going."

They rode at a long trot toward the Winchester ranch, and on the way Ira spilled his soul. After he had explained everything he knew about the plans of the anonymous ringleader, revealed now as Ward Brassman, to destroy Irving Wolfe's life, McShannock told Ira what Mary had heard Brassman say about getting his hands on Kate. Ira's face went grim.

With one mile yet to go, they kicked their horses up to a gallop, and there were no more words. With the noise and jolt of the pounding horses, they couldn't have carried on a conversation anyway. They occupied their own thoughts as they rode along through the moonlit dark. They knew they couldn't be more than twenty minutes behind Brassman; they had to stop him before he reached the ranch!

As for Ira Winchester, he didn't want to talk. After what McShannock had told him, he knew Kate might be in grave danger. He hadn't been there for his wife for so long, but he had to be there now. If she no longer loved him, he could understand that. But he would not let her die.

When the posse arrived at the Winchester ranch, the only ones to greet them were four scared youngsters whose mother had disappeared. Ira held each of them and told them how sorry he was, but he had no time to tell them more. In less than a minute, he and the others were pounding up the road as fast as they could ride toward the Twin Wolfe Ranch. Ira ached deep inside. Somehow he knew it would be too late. How could he raise a family alone? That is, if the law allowed him to try . . .

Ward Brassman's face paled a little as he looked over his sights at Kathryn Winchester. His lips quivered as his thumb touched the cross-hatched tip of the hammer. Kate watched him with her heart in her throat. But she couldn't feel it beating. It seemed to have stopped.

"You would really kill me?"

Kate's own voice startled her in the deathly silent room. Brassman's eyes changed, ever so slightly, and his gun started to lower. After several seconds, the weapon came back up. "I have to."

"Then at least tell me one thing. Why Ira? Why did you try to have him killed?"

Brassman sighed and lowered his pistol. "You married a fool, Kathryn. A fool. He was in the middle of it. He needed money, and I had money. We offered him money for helping us poison and shoot the cattle and keep his mouth shut. He wanted Wolfe gone as badly as anyone. But he claimed he had a conscience. A conscience!" he said, shaking his head. "Over . . . that." With a sneer, he took in Irving Wolfe's frightened face. "But it wasn't really a conscience. All he wanted was money. He wanted to be paid to keep him from going to the sheriff about my plan. It wasn't any conscience. It was pure greed."

"They tell me he's still alive, your husband," Brassman said. "It's sad that he should live now and you should die."

"So you sent your men after Ira so you wouldn't have to pay him anymore," Kate said quietly.

"Not quite. I guess he did gain a conscious there at the end. He told my men he was going to the sheriff. After that . . . Well, there wasn't any other way."

From the corner of her eye, Kate saw a slight form move across the room. Without looking directly at it, she recognized the willowy shape of Arthur Wolfe. He was moving toward Brassman. His stocking feet made no sound upon the hardwood floor.

"Have you thought about Vala and Cheyenne and the other children?" Kathryn asked suddenly. "What will happen to them?" She was only stalling for time.

Brassman looked at her oddly. "That isn't my problem."

Irving Wolfe was also watching the shape behind Brassman, and he stared at the banker and at the gun he held on Kate. That poor woman had done nothing. Wolfe had misunderstood many things, and so had she, but now that Wolfe knew the truth he held no ire for Mrs. Winchester. It wasn't right for her to die when she was innocent of everything.

But worse than that, he couldn't stand to see his boy die. That boy was his life. That boy had hurt no one. But now he held a butcher knife, and his intentions were plain. He must have heard Brassman talking about his mother. And the boy had vowed to Wolfe he would kill the man who had made her take her life. Now, here the man was, standing with his back to him. But the boy could never do it. He didn't have the nerve. Never had. He couldn't kill another human being in cold blood. He probably couldn't do it even in self-defense. He was that kind of boy. Yet if he kept coming on Brassman was sure to hear him. He was sure to turn on him, to see that knife. And Brassman would kill the boy. He would kill him because he was a part of Irving Wolfe, the man the banker obviously hated more than anyone else in the world. And he would kill him because Ward Brassman was a man with no heart.

"Why would you want to shoot Mrs. Winchester?" Wolfe asked suddenly. "She hasn't hurt anyone."

Kate glanced at Wolfe with a surprised look on her face.

Wolfe fixed his eyes on Brassman's face, not wanting to draw attention to his son. Arthur drew closer and closer to the banker.

"It isn't as if I have a choice, Wolfe," said Brassman. "Mrs. Winchester is a witness now."

Arthur Wolfe wasn't more than seven feet away from Brassman now, his socks sliding quietly along the floor. The boy's eyes, blurred by tears, were intent on the back of his intended victim.

"What if I pay you to let us go?" Wolfe asked, his face flushed.

Arthur closed. Five feet to go. Four. He was nearly close enough. But Irving Wolfe knew the boy could never act. His nerve would give out. Brassman would detect him. He would turn and kill him.

Brassman laughed, lowering the gun momentarily from Kate. "You're a fool, Wolfe. Out of everyone you know, I'm the one who knows you don't own a thing anymore."

Wolfe couldn't answer. He only stared at the bore of the Colt that Brassman raised again to point at Kate Winchester's chest. Irving Wolfe had forgotten about everything, even his own life. He had one chance to do something good, to make his name live on. That one chance was to save his boy. He couldn't let Arthur get closer. The only chance the boy had was to quietly go away, to leave the house and run.

Praying Brassman was too intent on Kate Winchester to notice anyone else, Irving Wolfe looked at his boy and mouthed the words, *No! Run!*

Brassman saw the movement of Wolfe's lips. His eyes flickered toward him. He saw that Wolfe wasn't even looking at him, but behind him. He started to turn.

Arthur Wolfe stared at Ward Brassman's back. Tears rolled down his cheeks. He was shaking like a reed in high winds. His hand had paused at his side. It was as if someone held onto his arm and wouldn't let it go forward.

Brassman turned fully around. With shocked eyes he saw the little boy standing there. Suddenly, he felt a burn deep in his stomach. His pistol fired, striking the far wall. He looked down, and there was a knife handle protruding beneath his ribs. And then he looked again, and there was the boy, shaking like a whipped dog in front of him. A wisp of a boy with big eyes and pale skin and a large pink mouth opened in terror. He cocked the pistol and leveled it at this boy. It was Irving Wolfe's boy. He was the image of his father.

Arthur Wolfe stared at Ward Brassman with a look of horror on his face. He looked just like a boy who knew he was about to die. A boy who had been a coward all his life. The room was quiet but for the tick of the clock. Arthur Wolfe couldn't speak. He couldn't run. He was too scared to even plead for his life.

With his left hand, Ward Brassman clutched the handle of the knife. A confused look slowly came over his features while his gun sights still wavered on Arthur Wolfe's eyes. He shook his head in disbelief. He tried to breathe. The burning consumed his insides. He blinked his eyes and raised his eyebrows and cocked his head a little sadly.

Then he pulled the trigger.

Chapter Twenty-Five

The rush of air from the explosion made Arthur Wolfe's hair part, and he cringed and fell to the floor, crying. He held his hands over his ears, squeezing his eyes shut.

"He's only a boy," Brassman said, looking down at the shuddering heap, his enemy's son. The words were so quiet they were barely heard over the grandfather clock. "Only a boy . . ."

And with those words Ward Brassman dropped his smoking gun and fell forward onto the hilt of the knife.

They were sitting on the porch only five minutes later, backlit by a lantern that hung from its hook above them, when the little posse galloped into the yard. Kate studied her hands, thinking it had been a long time since they had been washed. It hadn't, of course. She just had to keep from thinking of other things, like how narrowly she had missed death. She closed her eyes and gingerly touched the tender spots on her face. It seemed like her entire face was one tender spot.

Irving Wolfe was holding onto his boy, and the boy was crying. There were tears on Wolfe's cheeks, but his jaws were clenched in apparent determination not to let anyone hear him cry out loud.

Harvey Manfred just sat there by himself, his cheeks drained and blood matted in the hair on one side of his head. He puffed furiously at a cigarette, trying to draw its comfort down into his toes. Kate kept wondering when a spark from the cigarette would drop down onto the coal oil on his legs and set his pants on fire, but Manfred didn't seem to think about that.

Ira came out of his saddle before his horse had even stopped. He staggered to a halt there in the dark, dusty yard, his horse trotting away to the side of the house. Kate slowly, almost deliriously, raised her eyes to see the four men standing there in the yard looking at her.

Her eyes came to focus on Ira.

Later, she tried to understand the feeling of utter love and joy that washed through her when she saw those eyes, watching her uncertainly. She had found herself wondering at times if there was any love left between them. She had found her thoughts wandering to Vest McShannock, and—she thought of it now with horror—to Ward Brassman. But it only took one look at Ira Winchester to know none of her love had ever died. It had just been tested.

She stood up and walked to him with slow, measured steps, steps that were belied by the way she threw herself against him and kissed him passionately the moment he was within her reach. With tears pouring down her face, she heard him say he loved her.

Vest McShannock watched the two of them, and a sad smile drew back the sides of his mustache. He looked down and saw something shining dully in the dirt, and he leaned over to pick it up. It hadn't been his imagination. It was Kathryn's broach.

He nodded pensively and looked up at Kate and Ira, then over at Wolfe. Sheriff Hess had just walked up to the rancher and his boy. He heard Wolfe mumble something, and the sheriff looked toward the front door of the house. He looked back and saw McShannock and Clyde Hall watching him and motioned them over with his head.

The three of them went up onto the porch. McShannock was struck by the overpowering smell of coal oil as they came to the door and passed inside, seeing a man lying there. By his suit and fallen hat, McShannock knew it was Brassman.

The sheriff knelt and turned the body over, looking at the banker's sightless eyes. His falling weight had driven the knife as far into him as it could go, even burying part of the wooden grip in his abdomen.

Hess looked at him, then over at McShannock, who knelt beside him holding the banker's Colt. He thumbed open the loading gate, half-cocked it and found three cartridges freshly fired. Without comment, he let the hammer down and shut the loading gate, then handed the weapon butt first to Hess, who slid it down behind his gun belt.

They walked back out on the porch, out of the nauseating stench of the coal oil. Kate Winchester was still clutched in Ira's arms, and frail Arthur Wolfe was pressed to his father's chest. Harvey Manfred sucked voraciously on the stub of his cigarette and looked at them through the eyes of a man who might have come back from the dead.

When the three of them stepped off the porch, Kate Winchester turned and met the sheriff's eyes. She looked at Ira and smiled and said a quick prayer for him. She tried not to meet Vest McShannock's glance yet. She didn't know what to say to him.

Arch Hess looked at Kate, his expression soft. "Kate— Can I call you Kate?"

"Please do," she said.

"I think we can say you're safe now. There's a lot of sorting out to do, but let's take a few days first and try to get a hold of our lives." The sheriff gave Ira a serious glance. "I think we could all use it." He reached out and patted Kate's arm, and she took a step forward and hugged him.

Stepping away, she said, "I'm sorry I ever doubted you. I hope you can forgive me."

Hess just shook his head. "I forgave you long since."

Irving Wolfe and his boy had walked over, and Wolfe cleared his throat and looked at Kate. "I want you to know something, ma'am. I'm pleased to have you for a neighbor."

Kathryn smiled, and her eyes welled up with tears. "The feeling is mutual, Mr. Wolfe."

The rancher looked quickly down and wiped a hand across his mouth, then looked back up. "If there's anything I can do for you folks, just let me know."

Kate shook her head. "Oh, no. No, Mr. Wolfe. You are very kind, but . . ." She turned and looked at the sheriff and put her hand out to rest on Arthur's shoulder. "Sheriff, I want you to know that this is the young man who saved my life."

Arthur blushed and looked up at his father with his eyes full of tears. Kate squeezed his shoulder, and he stepped into her arms and hugged her almost fiercely, then turned and walked stiffly away, hiding his eyes. His shoulders were straighter than she had ever seen them.

Still not looking at McShannock, Kate turned to Clyde Hall and gave him a hug without saying a word. He patted her back. "You have your life back, my friend," he said.

Kate stood away from him, taking his big hands in hers and smiling through her tears. She raised a forearm to dry her eyes, and as she dried them they turned automatically to Vest McShannock, who stood there holding his hat.

"You didn't leave."

He tried to smile. "I came to Blackfoot to keep you safe. It wasn't time to leave."

Kate turned suddenly back toward Ira and held out her hand to him. He took it and squeezed, and she said, "Ira, I would like you to meet Vest McShannock."

Ira nodded and met McShannock's eyes. "I know him, Kate. He saved my life."

Kate's eyes shot quickly to McShannock, and she cocked her head questioningly. But she didn't ask. There were would be years of time to find out all about that and everything else.

"Mr. McShannock and I would like to talk for a minute," Kate said flatly. Looking over at McShannock she walked off toward the barn. She paused within sight of the others, but out of earshot, and turned to see McShannock stopping hesitantly beside her. His eyes darted back toward Ira, then rested uncomfortably on her.

"You lost something," he said. When she looked down at his hand that came up between them, she was surprised to see him holding her cameo broach. Her hand darted quickly to her throat and of course found an empty spot there.

She took the broach and looked at it carefully. There was blood on the tip of the pin. She hoped it was the last human blood she would ever shed. She looked up at McShannock.

"I'm glad you came back," she said.

"Why?"

"I had to tell you . . . to say I'm sorry."

"Nothing to be sorry for, ma'am. I gave you sort of a sudden shock."

"Yes. Yes, I suppose you did," she said. "When you said you killed my husband, I thought of Ira and . . . Well, I just wasn't thinking. I apologize."

"No, ma'am. I apologize—for leaving you a widow."

Kate quickly shook her head. "You saved my life the day you shot Conn Scarbrough. He would have killed me one day. And you saved my life again, with Lang Gutterage. And in Wolverine Canyon. You've spent an awful lot of time saving my life, Mr. McShannock. And my family's."

He smiled. "My pleasure, ma'am."

"Then stay until I can get your payment together. You've earned all of it. Every penny."

He lifted his eyes and looked out across the Blackfoot River Valley, at the distant sprinkling of stars and the full moon hanging over the black mountains that rimmed the bottom of the sky. Then his glance came back and met hers. "My payment was that you trusted me enough to let me stay there with you. You didn't know anything about me."

Now it was Kate's turn to smile. "Yes I did, Mr. McShannock. I knew you were kind and good-hearted and fair. You're not that much of a poker player. I read it all in your eyes."

"Then . . . did you also read . . ." He stopped himself and shook his head sadly, then started to turn away.

She caught his arm, and he turned back around, looking down at the soft skin of her hand. "Did I also read what?"

"I'm a selfish man," he said suddenly, in a husky voice.

"Selfish?"

He nodded. "I came here to help you, yes. But I came because . . . I had to see you again."

"Again?" she asked.

"I went to Scarbrough's funeral," he explained. "You smiled at me. It was the only time a real lady ever smiled at me. I've been in love with you ever since."

She cocked her head at him, a feeling of unexplainable sadness coming over her. Suddenly, she held out her arms and took him into them, and a little tear rolled down each of her cheeks. She held him for a long moment, as long as she dared, then kissed him softly on the mouth and stepped back.

"You see?" she said. "I'm not such a lady. I love my husband, and I wouldn't trade him for the world. But I've come to love you, too, Mr. McShannock. You've been my guardian angel."

He chuckled and bent the brim of his hat in nervous hands. Their eyes met, and he gave a little nod. "I'm afraid nothing you could do would convince me you aren't a lady." He placed a hand alongside her cheek and took one long last look in her eyes and said quietly, "Lady Winchester."

List of Characters

In Lady Winchester there are two groups of players. One consists of entirely fictional characters. The other is made up of people I know personally who have graciously allowed me to use their names and/or their likenesses in this book. I would like to make an acknowledgment to those friends of mine and those historical figures I made use of fictionally in *Lady Winchester*. For that reason and for clarity in following the flow of the book, we include this list.

Real characters

Kathryn Winchester (Geri Berg), Pocatello, Idaho
Sheriff Arch Hess (my grandfather)
Cheyenne Winchester (my daughter)
R.M. Sievers (Roger Sievers), Pocatello, Idaho
Susan Sievers, Pocatello, Idaho
Clyde Hall, Fort Hall, Idaho
Beaver—(his real name), California
Robert Lynch, South Carolina
Keith and Caroline Perkins, Gilbert, Arizona
Michael, Braden, Christian and Hunter—Perkins children
Elk—Clyde Hall's mother, Fort Hall, Idaho
John and Janet Webster, Pocatello, Idaho
Curtis and Annette Selders, Pocatello, Idaho

Historical figures

C.O. Sonnenkalb—Blackfoot's mayor at the time
Major Gallagher—the commander in charge at Ft. Hall at the time
Fred T. Dubois—one of Idaho's most famous statesmen of the era

Fictional characters

Countryfolk

Vala, Marshal, and Ellis Briggs
Vest McShannock
Irving Wolfe
Case Deckan—Coyote-faced man
Dunn Yates—Deckan's partner
Stewart "Calico" Lords—kidnapper from New York
"Star"—the cruel kidnapper
Sid "Neckerchief" Rolfe—kidnapper
Dub—kidnapper
Harvey Manfred—Wolfe's ranch hand
Judith Wolfe—Irving's wife
Arthur Wolfe—Irving's son
Howard McLaws—a Winchester neighbor
Dederscheck—a Winchester neighbor
Chris Dederscheck—Dederscheck's son
Kelly and Tracker Doyle—the killers of Tom Briggs
Lang Gutterage—Kate's dangerous "protector"

Townfolk

Ward Brassman—the banker
Luke Weaver—Hess's deputy
Dr. Martin Sims
Tryon Holt—the telegrapher
Thornton O'Toole—the undertaker

Kate's husbands

Dan Lauder—number one
Conn Scarbrough—number two
Tom Briggs—number three
Ira Winchester—number four

About the Author

Kirby Frank Jonas was born in Bozeman, Montana. He lived out of town in a remote area known as Bear Canyon, where sagebrush gave way to spruce and fir, and the wild country was forever ingrained in him. It was there he gained his love of the Old West, listening to his daddy tell stories and sing western ballads, and watching television Westerns such as *Gunsmoke, The Virginian* and *The Big Valley.*

Jonas next lived on a remote farm in the middle of Civil War battlefield country near Broad Run, Virginia. That was followed by a move to Shelley, Idaho, where he completed all of his school years, wrote his first book *(The Tumbleweed)* in the sixth grade and his second *(The Vigilante)* as a senior in high school. He has since written six published novels and one which is forthcoming, co-authored by his older brother, Jamie.

Besides writing novels, Jonas also paints wildlife and life in the West. He has done all of his cover art and hundreds of other pieces. He is a songwriter and guitar player and singer of old Western ballads and trail songs. Jonas enjoys the joking title given to him by his friends, "The Renaissance Cowboy," and the name given him by James Drury and the press, "The New Louis L'Amour."

After living in Arizona to research his first two books, and traveling through nine countries in Europe, to get his glimpse of the world, Jonas settled permanently in Pocatello, Idaho. He has made a living fighting forest fires for the Bureau of Land Management in five western states; worked for the Idaho Fish and Game Department; been a security guard and a guard for Wells Fargo in Phoenix, Arizona. He was employed as an officer for the Pocatello City Police and for the past seven years has been a municipal firefighter. He and his wife, Debbie, have four children, Cheyenne Kaycee, Jacob Talon, Clay Logan and Matthew Morgan.

Order the books and tapes at your local bookstore, through Amazon.com, on Kirby Jonas's website, or use this handy coupon:

Howling Wolf Publishing (www.kirbyjonas.com)
P.O. Box 1045
Pocatello, Idaho 83204

Please send me:

❑——— Copy/copies of: Season of the Vigilante, Book One: The Bloody Season ($12.95)*
❑——— Copy/copies of: Season of the Vigilante, Book Two: Season's End ($12.95)*
❑——— Copy/copies of: The Dansing Star ($10.95)
❑——— Copy/copies of: Death of an Eagle ($12.95)
❑——— Copy/copies of: Legend of the Tumbleweed ($12.95)
❑———Copy/copies of: Lady Winchester, soft ($12.95)
❑———Copy/copies of: Lady Winchester, hard ($23.95)

Books on tape read by James Drury, The Virginian

❑——— Copy/copies of: The Dansing Star ($60.00)
❑——— Copy/copies of: Death of an Eagle ($60.00)
❑——— Copy/copies of: Legend of the Tumbleweed ($60.00)
❑——— Copy/copies of: Lady Winchester ($60.00)

Check or money order—no C.O.D.'s, please.
Idaho residents add 5% sales tax
I am enclosing $———— .

Name ————————————————————————

Address ————————————————————————

City, State, Zip ————————————————————

Please allow three to four weeks for delivery.

UPRISING IN
EAST GERMANY:
JUNE 17, 1953

UPRISING IN EAST GERMANY: JUNE 17, 1953

BY ARNULF BARING

Translated from the German by Gerald Onn
With an Introduction by David Schoenbaum
and a Foreword by Richard Lowenthal

Cornell University Press | ITHACA AND LONDON

First published 1972 by Cornell University Press.
Published in the United Kingdom by Cornell University Press Ltd., 2–4 Brook Street, London W1Y 1AA.

International Standard Book Number 0-8014-0703-6
Library of Congress Catalog Card Number 70-38284

PRINTED IN THE UNITED STATES OF AMERICA
BY VAIL-BALLOU PRESS, INC.

Librarians: Library of Congress cataloging information appears on the last page of the book.

Contents

Introduction ~~~~~

by DAVID SCHOENBAUM

History books have their own histories. This one originated, a little improbably, as a master's essay in political
science at Columbia University in the mid-50's. But it appeared in its mature version in West Germany in 1965,
nearly on the eve of an election that the incumbent chancellor, Ludwig Erhard, was to characterize as the end of
the postwar era.

The election was, in fact, to be the last hurrah of West
Germany's first postwar political generation. As so often
in German history, there was no neat break between the
old and the new. But the landmarks of postwar life were
already disintegrating, and there was no route back to the
familiar scenery of the preceding years.

The landscape of West German foreign policy had
frozen into durable contours by 1952, before the end of
Konrad Adenauer's first term as chancellor. It withstood
erosion into the 60's, almost until his departure from office.
The principal features of Adenauer's world were the Atlantic Alliance and the integration of western Europe that
was assumed to be virtually inseparable from it.

Diplomatic navigation proceeded from two fixed points.
One was "negotiation from strength," the common western

formula of the era. The other was a constitutional commitment to German reunification. But in practice reunification was secondary.

Eastern Europe figured only as an extension of the Soviet Union, itself perceived as an undifferentiated glacier. Eastern Germany remained "the Soviet Zone of occupation." West Germany was the only Germany. Yugoslavia provoked an instructive test case in 1959 by recognizing East Germany. It vanished therewith from West German maps.

Among the landmarks of the era, to an extent now difficult for even a new generation of Germans to realize, was the official version of the East German rising of June 17, 1953. Every nation has it historical myths. But some are more historical, some more mythological, than others.

In official western and eastern versions alike, the myth of June 17 had a kind of instrumental function as both symbol and foundation of a whole view of political reality and international relations. After a momentary phase of self-criticism, the eastern version crystallized around putative neo-Nazis, unreconstructed bourgeois elements, and western provocation. Albert Camus noted with regret in a speech in Paris shortly after June 17 that the eastern view was hardly confined to the east.

The western version, of an ostensibly general and popular rising finally crushed only by the ruthless intervention of Soviet force, was enshrined in city maps and even the calendar. Somehow symbolic of a whole age of German history, Berlin's Siegesallee (Victory Avenue), built to commemorate the nation-building triumphs of 1864–1871, was renamed the Street of June 17. No less symbolically, the Street of June 17 has led since August 13, 1961, to a dead end at the wall before the Brandenburg Gate.

Since 1954, June 17 has been observed as a West German legal holiday. Originally attended by emotional speeches and performances of *Fidelio,* the holiday has latterly been an occasion for rueful editorials and family picnics. As Baring's book appeared, the father of a school boy in Rheydt, on the lower Rhine, challenged school officials by declaring his intent of taking his son with the family for the holiday instead of sending him to the official school ceremony. School officials replied with the threat of expulsion. It was an odd way to commemorate a rising whose objective had ultimately included freedom of conscience, of assembly, and of movement.

Yet the more things have remained the same, the more they have also changed. They were already visibly changing as the book appeared. Baring's book, like his career, was a preview of coming things. A native Berliner, himself 21 at the time of the rising, he was a kind of new German, come to consciousness among ruins both literal and political.

He had been educated in New York and Paris as well as Berlin and had already acquired a reputation in the early 60's with a series of brilliant pieces on Eastern Europe, an area still terra incognita to official West German policy when he wrote. His first book, with Christian Tautil, was a highly perceptive study of de Gaulle. In an article in *Der Monat* in 1962 he made a strong case for diplomatic recognition of East Germany. It was a position then taboo and still not self-evidently acceptable in Washington, London, and Paris, not to mention Bonn.

Since *Uprising in East Germany* appeared, the lucidity and sobriety of Baring's position have become so generally accepted that its originality, and even courage, needs to be recalled. Richard Lowenthal's discreet injunction in the original introduction, that western diplomacy *do* something, has been heeded—not only by those out of power in 1965, who sympathized at the time, but by the old order itself. Gerhard Schroeder, the hardest of hard-liners as Adenauer's interior minister, and afterward Erhard's foreign minister, was already undertaking the first steps as Lowenthal wrote.

Détente was written, *expressis verbis,* into official policy in January 1967, when a new government took office under Kurt Georg Kiesinger. The new chancellor had been the paladin of Christian Democratic orthodoxy in the great debates of the early 50's. Under his administration, "Soviet Zone of Occupation" vanished from West German lexicons, and "German Democratic Republic" emerged from its accompanying quotation marks into the light of official reality.

In 1971, Chancellor Willy Brandt, a junior Social Democratic politician in 1953, West Berlin's lord mayor during the shivery years 1956–1961, and Kiesinger's foreign minister from 1967 to 1969, was awarded the Nobel Peace prize for his government's efforts at détente—not only with Germany's East European neighbors, but with the Soviet Union and East Germany.

Baring, who had subsequently written a massive study of the origins of West German foreign policy in the domestic politics of the early postwar years and been appointed professor at the John F. Kennedy Institute of West Berlin's Free University, was an active partisan of the Brandt government. Lowenthal, professor of political science at the Free University since 1961, had been one of the chancellor's foreign policy advisers. Ironically, Baring and Lowenthal found themselves casualties of the university reform both had also helped initiate as the general thaw began. Everybody had learned a lesson from the years they described. But in a city remarkable, if not absolutely unique, for historical discontinuity, everybody had learned different lessons.

The Free University had been founded with generous American aid in 1947–1948 by secessionists from the old university in East Berlin. Twenty-five years later the student affiliate of East Germany's ruling Socialist Unity party showed signs of becoming the most successful campus political group. Among the younger generation of activists, Baring and Lowenthal, whose refusal to acquiesce in the conventional wisdom of either west or east is recorded in this book, now found themselves among the academic "class enemy."

If there was a victor, Walter Ulbricht, first secretary of the Socialist Unity party and chairman of the East German council of ministers, had been the victor of June 17. In 1971 he retired. There was little evidence that intrigue or factional struggle, let alone popular opposition, played a role in his departure. So far as one could tell, Ulbricht, now 77, had just resigned. The last of a Communist generation, he had politically survived Stalin, Malenkov and Khrushchev, Novotny and Rákosi, Gomulka, Dubček and Nagy.

He had escaped oblivion again in 1956, saved once more by the very forces that had apparently pushed him to the edge. "June 17 and the Hungarian revolt," *Der Spiegel* noted on his departure from office "made it possible for the party chief to establish the rule the Kremlin finally accepted: that the fall of proven captains, loyal to the Soviet Union, combined with course reversals of 180 degrees in the direction of reforms, only drive the steamer aground and onto the rocks under full steam."

The definitive crisis of his regime had come in 1961. The perennial threat to West Berlin, a particularly ferocious agricultural collectivization, East Germany's chronically stagnant economy, all had played their part. Emigration, Sebastian Haffner once observed, is the real form of German revolution. In 1960 the refugee volume had reached 200,000 in a population of about 17 million. By the beginning of August 1961 over 113,000 more refugees had turned up in West Berlin. There were over 17,000 between August 1 and 13, when the flow was finally stopped. By Ulbricht's own estimate, nearly half the refugees of 1960 were under 25, another quarter 25 to 45. Over 20 per cent of the fugitives from Germany's "first workers' and peasants' state" were skilled workers. In a famous piece in *The Reporter*, George Bailey characterized East Germany as "the disappearing satellite."

The wall appeared before the satellite disappeared. Ulbricht's monument appeared with and behind it. When he left office East Germany was the world's tenth largest industrial producer. In the decade since the wall its annual growth rates had averaged about 6½ per cent while average real wages had advanced slightly faster. The economy itself had been decentralized and radically reorganized. The Stalinallee had been renamed: Marxallee at one end, Frankfurterallee, its original name, at the other.

The construction worker of June 17 had come to enjoy

the highest standard of living in the eastern bloc, which meant a modest level of affluence even by western standards. His children, competitive and upwardly mobile, profited from an educational system even West Germans had come to admire. If he visited the West only via TV (66 per cent of East German households had TV by 1969 compared with 73 per cent in West Germany), he could at least meet western relatives on his home grounds. By the end of the decade over a million West Germans visited East Germany annually. About a million old-age pensioners were allowed to leave East Germany to visit the West.

The state-owned German Fashion Institute produced minis, maxis, and hot pants. The state-owned department stores occasionally sold a shipment of Lee jeans. Even small-town theaters showed an occasional American movie. "If you have to live here, you can live here," an East German surveyor observed to a western acquaintance late in 1971 after a third beer. No more, and no less. It could have been Ulbricht's political epitaph.

As it happened, 1971 was also a significant year for the President of the United States, who announced plans to extend the radius of presidential travel, which had already taken him to Rumania and Yugoslavia, to mainland China and the Soviet Union. His administration continued to pursue détente—indirectly, in its encouragement of Brandt's initiatives; directly, in the continuing arms control negotiations in Vienna and Helsinki. It also managed to achieve it in the new four-power statute on the status of Berlin concluded in late August. Nixon too, vice president of the United States in June 1953, had come a long way.

In his introduction to the original edition of this book,

Richard Lowenthal sketched the Soviet background of the events of June 17. Particularly for American readers, the contemporary American scene is also worth recalling.

In the months after Stalin's death, while the Soviet Union and its East German satellite were taking a "new course," the United States was adjusting to a "new look." But strategically the "new look" was largely an optical illusion, as Walter Lippmann pointed out at the time. Essentially the policies of the new administration were those of its Democratic predecessors, in turn a product of Stalin's last years.

Korea and the apprehensions of major allies limited American policy in basic ways. But the contingencies of domestic politics all but froze it. Even accepting sincerity of intent, there had been little intrinsically appealing to Washington in Stalin's proposals for German reunification on the basis of free elections and subsequent neutrality in spring 1952. Containment of communism, Atlantic and European integration, German rearmament, French ratification of the European Defense Community: these were the major goals of western policy. They still were a year later.

Theoretically western policy aspired to negotiation from strength. In fact, as Coral Bell and others have persuasively argued, the western position would never again be stronger than it was in mid-1953. In August the Soviet Union successfully tested its first H-bomb. Nor, on the face of it, was there significant public opposition to negotiation as such. Polls in May 1953, shortly after Churchill's proposal, reported 78 per cent of American respondents in favor of a summit meeting compared to 77 per cent in Britain.

But democratic politics is rarely plebiscitary. The realities of political life had drastically limited acting on any perception of strength by a Democratic administration under fire in 1952 from a Republican opposition resolved to exact vengeance for the apparently endless stalemate in Korea and the alleged sell-out at Yalta, not to mention failures and frustrations, real and imagined, going back to 1933. Nixon himself was declaring that "traitors in high councils of our own Government have made sure the deck is stacked on the Soviet side of the diplomatic tables." In the congressional election of 1954 he was still pointing out, now as vice president, that "real Democrats are outraged by the Truman-Acheson-Stevenson gang's defense of Communism in high places," that all three were "traitors to the high principles in which many of the nation's Democrats believed."

The dynamics of the 1952 campaign had, in turn, limited the options open to the newly elected Republicans. The alternatives followed, in effect, from an unstated syllogism. Democratic foreign policy was a failure. Democratic foreign policy was based on "containment." "Containment" was therefore a failure. This left two possibilities. The first, a return to isolationism, was rejected with the rejection of Senator Taft. The other was a kind of isolationism in reverse, the policy of "rollback" or "peaceful liberation." It was elaborated by the new secretary of state, John Foster Dulles, in a famous article in *Life* in May 1952, though he carefully specified, "We do not want a series of bloody uprisings and reprisals." Eisenhower himself echoed Dulles' views in the course of the campaign.

But even assuming some disposition to negotiate on the

part of Dulles and Eisenhower, there was fundamental opposition to summit diplomacy in any form among major Republicans in the Senate's new Republican majority. Early 1953 was the high tide of McCarthyism. The Wisconsin senator's myrmidons Roy Cohn and G. David Schine were permitted to disrupt United States Information Service libraries in Europe without reprimand. McCarthy himself let it be known in March that he had negotiated an agreement with Greek ship-owners to stop trading at certain Soviet and East European ports; i.e., a United States senator preempted the prerogatives of the executive branch, including the President whose coattails he had demonstrably ridden.

And Senator John W. Bricker introduced a constitutional amendment asserting the primacy of U.S. law over any international treaty. Dulles, who was active in the amendment's ultimate defeat, viewed it as a threat to the President's control of foreign policy. But Nixon, who later as president was so sturdily to resist congressional encroachment was among the amendment's supporters.

"Liberation" turned up postelection as one of three possibilities proposed for re-examination to senior presidential advisers on May 8, 1953. The alternatives to it were "containment," as practiced by the previous administration, and "massive retaliation," as Dulles was to propose it in 1954. In principle, the administration continued to speak of liberation and even, in a limited way, to pursue it in exotic places like Guatemala and Indo-China.

But in practice, as registered in NCS-162, the Planning Board's paper presented in October 1953, "containment" was basic policy with slight concessions to the "new look" policy of primary reliance on strategic air power. By that time, June 17 had come and gone as major events in Eastern Europe were to come and go again three years later. If historically interesting for no other reason, Baring's account is a sober reflection of American policy in the era of "peaceful liberation," as unlikely to comfort the followers of William Appleman Williams as the followers of John Foster Dulles.

But the book's value goes beyond its significance for diplomatic historians. Revolution is among the basic problems of modern history. Baring's book is also the story of a revolution. That it reads like John Reed in reverse, not the story of *Ten Days That Shook the World,* but of a day and a half that didn't, proves only that this revolution failed. Connoisseurs will recognize in Baring's closely documented, closely argued resconstruction of the context and course of June 17, the latter-day recapitulation of one of those revolutionary *journées* that have figured so spectacularly, and tragically, in the history of modern Europe.

Not the Burke or the Michelet of June 17, Baring seeks neither to praise the revolution nor to bury it; he wishes above all to demystify it in all its irony, profundity, and occasional frivolity. June 17 was a German workers' rising, the latest in a long series of German revolutions that failed. It was a historical turning point. But history failed to turn. It was a remarkable case of misunderstanding and self-deception in a remarkable number of places, many of them high. It was a kind of symposium of the deaf.

Germans alone can decide whether and how it should be celebrated. But it deserves to be remembered.

Iowa City, Iowa
1972

Foreword ~~~~~~

by RICHARD LOWENTHAL

The first comprehensive accounts of the East German rising of June 17 were written under the direct impact of events. Inevitably, every line of these works reflected the feelings of contemporary West Germans, who had witnessed the revolutionary incidents in the German Democratic Republic (GDR) as deeply sympathetic but powerless bystanders. No matter how conscientiously these early writers strove after objectivity, they could not avoid expressing their sense of human and political solidarity with the oppressed workers of the GDR, their indignation over the coercive methods that had provoked the demonstrations, their satisfaction at finding people capable of attempting the impossible by taking such sudden and completely spontaneous action, and their bitter disappointment over their own impotence—or failure?—and over the fruitless outcome of the rising.

Twelve years later, most of us still entertained such feelings. But, because we expressed them so often, they became unbearably hackneyed: protestations of indignation which do not lead to action must inevitably degenerate into meaningless rhetoric. At this time such rhetoric, far from illuminating the events of June 17, tends to obscure their true significance, especially for the younger generation that has grown up in the post-Stalin era. In his objective study, however, Baring deals with the historical aspects of June 17. He explains what actually happened, he analyzes the factors underlying the rising, and he discusses its consequences. And, having done so, he allows the reader to make his own value judgments.

It is now left to me to sketch in the international background of the specific events dealt with by Baring. This involves two principal factors: the economic and political crisis that began to emerge in the Soviet bloc in the months immediately following Stalin's death and the discussions entered into at that time with a view to reopening negotiations between the four great powers in order to resolve the German question.

When Stalin died on March 5, 1953, the economic resources of the Soviet Union and its European satellites were dangerously overstretched. Instead of trying to bring about a relaxation of tension following the breakdown of his postwar offensive in Europe in 1948–1949, Stalin had reacted to the failure of the Berlin Blockade, the secession of Yugoslavia, the ending of the Greek civil war, and the founding of NATO by persecuting the Titoist sympathizers in eastern Europe and by promoting the Korean War in 1950. His unwillingness to bring this war to an end was one of the principal reasons why the western powers, especially America, embarked on a massive rearmament program and made the decision to rearm the Federal Republic. In the closing years of his life Stalin vacillated between half-hearted attempts to establish a détente and frenzied efforts to rearm. And the peoples of the Soviet bloc had to pay for this policy. Quotas for armaments and heavy industries were increased again and again even though, once industrial reserves and reserves of raw materials had been used up, these projects could only be pursued by reducing to an absolute minimum the production program of the consumer goods and agricultural industries, which presupposed a similar reduction in the standard of living of the population. In the winter of 1952–1953 the growing food crisis led, in one satellite state after another, to a reduction of productivity even in heavy industries, where the workers were receiving preferential treatment. At this point Stalin's rearmament policy reached its absolute limit. The "combing out" of small industrial concerns, freelance craftsmen, and commercial firms in the Soviet zone of Germany within the framework of Ulbricht's program for the "establishment of socialism," which had such a tangible effect on East German living standards, was just a special instance of the general crisis in the Soviet bloc.

Because of this crisis Stalin's heirs received calls for help and warnings of impending disaster from the satellite states within months of taking office. They were quick to react to the worsening situation. In April 1953, Moscow began to evolve a new line which provided for concessions to the farmers, workers, and consumers and for foreign policy initiatives aimed at bringing about a relaxation of tension in international relations with a view to slowing down the arms race. Internal concessions went hand in hand with attempts to achieve an external détente. Thus, the speedy conclusion of the long-drawn-out armistice negotiations in Korea and Malenkov's assurances that, given the necessary good will, all international problems could be peacefully resolved were in complete accord with the new developments taking place throughout the Soviet bloc. These included the change of course forced on the Socialist Unity Party (Sozialistische Einheitspartei Deutschlands, SED) leadership on June 9; the relaxation of government pressure on the Czech workers following the disturbances in Pilsen, which were sparked off at the beginning of June by the confiscatory "currency reform" introduced by the Czech communist party; the establishment in Hungary on July 4 of Imre Nagy's first government, which proposed to increase the production of consumer goods and to allow the Hungarian farmers to opt out of the agricultural collectives; and, finally, "Malenkov's gifts" to the Soviet farmers (remission of tax arrears and the reduction of taxes on privately owned land), which were coupled with the announcement by the Soviet Premier to the Supreme Soviet, on August 8, of a decision to step up the production of consumer goods in the USSR. The decision made by the new leaders in Moscow to combat the crisis by reducing the economic pressure on the workers was also reflected in the changes effected in other Soviet bloc countries, where overambitious projects for heavy industry were canceled and concessions were granted to the working population.

But these proposed changes in Soviet economic and foreign policy had to be carried out in conditions of considerable uncertainty by men who were embroiled in an internal struggle for the succession. Under a leadership that was still far from firmly established and whose authority had been greatly diminished, to retreat too far from Stalin's policies could easily be interpreted as a sign of weakness. How far could the new men go with their liberalization plans without losing control of the situation? The attempt to bring about a détente abroad raised a similar question: to what extent were the western powers prepared to collaborate and what would they demand in return? Both in Moscow and, to a lesser degree, in the satellite states, power struggles within the communist leadership arose out of the question of how much liberalization should be allowed at home and how much détente abroad. It was the confluence of these and other related factors—as Baring points out in his study—that provoked the rising of June 17 in the GDR: the pent-up bitterness that was the legacy of the preceding period of extreme economic pressure, the abruptness of the change following Semyonov's directive of June 9, the arguments between Ulbricht and his critics in the Politburo of the SED over the extent of the change and the uncertainty that this created among the rank and file of the SED all combined to produce a revolutionary situation. Elsewhere in the Soviet bloc similar circumstances also led to a resurgence of individualistic activity, although not on the same scale as in the GDR: following the sudden change of government and the introduction of the new line in Hungary countless farmers decided to leave the agricultural collectives, with the result that the country's agricultural land, equipment, and stock were divided up in the middle of the harvest and in a completely haphazard fashion. Meanwhile, when the news of the East German rising reached the Soviet Union—where the authority of the state in general and the power of the secret police in particular had been greatly undermined following Beria's overthrow—it triggered a wave of strikes in the penal colonies, most of which were subsequently closed down as a direct consequence. Eventually the mass exodus from the collective farms in Hungary played an important part in the power struggle between the reform-minded head of the Hungarian government, Imre Nagy, and the Stalinist party leader, Rakosi, just as the rising of June 17 became one of the crucial factors in Ulbricht's victory over his rivals and in all probability contributed to Beria's downfall in Moscow.

The particularly close connection between the internal struggles fought out in the summer of 1953 by the leaders of the SED, on the one hand, and the leaders of the Soviet communist party, on the other, was due to the key position occupied by East Germany in the Soviet Union's policy of détente. Ever since the autumn of 1950 Stalin had been trying, without success, to prevent the rearming of the Federal Republic within the framework of NATO by making more or less vague offers of negotiations. When he died, the Bonn and Paris treaties had been signed but had not yet come into effect. Consequently, Stalin's heirs had to decide whether to enter into new negotiations with the other great powers on the German question and, if necessary, offer reunification in freedom in return for guarantees of German neutrality under the terms of a definitive peace treaty. By then they knew —from Churchill's speech of May 11, 1953—that the English Prime Minister wanted a four-power conference in the near future to negotiate just such a treaty. In this connection Churchill had spoken of a German Locarno.

There are many indications that, at the beginning of June 1953, not only Beria, but a majority of the Soviet party presidium led by Malenkov, was in favor of this proposal. The fact that Khrushchev subsequently accused his two vanquished rivals of wanting to sell out to the West in this way means little in itself. But everything that is known about Semyonov's behavior in Berlin in the days just before the rising fits in with this hypothesis. It seems certain, for example, that he encouraged Herrnstadt and Zaisser in their opposition to Ulbricht. Moreover, the rumors circulating at that time—even among the top functionaries of the SED—to the effect that the party might well have to go into opposition and might even be declared illegal seem to have originated in suggestions made by the Soviet High Commissar after his return from Moscow. The failure to discipline Semyonov after Beria's downfall suggests that his actions had been approved, not only by Beria, but also by the competent official departments. Moreover, this would explain why Herrnstadt and Zaisser, who were subsequently deprived of their party membership for forming factions within the party, were not also arraigned on a criminal charge of seditious complicity with Beria.

It seems that only after the events of June 17 did the majority of the Soviet party presidium, and especially Malenkov, come out against the proposed policy for the settlement of the German question, which was then condemned as "capitulationary" and, for a while, ascribed to Beria alone. Although Beria's arrest was not announced to the public until July 9, we know from subsequent official statements that the decision to move against him was made on June 26. The other members of the presidium doubtless had many reasons for wanting to overthrow the powerful chief of the secret police. But the time chosen for this action would suggest that he had been isolated at a critical moment by the failure of the

German policy that he had been actively promoting. What is quite certain is that Ulbricht's opponents in the Polit-buro of the SED continued their struggle even after June 17 and were not subdued until after Beria's downfall. In short, the Soviet leadership began to have second thoughts about the proposal for a "Solution of the German Question through Negotiations" after the East German rising and finally rejected it following Beria's elimination.

Does it follow from this that the popular rising of June 17 was the principal reason for the Soviets' change of course? If so, it would mean that the striking and demonstrating workers in the Soviet zone had tragically achieved the precise opposite of what they had come to regard in the course of the rising as their ultimate aim. Certainly, the Soviet leaders were influenced by the events of June 17. But these were no more than the proximate cause of their change of policy. The underlying and far more important cause was the passivity of western and West German foreign policy in the critical months following Stalin's death. Moscow had taken note of Churchill's initiative; the western and West German government departments had not. The State Department and the Office of the Federal Chancellor, the Quai D'Orsay, and even Churchill's own Foreign Office showed no inclination to jeopardize the incorporation of the Federal Republic into the western alliance, which had already been decided but still awaited ratification, by entering into discussions of the German question at a four-power conference. Meanwhile, Churchill himself was taken ill shortly after making his speech of May 11, and was unable to pursue this proposal any further. Under the circumstances the prospects of a compromise settlement of the German question, which his initiative had seemed to hold out, must have appeared less promising from week to week. And the dangers of adopting a vacillatory policy over Germany, which were clearly demonstrated on June 17, would have impressed themselves on the Soviet leaders all the more forcefully the more these prospects faded.

Considered in these terms, June 17 was not only a day of crisis for the Soviet Union but also a missed opportunity for the western powers. Such opportunities never recur in the same form, but they do contain lessons for those prepared to learn from them. At the present writing Russia again has a collective government, in which the distribution of power still seems uncertain and temporary. One of the problems on which its members will have to adopt a common attitude is the same as that which faced Stalin's heirs: the extent of a possible détente between East and West and the significance of the German question within that process. Today, of course, there are no signs of a popular rising in the German Democratic Republic or of a new opportunity to resolve the whole of the German question by diplomatic measures. But even the more modest opportunities open to us can only be put to profitable use if, instead of waiting for the Soviet leadership to clarify its position, the western powers try to influence that process by putting forward constructive proposals. In Germany today people have far greater knowledge of the factors involved than they had in 1953; by studying this history of June 17 they can increase their knowledge still further.

1965

/

THE EVENTS
LEADING UP
TO JUNE 17

The Second Party Conference
and Its Consequences

The events that led up to the uprising of June 17, 1953, began a year before. At the Second Party Conference of the SED (Socialist Unity Party, Sozialistische Einheitspartei Deutschlands), held in Berlin from July 9 to 12, 1952, Walter Ulbricht announced as a goal the "establishment of socialism." The conference then passed a resolution stating that "the political and economic conditions and the attitude of the working class and of the majority of the workers . . . had progressed to a point where the establishment of socialism had become the fundamental task [facing the state]." [1]

This declaration of intent did not mean, however, that the transition to socialism was actually under way but merely that the process of change, which had begun some years before, was to be accelerated.

In the postwar years until about 1948, the Russians had concentrated on a policy of reparations, drawing off as much as they possibly could from what was then their zone. During that period—for whatever reasons—they postponed their socialist plans and confined themselves to laying a firm foundation for future developments with

3

their so-called anti-fascist, democratic order. This policy was completely reversed in 1948–1949, and the Russians speedily transformed what had been their occupation zone into a people's democracy. In 1948 the first budget was introduced. In October 1949 the German Democratic Republic was founded. By 1950 the socialist sector—the industries taken over by the state—was responsible for 51 per cent of the gross national product (as compared with 20 per cent in 1946). As early as the mid-1950's the SED stated officially [2] that, with the creation of the GDR as an independent state, the introduction of comprehensive economic planning, the ascendancy of the public over the private sector and the elimination of party rivalry following the formation of the National Front (which embraced all parties and organizations under the leadership of the SED), the popular democratic phase of government had been instituted in 1949–1950. The German communists tackled the economic and social reconstruction of their territory with a program of strictly controlled economic redevelopment and a mass propaganda campaign. But they were greatly hindered from the outset by the inadequate supplies of raw materials and the low industrial potential of the GDR, by their patently obvious links with Moscow, and by the existence of two parallel and partial German states.

The second phase of the revolutionary process was instituted at the second Party Conference in the summer of 1952.[3] The first agricultural collectives were formed in July and were soon followed by craftsmen's collectives; the machinery of government was also completely transformed by the rearrangement of the territorial divisions within the GDR, whereby the existing five provinces were replaced by fourteen districts. Shortly before the GDR had taken steps to protect itself from external influences: following the signing of the European Defense Treaty the zonal frontier was declared a national frontier, travel was restricted, the telephone and road networks in Berlin were cut off at the sector boundaries, and West Berliners were forbidden to enter the GDR. The exclusion of the outside world was accompanied by greater vigilance at home: agents, disruptive elements, spies, and saboteurs were unmasked on all sides. Young people who joined the Young Christian Association (*Junge Gemeinde*) were expelled from school or from the universities, and numerous priests were called to account for alleged criminal offenses. Moreover, thousands of entrepreneurs, manufacturers and farmers were arrested on suspicion of tax evasion (or in extreme cases of subversive activity), condemned by the courts, and stripped of their possessions. It is hardly surprising that the economic difficulties with which the GDR had to contend should have increased considerably toward the end of 1952.

But there were other reasons for these difficulties. According to the law of systematic politico-economic development—which was evolved by Stalin on the basis of Marx's theory of production—those branches of industry which provide the state with the basic means of production (such as raw materials and machines) have to be developed more quickly than those which produce consumer goods. Consequently, the first five-year plan for the GDR (1951–1955) was concerned primarily with the establishment of heavy industry on a significant scale.

We have not been told how much of the industrial output of the GDR is given over to the provision of raw

materials and machines, but according to western estimates in the sixties, these accounted for about two thirds
of total production. Especially in the early stages, the
GDR encountered considerable difficulties in the ambi-
tious and costly project for socialist industrialization,
since it possessed few natural resources and its industry
had been undermined by the dismantling of factories for
reparations.

This is clearly demonstrated by the figures for steel
production: in 1936 the annual output of ingot steel and
rolled steel in what is now the GDR was 1.2 million tons
and 898,000 tons respectively. By 1955 it was planned to
increase these amounts to 3.4 and 2.2 million tons.

But in 1946 the production capacity of the steel industry in the GDR was reduced by 85 per cent owing
to the dismantling of factories. As a result the production
of ingot steel dropped to 97,000 tons and that of rolled
steel to 76,000 tons, which was less than 10 per cent of the
prewar output. The situation was aggravated still further
by the fact that, before the war, this part of Germany
had produced only one quarter of its coal and only 140,000
tons of iron ore from its own mines. From these figures
alone it is clear that, if the GDR was to build up its heavy
industry, it had to increase its mining output and open
up new industrial sites. And so the first task facing the
East German leaders was to provide adequate funds for
investment. At the same time they had to promote exports
so as to be able to import iron ore and coal to make up
for the deficiency that would remain even after they had
boosted their own production. Finally, they had to increase productivity. It was, of course, no accident that

in trying to do so they should have concentrated on the coal mining industry, where Hennecke's overfulfillment of his quota by 380 per cent led to a general increase in work norms.

In 1950 and 1951—by cutting back sharply on consumer goods and investing in heavy industry—the GDR actually did achieve a significant increase in the production of ore, in the output of iron and steel, and in the manufacture of heavy machinery. The production of ingot steel, for example, rose to almost 1.9 million tons, which was 50 per cent more than in 1936 and constituted a really remarkable achievement in view of the large number of rolling mills that had been dismantled.

But toward the end of 1952 it became apparent that exports were lagging far behind imports and that, while the production quotas set for 1952 under the terms of the five-year plan had not been achieved, wages had risen far in excess of the stipulated levels.

But these higher wages were not the only strain on the economy at that time. The budget for the second half of the year was also put under severe pressure when the government found it necessary to spend "considerable, unexpected sums" on the formation and fitting out of the paramilitary People's Police to counter the "aggressive military preparations" then being made against the GDR.

Moreover, this increased expenditure was accompanied by a drop in state revenue. Following the Second Party Conference, which had stressed the importance of continuing the class struggle, large numbers of people engaged in business on their own account—small industrialists, tradesmen, and farmers—had fled to the West, thus reducing the level of state income from taxation. The tax concessions granted to the newly founded agricultural collectives had a similar effect.

The party leaders felt that, if the establishment of socialism was to be successful, then there could be no reduction in investment, no letup in the formation of agricultural collectives, and no slowing down in the build-up of the paramilitary People's Police, the new secret army. Consequently, they decided to direct their energies to bridging the widening gap between wages and productivity. The SED was of the opinion that the inadequate rise in productivity was due to the indulgent attitude adopted toward the workers since the autumn of 1951 and considered that the time had come to abandon this "conciliatory" line. For, whereas industrialists, businessmen and craftsmen, the middle and lower middle classes and, increasingly, farmers, had all been made to feel the impact of socialist reconstruction and had lost their independence in the process, the workers had escaped the direct repercussions of the SED resolutions of July 1952. There were good reasons for this.

Disputes over the Collective Agreements

The first serious disputes between the workers and the regime took place in 1951. They were triggered by the skeleton and specimen collective agreements introduced into the GDR at that time, which were based on Soviet models and constituted an entirely new facet of German industrial law.

The first collective agreements in the USSR date from 1922. They were concluded between the unions and the industrial managements and initially they served a purpose similar to that fulfilled by the tariff agreements of the western world, since they incorporated protective legislation and regulated hours of work, rates of pay and so on. But in the second half of the 1920's, when working conditions in the Soviet Union were fixed by the state (usually within the framework of the economic plans), these collective agreements lost their significance as instruments of industrial law. Subsequently, they were used simply as a means of specifying, in greater or lesser detail, the terms of the laws and decrees promulgated by the state legislature. Finally, in 1934, collective agreements were dispensed with entirely.

It was not until 1947 that they were reintroduced. Then, however, they assumed a completely different form and served a completely different purpose. According to a manual of Soviet industrial law published in the GDR in 1952 the principal feature of the collective agreements concluded during the second phase of the socialist state was their insistence on "specific obligations binding on all parties for the implementation of any measures which contribute to the fulfillment and overfulfillment of the economic plans . . . " The purpose of these collective agreements—to define in contractual form the obligations freely entered into by the workers for improving productivity—was supposed to reflect the new relationship to work obtaining in the socialist state. The new outlook of "socialist man after his emancipation from exploitation," it was argued, would inevitably lead to a constant growth in productivity and so fulfill the one essential condition for the establishment of communism.

Like the collective agreements drafted in the USSR in

the second half of the 1920's, those produced in the GDR in the early 1950's (on the basis of the decree of February 15, 1951) were essentially stereotype copies of the skeleton and specimen collective agreements. They had been drawn up by the government ministries in conjunction with the Free German Trade Unions (Freier Deutscher Gewerkschaftsbund, FDGB). No collective agreement was allowed to depart from the guidelines laid down in the original skeleton agreement.

The purpose served by the collective agreements in the USSR during the first socialist phase—that of explaining to the workers the content of government legislation —probably played no part in Germany. It would seem that in the GDR the decision to reproduce in a more elaborate form the binding provisions of the specimen collective agreements, by drawing up hundreds of individual collective agreements, was prompted by a desire to lessen the impact of the transition from the earlier tariff agreements, which had been negotiated freely between unions and managements, to the new system of labor relations, in which working conditions were dictated by the government. In fact, the collective agreements concluded in the GDR in 1951 were essentially the same as the new type of Soviet collective agreement. By their terms the workers undertook, both individually and collectively, either to increase their output or to achieve the production target laid down by the state ahead of schedule.

Before the agreements could come into effect they had to be endorsed by the workers, and it quickly became apparent that this was going to pose difficulties for the regime. Although great pressure was brought to bear, it proved quite impossible to get all the agreements concluded by January 31, 1951, as had been planned. This terminal date had to be extended several times because employees at numerous factories refused to give their approval, even though this was sought in open ballots watched over by SED functionaries. It was not the collective agreements as such to which the workers took exception. (At that time the implications of these agreements were not fully appreciated in Germany; people had not yet realized what the Russians had been trying to do in the USSR since 1947 or what they intended to do in the GDR in the future.) What the workers actually objected to at that stage was the fact that under the new collective agreements they would be worse off than under the old tariff arrangements.

The dispute over the collective agreements showed how unwilling the workers were to follow the regime along its chosen path. It also impressed on them that they could successfully oppose the regime so long as they remained united. This realization was clearly one of the motivating factors underlying their decision to stage an open protest in June 1953.

In 1952 the regime decided that it must try to remove the difficulties which had arisen in the previous year by making concessions to the workers, since without their loyal cooperation the objectives of the five-year plan could never be achieved.

And so rates of pay and working conditions were taken out of the specimen and collective agreements and determined by statute. These statutory settlements were "far more favorable for the workers in material terms than the corresponding settlements stipulated in the collective agreements of 1951," [4] and went a long way toward meeting the demands made by the workers in the disputes of the previous year. In the collective agreements of 1952 the workers were asked to enter, both individually and corporately, into voluntary undertakings and, since little pressure was brought to bear to make them do so, the agreements were concluded with considerably less friction than in the previous year. The SED then tried to exploit this favorable climate in order to restore the popularity of the FDGB, which had helped to draw up and put through the collective agreements of 1951 and consequently had been seen by the workers for what it was, a mere instrument of the state apparatus. To this end *Das Neue Deutschland* published an article by Rudolf Herrnstadt, its chief editor and a candidate member of the Politburo, in which it was admitted that the conclusion of the collective agreements of 1951 had led to bitterness and resentment among the workers.[5] The reason for this bitterness, Herrnstadt suggested, was the lack of consideration shown for the workers' interests by the FDGB. But he laid most of the blame on the SED for failing to appreciate the situation and disregarding the workers' complaints. There had been a conscious attempt, he said, to disguise the fact that popular attitudes had not kept pace with the economic development. The state had tried to influence the workers by "ordering them about" and "even by intimidation" instead of offering them ideological enlightenment and bringing their attitude into line with the new social conditions.

Herrnstadt's article was the signal for a press campaign in the SED and FDGB newspapers. Although the reporters were not allowed to criticize the industrial and social policy of the GDR as such, they openly attacked industrial managements and labor unions and even ministers and secretaries of state for the abuses in their respective spheres. As a result relations between the workers and both the FDGB and the SED became more relaxed, and in the elections to the union managements at the industry and national levels in the autumn of 1952, nearly 70 per cent of the candidates were not party members.

But now the development of socialism had begun, and because of the economic difficulties which this created, the SED was obliged to drop its conciliatory attitude toward the workers.

Increased Quotas

On January 15, 1953 the SED press office put out a statement in which the official union organ, *Die Tribüne,* was accused of "ideological laxness" and the union itself was censured for its failure to prosecute the "struggle for ideological clarity" and for concentrating on promoting its members' interests instead of adopting a "correct attitude toward work quotas and piece rates."

The FDGB fitted in with the new line at once. Under the twin slogans of "higher quotas" and "strict economy" a campaign was launched to preserve the "socialist content" of the 1953 collective agreements which—as *Die Tägliche Rundschau* put it—had to be transformed into "real weapons in the struggle for a strict economy regime." [6]

The object of the campaign was to effect a rise in the work quotas, which would lead either to increased productivity or to lower production costs in the state-run industries and would, therefore, mean a reduction in state expenditure. If the higher quotas did not result in higher productivity, then they would have the effect of cutting back on wages, thus relieving the burden on the treasury and counteracting the constant growth in purchasing power. In the summer of 1952 the government had authorized wage increases, many of them quite substantial. But these wage increases had not been matched by an increase in supplies of consumer goods, partly because this would have run counter to an official policy which was geared to the needs of heavy industry, and partly because so many of the businessmen working in the private sector, which was largely responsible for the production of consumer goods, had sought refuge in the West.

In actual fact, the government's insistence on higher quotas was not as unreasonable as it might appear at first sight. After the war productivity in the Soviet zone —as in the other zones—dropped considerably. This decline was due to the general disorganization of the economy, the dismantling of factories, and the severe shortage of raw materials and of food. By the end of 1947 production had sunk to a mere fraction of its prewar level despite the fact that the total number of persons employed had risen by some 180,000.

Unfortunately, there are no proper records which show how the problem of overmanning affected the assessment of the work quotas. The only information available to us in this respect comes from occasional newspaper reports published in the Soviet zone at the time.

We are told that the index of work quotas set up for the Bau/Holz union of the FDGB in May 1949 was based on the assumption that productivity would be lower than before the war. The same principle was adopted at the potassium mines in Thuringia, while in the copper mines in Mansfeld the miners' quotas were set at 70 per cent of the prewar level. In the Max-Hütte output was fixed at 148 tons per shift although 190–200 tons would have been entirely feasible. As a result wages in the Max-Hütte rose by 64 per cent in the course of a single year; in the same period productivity sank by roughly 24 per cent.

Although the heads of the Soviet Military Administration had already called for higher productivity in their resolution of October 9, 1947 (No. 234) and although the agencies responsible for establishing "technically based work quotas" had been set up as early as September 1948 and were fully coordinated under a central administration by January 1949, it seems that little real progress was made in the initial stages. In a speech delivered on June 14, 1951 Gerhard Ziller stated that of the 8 million norms laid down for machine construction only 15 to 20 per cent were based on technical criteria. The figures given in May 1953 by Heinrich Rau, the deputy minister president, were 27 per cent for general machine construction and only 13.5 per cent for heavy machine construction. According to Rau no more than 37.2 per cent of industrial norms were technically based at that time. It is, of course, possible that the SED may have doctored these figures in order to justify their policy. But, even allowing for this, it is quite obvious that the introduction of such quotas had been a very slow process. We must bear in mind, however, that the "technically based work quotas" set up in the GDR lay "roughly midway between average and maximum output." In other words, the SED was intent on establishing "progressive work quotas as a mean." We should also remember that, according to communist ideology, the raising of work norms is a never-

ending process: each new technical installation supposedly makes for better working conditions and these
in turn supposedly make for greater productivity. But,
be that as it may, what happened in the GDR was that
for years on end numerous works remained completely
unaffected by the new policy; no technically based quotas
were introduced in these works, which continued to use
traditional quotas based on the productivity statistics of
previous years.

The slow progress made in the introduction of technically based norms was doubtless due in no small measure to the recalcitrance of the workers and of many
works and union managements. According to a report in
Die Tägliche Rundschau of June 3, 1949 various works
managements in the smelting, mining, and chemical industries had not even begun to revise their quotas a full
nine months after the publication of the relevant regulations. In Mecklenburg (again according to *Die Tägliche
Rundschau*) a union official, who argued for the retention
of the old "low" quotas, pointed out quite correctly that
in their time the capitalists had also introduced new
methods of increasing productivity only to use them as an
excuse for oppressing the workers by imposing higher
work quotas. As late as May 1953, *Die Einheit*, the theoretical party magazine, reported that in many places die-
hard attitudes prevailed and that in the course of the preceding twelve months the number of technically based
quotas in use had actually decreased.[7]

In view of all this, it is understandable that the party
tried to raise work quotas in the GDR. On the other
hand, it must be remembered that the only way in which
certain groups of workers could ensure even a moderate

livelihood was by overfulfilling their low quotas, thus obtaining a higher wage. Low-paid, simple jobs, for example, had been excluded from the pay increases granted in 1952 and the wages of the workers in these groups were so low that without such bonuses they could not hope to make ends meet. Owing to sharp increases in the cost of living, many of those in the better-paid groups also depended on this additional income. But the principal reason why the demand for higher quotas met with such determined resistance from the workers was the shortage of food, which had become particularly acute from the autumn of 1952 onward. That year the harvest had fallen far below expectations. In fact, the yield had been so low that no returns were ever published: the report of the state planning commission, which appeared in 1953, made no reference whatsoever to agriculture. The bad harvest was partly due to a combination of spring frosts and a wet autumn, but in particular to the exodus of several thousand farmers, who had fled from the GDR because they could not cope with the crippling burden of taxation, because they were unable to fulfill their quotas, or because they did not want to join an agricultural cooperative.

In 1951 a total of 4,343 farmers fled to the West; in 1952 the figure was 14,141. By the end of 1952 some 300,000 acres, roughly 13 per cent of the agricultural land in the GDR, had been abandoned in this way and subsequently taken over by the state. Meanwhile, the exodus of farmers continued, and in 1953 no fewer than 37,296 left the GDR.*

Two more reasons for the shortage of food in the shops

* These figures do not include the farmers' relatives, who accompanied them to the West.

were the government's decision in 1952 to stockpile large quantities of foodstuffs and the growing needs of the police forces, who received better rations than the rest of the population.

The regime tried to lay the responsibility for the food crisis at the door of the remaining representatives of capitalist society in the GDR. The "big farmers" (those owning more than eight acres, who were regarded as capitalists because they employed laborers) found themselves exposed to violent attacks in the press, to sudden arrest and expropriation. But there were other scapegoats as well: the SED claimed that "capitalist elements" had even infiltrated the government and systematically sabotaged the distribution of food; the Minister of Trade and Food, Dr. Hamann (LDP) and the Secretaries of State Albrecht (DBD) and Baender (SED) were arrested in the late autumn of 1952 and subsequently tried and condemned.

Ulbricht regarded such crises as inevitable. Had not Stalin repeatedly maintained that the class struggle would grow more acute during the transition to socialism? Ulbricht agreed with Stalin wholeheartedly. For him it was "an obvious fact and completely in keeping with the laws [of historical development] that the disruptions originated in the sphere of capitalist production;" he did not doubt for a moment that "with regard to the difficulties encountered in the production and distribution of food the representatives of the spent capitalist forces . . . tried to exploit the economic laws of capitalism in every possible way in their campaign to prevent the establishment of the foundations of socialism" or that "the capitalist forces will step up this campaign in order to hinder the full realization of the agricultural potential [of the

GDR] by the development of the agricultural coopera-
tives." [8]

The crisis grew still more acute. Before the Second
Party Conference, in the first six months of 1952, 72,000
people left the GDR. In the second half of the same year
this figure rose to 110,000 and in the first half of 1953 to
225,000. By the end of April 1953 the Central Office for
National Statistics was forced to admit that the economic
plan for the first quarter of 1953 (which had been encumbered with deficits carried forward from the previous
year) had not been fulfilled: the output of a large number of important products had fallen far short of the stipulated target. For the first time since 1947 there was a real
food crisis. By its "Decree to Prevent Speculation in Foodstuffs and Industrial Goods" of November 1952 the government prohibited sales to West Berliners, which until
then had been encouraged since they demonstrated the
viability and attractiveness of the socialist economic
system.

But a far more serious measure was the "Decree Relat-
ing to the Issue of Ration Cards in the GDR and in the
Democratic Sector of Greater Berlin," which came into
force at the beginning of April 1953. By the terms of this
decree, ration cards were withdrawn from all self-employed persons, for the most part small retailers, craftsmen and people in freelance professions, who were then
obliged to buy "free" goods in the HO at much higher
prices. Some two million people were affected by this
measure, for it applied, not only to all self-employed
persons, but also to their families. At the same time the
regime sought to ensure that the workers were adequately
fed by launching a government program—"Preferential

Treatment for Important Branches of Industry"—whereby special stores were opened up on factory and works sites. But these measures appear to have made little impact, for in the spring of 1953 the personnel in a whole series of works walked off the job in protest against the food shortage and the higher quotas demanded by the regime.

This catastrophic situation had not gone unnoticed by the SED leadership. As early as February 1953 the majority of the members of the Politburo recognized that speedy action was needed to bring about an improvement. But they also realized that this could not be effected by the GDR itself.

When Stalin died on March 5, Grotewohl headed the GDR delegation to the funeral ceremonies and, while in Moscow, he put out feelers. But he was told that the GDR could not expect to receive any large scale supplies of food from the Soviet Union and would have to solve its own problems as best it could. At the beginning of April the party leadership made an official appeal for help, in which it asked Moscow "to consider the situation that had arisen and to provide both moral and material support." [9] In their reply on April 15 the Soviet leaders informed their German comrades that there could be no question of financial or material aid and urged them to adopt a softer line.

But Ulbricht and his followers paid no heed to this advice. In a speech published in *Das Neue Deutschland* on April 16, 1953 the General Secretary of the SED paid tribute to "the wise leader of socialist development, J. W. Stalin," and called for "greater vigilance" and "the unmasking of agents and disruptive elements;" he attributed all current difficulties to "sabotage, arson and espionage," and declared that the most urgent task facing the state was the "abolition of outmoded work norms."

When the Central Committee of the SED convened for its thirteenth session on May 14, it first discussed the latest ramifications of the Slansky trial in Prague.[10] The resolution passed as a result of this discussion illustrates the spirit of the Central Committee at that time. It also casts a revealing light on the political climate of the GDR in May 1953 and proves beyond all doubt that, far from taking Moscow's advice and following a new line, the SED was actually trying to step up its old Stalinist line. In this document the members of the Central Committee stressed the fact that "the path to socialism is a hard struggle against the desperate attempts of the class enemy to reimpose the old accursed system of capitalism;" they attacked the destructive activities of "bourgeois elements and of the whole iniquitous rabble of Trotskyites, Zionists, freemasons, traitors and morally depraved individuals;" they branded the "socalled theory of the weakening class struggle," said to be a concomitant of the establishment of socialism, as a fiction put out by enemies of the state; they discovered "blindness," "slovenliness," and "lack of vigilance" on all sides and declared war on "saboteurs," "parasites," and "traitors." [11]

The Committee then turned to the question of higher quotas. Since appeals for voluntary cooperation had proved ineffectual, it was decided that the ministers and secretaries of state should be instructed to take "all necessary steps to remedy the abuses in the sphere of work quotas at a normal level and to raise those of crucial importance to [national] production by an average of at least 10 per cent before June 1, 1953." [12] This resolution of the Central Committee was endorsed by the Council of Ministers of the GDR, which decreed that the quotas in all publicly owned works were to be raised by a minimum of 10 per cent by June 30, 1953. There are two points worth noting here. Contrary to customary practice, the resolution passed by the Central Committee was not dealt with by the Council of Ministers until fully two weeks later; and then, when it was implemented, the date fixed for raising the quotas was not June 1—as stipulated by the Central Committee—but June 30. Presumably the Council of Ministers was better aware of the problems attendant on this decision. Certainly, it felt the need for a transitional period, in which to persuade the workers of the desirability of the new quotas. But there was a further reason why June 30, 1953, was a particularly suitable choice. It was Ulbricht's sixtieth birthday, a political red letter day, on which the Council of Ministers hoped to demonstrate the success of its campaign to engender a spirit of commitment and friendly competition among the workers.

The New Line

Stalin's death had brought new men to power in Moscow. Although we now know that the new Soviet leaders were constantly vying with one another at that time, political infighting was necessarily subordinated to the general aim of safeguarding the Kremlin's position both at home and abroad during this difficult transitional period.

Externally, the Soviet Union found itself isolated. By

reestablishing diplomatic relations and removing possible grounds for conflict in the international sphere it was hoped that the country's external position would be strengthened, its prestige increased, and the tension between the great powers reduced, thus affording the new administration a breathing space in which to resolve its difficulties at home. Within a week of Stalin's death the Soviets proposed a three power conference to discuss questions of air safety in German air space following the Anglo-Soviet incident in the Berlin corridor of March 12. They also withdrew their objections to the new Secretary General of the United Nations, Dag Hammarskjöld, renounced their territorial claims on Turkey and reestablished diplomatic relations with Israel and Yugoslavia. Most important of all, they gave a fresh impetus to the armistice negotiations in Korea, which had become bogged down: by the end of March the Chinese and North Koreans agreed to an exchange of wounded; shortly afterward they gave their assent to a proposal whereby Chinese and North Korean prisoners should be allowed to choose between repatriation to China or North Korea and emigration to Formosa or South Korea; on July 27, 1953 the armistice was duly signed.

All these Soviet initiatives were followed with great interest in the West, where the leading statesmen of the day, hopeful that the Soviet Union was embarking on a more realistic policy, began to consider the possibility of a summit conference. President Eisenhower's major speech of April 16, in which feelers were put out to establish the feasibility of a détente, was reproduced in *Pravda* without distortion or editorial ridicule; the Soviet Union announced that it was prepared to participate in discussions of any issues that were a cause of concern. On April 28 *Pravda* advocated a nonaggression pact between the four great powers, and on May 24 responded favorably to Churchill's suggestion in the House of Commons on April 20, and again on May 11, that a summit conference should be convened.

Meanwhile, in its internal affairs the Soviet Union quietly pursued a policy of de-Stalinization. An amnesty was declared for political detainees, the Kremlin doctors (who had been arrested in November 1952 on suspicion of having murdered top Soviet leaders) were rehabilitated, the state security service was censured, and a campaign was launched for greater social justice. But the principal innovation made by the new Soviet leaders was in the economic sphere. One of the first things Malenkov did when he came to power was to promise to step up the production of consumer goods, a promise that was fulfilled insofar as the growth rate of the consumer goods industry exceeded that of heavy industry in 1953 for the first time in many years. By denying the preeminence of the means of production, the new leaders departed, albeit temporarily, from the principle which Stalin had laid down in his political testament of 1952 as a necessary condition of constant economic growth.

For the time being the Soviet leaders were clearly intent on bringing about a general relaxation of tension: in the sphere of foreign policy they entered into negotiations with the western powers while at home they granted greater individual freedom and provided more consumer goods, both for their own people and for the peoples of the eastern bloc countries. The Soviets hoped to create a favorable impression abroad which would open up new possibilities for Soviet foreign policy initiatives, and it seems distinctly possible that Germany was selected as a guinea pig for this project. Certainly, the "new line" was first introduced in the GDR, which was then in a particularly precarious situation, due partly to the ill-considered and harsh policy which it had pursued since the second Party Conference and partly to its long open frontier in the west. Shortly afterwards the new line was adopted by Hungary, then by Rumania and Bulgaria, by Czechoslovakia and, finally, by Poland.

On April 22 the political adviser to the Soviet Control Commission in Berlin, Vladimir Semyonov, was recalled to Moscow, apparently to report on the German situation. On May 28—the day on which the Council of Ministers of the GDR put in effect the resolution calling for higher norms—the Soviet government withdrew its control commission and replaced it by a high commission headed by Semyonov, who returned to Berlin on June 5.

The Soviet leaders then made another approach to the Politburo of the SED, reiterating the doubts and concern which they felt with regard to current developments in the GDR and insisting on a revision of policy. The Politburo was told that it could expect no special aid from the Soviet Union, which needed all the resources it could muster in order to raise the standard of living of its own people. Consequently, the SED would have to change its economic policy and take any measures calculated to improve living conditions in the GDR as quickly as possible. Instead of attaching such great importance to the celebrations for his sixtieth birthday (for which preparations had been underway for months on end in every part of the GDR) the Soviet leaders recommended to their German comrades that Ulbricht would do better to take a leaf out of Lenin's book, who—as Semyonov smilingly reminded the members of the Politburo—had celebrated his sixtieth birthday by inviting a few friends around for the evening. Semyonov also submitted to the Politburo a document outlining the principal points of the resolutions which Moscow expected the SED leaders to pass. These were accepted without demur.

On June 9, 1953, the Politburo of the SED, which had been in permanent session ever since Semyonov's return, decided to recommend to the government of the GDR that it should implement a series of measures calculated to bring about the necessary improvement in the standard of living of all sections of the population and to strengthen their legal rights. The government was advised to make cuts in its program for the build-up of heavy industry and to step up the production of consumer goods. The oppressive taxes levied on farmers, craftsmen, wholesalers and retailers and on industrial, construction and transportation firms were to be abolished; private businesses closed down by the authorities were to be allowed to start up again; farmers who had fled to the West and wished to return were to have their lands restored and to receive help in the form of credit, machines and seed; in fact, all refugees returning from the West were to be helped in every possible way and reinstated in their former possessions. Interzonal passes and permits for West Germans to visit the GDR were to be issued more freely in future and scientists and artists living in the GDR were to be allowed to attend conferences and meetings in West Germany. Children removed from school because of their religious beliefs were to be readmitted and allowed to take any examinations they had missed during their absence. Students expelled from the universities were to be reenrolled. Prisoners on remand accused of minor offenses were to be released; those already sentenced were to be pardoned. In the future all citizens were to be entitled to ration cards. Recent price rises were to be withdrawn and reduced fares and cheap return tickets reintroduced for certain types of journey on public transport. In short, most of the coercive measures taken during the preceding twelve months were to be rescinded and the transformation of the GDR into a people's democracy, which had been gathering speed since July 1952, was to be halted. The Politburo openly admitted that "the interests of certain sections of the population such as small farmers, retailers, tradesmen and the intelligentsia" had been neglected with the result that many people had left the Republic. After insisting that this state of affairs could not be allowed to continue, the Politburo stated quite categorically that it was dedicated to the "great goal of German reunification," which called for measures on both sides that would "materially facilitate a rapprochement between the two parts of Germany." In its resolution the Politburo also admitted that the SED and the government of the GDR had perpetrated "a series of errors in the past," an admission that was echoed by *Die Tägliche Rundschau,* the mouthpiece of the Soviet occupation forces, in a leading article on June 13, which stated that the former Soviet control commission had been "responsible to some extent for the errors that had been committed."

On June 11 the Politburo's resolution appeared without any editorial comment in *Das Neue Deutschland.* On the same day the Council of Ministers put in effect all the measures proposed by the Soviet authorities.

But, although no attempt was made to prepare by advance propaganda for this change of course, neither the abruptness of the change nor the change itself constituted the principal cause of the disturbances which broke out a week later, on June 16 and 17, 1953. The major motivating factor here was provided by two attendant circumstances, both of which could have been avoided.

An Autocratic Decision

The fact that the new line was introduced by a resolution taken in the Politburo was to have dire consequences for the SED.

Although the Politburo is described in the party statutes of the SED as a political bureau set up by the Central Committee to carry out any necessary "political work" when the Committee is not in session, it is well known to students of politics—notably from the history of the communist party in the Soviet Union—that in communist countries real power is invariably vested in the Politburo.

But up to June 9, 1953 the party leaders in the GDR had taken great care to conceal this fact from the man in the street. In the majority of cases the resolutions passed by the all-powerful Politburo in its weekly sessions were kept secret. On the rare occasions when they were intended for publication—as in the case of the directive instructing the Council of Ministers to legislate for higher quotas—they appeared as resolutions of the Central Committee. For, according to the SED statute, "between Party Congresses" (which are normally convened every four years) the Central Committee is "the supreme organ of the party." Theoretically, therefore, it functions as a kind of parliament for the party.

But not even the Central Committee was authorized to legislate for the kind of changes made on June 9. Because of the broad scope and the fundamental importance of these proposals a Party Congress or, failing this, a Party Conference should have been convened. According to the SED statutes Party Congresses "decide the party program and determine the general line and the tactics of the party" while Party Conferences (which, unlike Party Congresses, can be arranged at short notice) deal with "urgent" questions of party policy and tactics. Since the establishment of socialism had been authorized by the Party Conference of July 1952 and since it was clearly impracticable to wait for a Party Congress to be arranged (although, strictly speaking, this was the only body really competent to deal with such matters), the SED leaders should have convened a further Party Conference when they decided to call a temporary halt to this project.

There were, of course, good reasons why the Politburo did not call a conference or even arrange a session of the Central Committee. If it had done so, every aspect of SED policy would have come up for discussion, and it would have been quite impossible to reconcile the program for the development of socialism with the new line that had ousted it. Since this was so, how could the leaders have avoided apportioning blame for the failure of their socialist policy? In the early days of June rumors circulated among the SED functionaries in Berlin that Semyonov had severely censured the present leaders of the party and that Rudolf Herrnstadt had been asked to submit a list of alternate candidates for the top positions in the SED. But Ulbricht and his followers were also faced with another and more immediate threat at that time: Franz Dahlem, who had been an opponent of Walter Ulbricht's for decades, had been expelled from the Central Committee at its last plenary session on May 14, 1953, and consequently from the Politburo, where he had been the most important figure apart from the General Secretary, on the flimsy pretext that he had failed to detect "the attempts of imperialist agents to penetrate the party." Dahlem, who had been responsible for party organization and personnel and for SED activities in West Germany, had fought in Spain, emigrated to the West, and been detained in a National Socialist concentration camp, was highly regarded by all those party members who were opposed to the "Moscow emigrants" and, above all, to Ulbricht. It seemed probable, therefore, that Dahlem's friends would try to exploit the present leadership crisis in order to reopen his case.

But the New Quotas Remain

However, although the threat of public recriminations would have been reason enough for refusing to convene the Central Committee, the party leaders also had other equally cogent grounds for doing so, since they were determined to avoid a discussion of the new quotas at all costs. At a meeting of the Berlin District Headquarters of the SED, Fritz Ebert, the Oberbürgermeister of East Berlin and a member of the Politburo, openly admitted that the reason why the Central Committee was not being convened was that the party wished to avoid a discussion of the Dahlem case and of the new quotas. Those who opposed the higher quotas, he said, were undermining the new line.

In actual fact, Ebert's argument was perfectly logical. If the standard of living was to be suddenly raised in an impoverished and exhausted country like the GDR without material support from the Soviet Union, and if—as Bruno Leuschner ironically observed at a collegiate meeting of the Planning Commission[13]—the Politburo suddenly wanted to see "larks falling ready roasted from a Utopian sky," then higher productivity was even more necessary than before. In fact, the Planning Commission doubted whether the GDR could afford this expensive new program; they first asked themselves whether these undertakings would not have to be withdrawn at some future date. Consequently, it was no accident that the new legislation authorizing the imposition of higher quotas was the only one of the coercive measures introduced during the period of socialist development not to be mentioned—let alone revoked—in the resolutions passed by the Politburo and the Council of Ministers. On the contrary, it was a carefuly considered policy. But the decision to retain the new quotas also shows how completely out of touch with popular feeling the party leaders were. For it was believed in many quarters, especially among the workers, that these quotas should be revised and that the party and the government, having made concessions to capitalist groups such as the big farmers and private industrialists, should also adopt a more accommodating attitude to the working class. This was also the view of many party members.

It was at this point that the secret policies pursued by

the Politburo came home to roost. For its premature change of course, for which not even party members had been prepared, created total confusion at all levels of the party, of industry and of government administration.

The uncertainty within the party and the ambiguity of the new line were both reflected in an article that appeared in *Das Neue Deutschland* on June 14. Under the title "It is Time to Lay Aside the Bludgeon" the way in which the new quotas had been introduced was severely criticized. Bruno Baum, a member of the Secretariat of the Berlin SED District Headquarters, was actually mentioned by name and censured for having stated in the course of a discussion with party functionaries of the Berlin construction industry at the end of May (some two weeks before the introduction of the new line) that it is "sometimes necessary to make examples" and for suggesting that one of the brigades of construction workers that had disrupted work discipline on its work site (by demonstrating against the higher quotas) should be dismissed without notice. This suggestion was not endorsed by *Das Neue Deutschland* (the principal mouthpiece of the SED) which stated that the government and party resolutions calling for higher quotas should not be imposed "dictatorially." The time had come, the author of the article suggested, to cast aside "false optimism," "self-deception," and "arrogance." Higher quotas, he said, should only be made legally binding after the workers had been "convinced" of their necessity. To proceed in any other way would cause resentment among the workers to the detriment of industry.

What was this supposed to mean? Although neither the resolution of the Central Committee of May 14 nor the

directive of the Council of Ministers of May 28 were referred to as such in *Das Neue Deutschland,* their contents
—the raising of the work quotas by legislative order—
were certainly called into question. Prior to May 28 the
party had tried in vain over a period of many months
to persuade the workers to accept the higher quotas
voluntarily. And now that *Das Neue Deutschland* was insisting that the quotas should not be raised until the
workers had been "convinced" of the importance of this
measure, it looked very much as if the SED intended to
return to this voluntary procedure in the implementation
of its new line.

At all events, on Monday, May 15, this article was
passed from hand to hand among the construction workers on the Stalin-Allee, who were encouraged to learn
that the "bludgeoning methods" used in the past had
been condemned in print. Consequently, when reports
reached the Politburo on June 16 that the construction
workers were demonstrating, the senior editor of *Das
Neue Deutschland,* Rudolf Herrnstadt, was told by his
colleagues in the Politburo that his article of June 14 was
the cause of all the trouble.

But this charge was only partially justified. On June 16
Die Tribüne (the union mouthpiece) had also published
an article in which Otto Lehmann, a member of the
FDGB executive, stated unequivocally that the resolutions of May 28 authorizing higher quotas were "completely in order," would be retained, and must be put
into effect. It was this article that actually sparked off
the demonstration by the building workers on the Stalin-
Allee. Otto Nuschke, the deputy Minister President of the
GDR, subsequently admitted in a radio interview with

RIAS (Radio in the American Sector) that this had "sparked off the wave of unrest."

It was the combined effect of several different factors that brought about a situation in the GDR in the middle of June 1953 that was conducive to demonstrations by the workers: the sudden change of policy by the Politburo, the confusion which this created among the communist functionaries and the widespread uncertainty among the population at large about what was going to happen about the new quotas.

But why were the construction workers the first to act?

The Construction Workers

To answer this question it is necessary to consider the special working conditions that obtained in the construction industry. As a group construction workers differ from the great majority of other workers in one essential respect: theirs is a seasonal trade and, when winter comes, they are invariably laid off. Consequently, they have never been bound by considerations of loyalty to a specific firm or a specific employer. In fact, their inevitable redundancy in the autumn has always forced the building workers to defend their interests resolutely during the summer months, so as to have sufficient funds to see them through the winter. They have always been prepared to take strike action when necessary, even if it meant sacrificing several months' pay. This explains the militant reputation enjoyed by the German construction trade unions. (The workers' associations known in Germany prior to 1933 as *Gelbe Verbände* [Yellow Associations], which received financial support from the employers and consequently never had recourse to strike action when negotiating working conditions for their members, were not to be found in the construction industry.) In their strikes and demonstrations the construction workers were fortunate in that most of them were very hardy, having been accustomed to working in the open air in every kind of weather. This was an important factor in June 1953, for on June 16 it poured down rain.

In the light of what has been said it is understandable that the construction workers in the GDR and in East Berlin should have offered fierce resistance to any attempts to undermine their tariff rights by the introduction of "modern" productivity rates.

In East Berlin they successfully defended their old piece rates and time allowances in the face of bitter attacks in the SED and FDGB press, which called for the introduction of technically based quotas. In one newspaper article Minister Gerhard Ziller, who later became Secretary of the Central Committee of the SED, pointed out that on certain construction sites the workers were consistently overfulfilling their quotas by 300 to 350 per cent with the result that men laying composition floors were earning between five and nine marks an hour; even unskilled laborers were receiving three marks an hour. In this article Ziller also revealed why it was that the construction workers had been so successful in opposing the SED and the FDGB. He explained that many of the functionaries in the carpenter's union were "old diehards," that the workers had staged a deliberate "slowdown" when the authorities had tried to establish realistic norms and that, in the end, the officials concerned had simply "capitulated" in the face of the "antiquated views of their colleagues." [14]

The fact that the construction industry was the last major branch of industry to be nationalized in the GDR was also due in no small measure to the energetic support given by the building workers to individual employers, who were allowed to continue trading for some considerable time without undue interference from the state.

The party and union functionaries responsible for concluding the collective agreements within the construction industry in 1951 found they had a particularly difficult task on their hands. Of the 350 collective agreements due to be concluded by the Bau/Holz union only 5 had been approved by the end of July, which was less than 2 per cent of the total. This meant that construction lagged behind all other industries, for by that time the chemical industry had concluded 6 per cent of its collective agreements, the textile and leather industry 12 per cent, the metallurgical industry 20 per cent and the mining industry no less than 67 per cent.

In 1952, when the collective agreements were still essentially voluntary, the commitments entered into by the nationalized construction firms were smaller than those undertaken by other branches of industry: the construction workers promised to raise gross production by 17 per cent and productivity by 10 per cent and to reduce costs by 11 per cent whereas the iron ore miners and foundry workers proposed to boost their gross production by 28 per cent and to reduce costs by 14.6 per cent.

Moreover, the construction workers failed to fulfill even these relatively modest commitments. Building costs were not reduced. On the contrary, the cost of new homes rose by 35 to 40 per cent between 1950 and 1953. The losses incurred by the Berlin *Bau-Union* during this period were so great that this concern had to be liquidated in January 1953.

It is hardly surprising, in view of the unsatisfactory situation in the construction industry, that from January 1953 onward the communist press should have regarded the introduction of higher norms for construction workers as a matter of particular urgency.

The reaction of the workers to this demand was revealed by an article in *Der Neue Weg*, a journal concerned with the practical ramifications of SED policy. According to this article, it took eighteen months of "fierce discussion and hard struggle" before the workers of the Berlin Builders' Union agreed to work a new system that would cut down on costs, and even then a "number of the workers adopted a negative, if not indeed a hostile, attitude" because "the introduction of new methods invariably leads to higher quotas, which could result in lower wages." [15]

But, despite the introduction of this new system, which the authorities claimed was eventually to be used on every construction site in Berlin, it seems that the construction workers were still loth to accept higher quotas. At the beginning of April 1953 *Der Neue Weg* likened the building procedures in the GDR to those employed in Ancient Egypt for "the building of the pyramids" [16] while on April 10 *Das Neue Deutschland* complained that nobody on the Stalin-Allee was doing anything about the "inappropriate and unhealthy quotas" even though these were being overfulfilled by "upwards of 200 per cent" and even though the construction firms engaged on the Stalin-Allee project had incurred an overall loss of 3.8 million marks in the first two months of 1953 alone.[17] In the same article *Das Neue Deutschland* also reported on a party activist meeting held on the Stalin-Allee, at which the leaders of the various workers' brigades undertook to "persuade their men to raise the work norms by an average of 15 per cent by May 1." But nothing came of this undertaking either.

There were good reasons why the construction workers were able to turn a deaf ear to the demands of the party. By the beginning of 1953 there was a shortage of some 40,000 workers in the East German construction industry. Many had fled to the West and many more, who lived in East Berlin, had found no difficulty in obtaining employment in West Berlin. Until the wall was erected in 1961 many thousands of East German building workers commuted between the city sectors in this way. From 1951 onwards there had been a large scale building program in West Berlin and consequently there was a critical shortage of construction workers throughout the entire city. It was because it had to compete with private firms in West Berlin that the SED was so chary about bringing pressure to bear on its workers. The regime attached great importance to the completion of the Stalin-Allee. This was the "first Socialist street in Germany" and it was imperative, for propaganda reasons, that the work there should proceed quickly. And so for a long time the SED was prepared to accept a relatively low standard of productivity and pay high wages (between 450 and 650 marks per month, which was a lot of money at that time). On May 28 the question of higher quotas was discussed once again, this time at a meeting of brigade leaders and activists * of the VEB Wohnungsbau (nationalized in-

* In the Soviet Zone workers distinguished for above-average output were called activists.

dustry for the erection of private dwellings), whose workers were engaged on the Stalin-Allee project. After the meeting *Das Neue Deutschland* was obliged to report that the majority of those present had voted against a general increase in work quotas.[18] Toward the end of May the workers on a number of sites walked off the job when an attempt was made to pressure them into accepting higher quotas on a voluntary basis. Meanwhile, the Council of Ministers published its directive of May 28 imposing a general increase of 10 per cent in all work quotas, which was to be implemented by June 30. The imposition of higher quotas and the consequent threat of wage reductions produced unrest, stoppages and finally, on June 16, strike action.

June 16

In the aftermath of June 17 the communists repeatedly claimed that the events of that day were the outcome of a well-prepared and deeplaid plot, that June 17 was in fact a sort of D-day for the western powers. Later we shall discuss the influence exerted by the West on the events in the GDR on June 17 after the news of the previous day's demonstrations had broken. Meanwhile, if we consider the outbreak and course of the demonstrations of June 16, we find no evidence whatsoever to suggest that any attempt was made by western agents to influence the construction workers of the GDR either on or before that day. This is also apparent from the initial reactions of various members of the GDR government, who stated publicly that the demonstrations were completely permissible and even suggested that they were justified. The Minister for Industry Fritz Selbmann (SED) in a speech before the House of Ministries of June 16, the deputy Minister President Otto Nuschke in his RIAS interview of June 17, the Minister President Otto Grotewohl in various speeches to works personnel after June 17 and, finally, the Minister of Justice Max Fechner (SED) in an interview that was printed in *Das Neue Deutschland* on June 30 after first being cleared by the Minister President's press office—they all conceded that, in staging their demonstration, the construction workers had acted on their own initiative and not at the instigation of western agents provocateurs.

But whether the demonstrations were completely spontaneous or whether they were planned in advance by the construction workers themselves is not so easily determined. We know that from June 1 onward there had been individual instances of unrest on various construction sites, but these had all been settled at a local level by FDGB and SED functionaries, who had set up small discussion groups. We also know that the question of higher quotas and the possibility of a walk-off were discussed by members of the VEB Industriebau (nationalized industry for the erection of industrial installations) and the VEB Wohnungsbau on a steamer excursion which was made on June 13 but which had been planned several weeks in advance. What we do not know is whether, on this excursion, the workers arranged to stage simultaneous stoppages at a wide variety of sites on the following Monday, June 15. This is not indicated by western sources. Nor can it be inferred from the eyewitness reports.

In May 1954, when a number of construction workers from the Stalin-Allee were charged with conspiracy before the East Berlin municipal court, the authorities attempted to prove that on this outing a firm decision was

taken to call a stoppage for June 15.[19] But this attempt
failed. Even assuming that all the incidents described by
the prosecution actually took place, this merely means
that the possibility of staging a walkoff was discussed and
was advocated by some of those present. It does not mean
that a firm decision was taken. In point of fact, as was
recorded in the transcript of the trial, the only workers
who refused to start work were those engaged on the construction of the new hospital in Friedrichshain. On all
other sites in East Berlin the day started normally. It was
only when they heard that their colleagues on the hospital
site in Friedrichshain had come out that the workers on
two other construction sites—Block 40 on the Stalin-
Allee and the new administrative block for the People's
Police in Friedrichshain—walked off. On both of these
sites the workers held meetings to discuss the terms of a
petition dealing with the question of work quotas which
they proposed to present to Minister President Otto
Grotewohl.

At Block 40 two delegates were selected to present to
the government a petition in which the workers asked for
the new norms to be withdrawn. But at that point the
union leaders on the site asked the delegates to await the
arrival of a representative from their central office who
was supposed to be on his way to clarify the whole question of the work norms. Thinking that this representative
might perhaps have been authorized to announce the
withdrawal of the new quotas the two delegates agreed
to wait. But they waited in vain. By the end of the day
the representative had still not put in an appearance,
whereupon the workers at Block 40 and their two delegates made their way home.

The construction workers in Friedrichshain had already

submitted their petition to the Minister President. On the evening of June 15 Otto Grotewohl's secretary appeared at the SED District Headquarters in Berlin with a letter signed by the workers employed on the hospital site in Friedrichshain, which called for the immediate withdrawal of the higher quotas. The workers complained that the only people to benefit from the new line were the capitalists. They declared their intention of sending a delegation to the Minister President on the next day, Tuesday June 16, and threatened strike action unless the new quotas were withdrawn by then.

Through his secretary Grotewohl asked the officials at SED Headquarters, who were better acquainted with local conditions, to assess the situation and advise him as to what action should be taken. In reply Bruno Baum suggested that there was nothing to be feared provided the party did not panic and a firm line was adopted from the outset. He was of the opinion that, once the delegation entered the hallowed precincts of the Minister President's official residence, its members would be so overawed that they would prove quite docile. After all, that sort of thing had happened often enough under the capitalists: time and again in the past, workers' delegates had been fobbed off with a few empty phrases and had then basked in pride for the rest of their lives because they had been received by a government official. And so Baum advised Grotewohl to remain calm, to disregard the letter and, when he received the delegates, to treat them with courtesy but refuse to yield on the one essential point: the absolute necessity for higher quotas and strict economy. When Grotewohl's secretary left SED Headquarters she was much relieved.

On the morning of June 16, instead of sending their delegates to Grotewohl as intended, the workers at Block 40 on the Stalin-Allee formed a procession and marched in a body to the union and government headquarters in order to press their demands. There were two reasons for this change of plan.

In the first place Otto Lehmann's article, which had appeared that morning and was read out by one of the union representatives on the site, had raised the workers' anger to a new pitch and greatly increased their determination to take some kind of action against the new quotas. In the second place the workers decided, after lengthy discussions, that the two delegates chosen to represent them on the previous day should not be sent to deal with the union and the government on their own lest they should be arrested. Once this had been agreed, it was not long before the workers came round to the idea that they would all have to go: one man said the time had come for action, another suggested that all those who wanted action should move off to the right when the meeting broke up, whereupon, as one of the workers subsequently reported, "the whole crowd moved off to the right." Within a matter of minutes 300 construction workers from Block 40 were on the march. They carried a banner bearing the caption: "We Demand Lower Quotas."

Meanwhile, the workers from the hospital site in Friedrichshain had also decided to accompany their delegation to the Minister President in order to lend greater weight to their petition.

From the very outset the construction workers lacked firm leadership, for neither of the sites had elected a strike committee. We shall come to see in the further course of our study just how much the development of these demonstrations was determined by chance.

The first thing the construction workers from Block 40 and the hospital site in Friedrichshain did was to march to other sites on and near the Stalin-Allee to persuade their colleagues to join them in their demonstration. Then, greatly swollen, the procession moved on to the FDGB headquarters on the Wallstrasse. At this point the demonstrators' sole object was to press for the withdrawal of the new quotas.

When they discovered that the FDGB building was closed and none of the union officials was prepared to negotiate with them, the workers marched off to the House of the Ministries on the Leipziger Strasse. All this time the procession had been attracting new recruits. Nonetheless, even after it had left the Stalin-Allee, its hard core still consisted of construction workers, the entire personnel of various sites in the central districts of Berlin having joined the march en route. By the time the demonstrators had gathered in front of the House of the Ministries their strength was estimated at some ten thousand men. There too they found all doors barred and no sign of a negotiator, a fact which greatly incensed this large crowd.

Eventually Secretary of State Walther appeared but was mistaken for Walter Ulbricht's secretary and shouted down by the workers who wanted to hear from Ulbricht himself. Minister Selbmann (the only one of the top SED functionaries that day who had the courage to go out and face the workers) was also shouted down and subjected to personal abuse. "The next functionary to mount the speaker's rostrum," one of the demonstrators subsequently reported, "introduced himself as Professor Havemann." Havemann, it seems, tried to deliver a lecture to the workers on the basic facts and anomalies of their economic position. But, the demonstrator went on to say: "We didn't trust him. The meeting got noisier and noisier. And he was booed off, too."

The fact that they had disposed of a minister and a professor in such rapid succession doubtless increased the sense of corporate power felt by the massed demonstrators. They enjoyed themselves enormously, hurled streams of abuse and chanted for Grotewohl and Ulbricht to appear.

Meanwhile, as the protest meeting, which had started out as a perfectly orderly gathering, degenerated into rowdyism, it gradually became apparent that the workers did not really know what to do next.

A number of them sensed that the government was completely nonplussed by the course of events and felt that this weakness should be exploited; they also realized that they had a golden opportunity to obtain, not only a revision of the quotas, but new and more far reaching concessions of a political nature as well. These new political objectives were in fact formulated by various speakers, each of whom was greeted with tumultuous applause. But there was no one capable of taking charge of the meeting and directing the course of events, and the demonstration began to lose its impetus.

When Selbmann reappeared at two P.M. to explain that the Council of Ministers had withdrawn its decision to increase the work quotas by administrative order because it now realized that this had been a mistake, one of the construction workers pushed him aside and announced that a revision of the quotas was no longer enough: the government would have to accept the consequences of its mistaken policies and resign.

But it is typical of the uncertainty which had beset the demonstrators that, following this spirited call to action, nothing happened. When the general enthusiasm had subsided, no other speaker came forward and the crowd again grew uncertain.

Eventually another worker climbed on to the rostrum and again called on the government to resign. He said that they had waited long enough and suggested that, if Grotewohl or Ulbricht did not appear within half an hour, they should march off and proclaim a general strike.

This speaker was loudly acclaimed. But then the uncertainty returned and five minutes later the meeting broke up and the demonstrators marched back to their work sites.

On the way to the Stalin-Allee they met loudspeaker vans, which had been sent out by the government to announce the withdrawal of the new quotas. Many of the announcers in these vans expressed themselves in the legalistic and ambiguous jargon employed by the Politburo for the special resolution which it had drafted at noon. In that resolution, after stating that "better living conditions both for the workers and for the population as a whole [would only be] possible on the basis of higher productivity and greater production" the SED leaders stressed that work quotas could not, and should not, be raised by a legislative act but "only on the basis of conviction and voluntary cooperation." Consequently, it was recommended that "the obligatory increase in the work quotas imposed by individual ministries should be withdrawn . . . The government resolution of May 28 [would then be] reconsidered in collaboration with the unions." Was the increase in the work quotas to be withdrawn or merely reconsidered? And, if examination showed that they were justified, were they perhaps to be retained after all? And then again, why was the Politburo talking about a recommendation? Had not Selbmann already announced the withdrawal of the new quotas as an accomplished fact? The demonstrators who met the loudspeaker vans began to wonder if the authorities had been lying to them. Either the new quotas had been withdrawn, in which case there was no need to reconsider them, or else they had not, in which case Selbmann, acting as spokesman for the Council of Ministers, had told them a deliberate lie.

In actual fact, the Council of Ministers had probably not even convened at the time when Selbmann informed the workers that the government had withdrawn its resolution of May 28, for its senior members had been attending the weekly session of the Politburo, which was held every Tuesday morning and which, on that particular day, had gone on until late in the afternoon. But, despite its ambiguities, the text of the resolution promulgated by the Politburo on June 16 shows upon careful scrutiny that the party had no intention of adhering to its original plan of imposing higher quotas by administrative order. However, the Politburo was a creation of the party and as such had no legal powers of its own. Consequently, it could not withdraw a resolution that had been passed by the Council of Ministers; all it could do was recommend its withdrawal. But since, on the other hand, it was absolutely certain that the Council of Ministers would approve this

"recommendation" at the earliest possible moment Selbmann doubtless felt justified, after being informed of the
Politburo's decision over the telephone, in presenting the
withdrawal of the new norms to the workers as an established fact. This he did, with the result that the demonstration lost much of its impetus.

He could not know that the workers would be thrown
into confusion by the statements put out by the loudspeaker vans. In actual fact, therefore, it was not Selbmann who was at fault but the members of the Politburo.
Did they really expect the demonstrators to place the correct construction on their ambiguous text?

Meanwhile, scuffles had broken out. One loudspeaker
van was taken over by the demonstrators, who decided
that the time had come to make *their* opinion known.
They then tried out various speakers until, eventually,
they found one who knew what he was about.

This speaker was a key figure in the development of
the East German rising, for he hit upon the idea of using
the loudspeaker van to proclaim a general strike. Again
and again he called on the workers of East Berlin to
assemble at the Strausberger Platz on the morning of
June 17.

One of the demonstrators in front of the House of
Ministries had, of course, already called for a general
strike and his call was subsequently taken up by the other
construction workers who chanted it as they marched
back to the Stalin-Allee. At 4:30 P.M. on June 16, RIAS
also made a passing reference to the fact that individual
demonstrators had demanded a general strike outside the
House of Ministries, but this reference was withdrawn
from all subsequent news bulletins at the request of the

American authorities, who insisted that nothing capable of provoking strikes or demonstrations in the GDR should be included in RIAS programs.

It was not until the hijacked loudspeaker van began to put out its message that really substantial numbers of East Berliners learned of the workers' intention to continue their demonstrations. Those who heard the message hurried to friends and colleagues to discuss the situation and to work out ways and means of advising other workers within the city sector, who had not taken part in the demonstrations of June 16, of the action planned for the following day. And so, thanks to this one loudspeaker van, the call for a general strike spread through East Berlin like wildfire in the night of June 16 to 17.

Meanwhile, at about five o'clock on the afternoon of June 16, the demonstrators arrived back on the Stalin-Allee. The huge procession then broke up, the loudspeaker van was handed back and the workers made their way home.

JUNE 17

The demonstrations of June 16 all took place in East Berlin and were largely restricted to the construction workers. On June 17 there were strikes and demonstrations in more than 250 towns in the GDR. For many of these towns we possess no eyewitness accounts at all, and for many others we possess conflicting accounts. Only in relatively few cases, therefore, are we able to form an accurate assessment of what actually happened on June 17. This even holds true of the larger centers, such as East Berlin, where—despite the numerous eyewitness accounts available to us—the size of the area involved and the extensive nature of the strike action make for confusion. In fact, any attempt to present a comprehensive and detailed record of the countless highly varied incidents that took place both in Berlin and in the GDR could not possibly succeed, because of the lack of firsthand information. Nevertheless, from a careful analysis of the available material it is possible to construct a general picture of the rising, for, despite local variations, the events of June 17 tended to follow a basically similar pattern in all parts of the GDR.

A Résumé of the Rising

Extent of the Rising

Eastern and western sources are more or less in agreement as to the extent of the strike action of June 17. In July 1953 Grotewohl stated officially that strikes had occurred in 272 towns and that 300,000 workers had been involved,[20] while western estimates list 274 towns and 372,000 strikers.[21] The total work force in the GDR (excluding apprentices) at that time was 5.5 million.[22] It is immediately apparent, therefore, that only a relatively small proportion of the work force took part in the events of June 17: according to Grotewohl's version 5.5 per cent, according to the western version 6.8 per cent.

There are no official estimates, either from the East or from the West, as to how many members of the general public joined in the workers' demonstrations. The estimates made by eyewitnesses, which cannot of course be verified, are highly contradictory. For example, the number of people taking part in the demonstration at the Hallmarkt in Halle (Saale) was variously assessed at 60,000, 70,000, 80,000 and even 90,000.

But do such estimates really matter? There is a danger in paying too much attention to the large scale demonstrations which took place in certain towns, for they tend to create the impression that June 17 was a popular rising. In fact, the eyewitness reports prove conclusively that this was not the case. It was the industrial workers—actively supported by the youth of the GDR—who were responsible for the events of June 17. They started the rising and they were the dominant factor in every major demonstration. By contrast, the farmers were involved only in isolated incidents, and the middle classes and the intelligentsia played little or no part in the day's events. There were a few towns (Görlitz, for example) where intellectuals joined in the demonstrations, but these were the exception rather than the rule. On the face of it, this seems surprising, for the middle classes, the intelligentsia and the farmers were even more harshly treated than the workers. Why, then, were the workers the ones to strike?

Some twelve months before the June rising, Professor Hans Köhler, published a paper in which he argued that, far from being undermined by their bitter experiences, the solidarity of the workers in the eastern zone had actually been reinforced. This was why they had resisted the collective agreements so resolutely and why all attempts at intimidation on the part of the regime were bound to miscarry for, since the workers had nothing to lose, oppressive measures would only strengthen them in their opposition. Köhler detected a similar attitude among the farmers of the GDR, most of whom were in any case natural conservatives and consequently anti-SED, and all of whom had good reason to hate the communist state, which was seeking to confiscate their property and deprive them of their independence. But, as Köhler pointed out, the conditions of rural life were such that it was much easier for the authorities to keep a close watch on the activities of individuals in the country with the result that, at least apparently, the farmers had been obliged to conform to a far greater degree than had the industrial workers. As for the middle classes and the old intelligentsia, whose numbers had been greatly diminished by the flight of so many of their members to the West and whose social position had been undermined as a result of the economic and political programs instituted by the regime, Köhler regarded them as a completely demoralized force. Having allowed themselves to be intimidated by government pressures and threats, these two groups were prepared to make a deal with the regime in the hope of preserving what was left of their former status. Köhler wrote at the time: "The workers are prepared to act, the middle classes are not; they are hoping for help from outside." [23] In my view Köhler's assessment of the workers' attitude in 1952–1953 was entirely correct. Long before June 17, 1953, he pointed to the underlying reason why even those farmers who heard the strike call in time found it difficult to show their solidarity with the industrial workers. This, coupled with the fact that small rural communities simply do not lend themselves to strikes and demonstrations (which need the kind of mass audience provided by the big city if they are to be really effective), explains the farmers' failure to participate. As for Köhler's assessment of the middle classes, this was completely endorsed by the events of June 17. It has been suggested that the reticence shown by the middle classes on June 17 was because the higher quotas, which had been the original bone of contention, were primarily a matter of concern to the workers and that consequently the rising had "nothing to do with the middle classes." But this argument is specious. It has also been said that the middle classes were unaware that a strike had been called until the Soviet troops appeared on the streets. This simply is not true. It is quite obvious from the eyewitness accounts that news of what was happening spread with almost unbelievable speed.

The indecisiveness of the middle classes on June 17

seems to have been characteristic of their general attitude. Köhler tells us that, even prior to 1953, the members of this social group seldom became involved in political disputes. Was this because they had formed a more accurate assessment of future developments in the GDR or was it because they were afraid to take risks? Foresight and fear are often interdependent, and it could well be that the middle classes of East Germany were motivated by both. Nevertheless, the fact remains that they were far too enervated to enter into any commitment on their own account. They had seen that the wind of change was blowing in the GDR and had decided to knuckle under in the interests of survival. Instead of placing their trust in their own endeavors, they waited in the hope that things would improve, either as a result of a change in the leadership or as a result of western intervention.

Centers of Revolt

Apart from Berlin and its environs, the principal centers of revolt were to be found in the industrial areas of Central Germany (Bitterfeld, Halle, Leipzig, and Merseburg), in the Magdeburg district and, to a lesser extent, in the districts of Jena/Gera, Brandenburg, and Görlitz. 61,000 workers struck in and around East Berlin, 121,000 in the industrial areas of Central Germany, 38,000 in Magdeburg, 24,000 in Jena, 13,000 in Brandenburg and 10,000 in Görlitz. The strikes in all these districts and towns started in large industrial installations, which was the principal reason for their initial success. When the personnel of these big industrial concerns, such as the Leuna plant (28,000 men), the Buna plant (18,000 men), the Wolfen Paint Factory (12,000 men), and the Hennigsdorf plant (12,000 men), marched on to the streets in an orderly fashion, the local party and government functionaries were at a total loss. In other places, where there were no large factories or where these disregarded the strike call (in Dresden, for example), the demonstrations were either suppressed before they could get under way or were dispersed by SED functionaries skilled in the art of argument, who entered into discussions with the demonstrators and then talked them to a standstill.

There was almost no liaison between the various strike centers, although an ineffectual attempt was made to coordinate the strike action in the towns of Halle, Merseburg and Bitterfeld: the workers in Halle tried to get pamphlets printed, they discussed the feasibility of proclaiming a general strike for the whole of the GDR and they made telephone contact with the strike leaders in neighboring towns. But time ran out on them long before their initiatives could influence the course of events.

Industries Involved in the Strike

Of the many branches of East German industry involved in the strike by far the most prominent were the construction industry, the mining industry, the machine construction industry, and the chemical and iron-ore-producing industries. I have already mentioned the construction workers in the section dealing with the events of June 16 but there are two further points which need to be made in this connection.

The vast majority of the East German construction workers who struck on June 17 belonged to the industrial construction unions, which were engaged on special construction projects forming part of the general program of socialist development. Many of the construction sites concerned were situated in isolated areas, where nobody had ever built before and where the regime had decided to erect industrial installations and socialist new towns in the early 1950's. The workers who came to build these ideal socialist homes of the future were themselves accommodated in extremely primitive huts. Moreover, in these desolate and remote districts there were no diversions (such as cinemas or dance halls), very few women and, on the not infrequent occasions when there was a breakdown in organization, not even adequate food. It is hardly surprising that in such conditions and in such a milieu—a perfect breeding ground for discontent and resentment—the higher quotas stipulated by the government should have led to strike action.

Those construction workers employed in the provincial towns struck for an entirely different reason: when they heard that their colleagues in East Berlin had been demonstrating, the construction workers in numerous towns throughout the GDR came out in sympathy. Thus, the feeling of solidarity that had been such an important factor on June 16 at a site level re-emerged on June 17 at an inter-site level, which meant that the workers of a whole industry were united by this common bond. But this feeling of unity went still further, for the personnel of various other industries also demonstrated their solidarity with the construction workers of East Berlin.

This was an important development and one that casts a significant light on the situation in the GDR for it shows that, although the unions had lost their original function and no longer served as a vehicle for united action, a large number of workers had evidently retained their sense of solidarity.

If we consider the strike situation in the mining industry we find that in both the iron ore and the potassium mines there were extensive stoppages whereas in the coal and uranium mines there was practically no strike action at all. This is accounted for, in part at least, by certain essential differences between these branches of the mining industry. In the copper mining industry, with its centuries-old tradition, the workers revealed a high degree of solidarity that enabled them to join forces and offer concerted resistance to the regime. (Not surprisingly the town of Mansfeld, where copper mining has been going on for the past six hundred years, was one of the major centers of the strike.) By contrast, the uranium mines, which were started after the Second World War at the instigation of the Soviet Control Commission and which drew their labor from all parts of the GDR, had inspired no real sense of community, which precluded all possibility of solidarity among the workers. Moreover, the uranium miners received far higher wages and far better food than most other categories of workers, which meant that they had little personal incentive for taking strike action. In the coal mines of Saxony, which were expanded and modernized after the war, the situation was much the same.

On the face of it, therefore, it would appear that the failure of the uranium and coal miners to take strike action on June 17 was due to a combination of material welfare and a lack of solidarity. This seems all the more likely if we consider the iron industry, for example: a new and extremely large foundry (Eisenhüttenkombinat Ost) built after the war where the workers enjoyed conditions comparable to those obtaining in the uranium and coal mines, also continued work on June 17.

It is also true that the workers in the uranium district were notorious for their riotous behavior. Until quite late in the 1950's they regularly attacked police stations and beat up SED functionaries. However, these actions were hardly ever prompted by political considerations, and it was only on relatively rare occasions that the uranium miners protested against their economic situation. The truth of the matter is that, in this particular district of the GDR, conditions were rather like those found in the western United States at the time of the gold-rush: money was quickly earned and just as quickly lost, morals were lax, and heavy drinking often led to brawls and even bloodshed. Prior to June 17 there had been more stoppages in the uranium mines than in any other industry in the GDR, and in the circumstances, one would have expected these workers to have been the first to strike.

One factor in their apparent inertia was that, in those days, it was almost impossible to receive western radio transmissions in the Erzgebirge, which is where the uranium mines were situated. As a result it was several days before many of the miners heard about the July 16 demonstrations in East Berlin, and by then it was too late.

But the principal reason why the uranium and, for that matter, the coal miners of Saxony played such a minor part in the strike was that in Saxony, as in the harbors on the Baltic coast, the Soviets intervened very quickly to nip any incipient disturbances in the bud. It seems that, even during their June maneuvers, the Soviets maintained garrisons in areas of major importance such as the uranium district of southern Saxony and the shipyards on the Baltic. Consequently, they were able to act at a moment's notice in these areas, whereas in other parts of the GDR there was a time lag of several hours because the troops had to be transported from their field maneuvers to the various trouble spots.

Along with the iron ore and potassium miners and the construction workers, the workers in heavy industry also played an important part in the strike. So too did those in various essential industries. In nine out of ten of the major iron and steel works in the GDR, for example, there were stoppages or riots. At first sight it seems surprising to find that it was these highly paid workers who took strike action and not those employed in the less remunerative sectors of the economy, such as the state controlled trading concerns or the hotel, food and textile industries. But there were good reasons for this.

In the first place, the workers in the essential industries had been subjected to particularly heavy pressure during the government's propaganda campaign for a voluntary increase in work quotas. The state economists had argued forcibly that, since wages were high in these industries, productivity should be correspondingly high. Between January 1952 and June 1953 *Der Neue Weg*, a journal concerned with the practical application of party policy, published twenty-three articles on productivity in the iron and steel producing plants in the GDR, twenty-six articles on productivity in the coal, electricity and gas industries and in various works producing raw materials for the chemical industry, thirty-six articles on productivity in works engaged in heavy machine construction but only one article on productivity in a branch of the publicly owned HO.

However, the pressure brought to bear on these workers to increase their productivity (despite the progressive decline in their living standards) was only one of the reasons why they opted for strike action. They also struck because they knew they were indispensable.

Like the construction workers on the Stalin-Allee, they were fully aware that the regime needed them in order to fulfill its economic plans. If necessary, administrative and commercial workers could be replaced. So could the workers in the consumer industries. And if the quantity and quality of the consumer goods produced in the GDR failed to meet the people's needs or if the efficiency of the state trading organizations constantly declined, then these were not matters of great concern to the SED regime. But the program for heavy industry was of the utmost importance, and it could not be achieved without skilled workers. This was why higher wages had been paid in the essential industries, and it was why special shops had been installed on factory and work sites in February 1953 when there was a shortage of food. It was also why the SED had been forced to accept the fact that far fewer industrial workers had become party members than it would have liked. Undoubtedly, these workers would have known that the regime depended absolutely on their loyal cooperation and simply could not afford to have them shot down in the streets, since this would have resulted in the total collapse of the economic structure of the GDR.

Over and above this, of course, the workers must also

have known that, for purely ideological reasons, the regime would want to avoid using force at all costs. For the SED campaign for the build-up of heavy industry had been conceived as a program of socialist industrialization. In other words, it was to have established socialist working conditions in the GDR. Opposition on the part of independent craftsmen or small commercial firms would merely have served to confirm the government's thesis that the transition to socialism would necessarily involve a bitter class struggle. But resistance by the workers—especially those employed in essential industries—would undermine its whole conception of the state, in which the working and agricultural classes were to have become the ruling class and to have played the central role. After all, the GDR was supposed to be a workers' state and the government of the GDR merely an instrument for the representation of the workers' interests.

There was only one big works engaged in heavy industry that did not join the strike. This was the Eisenhüttenkombinat Ost, the new foundry then in course of construction at Stalinstadt (now Eisenhüttenstadt) near Frankfort on the Oder, where it was ideally situated to receive supplies of coal from the East and iron ore from Sweden.

In 1953, Stalinstadt was the largest industrial installation in the GDR. But, quite apart from its importance to the economy, this enormous project—which was described at the time as "the first socialist town in Germany" —also fulfilled a political function, for it constituted the first systematic attempt to restructure a cross-section of German society. Stalinstadt was supposed to become what Stammer has called a "socialist fortress," in other words a model of the new socialist way of life that would break down the old capitalist structure and then reshape it along entirely different lines.

In 1953 the wages in Stalinstadt were higher than those in any other town in the GDR. Because of this and because of the novelty value of living in a "socialist town" there was a large influx of workers. Most of these were young men, many of whom came from the former German territories east of the Oder. In 1954, the proportion of refugee workers living in Stalinstadt was estimated at nearly 50 per cent of the total work force.[24] Previously, when they had been living in other towns in the GDR, these refugees had found it difficult to compete with the indigenous workers and had tended to get the worst-paid jobs. This explains why they showed a greater willingness to offer themselves as guinea pigs for this socialist experiment than their native counterparts, most of whom preferred to remain in their familiar and trusted environment, even when a financial sacrifice was involved.

We see, therefore, that the workers in Stalinstadt had little financial incentive to join the strike. But they were not only far better paid than the other workers in the GDR; they also lacked the sort of cohesion found among the personnel of established concerns, which is one of the prerequisites of concerted action. This was due partly to the fact that the entire work force consisted of newcomers, the vast majority of whom had been strangers to one another before their arrival, and partly to the sharp watch kept by the party on the political attitudes of these workers. Neither of these factors made for close human relationships and it is hardly surprising that the industrial workers of Stalinstadt showed no sense of solidarity with their colleagues in other parts of the GDR. The only demonstrations in this town on June 17 were those staged by the itinerant construction workers.

Consequently, when the troubles were over, the regime was able to comfort itself with the thought that the new experimental town at least had remained true to its socialist principles. In actual fact, of course, the reason why the industrial workers of Stalinstadt failed to strike was that they lacked the necessary sense of solidarity. Unlike the workers in so many of the older industrial centers (who were also receiving comparatively high wages but who nonetheless took strike action on June 17) they were rendered incapable of concerted action by their feelings of isolation. It remains to be seen whether the workers of the large new industrial centers that have now been developed in the GDR acquire a sense of solidarity in the years to come. If they do, and if they should decide to oppose the government *en bloc,* the SED could find itself in a highly precarious situation.

The Significance of Tradition

The solidarity of the workers, whose effectiveness had already been demonstrated in the dispute over the collective agreements, was the principal reason for the initial success of the events of June 16 and 17.

It is difficult to assess the extent to which this new postwar solidarity was influenced by trade union or political tradition. Certainly, the biggest demonstrations were mounted in places like Magdeburg, Leipzig and Halle, which had always been centers of the working class movement. And even if the members of the younger generation —who were responsible for setting up most of the strike committees and were in fact the mainstay of the whole strike—had no firsthand knowledge of the old working class movement, they may quite conceivably have been told about the aims and beliefs of the movement by their parents and older colleagues. Nonetheless, I have been unable to discover in the reports to which I had access any reference to the "traditional accounts of the old social and political working class movement" which, according to Willy Brandt,[25] exerted a considerable influence on the events of June 17. Perhaps they did. But there is no way of proving it.

What is quite certain, however, is that the demonstrations in the traditionally communist districts of the GDR were no less vehement than those in the old Social Democrat districts. It seems as if all ancient conflicts were resolved by the common bond of opposition to the new regime. This was already apparent at the elections for the Berlin municipal parliament in 1946 when the communists, who had obtained more votes than the Social Democrats in Berlin during the closing phase of the Weimar Republic, suffered a heavy defeat at the hands of the German Social Democratic Party (SPD): 48.7 per cent of the valid votes cast went to the SPD and only 19.8 per cent to the SED.

At the first postwar election in the Russian zone the SPD and The German Communist Party (KPD) shared the same platform, which meant that the electors in the zone—unlike those in Berlin—were not able to vote SPD without voting KPD. None the less, the bourgeois parties did remarkably well, for in none of the provincial assemblies did the SED obtain an absolute majority. In Sachsen-Anhalt, a province consisting of a sparsely populated, mainly agricultural area in the north and a densely populated, industrial area in the south (centered on the towns of Magdeburg, Halle, Merseburg and Bitterfeld), the SED received 45.8 per cent of the valid votes in the provincial election, the Christian Democratic Union (CDU) 21.9 per cent and the Farmer's Association for Mutual Aid (VdgB) 2.4 per cent. With its bourgeois majority the provincial assembly of Sachsen-Anhalt had a Liberal Democratic Prime Minister in 1946. In view of the success of the bourgeois parties and the high percentage of spoiled votes cast at that time it seems reasonable to assume that a considerable number of the workers will have voted for the CDU or Liberal Democratic Party (LDP) or else have spoiled their ballot papers.

In any event, it was in the district of Halle and Merseburg, where the communists had been the strongest single party during the Weimar period, that the largest demonstrations were staged. Other strike centers, such as Magdeburg and Leipzig, had of course been Social Democrat strongholds prior to 1933. In the early 1950's when they heard Ernst Reuter speaking on the radio, many Magdeburgers will have recalled their former Oberbürgermeister. Only a month before the rising—on May 19, 1953—the Central Committee published a detailed resolution, in which it censured the local SED leaders in the Magdeburg district for failing to pursue the socialist restructuring of the city with sufficient force. And, after June 17, Otto Grotewohl was obliged to explain that "in certain towns, such as Magdeburg, Leipzig and others" there were "illegal organizations of former SPD members, who still cling to Social Democrat conceptions that are inimical to the workers." This theme was one that was subsequently taken up by the Central Committee of the party.[26]

We know from various sources—many of them unimportant in themselves—that in both the former communist district of Halle (where the Leuna Works are situated) and in the former Social Democrat district of Magdeburg even the SED party members were no more than lukewarm in their advocacy of the SED brand of socialism. Thus, in its issue of December 1952, *Der Neue Weg* severely criticized the party members employed at the Leuna Works and those living in the towns of Halle and Magdeburg for buying so few communist journals. It appears that only 19.5 per cent of all party members in Halle, 18.7 per cent in Magdeburg and 11.8 per cent at the Leuna Works were regular subscribers to *Der Neue Weg*. These were the lowest figures in the whole of the GDR, which meant that Halle, Magdeburg and Leuna were failing in their duty to support this important organ for the dissemination of information about the practical aspects of party work.[27]

The Course Taken by the Rising

The Trigger: Western Radio Bulletins

By and large the events of June 17 were triggered by western radio bulletins (especially those put out by RIAS) which described the incidents in East Berlin of the preceding day. But the communications services of the GDR also helped to spread the news. It appears from a number of reports that during the afternoon of June 16 the railway telephone network (BASA), which links all the stations in the GDR, and the telex network of the

German Home and Foreign Trade Organization (Deutscher Innen- und Aussenhandel, DIA) were used by the employees of the companies concerned to inform their colleagues in the zone of the incidents taking place in East Berlin.

The Crucial Factor

On the morning of June 17 the workers in nearly every part of the GDR excitedly discussed the events of the preceding day. Groups of gesticulating factory workers gathered spontaneously in their changing rooms and on the shop floors to discuss whether they could and should take action themselves. In many cases these small groups quickly grew until the whole of the factory personnel was assembled. But it would seem that the crucial factor at all of these spontaneous gatherings was whether, among the assembled company, there was one determined man capable of persuading his colleagues to walk off the job. Once one department of a factory had decided to strike, the other departments almost invariably followed suit, and once the personnel of a whole factory had marched out on to the streets, the men of other factories quickly joined them.

But this pattern did not develop everywhere. At a number of factories, although the possibility of a strike was discussed both at specially convened meetings and on the shop floors, no action resulted. Presumably this was because there was nobody with sufficient determination and drive to persuade his colleagues of the need to strike.

The composition of the strike committees was largely fortuitous; especially in the bigger factories, on which the success of the rising largely depended but where the workers were not on close personal terms with one another. It seems that nowhere in the GDR was a strike committee elected in the approved manner by secret ballot. Instead the members were chosen quite spontaneously by acclamation. Consequently, these committees consisted almost entirely of those workers who had played a leading part in the preliminary discussions. The fortuitous nature of this procedure was revealed by various eyewitnesses, who stated that at several of the larger works most of the men elected to serve on the committee were those who happened to have been standing near the microphone during the factory meeting. Because they were able to make themselves heard, it was generally assumed that they would know how to formulate demands. And so they were elected.

The Composition of the Strike Committees

The first point to be noted about the strike committees is that they were made up almost exclusively of men aged between twenty-five and forty. By and large the older men kept in the background, although whether they were motivated by fear or by a clearer realization of the hopelessness of the undertaking is not easy to decide.

In the vast majority of cases, membership was restricted to workers and a few lower-paid employees. The intellectuals among the salaried staff did not serve on the committees, partly because they did not want to, partly because the workers would not let them. This reticence on the part of the workers was due to the fact that—certainly during the initial postwar period—their traditional animosity toward the intelligentsia had been given a fresh impetus by the special privileges accorded to the East German technologists. Consequently, on June 17, 1953, the industrial workers of the GDR tended to regard the technological personnel as members of a new upper class that had been "bought" by the SED. And, in point of fact, if we consider the general behavior of the technologists during the rising it is difficult to escape the impression that they felt a certain debt of loyalty to the regime. By and large, the technological intelligentsia did not strike on June 17. There were, however, a few exceptions: in the Zeiss Works in Jena, in the Development and Research Center (Entwicklungs-und Forschungsbetreib, EFEM), in Berlin-Oberschöneweide and in the Nationalized Radio Works (VEB Funkwerk) in Berlin-Köpenick a large proportion of the technological personnel openly supported the workers, and some even took part in the demonstrations. In general, however, the technologists either sat quietly in their offices or made their way home when the workers grew restive. But, although they failed to show any real solidarity with the workers, they did not openly support the regime. In fact, their attitude on June 17 might best be described as one of "cool loyalty" to the government.

The third remarkable thing about the strike committees was the relatively large number of former professional soldiers—mostly noncommissioned officers—who served on them. Although this ex-military component never constituted more than ten per cent of the total membership of any committee, this is nonetheless a fairly high proportion and one that calls for some comment. The fact of the matter was that very many of the former professional soldiers working in East German industry after the war were violently opposed to communism in general and the SED regime in particular. There were two principal reasons for this. Judging by the kind of ex-professional soldier who fled to the West following the June rising, many of the members of this group appear to have held right wing political views while many others felt that the SED regime, having deprived them of their careers, had added insult to injury by maligning their chosen profession, the denigration of militarism being official SED policy at that time.

But, quite apart from the question of political or personal aversion to the regime, there was also the additional fact that soldiers are trained to assume leadership in any critical situation. And on the morning of June 17 the East German workers, who were determined to strike but lacked the leadership traditionally provided by the trades unions, found themselves in just such a critical situation. Not unnaturally, therefore, these former professional soldiers stepped into the breach.

Later, the communists cited the fact that ex-soldiers had been instrumental in organizing the rising in support of their theory that the events of June 17 had been the work of "militarists and fascists." In the resolution passed at its fifteenth session the Central Committee of the SED mentioned specific incidents in which "illegal fascist organizations" and "formerly active Nazis" supposedly played an important part. In my view the Central Committee came nearer the mark when it referred to the significant changes which had taken place in the composition of the East German work force. Among other things, it pointed out that "a large proportion of the most progressive workers" had been "transferred to government

and economic departments" and that "many non-prole-
tarian elements from bourgeois and petty bourgeois circles, including not a few fascist elements, in other words
civil servants and entrepreneurs who lost their privileged
positions in 1945 and who still dream of having their old
privileges restored," have obtained employment "in industry." [28]

But, although it is perfectly true that many members of
the old bourgeoisie, who were demoted in 1945, became
industrial workers, there is nothing in the reports available to us to suggest that these new "elements" tried to
incite their colleagues to strike action or were in any way
responsible for the day's events, as claimed by the communists. In any case, there were far too few of these
newcomers for them to have had any real effect on the
general development. Moreover, although local feeling
certainly played its part, it is quite clear that the really
crucial motivational factor was provided by the news from
Berlin. It was this, not agitation in the factories, that
triggered the strikes and demonstrations.

The Objectives

The extent to which the incidents in East Berlin of
June 16 influenced the events of the following day
throughout the GDR is clearly demonstrated by the fact
that the demands formulated by the workers on the
Stalin-Allee and subsequently reported by RIAS in its
news bulletins were taken over verbatim by the workers
in a large number of towns. These demands were: 1)
wages to be paid on the basis of the old norms with effect
from the next pay day; 2) the cost of living to be lowered

immediately; 3) free and secret elections; 4) no victimization of strikers or their spokesmen.

Like the building workers of East Berlin, the vast majority of the industrial workers in the zone were interested primarily in lower quotas and lower prices, especially food prices. The demand for free elections was far less urgent.

To some extent this order of preference merely reflected the sequence of events. Both in East Berlin on June 16 and in the GDR on June 17 the strikes were prompted in the first instance by economic considerations and it was not until the workers had massed on the streets and their ranks were swollen by passersby that they felt sufficiently elated to call for political changes.

With the emergence of political demands the demonstrations assumed a completely different character. Thus, in all parts of the GDR, the events of June 17 took place in two distinct stages.

In the first stage the industrial workers marched in orderly processions under the control of their strike leaders from their works sites in the outer suburbs to their respective city centers. En route they tore down pictures of the party leaders, political posters and banners and destroyed or set fire to propaganda kiosks. Then, after reaching the city center, they occupied the town hall and other public buildings and tried to release political prisoners. But in everything they did the workers displayed remarkable discipline and a marked sense of order, which were doubtless due to the influence of the strike committees. During this initial stage there was virtually no looting and no rioting; any tendency towards riotous behavior was quickly checked by the workers themselves.

During the second stage, when members of the general

public—especially women and juveniles—joined the workers, the demonstrations assumed the character of a popular rising. As a result control passed from the hands of the workers' strike committees, which were replaced in many towns by central strike committees. These central committees—in which outsiders and even outright demagogues made their voices heard—did not have the authority of the workers' committees and so were unable to exercize effective control.

The first stage of the demonstrations was concerned primarily with demands for better economic conditions and the release of political prisoners (especially those who had been engaged in industry); the second stage saw the emergence of political slogans, which gradually acquired major significance. But this was not the only difference. During the first stage the demonstrators in many towns consisted of homogeneous and disciplined groups of workers from the same industrial concern, whose orderly and systematic approach to the task in hand enabled them to occupy the local administrative offices with a minimal use of force and without recourse to weapons. (Captured weapons were invariably placed under lock and key and, in some cases, were even dismantled.) But in the second stage the revolutionary wave flowed quite indiscriminately. This was due partly to the lack of adequate leadership during this period and partly to the heterogeneous composition of the demonstrating crowds. In the second stage—which set in at about noon on June 17 in most parts of the GDR—there was looting, and there were cases of arson and lynchings. Thus, the afternoon was in marked contrast to the morning.

It is, of course, perfectly true that even in the morning

a number of government and party functionaries were beaten up by the workers. But these workers always distinguished between the office and the man with the result that ardent supporters of the regime were left unmolested if they were known to have behaved decently in the past. In the afternoon no such distinctions were made and anyone wearing a party badge on his lapel was immediately seized and beaten up.

Thus, in the course of the day the rising became progressively more radical. This development is also demonstrated by the different attitudes adopted to the release of prisoners in the course of the day. For the most part the industrial workers who appeared at the gates of the prisons and penal colonies in the morning asked only for the release of individual prisoners, whose names they submitted to the prison authorities (although in certain cases this demand was extended to cover all political detainees). Moreover, in the vast majority of the prisons to which the workers succeeded in gaining entry the prison staff readily agreed to show them the prison records and actively cooperated in the release of the prisoners.

In the afternoon the situation was completely different. Uncontrollable crowds of demonstrators found their way into the prisons and opened the cell doors with no sense of discrimination and with the inevitable result that, in many cases, criminal elements were restored to liberty. In their subsequent propaganda the communists made great play with this.

The orderly demonstrations staged by the workers were transformed into a popular revolt before Soviet troops, supported by units of the paramilitary police, were sent in to put down the disturbances. Although in a few

isolated cases the rioting appeared as a direct consequence of Soviet intervention, broadly speaking it was
only after the demonstrations had attracted wide popular
support and had assumed a distinctly political character
that the Soviets decided to use troops to disperse the
crowds.

But let no one imagine that the rising was actually
put down by the Soviet troops. By the time they were de-
ployed the revolutionary wave had already begun to ebb.
The Soviet intervention was not a turning point, it merely
served to mark the end of the day's events: the demonstrators had run out of steam; their rising had come to a
standstill before it had really got off the ground.

This became quite evident following the mass meetings held in the afternoon in all the larger towns where
the workers had struck. At these mass meetings, many of
which were attended by tens of thousands, the demonstrations reached their climax—and their conclusion. The
only significance of these meetings lay in the fact that
they enabled those taking part to show to the world at
large the widespread, almost nationwide, dissatisfaction
of the population with the kind of conditions obtaining in
the GDR. Numerous speakers mounted the rostrum to
make economic and political demands which were
greeted with wild applause. But when the meetings were
over the groups of industrial workers marched back to their
factories and the other participants (juveniles, women and
bystanders) dispersed to their homes. In the eyewitness
accounts we are told time and again that, once the mass
meetings were over, people had the feeling that "nothing else would happen," that the movement had "faded
away."

It soon became apparent that no one had made any contingency plans for continuing the rising. This applied even to places like Berlin, where the demonstrators were driven from the streets by Russian tanks. Fritz Schenk who, as personal assistant to Bruno Leuschner, spent June 17 in the House of Ministries, from which he was able to observe the incidents in the city center, gave a graphic description of the way in which the great crowds of demonstrators (reinforced by numerous sightseers from West Berlin) stood outside the government building: packed tightly together, well-disciplined and completely inactive, they waited "almost patiently" [29] for Grotewohl and Ulbricht to appear—only to be dispersed to their homes by the Soviet tanks. This is hardly the sort of thing we would expect to find in a genuine revolt.

However, there is a simple explanation for this inertia. After the workers had achieved their immediate objective by forcing the government to withdraw the new quotas the demonstrations entered into their popular phase and control of events passed from the industrial to the central strike committees. But these central committees were badly organized and had no clear-cut plan of campaign just as the masses whom they represented had no clear-cut communal objective. Unlike Poland and Hungary, which threshed out the issues confronting them in a period of lively intellectual debate prior to their risings in 1956, the GDR was taken completely unawares. Stalin's death had roused vague expectations and hopes. But, apart from a few of the top SED leaders, nobody had worked out detailed practical objectives. Moreover, nobody knew just how Moscow would react to a change of policy in the GDR. It was against this background that the SED suddenly introduced its new line, which was followed by the unexpectedly successful demonstrations of June 16 and 17. But in the brief lull which these procured, the strike leaders were not even able to form an objective assessment of the situation, let alone establish a new government that would have been acceptable both to the people of the GDR and to the Soviet Union: the GDR had no Gomulka and no Nagy; it had nobody capable of assuming the leadership.

If proof is needed of the spontaneity and naïveté of the East German rising, it is to be found in the fact that, whereas in towns virtually throughout the GDR the demonstrators tried to release political prisoners, little or no attempt was made to get control of the traffic and telecommunications networks, which would have been an essential prerequisite for any serious bid to take over the government of the country. The only exception to this general rule was in Dresden, where the workers tried to storm the Central Post Office. On the other hand, if the demonstrators had realized what was required of them, they would probably have drawn back in fear and there would have been no June 17. After all, the outcome was predictable: as soon as the regime began to totter, the Soviets would be forced to intervene, for they could not allow the SED to be overthrown.

The Soviet Reaction to June 17

Although the Soviet army did not proceed against the demonstrators until very late in the day—in many towns no military action was taken until several hours after the declaration of a state of emergency—all the important strategic positions in the GDR, such as the railway stations and post offices in the larger towns, the docks and harbors on the Baltic and the uranium mines in the Erzgebirge, had been occupied by Soviet troops since the early hours of June 17.

It would seem, therefore, that at the outset the Soviet occupation forces were intent simply on keeping control of the traffic and telecommunications networks, thus effectively preventing the various local strike committees from coordinating their efforts. It was only when the orderly demonstrations staged by the workers turned into a popular rising that they decided to disperse the crowds by force.

On the morning of June 16, when Waldemar Schmidt (SED), then President of Police in East Berlin, asked the Soviet authorities for permission to disperse the as yet relatively small crowd of demonstrators on the Stalin-Allee and to arrest their ringleaders, he was forbidden to do so. It could be that the reason why the Soviet commanders did not decide to use troops until the following day was that until late in the morning of June 17 they had failed to appreciate the actual extent of the revolt. On the other hand, the moderate attitude adopted by the demonstrators towards the occupation forces may also have persuaded them to stay their hand. Apart from a few isolated incidents, in which small groups of demonstrators—most of them East Berliners—had hurled bricks at Soviet tanks and clawed at them with their bare hands, the occupation forces were not even criticized, let alone attacked. Both the strike leaders and the speakers at the mass meetings declared time and again that the strike was directed against the SED and not against the Soviets.

Finally, it is possible that the purely practical problem of transporting troops from their field maneuvers to the various trouble spots may also have caused a delay of several hours. (It would be interesting to know in which parts of the GDR the Soviet troops were stationed during the June maneuvers, for this might well explain why it was that the demonstrations followed a different course in different areas. Unfortunately, the information available to us in this respect is far from complete and it is not possible to form an accurate picture.) What is quite certain, however, is that even after a state of emergency had been declared the Soviet troops acted with great restraint and had obviously been instructed to avoid bloodshed. In Halle, for example, where a mass meeting was called for six P.M. on the Hallmarkt, the Soviet military commander allowed tens of thousands of demonstrators to gather on the square, which was already surrounded by tanks and infantry. It was only after the meeting that the troops dispersed the crowd. And in every town in the GDR where Soviet tanks were used to break up demonstrations, they advanced very slowly so as to give the people time to get away. As the deputy Minister President Otto Nuschke said in his RIAS interview, the tanks were "also demonstrating." Moreover, when Soviet soldiers opened fire, they almost invariably fired in the air. This explains why there were only 21 people killed on June 17 in the whole of the GDR, a very low figure considering the size of the demonstrations.[30] It also explains why a few German youths were able to pull down the red flag from the Brandenburg Gate, which had been hoisted there in 1945, despite the fact that three companies of Soviet soldiers were stationed on the eastern side of the

Gate at the time: the soldiers opened fire, but they fired in the air.

However, although the Soviets reacted to the East German rising with equanimity and prudence, the fact that the workers had demonstrated in such large numbers against the Soviet-backed SED regime appears to have made a deep impression on them. Certainly, it would seem that the news of the rising was carried through the eastern bloc and the USSR like wildfire. The eastern bloc press devoted most of its news space to comment on the events in East Germany, and the leaders of the eastern bloc countries felt constrained to hold mass meetings to explain the situation to their people, thus providing even wider coverage.

We do not know how the people of the USSR reacted to the events of June 17, nor do we know what effect it had on the Soviet soldiers when they were ordered to disperse demonstrators in a "workers' and peasants' state." Certainly, the news from the GDR led to extensive and protracted work stoppages in a number of Soviet forced labor camps, such as Workuta (USSR). Here too the Soviet leadership proceeded with extreme caution, trying to resolve the disputes—in which both Russian and foreign prisoners were involved—by peaceful means. In this it succeeded, but only after weeks of painstaking negotiations.

The West on June 17

In my opinion both the West Germans and the western allies were taken completely unawares by the events in the GDR. At the beginning of June—in other words, after the administrative increase in the East German work quotas of May 28 but before the Politburo resolution of June 9—a conference was held in West Berlin which was attended by representatives of the western press and radio networks, by members of the department for scientific research into eastern affairs, by trade union delegates and by various deputies of the Federal Parliament in Bonn. Conferences of this kind were held every few months to facilitate the exchange of information and views on the situation in the GDR. One of the items on the agenda at this particular conference was the administrative increase in the East German work quotas and when this subject was discussed Dr. Marie-Elisabeth Lüders suggested that the new SED policy might well provoke extensive strike action. Dr. Lüders subsequently informed me that her assumption had been based on "private letters received from the zone and from East Berlin and on conclusions drawn from a close study of various events which indicated that such a development was possible. For every experienced and perceptive observer of the political scene there could scarcely be any doubt about it . . . " But apparently Dr. Lüders was unable to convince the other delegates to the conference, who seem to have formed an entirely different assessment of the situation in the GDR. In fact, they considered her suggestions so improbable that the possibility of work stoppages in the GDR was not even mentioned in their final report.

This attitude still prevailed in the West on the eve of the demonstrations on the Stalin-Allee. At 7:30 P.M. on June 15, RIAS reported that there had been unrest on various building sites in East Berlin, but none of the western news agencies took up the story because they thought it could not possibly be true. Even on June 16, RIAS was the only western news service to take an interest in events in East Berlin until quite late in the day. News of the strikes and demonstrations on the Stalin-Allee first reached RIAS towards noon and was confirmed shortly afterwards by a group of building workers, who appeared in the RIAS building to ask if they could broadcast to their colleagues in the eastern sector and zone. This, they said, was the only way of bringing the workers together and ensuring that the call for a general strike made that morning in front of the House of Ministries was heard throughout the GDR.

As a result of this visit RIAS put out its first bulletin about the incidents in East Berlin at 1:30 P.M. This was followed at 4:30 P.M. by a detailed report, in which reference was made to the fact that various individuals taking part in the demonstrations had called for a general strike. Meanwhile, however, the American Director of RIAS refused to allow the building workers to use the RIAS broadcasting facilities, presumably because he feared the Soviets might regard this as a provocative act. Later that afternoon the American headquarters staff in Mehlem issued strict instructions to the effect that RIAS was to limit its programs to straightforward news coverage and was on no account to put out statements likely to provoke strikes or demonstrations. Moreover, the expression "general strike" was not to be mentioned in any future broadcasts. In the special hourly news bulletins transmitted from 11:00 P.M. onwards reference was made to the fact that the workers of all branches of industry in East Berlin had called upon the inhabitants of East Berlin to assemble on the Strausberger Platz at 7:00 A.M. on June 17. The decision to include this item of news was taken by the American Director of RIAS.

Meanwhile, there was no official reaction from Bonn or West Berlin. June 16 passed without comment from the West German authorities. No politicians, no political parties and no organizations of any kind declared their solidarity with the workers of East Berlin. Apparently, western observers suspected at first that the demonstrations had been stage-managed by the SED and constituted part of the new line which had been introduced on June 11.

This new line had been received with mixed feelings in the Federal Republic. Most newspapers and the leading politicians of all parties regarded it as proof of the bankruptcy of the SED's earlier policy but welcomed it insofar as it promised to make life easier for the people of the GDR. Leading Christian Democratic and Christian Socialist representatives claimed that it justified their *Ostpolitik.* At the same time government circles obviously feared that the Soviet Union would try to use this new line and the new four power conference that was then being mooted to sabotage the incorporation of the Federal Republic into the western alliance, thus weakening the CDU, giving a boost to the SPD and its reunification policies and impairing the CDU's chances of being returned to power at the second Federal election on September 6. The Federal Republic had opted definitively for integration with the West on March 15, 1953, the day on which the Federal Parliament had first approved the European Defence Treaty and the agreement with the western powers ending the occupation. On May 19, 1953, about a month before the East German rising, the Federal

Council had ratified these treaties. But other parties—including France—had yet to do so and meanwhile both the Soviet Union and the Foreign Policy Committee of the French National Assembly had welcomed Churchill's proposal for a summit conference to discuss any issues that were a cause of concern. Clearly, the German peace treaty was such an issue. In order to check this development, which he considered to be dangerous, Chancellor Adenauer submitted a memorandum to the President of the United States on May 29, in which he stressed the necessity for reunification in freedom, in other words for a peace treaty freely entered into that would permit a reunited Germany to negotiate alliances of her own choosing. In this connection Chancellor Adenauer spoke of "the right of a free and equal nation to join forces with other nations for peaceful purposes," [31] by which he undoubtedly meant to imply that a reunited Germany would belong to the European Defense Community. Shortly afterward, on June 9, the SPD minority in the Federal Parliament urged the Federal government to do all in its power to promote new four power negotiations on the question of German reunification.

After first assuming that the demonstrations of June 16 were part and parcel of the new line and might even be one of the elements of a new Soviet initiative in Germany, western observers came round to the view that the people of the GDR actually were rising against the SED regime. As more news came in from East Berlin and it became apparent that the communist leaders could not possibly have engineered strike action on such a scale, surprise and incredulity gave way to cautious acceptance. Like the Americans, the West Germans were now convinced that any actions likely to be interpreted by the Soviets as interference in their affairs must be avoided at all costs. Accordingly Jakob Kaiser, the Federal Minister for All-German Affairs, made a broadcast late on the evening of June 16, in which he appealed to the East Germans not to allow themselves to be induced to "rash" or "dangerous actions" at a time when our "reunification policies have at last started to make progress." "Caution coupled with trust in our sense of solidarity," Kaiser suggested, should be the watchword. The West Berlin trade union leader Ernst Scharnowski, on the other hand, appealed over RIAS to the workers and people of the eastern zone to demonstrate their solidarity with the building workers of East Berlin and called upon the inhabitants in all parts of the GDR to assemble on their local "Strausberger Platz." This appeal, which was described both by a spokesman for the Federal Council and by the Social-Democrat Executive Committee as a "suicidal provocation and an act of incredible irresponsibility," [32] was taped in the RIAS studios on the evening of June 16 but was not broadcast at once because the RIAS officials wanted to obtain the authorization of the American Headquarters in Mehlem. Accordingly, they informed the Americans that they proposed to postpone transmission until 5:00 A.M. on June 17: if they did not hear from Mehlem by then, they would go ahead with the broadcast. There was no reply from the Americans, who were evidently undecided as to what to do.

As the day wore on it became more and more apparent that the allied control commissions and the West German and West Berlin politicians were determined to avoid any course of action that might be regarded as interference in the internal affairs of the GDR. In Bonn Chancellor Adenauer made a cautious and dilatory statement to the Federal Parliament. In West Berlin the authorities did their best to stop the demonstrations from spreading to their part of the city and to prevent West Berliners from joining in the demonstrations in East Berlin or from influencing their development. The allied and German police forces stopped all public transport in West Berlin in the immediate vicinity of the eastern sector and blocked all access roads in order to halt the great crowds of West Berliners making for the border. British military police took up positions in front of the Soviet war memorial in the British sector to protect it from attack while the French military government tried—but failed—to prevent the personnel of the Hennigsdorf Steel Works in the northern outskirts of Berlin from passing through the French sector on their march to the city center. Ernst Reuter, who had been attending a conference in Vienna, tried to return to Berlin as soon as he was informed of the demonstrations in the eastern sector, but was refused a seat on a military aircraft by the American authorities. An address directed at the soldiers of the Red Army, which Reuter had written and recorded in Russian, was not accepted for transmission, although it contained nothing more sinister than an appeal not to shoot at unarmed German workers. A loudspeaker car, which was sent out by a Russian émigré organization to patrol the borders of the western sectors and advise any Soviet soldiers within earshot that the demonstrators they were being asked to disperse were German workers and not fascist agents, was impounded by the allied authorities. And from noon onwards on June 17 hundreds of German and allied policemen were stationed along the sector borders to disperse the great crowds of West Berliners, who had gathered there to see what was happening in the eastern sector of their city.

This police action was only partially successful. Large numbers of these West Berliners, who had appeared on the scene quite spontaneously, undoubtedly crossed over into the eastern sector and joined in the demonstrations staged in the city center of East Berlin, which is situated close to the sector borders. There were also isolated acts by West Berliners which were clearly premeditated. Thus, although the Federal Ministry for All-German Affairs was completely unprepared for June 17 and quite incapable of taking speedy decisions, although Ministerialdirigent Magen—one of the top officials in the Berlin branch of the ministry—sat in his car on the Potsdamer Platz observing the course of events without being able to do anything about them, there were others who took the initiative. For example, members of the West Berlin branch of the Federation of German Trades Unions tried—with considerable success—to persuade the personnel of the municipal transport system in East Berlin to stop work. Moreover, it seems highly probable that, once the disturbances had broken out in the eastern sector, the numerous western secret service organizations operating from Berlin will have done their utmost to bring their influence to bear. Although there is no actual proof of secret service involvement—there seldom is— Andrew Tully, the American author, has conjectured plausibly along these lines.[33]

But, by and large, the western attitude, which was primarily designed to avoid conflict with the Soviet

Union, was one of cautious reserve. Consequently, it disappointed the inhabitants of the GDR, as is evident from the reports of East German demonstrators who subsequently fled to the West. Apparently, many East Germans had thought that the western powers would use the rising as a pretext for intervention; many more had assumed from the reports put out by the western radio stations that, if necessary, western forces would come to the aid of the East German insurgents. It should be added, however, that these hopes were entertained, not by the workers—who bore the main brunt of the demonstrations —but by the members of the middle class. Their confidence was badly shaken by the western attitude.

The SED and June 17

On Tuesday, June 16, 1953, the Politburo of the SED was holding its weekly session in the East Berlin House of Unity, the seat of the Central Committee, on what is now the Wilhelm-Pieck-Strasse. The debate was heated for the members were discussing the new line and its consequences both for the economy and for the future composition of the government: in the economic sphere immediate and large scale changes had to be made to the current five-year plan; in the personal sphere Walter Ulbricht's position as General Secretary was being called into question by a powerful faction within the Politburo. Erich Honecker, a faithful follower of Ulbricht's, is supposed to have said to one of his colleagues after this session: "Things look bad for Walter."

Not long after the Politburo had opened its session Heinz Brandt, the Secretary for Agitation and Propaganda on the SED Headquarters staff in Berlin, sent a messenger into the conference room to ask Hans Jendretzky, the First Secretary on the Headquarters staff, to leave the meeting and speak to him in the antechamber. Jendretzky came out immediately, accompanied by Rudolf Herrnstadt. Brandt then informed them that party agents employed on the Stalin-Allee had hot-footed it to the SED District Headquarters with the news that processions of demonstrators had formed at the hospital site in Friedrichshain and at Block 40 on the Stalin-Allee and were constantly being swollen by new recruits, for there was unrest on every building site in the area and the workers were determined to strike. He then impressed on Jendretzky and Herrnstadt that, unless action was taken at once, there would be a gigantic demonstration, adding that he and his colleagues at District Headquarters saw only one possible solution: the Politburo must withdraw the new norms at once. "You mean," Herrnstadt asked, "that we should back the workers' claims—that they are in fact justified?" When Brandt confirmed this, both Herrnstadt and Jendretzky agreed to put this argument to the Politburo.

It was some time before a decision was reached. Eventually an agitated Ulbricht emerged from the conference room, accompanied by Jendretzky, and told Brandt that the Politburo had approved the suggestion made by the SED, adding that Bruno Baum (another secretary on the District Headquarters staff) was to inform the building workers of this decision and so break up the demonstration.

By the time Baum and Brandt caught up with the procession on the Alexanderplatz it was several thousand strong and steadily growing, for building workers from other sites, industrial workers and passersby were constantly joining its ranks. Baum saw at once that there was no point in even attempting to carry out Ulbricht's orders. He realized that what was afoot in East Berlin could not possibly be halted by an improvised speech. Shortly afterwards the Minister for Industry Selbmann telephoned the Politburo. By then the demonstrators had passed along the Leipziger Strasse and gathered outside the House of Ministries, where they chanted for Grotewohl and Ulbricht to appear. Selbmann, who was one of the few officials in the government building to keep his nerve, asked to be connected with Ulbricht and urged him to come and speak to the workers. Ulbricht refused, apparently on the grounds that he could not leave the Politburo meeting; and, when Selbmann tried to impress on him that the situation was serious and required his presence, he is said to have replied that, since it was raining, the demonstrators would soon disperse in any case.

The party leaders evidently considered that the statement put out by the Politburo announcing the withdrawal of the new norms had banished all danger of further demonstrations. After Selbmann had informed the workers in front of the House of Ministries of the party's decision and they had begun to make their way home it was widely assumed in the higher echelons of the party and the government that, to all intents and purposes, the disturbances had come to an end. The SED leaders in Berlin were in any case fully occupied with the preparations for a meeting of party activists, which had been arranged only two days before and which took place on the evening of June 16 in the Friedrichstadt-Palast in Berlin. It was a macabre meeting. As Grotewohl and Ulbricht subjected the assembled delegates to longwinded explanations of the sudden change of policy of June 9, making only a passing reference to the morning's events, the workers were parading the streets of East Berlin calling for a general strike. The People's Police in numerous districts of East Berlin reported that the call for a general strike and the projected demonstration on the Strausberger Platz were being openly discussed by groups of excited people.

As a result the East Berlin radio was instructed to transmit frequent repeats of the official announcement calling on all workers in the city to disregard the "misleading rumors" that had been circulated and to report to work as usual on the following morning, where special meetings would be held to clarify the situation. The SED District Headquarters in Berlin had already decided in the course of the afternoon that each member of the secretariat was to visit one of the large building or industrial sites to explain the new line and the withdrawal of the higher quotas.

At this point the party and government leaders believed that, even if the strikes and demonstrations were continued on June 17, they would be confined to Berlin. Earlier that afternoon the Minister of State Security Zaisser had sent a memorandum to all security departments in the GDR, ordering numerous security officials, including heads of departments and section leaders, to report to the Ministry of State Security in Berlin. Late in the evening of June 16, Zaisser sent out a second memorandum ordering further security men to Berlin to support the party and union functionaries at the works meetings on the following morning. As a result some seven hundred members of the State Security Service arrived in Berlin in the course of the night. It seems highly improbable that the Minister for State Security would have concentrated so many of his men in Berlin if he had suspected that on June 17 disturbances would break out, not only in the capital, but in hundreds of provincial towns as well.

Many of the provincial functionaries had formed a more accurate assessment of the situation. During the afternoon and evening of June 16, Fritz Schenk, acting on instructions from Leuschner, ordered all the ministers, heads of district committees and leading functionaries concerned with the administration of the economy to proceed to Berlin together with their chief advisers. There they were to attend a conference called by the Politburo for June 17 to determine the principal changes which would have to be made in the current five-year plan as a result of the decision to introduce the new line. (Basically, the party leaders wanted to halt any major investment projects and devote all available resources to the production of consumer goods and the building of new homes.) It was no easy matter to convince the heads of the district committees that they must travel post haste to Berlin. Those in Dresden, Chemnitz, Halle, Leipzig and Magdeburg had already anticipated, on the evening of June 16, the disturbances that were due to break out on the following day. Time and again Schenk was told over the telephone that the people in Berlin had no idea of what things looked like in the provinces.

In any case, the party and government leaders made no contingency plans for the provinces on June 17 and very few for Berlin, which would suggest that they were taken completely unawares both by the unrest in the country at large and by the extent of the disturbances in the capital. The regime's two principal instruments of power, the secret police and the People's Police, proved utterly ineffectual. During the morning of June 17 the Ministry of State Security in Berlin lost contact with one after another of its provincial units and by midday was virtually isolated, while the People's Police made no attempt to intervene until ordered to do so by the Soviet authorities.

For the most part, the local party and government functionaries also failed to take action against the demonstrators on June 17. The introduction of the new line on June 9 had thrown them into utter confusion, for they had been given no explanation for this abrupt change of policy. The only directive they had received since then was one from Hermann Axen, the Secretary for Agitation in the Central Committee, who had instructed them to remove—immediately but unobtrusively—all political banners which were designed to promote the development of socialism or which even contained the word "socialism." This, of course, merely served to increase their uncertainty. Had the party leaders merely deferred the creation of a socialist society or had they renounced it altogether? Was everything they had been trying to achieve for the past twelve months in the face of mounting difficulties and multiple resistance wrong? And if it was wrong, then what was right? These were the sort of questions the junior functionaries were asking themselves on June 17. They had long since lost the ability to think for themselves and so, when faced with a strike situation, were quite incapable of acting on their own initiative. Many of the functionaries felt so insecure that they readily complied with the demonstrators' demands; others actually made common cause with them, and consequently—according to the communiqué issued by the Central Committee after its fifteenth plenary session—found themselves "taken in tow by the agents provocateurs." The dominant feeling in the provincial party and administrative centers on June 17 was one of helplessness. Later many functionaries openly admitted that they simply had not known how to deal with such a rising. In its communique the SED Central Committee complained that "numerous deficiencies and weaknesses" had been revealed and that party functionaries and party members had been "thoughtless and unorganized" during the rising. Party members, it was said, "had panicked and slid back into capitulationary and opportunistic attitudes toward the enemies of the party and fascist agents provocateurs." [34] In other words: party members and functionaries working for local administration departments had either given in to the demonstrators and simply handed over the keys to prisons, document cupboards and card indexes or else had tried to save their own skins by locking themselves in their offices, barricading the doors and putting up the steel shutters. (In a number of cases the demonstrators seem to have anticipated such behavior, for they brought oxyacetylene torches with them and cut their way in through the windows.)

Things were much the same where the regular police were concerned: in the majority of cases the men of the provincial units were either unable or unwilling to oppose the demonstrators. Time and again, it seems, the police entered into protracted discussions with the strikers and then stood back with lowered truncheons to allow the long columns to go on their way. Most of them sympathized with the strikers and some gave tangible expression to their feelings by throwing their weapons away. Others actually joined in the demonstrations.

The paramilitary police, however, did not side with the demonstrators. On the contrary, they afforded the authorities able support. This was doubtless due in part to the fact that they did not appear on the streets until after a state of emergency had been declared, by which time they had been placed under Soviet command. After all, it would have been difficult for the paramilitary units to show their solidarity with the demonstrators while working alongside the soldiers of the Red Army. But there was also a further factor, which will almost certainly have played a part in this respect. By and large the members of the regular People's Police were recruited from the towns or communities in which they subsequently served and consequently felt a natural bond of loyalty to the local inhabitants. This was not the case with the men of the paramilitary units, who were drawn from all parts of the GDR. Time and again, eyewitnesses spoke of local policemen who decided to join in the demonstrations after seeing friends or relations in the processions. But, even where no such meetings took place, members of the regular police may well have been prompted to show their solidarity with the strikers by the mere mention of some wellknown and respected local firm, whose personnel were taking part in the demonstrations. The paramilitary police, on the other hand, who knew nothing of local conditions, found it much more difficult to grasp the true situation and see through the flimsy grounds on which the authorities had tried to justify the use of troops: a putsch engineered by the western powers had to be put down.

Like the workers of the Eisenhüttenkombinat Ost, the paramilitary police had been deprived of the will to oppose, and even of any inclination to protest against, official policies by a process of isolation and political indoctrination combined with above average pay and conditions. The events of June 17 showed that the future prospects of the communist regime in the GDR were good, provided the authorities were able to isolate their citizens from one another and subject them to political indoctrination, effecting at the same time a marked improvement in their standard of living.

Immediately after the rising, of course, the East German communists still had a long way to go before they could hope to reach this goal. Their reaction to the events of June 17 showed that they were fully aware of the true extent of the reversal which they had suffered and that they proposed to solve their problems, not by introducing a reign of terror, but by striving for conciliation.

Aware that the catastrophic economic situation in the first half of 1953 had been one of the major factors contributing to the outbreak of civil disturbances, the regime was determined to improve the supply of foodstuffs. Consequently the new line, which had been introduced on June 11 with the announcement of a number of new economic measures, was maintained after the rising of June 17 and subsequently extended by two series of ministerial decrees and directives designed to bring about "a further improvement in the standard of living of the population," which were announced on June 25 and July 23 respectively. Among other things, these measures were designed to provide assistance for the agricultural industry; relief for independent craftsmen and workers in private industrial concerns (by means of lower taxes and higher wages, especially for the workers in groups 1 to 4, who had received very low wages until then); higher pensions; and the release of publicly owned stocks of food and export goods for home consumption.

But, above all, the regime adhered rigidly to the most important provision in the Politburo resolution of June 9 by promoting the production of consumer goods and investing more money in this field than in heavy industry. This it was now able to do, for as a result of the rising the Soviet Union was prepared to offer "every assistance" to the GDR (after having repeatedly refused to help their German comrades in any way). The statements made at the fifteenth plenary session of the Central Committee between July 24 and 26, 1953 also strengthened the party in its resolve to abandon its ideological objections to the middle class property owners by allowing commercial firms and craftsmen to operate on a free-enterprise basis, by supporting the independent farmers and by forming no further agricultural collectives.

But, of course, the dissatisfaction, indeed despair, of the bourgeois sections of the population was not due to economic factors alone. Consequently, the relief afforded by the new line was not restricted to the economic sphere. To the contrary, the party adopted a more conciliatory attitude in every respect: the *Volkskammer* (the East German parliament) and the block parties (the junior partners of the SED) found themselves upgraded, relations between the state and the church became more relaxed, greater consideration was given to the people's need for entertainment and those engaged in scholarly and cultural pursuits were allowed rather more freedom than in the past.

This new development did not pass unheeded. That is quite evident from the remarkable politico-cultural resolution passed by the German Academy of the Arts on June 30, 1953 and, above all, from the resolution passed by the praesidium of the Cultural Union under the chairmanship of Johannes R. Becher, which called for freedom of thought in all scholastic discussions, in all artistic pursuits and in research work and education, for reliable information in the press and radio and for "justice based on the inviolable constitution of the Republic." The astonishing outcome of this resolution—one that would have been inconceivable in more normal times—was a promise made by Walter Ulbricht at the fifteenth session of the Central Committee to the effect that the "major part" of these demands could be implemented. But the new line produced more than resolutions. Although the party carefully avoided making any real concessions and the most that its leading functionaries were prepared to concede were half-truths, a number of outspoken articles were none the less published at that time: Johannes R. Becher and Bertolt Brecht, Peter Huchel, Erwin Strittmatter and Arnold Zweig all expressed more or less candid, more or less severe and invariably critical opinions. Günther Cwojdrak's rousing appeal to the writers of the GDR under the title "Write the Truth!," Wolfgang Harich's vehement attack on the State Commission for the Arts and Erich Loest's destructive critique of the press showed how deeply the members of the postwar generation, the new social intelligentsia, had been moved by the workers' rising of June 17 and what high hopes these young socialists had invested in the new line and the restructuring of the party.[35] But their hopes proved illusory; it was no accident that Harich and Loest should have been arrested in 1956 and 1957 and sentenced to long terms of penal servitude.

The fact of the matter was that the new line was not supposed to bring about a permanent relaxation of state authority in the GDR. It was merely a tactical move designed to relieve the immediate short term pressure of public demand. The party had no intention of relinquishing its position of power. It just wanted to disguise it more effectively. In the summer of 1953, Grotewohl drew a significant parallel between the new line that had been introduced in the GDR and the new economic policy pursued by the Soviet Union between 1921 and 1925. Although some of the new principles adopted by the East German leadership were retained for some time, others—including the principle of according primacy to the production of consumer goods—were soon abandoned. As early as July 1953, the Central Committee had stated quite openly at its fifteenth plenary session that the whole object of the exercise was to give the party room to breathe. The party, it said, was quite right to have led Germany on the path of socialism by beginning to create the foundations of socialism in the GDR: "This general line . . . was and still is correct." [36]

Under the new line of June 9, 1953, the SED leadership proposed the abandonment of terrorism as an instrument of policy, which meant that excessively heavy sentences would no longer be imposed on political opponents by way of a deterrent, previous sentences of this kind would be reduced, amnesties would be announced for certain categories of crime and an attempt would be made to strengthen the legal rights of the individual in general.

Such proposals were calculated to win over the strikers and demonstrators of June 17 and, in point of fact, we find that in the first instance the regime exercised considerable restraint where they were concerned. In an interview which was reproduced in *Das Neue Deutschland* on June 30 and in the Soviet run *Die Tägliche Rundschau* on July 1 the East German Minister of Justice Max Fechner (SED) stated that the right to strike was written into the constitution of the GDR and that, consequently, neither those who had taken strike action on June 17 nor those who had played a leading part in the strike committees were guilty of a criminal offense. But on July 16, 1953, Fechner (who was a longstanding adversary of Walter Ulbricht's) was dismissed from his post and arrested. In her inaugural speech Fechner's successor, Hilde Benjamin, made great play with this interview, arguing that in it Fechner had committed the fundamental error of "trying to justify an attempted *coup d'état* and fascist putsch as a strike." [37] The precise number of strikers and demonstrators subsequently arrested and sentenced on trumped up charges—such as disturbing the peace, inciting a boycott or maligning the state—is not known. According to western records over 1300 people were indicted on such grounds, of whom four were given life sentences and six were condemned to death and the rest sent to prison for periods of several years. It seems surprising that the regime should have adopted such a harsh attitude, for it had good reason to fear that large scale arrests would trigger new strikes, which would have had a serious effect on production. And in fact the personnel of numerous works took further strike action after June 17 in order to obtain the release of arrested colleagues.

But economic improvements and the arrest of the (alleged) ringleaders were not a complete answer. The SED had to form a speedy and accurate "assessment" of the events of June 17 which could be made acceptable to the population and, above all, the workers of the GDR.

Apparently, the majority of the members of the Politburo and the Central Committee considered it quite impossible to discuss the true situation in public. At all events, when the Central Committee of the SED held its fourteenth session on June 21—just four days after the rising—it issued a communiqué "On the Present Situation and the Immediate Tasks facing the Party," in which it described June 17 as a D day for which the West had long been preparing and tried to prove that at that particular point of time the international situation had been such that the western powers had been forced to provoke disturbances in the GDR. This interpretation of the day's events was endorsed and complemented by the communiqué put out by the Central Committee of the SED after its fifteenth session, which formed the basis of party policy from then onwards. Meanwhile, press and radio took their lead from the communique of June 21. Immediately after the rising and prior to the publication of this document a number of newspapers had tried to reconcile the two conflicting views of the day's events by arguing that they had involved both genuine demonstrations and an attempted putsch. Some commentators maintained that the West had seized upon the demonstrations and exploited them for its own ends, while others asserted that the provocation of western agents had elicited a partial response from certain discontented workers. But such interpretations evidently did not meet with the approval of the SED leadership and soon disappeared from newspaper reports and editorials. At the mass meetings held at the end of June in all the major cities of the GDR to demonstrate the nationwide support of the population for the government and the party the arguments put forward by the speakers were firmly based on the two leitmotifs of the Central Committee's communiqués: (1) the events of June 17 were due exclusively to the activities of western agents provocateurs, and (2) the measures introduced or planned by the government would ensure a speedy improvement in the general standard of living.

However, it would seem that the SED leaders were by no means convinced that their views would meet with a sympathetic response from the people and, more particularly, from the workers, who had played an active part in the demonstrations of June 17.

Their doubts on this account led them to undertake an interesting and significant experiment designed to improve their popularity: between June 20 and the beginning of July leading party functionaries visited a number of the larger industrial sites, where they entered into long, self-critical and, in nearly all cases, extremely open discussions with the workers in an attempt to regain their confidence.

Das Neue Deutschland and *Die Tägliche Rundschau* carried reports on twenty-nine discussions of this kind which were held in districts where the disturbances had been particularly serious. Thus, fourteen were staged in Berlin, nine in industrial concerns, and five on building sites (four of them on the Stalin-Allee), while a further six discussions were held in Saxony and four in Sachsen-Anhalt.

The journalists reporting these events were careful to

point out that in three of the works where discussions were held there had been no strike action on June 17. However, from the general tenor of their articles it is quite apparent that the personnel of the other twenty-six works concerned did play an active and, in some cases, a leading part in the strikes and demonstrations. The Ammendorf Waggonfabrik (Railway Coach Factory), the Leuna-Werk, the Thälmann-Werk in Magdeburg, the Marx-Werk in Potsdam and the Neptun-Warnow Docks in Rostock, all of which were visited by party speakers, were among the most prominent industrial concerns involved in the rising. And so the top members of the SED leadership hurried off to the factories and building sites. Apart from numerous members of the Central Committee, eleven of the fourteen members and candidate members of the Politburo took part in these discussions. Only Zaisser, Jendretzky (who was said to be ill) and Pieck (who was convalescing in the Soviet Union) failed to do so.

This campaign was a definite success. For the most part the discussions appear to have been both open and detailed. In certain cases they went on until quite late at night and, judging by the newspaper reports, it would seem that the workers were not afraid to speak up for themselves. Material worries, objections to the working methods in the factories and political criticisms were all debated and the debates were reported (in an edited form no doubt) in the press. Apparently the party leadership was well satisfied with the outcome of these discussions and considered that the danger of further risings had been banished. Consequently, the campaign was discontinued at the beginning of July.

But, if we compare the speeches made by the leading

SED politicians in the various discussions we see that, at that time, there was a marked divergence of opinion within the leadership. For, although the majority of the speakers based their remarks exclusively on the assertion made by the Central Committee at its fourteenth session that the June rising had been provoked by western agents, there were some who paid little or no attention to this party directive.

If we disregard Zaisser and Jendretzky, who did not take part in the discussions although they were both in the GDR at the time, then Rudolf Herrnstadt, a candidate member of the Politburo and the chief editor of *Das Neue Deutschland*, appears to have deviated most noticeably from the party line. He openly conceded that the workers had had good reasons for taking strike action, although he regretted the fact that, in doing so, they had become embroiled in a western putsch attempt and so—quite inadvertently—had helped to further foreign interests. The SED writer KUBA (Kurt Babels) argued along similar lines although with rather less finesse. After admitting that real abuses had existed he went on to suggest that the use of force had really been quite unnecessary in view of the new line introduced by the government on June 9.

Anton Ackermann, a candidate member of the Politburo and Secretary of State in the Foreign Ministry, and—more significantly—the Minister President Otto Grotewohl also conceded governmental responsibility for the miserable state of the economy in the spring of 1953. Because it had committed errors, they said, the government had been obliged to introduce the new line, which had then been misconstrued by the public as an open admission of bankruptcy. Neither of these speakers made any reference to western provocation, thus greatly undermining the official party line.

Finally, there was a third group of speakers who maintained a strict silence on the subject of the rising and the events leading up to it, restricting their comment to the sociopolitical and politicoeconomic demands of the workers. This essentially practical approach is best illustrated by the five speeches delivered by the deputy Minister President Heinrich Rau. (See documents).

It was not until the end of July that the differences of opinion and the struggle for power within the SED leadership became apparent to outside observers and, although Ulbricht had little difficulty in forcing his two principal opponents, Herrnstadt and Zaisser, out of the Politburo, it took him several months to have them expelled from the party. We still know very little about the precise aims then pursued by the opposition forces or about the methods which they used to achieve them. Above all, we have only a vague idea about when they first evolved their alternative policies. This is scarcely surprising since the speeches in which the members of the victorious Ulbricht group commented on their vanquished opponents are our sole source of information; in the circumstances it seems questionable whether they will have given a balanced and just account. Nonetheless, we are still able to form a general impression of the aims and activities of the opposition group.

According to the communiqué issued by the Central Committee after its fifteenth session Rudolf Herrnstadt and Wilhelm Zaisser, aided on occasions by Anton Ackermann and Elli Schmidt (who was later accused of referring to Ulbricht in the Politburo by "one of the coarsest expressions") and protected by the "conciliators" Hans Jendretzky and Heinrich Rau, "formed an anti-party faction with a defeatist policy calculated to undermine party unity . . . and adopted a defamatory platform with the object of splitting the party leadership." But what lay behind these vague and misleading statements? The platform referred to in the communiqué was real enough. It was a written memorandum, intended to serve as a basis for internal discussion, and which actually was discussed by the Politburo on June 16, 1953, at the precise moment when the building workers of East Berlin were preparing to demonstrate. This memorandum contained a severe criticism of SED policy to date, it called for reforms both in the economy and in the machinery of government and, above all, it urged the regime to carry out a thorough reorganization of the party. The opposition group wanted the SED to become what Hermann Matern, speaking at the Fourth Party Congress, had called a "party of the people," one that would "also represent the just interests of other classes and class groups." But if these demands were to be met, then Ulbricht, who was the original architect and perfect exemplar of the old party line, would have to go. Ulbricht and his followers later maintained that if the program of reforms proposed by the Herrnstadt-Zaisser group had been carried out, it would have been tantamount to the restoration of capitalism in the GDR; they even claimed that Zaisser had toyed with the idea of handing over the GDR in order to preserve international peace, an idea that Beria is known to have entertained. Zaisser himself repudiated this charge completely. On the face of it, it seems hardly likely that the opposition group within the SED would have formed such a pessimistic assessment of their country's prospects. They were in complete agreement with Ulbricht over the need to build a socialist Germany. They only disagreed over the means whereby this end was to be achieved.

Herrnstadt and Zaisser probably had better connections in the USSR than any other East German politician except Ulbricht, and no doubt had taken all possible steps to obtain Russian backing for their program. The fact that they nonetheless failed to impose their will on the SED leadership had two principal causes.

In the first place Beria's downfall, which came just a few days after the June rising, placed the opposition group within the SED in a difficult position and greatly undermined their chances.

At the end of July Ulbricht claimed that Beria had conducted negotiations in East Berlin through two special envoys without informing the Politburo, and had instructed Herrnstadt and Zaisser to bring about Ulbricht's downfall. But in his speech at the Fourth Party Congress Hermann Matern stated quite categorically that, when the members of the Central Control Commission of the SED had investigated this matter, they had discovered "no indications of direct influence by the criminal Beria." [38] They had merely suggested that the "divisive activities of Herrnstadt and Zaisser" should be considered in the light of the facts which had emerged from the reports of the Beria trial. The facts referred to here were the accusations which had been levelled against Beria and which were essentially the same as those made against Herrnstadt and Zaisser by Ulbricht. According to an internal Russian memorandum, to which the members of the Central Committee of the SED had had access at their fifteenth session, Beria had been accused of pursuing a "capitulationary" policy, which was designed to restore the capitalist system, of opposing the Agricultural Collectives and the development of socialism in the GDR and of carrying his desire for compromise to such lengths that his policies might have led to the abolition of East German socialism. Subsequently, after Beria's downfall, Malenkov was also accused of these crimes.[39] The validity of such charges is, of course, extremely dubious since the accusers had such an obvious vested interest: to strengthen their own position by discrediting a toppled rival. For many years now there has been a kind of inverted personality cult in the USSR, in which Beria presently occupies the position once held by Trotsky.[40] Consequently, when contemporary politicians in the eastern bloc countries wish to charge an opponent with deviationist practices, one of their favorite ways of doing so is to accuse him of wanting to betray the interests of the GDR and, if necessary, to sacrifice the country for the sake of some new policy. The accusations and counteraccusations which have been made by the Russians and Chinese of recent years are typical of this kind of procedure. However, whether Herrnstadt and Zaisser were acting on instructions from Beria or not, the fact that Ulbricht was able to impute such a motivation made it much easier for him to deal with the opposition to his leadership within the GDR.

But it is nonetheless distinctly possible that Ulbricht would not have survived the failure of his policy and the defeat of his party but for the fact that Moscow was clearly loth to allow him to be replaced in the immediate aftermath of the rising. For the removal of Ulbricht might well have been interpreted as a concession by the insurgents and consequently have encouraged them to make further demands. This is the second and the more important reason for the failure of the opposition forces within the SED to topple Ulbricht from his position as leader of the party. Ulbricht did not survive in spite of the weakness revealed by his government on June 17. He survived because of that weakness, because Moscow could not afford to take the risk of having him replaced. Instead of bringing about his downfall the protesting workers and the conspiratorial SED functionaries unwittingly contrived to prevent it.

Conclusion

On several occasions Lenin analyzed the conditions necessary for the emergence of a "concrete revolutionary situation." The classical description of this process is in his "Collapse of the Second International" of 1915, in which he pinpointed three principal features of a revolutionary situation:

"1) The inability of the ruling classes to maintain their rule unchanged; some crisis or other among the 'top ranks,' a political crisis within the ruling class that creates a cleft, through which the discontent and indignation of the suppressed classes erupt. . . .

"2) The intensification of the distress and misery of the suppressed classes beyond what they are accustomed to.

"3) For the above reasons considerable activity on the part of the masses, who readily allow themselves to be exploited in a 'peaceful' epoch but who are induced to take independent historical action in stormy periods . . . as a result of the critical conditions." [41]

These three features were present in the GDR in the spring of 1953.

1) The GDR was the first country in the eastern bloc in which there was a significant change in official policy following Stalin's death: the establishment of socialism, which had been pursued ruthlessly until then, was halted and some of the programs of the Stalinist period were abandoned. Initially, it was impossible to assess the significance of this change of policy or to predict its consequences. As a result it produced a profound sense of insecurity among the party functionaries both at the SED District Headquarters in Berlin and in the small provincial units, both in the party machine and in the administration, and even in the armed forces.

2) The change of policy was necessary because the economic and financial resources of the GDR were inadequate for the task of transforming the territory into a people's republic. The marked increase in the number of refugees and the severe shortage of food beginning in the autumn of 1952 had shown quite clearly that the SED had overreached itself.

3) When the higher quotas, which had been fixed at the end of May 1953 against the express wishes of the workers, were not withdrawn following the introduction of the new line, the workers grew restive and gave vent to their dissatisfaction by staging strikes and—in conjunction with other sections of the population—demonstrations on June 16 and 17.

These three factors undoubtedly provided the principal

motivation for the East German rising. Other factors, such as programs transmitted by western radio stations, were only of secondary significance. To my mind Lenin's thesis—which he would scarcely have expected to find applied to such a situation—defines the major causes underlying the events of June 17 with complete accuracy: the insecurity at all levels of the communist leadership, the extremely critical economic situation and the pent-up discontent of the workers that was searching for an outlet. For a theoretical and practical revolutionary like Lenin the failure of the rising would hardly have come as a surprise. He knew that "no single revolutionary movement can endure without a stable . . . leadership-organization." [42] The rebellious workers lacked such leadership, and they lacked such an organization. So did the GDR.

Could the events of June 17 recur in the GDR? Bearing in mind that shortly before the June rising the historians Gerhard Ritter and Walter Görlitz were arguing that there can be no popular movements against modern forms of tyranny, it is perhaps wiser to be sparing with prophecies. What is quite certain, however, is that the rising of June 17—like the later risings in other eastern bloc countries—was made possible only by a combination of several quite different factors. Such constellations are rare. Thus, when the new crisis over succession developed in the USSR following the fall of Khrushchev, the GDR was in a far better position than it had been twelve years earlier.

In those twelve years it overcame considerable difficulties, consolidating its position both at home and abroad. Since the summer of 1955 the Soviet Union has stated over and over again that the GDR is a second independent German state, whose approval must be sought for any permanent solution to the problems of Central Europe. Ulbricht and his followers have undisputed control of the party leadership. As far as we know, Ulbricht had the backing of Moscow and within the upper echelons of the SED—which are the only ones that matter—he had no opponents until the end of the sixties. He has in any case little to fear, for he has been pursuing a policy of reform in many different spheres for some time past, which has effectively silenced any opposition that might otherwise have found expression. Nothing could be further from the truth than the assertion that there are powerful forces in the GDR pressing for the deposition of the present ruling class and the introduction of an alternative system of government. The West's inactivity on June 17, 1953, in October 1956, and on August 13, 1961, was a bitter lesson that contributed to the resignation of the present generation of East Germans and helped to impress on them the need to come to terms with the SED regime, since they were likely to remain members of the eastern bloc for some time to come.

The situation is still largely in a state of flux, but the general line of development is clear enough. The time is ripe for evolution and not for revolutions.

DOCUMENTS

1. The Raising of the Quotas: Resolution of the Central Committee of the SED of May 14, 1953; "On the Raising of Productivity and the Introduction of Strict Economy"

According to the criteria established by the General Secretary of the German Socialist Unity Party, Comrade Walter Ulbricht, in his report on the ramifications of the XIXth Party Congress of the Communist Party of the Soviet Union, the resolution passed by the IInd Party Conference calling on the party to lay the foundations for the construction of socialism, necessitates the strengthening of socialist industry, in other words the reconstruction of existing socialist concerns and the construction of new socialist concerns, the development of heavy industry and machine construction in accordance with the laws governing the expansion of the socialist economy. The fulfillment of these tasks depends, above all, on an uninterrupted rise in productivity and a constant reduction of production costs.

These conditions can only be fulfilled by the introduction of a strict economy regime and the application of all available accumulated profits to the development of socialism in our German Democratic Republic. Only in this way can we progress towards the realization of the fundamental economic law on which socialism is based and which Comrade Stalin formulated as follows:

"The achievement of the maximum satisfaction of the constantly increasing material and cultural needs of the whole of society by the uninterrupted growth and the constant improvement of socialist production on the basis of highly developed techniques."

In many concerns the technological basis of production is outmoded and inadequate. Because the requirements of socialist development and the needs of the people have to be satisfied it is essential that work should be concentrated, far more than it has been in the past, on the construction of new concerns, the modernization and improvement of existing concerns and the building of new dwellings and cultural institutions, and that a considerable part of the profit resulting from the [nation's] work must be employed for the realization of these great tasks.

The accumulated resources needed for these purposes can only be built up as a result of higher productivity over a long period combined with lower production costs. One important means of achieving this is provided by the development and introduction of technically based work quotas.

The [present] totally unsatisfactory method of determining work quotas in the socialist concerns in all branches of our economy shows that too little attention has been paid to the realization of these ideas, which are so important for our economic development. The proportion of technically based work quotas is unsatisfactory while the quotas based on "past statistics" are out of keeping with modern technology, with the experience and achievements of the activists, with the organization of industrial processes and with the higher skill of [modern] workers. They have become a serious obstacle to our economic and social development in the German Democratic Republic.

The works managements and the officials in charge of departments dealing with economic matters are paying too little attention to the development and introduction of technically based work quotas and are allowing these important matters to follow their own impetus. This leads to the emergence of quotas which are against the public interest since they do not raise the standard of living of the population. Workers are [at present] over-fulfilling their quotas by 150 to 200 per cent without achieving any commensurate increase in productivity.

The establishment of work quotas based on false criteria is encouraged by the guidelines published by the Ministry of Labor for the development and introduction of technically based work quotas, according to which it is not admissible for wages to be reduced as a result of the introduction of new work quotas. This provision has proved to be a mistake and an obstacle to the whole project for the development and introduction of technically based work quotas and must be amended.

The Central Committee of the German Socialist Unity Party adopts the view that the ministers, secretaries of state and general foremen should initiate and carry through all necessary measures to remedy abuses in the sphere of work quotas with the object of establishing [all] work quotas at a normal level and raising those of crucial importance to [national] production by an average of at least 10 per cent before June 1, 1953.

[All] factory quotas are to be reviewed at once with a view to raising them and, after the factory party organizations and the comrades in the trade union organizations have carefully and conscientiously explained the situation to the workers, these higher quotas are to be introduced by the factory manager. The feasibility of this measure has been demonstrated by the fact that the workers in numerous factories have already requested higher quotas of their own accord and also by the many appeals submitted to the government of the GDR by works and workers' brigades calling for higher quotas throughout the country.

The splendid examples set by [so] many different concerns show quite clearly that this great achievement was only made possible by a cooperative effort and staunch opposition to all antiquated views coupled with improved working methods. It is essential that the party, trade union and economic organizations should now place themselves at the head of this great workers' movement and support it to the best of their ability. The educational work being carried out among the broad mass of the population to impress on our workers the necessity for higher quotas must be intensified and endeavors must be made to ensure that the initiative shown by the more progressive workers and brigades is shared by all the workers. It is the duty of our party members to take up their positions in the vanguard of this movement and to distinguish themselves both by their exemplary work in the modernization movement and in the calculation of technically based work quotas. The local trade union organizations in our industrial concerns can afford considerable support both in raising the present levels of work quotas and in the development of technically based work quotas by forming groups embracing "heroes of labor," "activists" and "modernizers," engineers, technicians and skilled workers.

The use of advanced techniques, the full exploitation of our available capacity, the obligatory introduction of new working methods, the thoroughgoing implementation of the piece rate principle and the constant raising of the workers' skills presuppose a fundamental improvement in work organization and a responsible and rational form of management. We know from the experiences of the Soviet Union that this is the only way to develop productivity in such a way as to provide optimum satisfaction of the workers' material and cultural needs.

If these measures are to be implemented the following six points must be observed: (1) The heads of ministries and secretariats of state must establish indices for the raising of work quotas based on calculations that would ensure a minimum average increase of 10 per cent. These higher quotas must be regarded as a first step towards the elimination of the present antiquated quotas and as the point of departure for a systematic procedure for the establishment of technically based quotas. (2) The higher quotas must be evolved by the factory foremen, the officials from the Department for Quotas and the technologists under the supervision of their factory director, who will bear the ultimate responsibility for their findings. These must take account of the actual fulfillment of individual work quotas, the results of time and motion studies, the elimination of any deficiencies revealed by the investigations and the experiences of activists and modernizers. (3) The resulting higher quotas must be endorsed by the factory director and announced to the workers before they are introduced. They should not then be altered until December 31, 1953, unless new large scale technical or organizational changes are made [in a particular works.] (4) The factory management must take all possible measures to enable the workers to fulfill and overfulfill the new quotas. These measures must be incorporated into the collective agreements, where these have yet to be concluded, or into special appendices to existing collective agreements in the form of binding undertakings on the part of the management. In addition, all department heads in all departments must evolve, in conjunction with all their workers, a schema of technical and organizational tasks, for which they will be responsible and whose implementation must be constantly watched over by the "directors for work" and the local trade union managements. This schema should embrace, above all, the improvement of work organization, the training of skilled workers, changes in technical procedures, the elimination of time losses and the improvement of the instruction given by foremen and brigade leaders. (5) In the period from June 1, 1953 to December 31, 1953 time allowances and technical and economic guide lines must be worked out by scientific methods so as to ensure that plans evolved in accordance with technically based work quotas can be introduced for the year 1954 and that the new planning year can start on January 1, 1954, with a minimum of 50 per cent of the work quotas technically based. These technically based work quotas must cover the economically most important processes in the factories. (6) The works party organizations and the comrades in the trade union organizations must explain to the workers the importance of these work norms and the need to review and raise them at the end of each year.

In order to facilitate the implementation of these political and economic measures, which is imperative if we are to raise the real level of wages or, alternatively, the standard of living of our workers and employees, the Central Committee of the German Socialist Unity Party calls upon all party members in industrial concerns, in the departments responsible for the administration of the economy, in the district and precinct headquarters and in the trades unions to carry out a large scale educational project among the workers to explain the importance of improving the work quotas so as to ensure the successful fulfillment and overfulfillment of the five-year plan and thus ensure a constant rise in the standard of living of the whole population.

Dokumente der SED, Vol. IV, pp. 410 ff.

2. *The New Line: The Decision. Communiqué Issued by the Politburo of the SED on June 9, 1953*

At its session of June 9, 1953 the Politburo of the SED passed a resolution recommending to the government of the GDR that it should implement a series of measures designed to bring about a marked improvement in the standard of living of all sections of the population and to strengthen the legal rights of the individual in the German Democratic Republic. The Politburo of the Central Committee of the SED took the view that both the SED and the government of the German Democratic Republic have committed a series of errors in the past, which have found expression in decrees and directives (such as the decree introducing new regulations for the distribution of ration cards and the decree authorizing the takeover of rundown agricultural holdings), in special census measures, in harsher taxation methods and so on. The interests of certain sections of the population, such as the independent farmers, private business men, craftsmen and intellectuals, were neglected. Moreover, serious errors were committed in the implementation of the abovementioned decrees and regulations in the districts, precincts and towns. One result of this has been that a large number of people have left the republic.

In passing its resolutions the Politburo has kept the great goal of German unity in mind, which calls for concrete measures from both sides designed to facilitate a rapprochement between the two parts of Germany.

For these reasons the Politburo of the Central Committee of the SED considers it essential that a series of measures should be introduced in the near future, in conjunction with the proposed modifications of the plan for heavy industry, which would correct these past errors and improve the standard of living of the workers and farmers, the intellectuals and tradesmen and all the other middle class groups. At its session on June 9 the Politburo decided on measures to deal with trade and agriculture and the supply of food and also on measures designed to ease travel between the German Democratic Republic and West Germany.

In order to increase the production of consumer goods, which are manufactured by small and medium sized private concerns, and in order to expand the trade network it is suggested that craftsmen, retail and wholesale traders and independent industrial, construction and transport concerns should be granted any short term credits they may need. The coercive measures introduced in the period up to the end of 1951 for the collection of arrears of income tax and social security contributions are to be waived for small, medium and big farmers, retail and wholesale businesses and independent industrial, construction and transport concerns, in other words for the whole of the private sector.

If any proprietors of businesses, who have recently closed or given up their businesses, should wish to reopen them, they are to be encouraged to do so. It is further proposed that the HO should conclude agency agreements with private retailers in order to provide a better service for the public.

The Politburo also recommends that the decrees authorizing the takeover of rundown agricultural holdings should be rescinded and that the practice of appointing managers for failure to fulfill the official quota or for incurring income tax arrears should be discontinued. Those farmers (small, medium and big farmers) who have left their holdings and fled to West Berlin or West Germany because of the difficulties they encountered in running their farms should be given an opportunity of returning to their farms. In exceptional cases, where this is not possible, the farmers concerned should be offered full compensation. Those who do return to their farms should be given credits and agricultural stock to help develop them. Sentences passed [on farmers] for failure to fulfill their quota or to meet income tax demands should be reviewed. It is recommended in this connection that the Minister for Agriculture and Forestry should be instructed to take all necessary measures to safeguard the interests of the agricultural collectives.

The Politburo further recommends that all persons who have fled the country and now wish to return to the territory of the German Democratic Republic or to the democratic sector of Berlin should have any property that was confiscated under the decree of July 17, 1952, to safeguard [East German] assets restored to them. If restoration proves impossible in individual cases, compensation should be given. There should be no discrimination against refugees returning to the republic. They should be reintegrated into the economic and social life [of the country] by the competent departments of the district or precinct councils concerned and should be granted full rights of citizenship (German identity card, ration card and so on). Information centers should be set up to provide those returning with any information and advice they may require.

The Politburo further considers that the regulations governing the issue of permits for West Germans and West Berliners to visit the GDR and of interzonal passes should be made less stringent, thus facilitating travel between East and West Germany. When West Germans or West Berliners apply for permits to visit the GDR or for interzonal passes, family reasons should also be recognized [as valid grounds]. Above all, scientists and artists should be enabled to attend conferences in West Germany, and artists from West Germany should also be allowed to take part in conferences in the German Democratic Republic.

The Politburo further recommends that all pupils suspended from higher modern schools as a result of the recent investigation of higher modern school pupils and the discussion of the activities of the *Junge Gemeinde* should be readmitted to their classes and allowed to take any examinations they may have missed. Moreover, any teachers dismissed or transferred as a result of the investigation of higher modern schools should be reinstated in their old positions. All cases of relegation from colleges and universities during the past few months should be reviewed immediately and a final decision reached before June 20, 1953. In the case of enrollments at colleges and universities there should be no discrimination against capable children from middle class homes.

The Politburo also recommends that the government of the German Democratic Republic should instruct the judicial departments to arrange for the immediate release of all prisoners sentenced to a period of one to three years imprisonment under the terms of the law passed for the protection of public property save in cases involving serious consequences [for the state].

It is also recommended that all persons remanded on charges under the law for the protection of public property whose sentences are not expected to exceed the legal minimum of one to three years should be released at once.

Finally, the Politburo has decided to recommend to the government of the German Democratic Republic that from July 1, 1953, ration cards should be issued to all citizens of the German Democratic Republic and the democratic sector of Greater Berlin according to the occupational categories established in law. It is also recommended that the increases in the price of jam, artificial honey and confectioneries introduced in April 1953 should be withdrawn as from June 15, 1953, that the fifty per cent reduction in workmen's return fares should, from July 1, 1953, be extended to all travelers in the relevant occupational categories irrespective of the size of their income, that reduced fares for schoolchildren and teachers, for certain classes of workers and for severely disabled persons, allotment holders and so on should be restored and the payment of fares by the social security authorities for visits to specialists reintroduced.

Dokumente der SED, Vol. IV, pp. 428 ff.

3. Announcement and Justification of the New Line: "On the Meeting of Party Activists in Berlin"—Speech by Comrade Otto Grotewohl

Comrades!

On June 9 the Politburo issued a communiqué of great importance. In this communiqué the Politburo set out the measures which, it considers, need to be implemented in the immediate future. At the same time the party and the government have openly and honestly corrected a number of existing errors.

We had no intention of putting these necessary measures into effect behind closed doors, in some quiet retreat. We have always taken the view that the people and the government are an entity. This view has remained unchanged. It applies in good times and, even more so, in serious times. The Politburo of our party and the government have no thought of avoiding this serious discussion with our people. We are firmly convinced that a relationship of real trust between the people, the party and the government can only exist if the path of open and serious discussion, which has been followed in the past, is also pursued in the future. There are people who say: why didn't the government listen to us? Naturally, we listened to all those voices. It was because we listened to them that we arrived at the proposals and measures with which we are now concerned. "For a government to identify its errors so openly and correct them so decisively and thoroughly, is most unusual." That is what one of our many correspondents wrote to us. And a professor in West Germany wrote: "We cannot conceive that the Bonn government would ever behave like that. If it possessed anything like the strength and honesty shown by the German Democratic Republic in admitting to its errors, then the Bonn system of war treaties could be abolished and, with them, the risk of a European war, and we could progress towards a united Germany with giant strides." I believe that is true. This comparison shows the enormous difference between a government, whose principal concern is to live and work in close contact with the people, and a government such as Adenauer's, which is bent on policies that are inimical to a closer understanding and pose a threat to peace. Our friends in West Germany should not forget: it is impossible to negotiate with Adenauer, Adenauer has to be overthrown. Our party and our government do not indulge in political maneuvers or stratagems. If errors have been committed and recognized, then it is in the interests of the people to correct them speedily and thoroughly. That is what we want to do and that is what we are doing. An hour ago, just before I set out for this meeting, I received a long and instructive letter from an old comrade of our party, who made many extremely critical observations but finally adopted a frank and honest attitude. At the end of his letter, which was written with passionate conviction, he said: "I am not a faultfinder or a malcontent, but I know the hardship of the poor only too well, and consequently have made myself their spokesman. Always listen to criticism from below and lend your ear to the people. That is right and fitting, only it must be more than mere theory. You have shown the whole world that you were able to put this theory into practice in the most magnificent way when you withdrew the decrees. You will, and must, be thanked for this with tokens of affection and confidence." Now, far be it from us to go fishing for laurels and recognition at a time like this. We are interested simply and purely in the cause of our people. That is why we are able to speak so openly and clearly about these matters. We are not seeking refuge in demagogic tricks, euphemisms or evasions. But our errors, which we openly admit, are not due to a lack of understanding. On the contrary, these errors have come about as a result of an honest attempt to speed up the developments designed to create a higher standard of living for the whole people. This was where the crucial error was made.

Our experiences since 1945 have shown that the transfer of works owned by monopolists, warmongers, and nazis to public ownership and the planning of the economy on this basis resulted in a development that is proof against crisis. In our country the productive forces develop, not as in the anarchical countries of the imperialist world, but in complete harmony and in a proper relationship to one another. Our nationalized economy is already showing a constant increase in production and has led to an increase in popular affluence. The basic discrepancy between our productive forces and the state of our production was already well on the way to being removed and had released the energies of the people. This was made possible by the vital development of our economy and by the opportunities which this provided for improving the standard of living of the population. During this period we increased and improved the turnover of [consumer] goods by reducing prices in the HO no less than twelve times. During this period we drafted important laws which made human beings and human labor the focal point of society. The progressiveness and boldness of this legislation is unequalled in the annals of Germany. Thanks to the devoted efforts of our workers and farmers, our scientists and technicians, this successful economic and cultural development in the German Democratic Republic was accomplished ahead of the schedule laid down in the five year plan. Despite all difficulties encountered in the acquisition of raw materials and primary commodities production levels rose constantly. In the agricultural sphere we exceeded the 1936 production figures per hectare of land. This steadily rising curve justified the assumption made in the spring that we had reached the point where we could proceed to create the basis for the establishment of socialism at a faster rate. But by then we had been encumbered by a number of financial and economic burdens which aggravated [the situation] and prevented us from attaining our objective. Some of these were imposed upon us by the aggressive military preparations made against the GDR; others resulted from the abuse of our laws in industrial works and in the middle grades of the administration. And so we were obliged to take measures to ward off the harmful repercussions [of these developments]. If, today, I mention only the most important and crucial of these matters, I hope the comrades will nonetheless obtain a clear and coherent view of the situation. The first major setback arose in the second half of 1952 [and was] due to the cold war policy pursued by Bonn insofar as we were forced to incur considerable unforeseen expenditure for the protection of our state and our achievements.

The second disruption of the normal course of the economy occurred as a result of the abuse of the resolutions which we had passed authorizing wage increases for the workers in the first four wage groups of our heavy industries. We were not aware of the full repercussions of this error until we came to assess the state of the country's finances at the end of 1952. The Politburo and the government had decided that these wage increases, which involved a total of 700 million marks, should be paid in two stages, the first in 1952 and the second in 1953. But this policy was completely changed in the middle grades of the administration and in the industrial works. This led to a complete distortion of the normal relationship between the wages fund and the production fund. The production fund was running at a level of 14 billion marks while by the end of 1952 the wages fund had already reached a level of 18 billion. This discrepancy of 4 billion marks between wages and production, which had been carefully concealed until it was suddenly discovered [by the auditors], inevitably led to a sharp decline in the production of consumer goods, which coincided with a shortage of food in the sugar and food markets due to the bad weather. Sabotage and faulty work then resulted in the supply difficulties which we all know about.

As if this were not enough, we had removed the development of our heavy industry and of other important sectors of the economy from the five-year plan and carried them forward to 1952. Our confident expectations were based on the assumption that, by stepping up the development of our heavy industry, we could also increase the production of manufactured and consumer goods, thus effecting a considerable improvement in our foreign trade. This assumption proved false and today we know that none of the stages in the development of the economy can be omitted. Fundamental laws of political economy cannot be suspended by resolutions. That has been made perfectly clear by the course of events. What we now have to do is draw the necessary conclusions from this fact.

But economic events are never isolated. On the contrary, they are invariably linked with great and profound social developments. In the implementation of all these measures we encountered fierce resistance from the opposition. The class struggle grew more bitter all along the line and in every aspect of social life. Persecution and slander were rife and resulted in the nonfulfillment of delivery quotas, artificially inflated tax assessments and secret and, in many cases, even open resistance to the economic and administrative measures taken by the state. In trying to eradicate these defects we relied almost entirely on administrative means. That was wrong. The administrative method—police action and harsh sentences —is wrong and stifles the productive forces of a people.

This was made apparent by the events that followed: the general restriction of supplies, the pernicious effect on retailers and on the middle class, the flight of the farmers to West Germany and the justified growth of discontent among the workers over the many measures taken in the social security field, over the abolition of cheap fares and so on. The flight to the West led to the creation of a vast army of propagandists in the West, who turned against the East, against the GDR. Moreover, the effects of these policies were calculated to widen the rift between the people in the western and eastern parts of Germany.

In the final analysis, of course, that is an intolerable error and an intolerable state of affairs, for it touches upon the most central and the most crucial problem facing the German nation. The unity of Germany is the firm base for a better future and for conditions of peace in Germany and Europe. When people turn away from us, when in addition to political and economic divisions we also find that the human relationships which still form a bond between Germans are being rent, then this policy is wrong. We now have to draw all the necessary conclusions, without fear or scruple. The vanguard of the German working class must unite still more closely with the masses, and it is up to us to promote this condition of unity. There is no other way—for all the reasons I have given. We have to make a change of course. It is not just a question of carrying through a program of small and insignificant tactical measures. What we have to do is make a complete change, one that has become essential and can no longer be deferred, with all due order and discipline.

The enemy speaks of collapse and catastrophe. There is no justification for either. We are making this change because it is necesary to protect the living conditions of our people in the GDR and because a proper understanding between Germans is a necessary condition of any solution to the great problems facing the German nation. People ask us why it is that we are suddenly able to do this. Well, you know, it seems to me that if, after a searching analysis, after searching criticism and self-criticism, the right path has been mapped out, then nothing can prevent a responsible party and government from successfully following that path together with the people.

We have taken a number of measures in an attempt to bring an immediate and beneficial influence to bear on the living conditions of the people and on their political consciousness. We took these measures with all speed and in all seriousness and are determined to take other far-reaching measures which will also have a favorable effect on the life of the people.

These further measures, which are now being evolved by the Politburo, will be submitted to the Central Committee for its approval and formal ratification. They are concerned with important changes in the national economic plan. The Central Committee of the party will issue a full and comprehensive statement listing all the errors that have been committed and outlining the measures needed for their eradication. The Politburo will be fully accountable to the Central Committee. No errors and no defects in either the party or the administration will remain concealed or be left undiscussed. The leading organ of our party, the Central Committee, will then make its decision. We are of the same blood as the working class and the same flesh as our people. With these bonds the party leadership and the government will overcome its errors, not only by serious theoretical endeavor, but also by practical action, and will work successfully for a better future, for the restoration of national unity and for peace. *Das Neue Deutschland,* June 18, 1953.

4. Ambiguities Concerning the Raising of the Quotas: "It Is Time to Lay Aside the Bludgeon"

70 brigades in the VEB Wohnungsbau* have voluntarily raised their norms! This claim was made in mid-April, and by May a further 50 brigades were supposed to have followed their example, making 125 in all. No other Berlin building concern was able to report comparable progress.

On May 28 a meeting was held at the VEB Wohnungs-

* Nationalized housing industry.

bau headquarters, in which brigade leaders and activists took part, to discuss a recommendation calling for a general increase in work norms averaging out at ten per cent for the whole of the concern. And what happened? The majority voted against a general increase.

At virtually the same time an alarming report was received from Section G-North on the Stalin-Allee to the effect that various carpenters' brigades had refused to start work that morning due to differences with the Department for Quotas. There were similar reports from the Strausberger Platz, where other carpenters' brigades from the VEB Wohnungsbau were employed.

One would have thought that these signs of dissatisfaction among the workers would have prompted the works and party managements at the VEB Wohnungsbau to enquire into their procedural methods and to check the validity of their earlier reports claiming that 125 brigades had voluntarily increased their work quotas. But not a bit of it! Party Secretary Paul Müller is as convinced as ever that the Department for Quotas at the VEB Wohnungsbau is working correctly but [considers that] the construction workers will always be suspicious of the activities of this department. "The discussion of the work quotas was carried out in an exemplary manner," he maintained, "there is absolutely no doubt about that. And the meeting to discuss a general increase in the work norms was wrecked by brigade leader Rocke."

Who Is the Bricklayers' Leader Rocke?

The bricklayers' brigade leader Rocke is one of the several hundred Berlin construction workers on the Stalin-Allee whose achievements last year were outstanding. It was thanks primarily to his initiative that it was possible to make good a considerable backlog of work on Block B-South. Brigade leader Rocke was one of the modernizers on the Stalin-Allee.

At the beginning of May Rocke's bricklayers' brigade started work on the large Ostseestrasse construction site of the VEB Wohnungsbau. "I had hardly been here 20 minutes," brigade leader Rocke told us, "to get everything fixed up for the new building site, when three men from Headquarters arrived and wanted to discuss the question of higher norms. One of them was Lembeck, an official from the Department for Quotas. I said they should wait until the whole brigade had arrived because half of my colleagues were still working on the site on the Mühlenstrasse. Then they told me that my colleagues on the Mühlenstrasse had already agreed to an increase in the work quotas and that the general foreman at the Mühlenstrasse had their signed statements approving the increase in his pocket. I told them they were lying, and I was right. But when they saw I wasn't falling for their trick, Lembeck told me that they would only allow brigades to work on the big building sites if they had raised their quotas. And so we raised our quotas by an average of 6.5 per cent. But in my view it was downright blackmail."

Brigade leader Rocke told his story at the meeting on May 28. And that is why Party Secretary Müller claimed that Rocke had "wrecked" the meeting! Comrade Paul Müller was then informed by comrade Förster, an official in the Work Division of the VEB Wohnungsbau, that Rocke's brigade had been criticized in the democratic press and that RIAS had used the incident for one of its propaganda tirades. Immediately "everything was clear" to Party Secretary Müller. He had no evidence, he had not even read the press article, but as far as he was concerned there was a definite link between the "wrecked meeting" and the inflammatory program transmitted by RIAS.

On May 29, the day after the unsuccessful meeting, comrade Müller visited Rocke's brigade during their lunch break. Completely beside himself, he harangued the men. Brigade leader Rocke, he said, had been named on RIAS; and there was no room for RIAS agents in a nationalized industry.

Today comrade Müller claims that he was speaking "in general terms." But the indignation felt by the members of Rocke's brigade at these monstrous allegations prove that this was not the case. The brigade knew nothing about the article in the democratic press or about the lies concocted by RIAS. Brigade leader Rocke has told us how he felt when he heard the accusations made against him. "When comrade Müller launched into his tirade, I felt as if someone had put a rope round my neck and was knocking my legs from under me," he said. "Yes, that is the state I was in then," he added. "If only somebody had spoken to us properly, we would have agreed to higher quotas without question. But nobody is going to hold a pistol to our heads."

Fuchs' plasterers' brigade received much the same sort of treatment. In their case too the authorities tried to play off one section of the brigade against the others in order to gain their ends.

The Vorwerk Brigade

The treatment meted out to the Vorwerk brigade at building site G-North on the Stalin-Allee provides a further example of the way in which the comrades on the Headquarters staff of the VEB Wohnungsbau think they can disregard the wishes and opinions of the building workers.

The Vorwerk brigade asked for a time and motion study on a particular job, which was carried out by comrade Rank, an official in the Department for Quotas. The workers waited almost three weeks for the results. In the end comrade Rank telephoned to say that the study had "produced no positive result" and that the old norm would be retained. Later, when he visited the building site in another connection and the brigade pressed him for further information, he said that he had no documents with him and so could not discuss the time and motion study. The construction workers then retaliated against this shameful treatment by stopping work. Suddenly comrade Rank was able to find time for the workers. He returned to the site and, after much argument, granted the brigade a handicap allowance of 17 per cent, whereupon the brigade went back to work.

But no sooner had he returned to headquarters than comrade Rank complained that he had been negotiating "under duress," picked up the telephone and withdrew the allowance from the safety of his office chair. And so, instead of the 17 per cent promised to them, the members of the brigade are actually receiving an allowance of one half per cent.

The workers have been deceived by comrade Rank's intrigues, and it testifies to a high degree of social consciousness when the leader of the Vorwerk brigade, who was asked why he had not done anything about this fraudulent treatment, replied: "What can we do, we have to get on with the building, we can't sit around for ever."

"You don't print the things we tell you in your paper!" These were the words with which we were greeted when we visited the excited members of Zock's brigade in their hut on the Strausberger Platz. When the wages for the members of this brigade were announced for the month of May it appeared that their average earnings had been only 1.63 DM per hour. They asked for the figures to be checked. Nothing was done about it. So they stopped work.

The irresponsible officials of the VEB Wohnungsbau then condescended to check the accounts. And what did they find? Their calculations were wrong and the workers had actually earned an average of 1.99 DM per hour.

"We've been arguing with the Department for Quotas for months," the members of the brigade told us. "Our accounts are never right. Do we have to beg for our wages as if they were charity?" After a lengthy discussion they finally said: "You must try to understand our feelings. We work hard enough and we want to be constructive. But what riles us is that nothing ever goes right at headquarters."

Bornemann's scaffolding brigade was subjected to the same sort of treatment.

The Department for Quotas Is Supposed to Help the Brigades

The quota assessors at the VEB Wohnungsbau no longer have any sense of solidarity with their colleagues on the construction sites. They treat them with arrogance and then wonder why the workers have no faith in them. If the quota assessors think they can ingratiate themselves with the company management by their dangerous tricks,

they are mistaken. For they have the construction workers against them, without whom the company can never
function smoothly. The Department for Quotas should
not delude itself into thinking that it can go on acting
against the interests of the construction workers with
impunity for very much longer.

The quota assessors must help the brigades and join
with them in establishing progressive quotas. Immediate
steps must be taken to ensure that the Department for
Quotas at the VEB Wohnungsbau is made fully aware
of this. Every member of this department must endeavor
to establish a relationship of mutual trust between the
department and the construction workers in order to
eliminate the present tensions, which they themselves
have created.

The Dictators

Colleague Paul Müller fondly imagines that the construction workers regard him as an ideal party functionary.
In fact, the opposite is the case.

Christen, the general foreman at the large construction
site on the Ostseestrasse, who is not a member of any
party, said of him: "Colleague Müller invariably behaves
like a dictator. He never finds the right approach, one
that would enable him to convince the building workers
of the need for new measures important for the work
program. He prefers to 'knock things into shape.'" When
we asked him why he, as a general foreman, was prepared
to tolerate such behavior Christen replied: "I don't dare
to say anything. Anyone who contradicts colleague Müller
is likely to be 'müllerized.' In my opinion, he is a man
who simply cannot take criticism. Now, our colleague

from the local SED Headquarters in Prenzlauer Berg is entirely different. Nobody has ever given me as much help and support as he. We always decide between us how our building site can best be helped. I would never discuss such matters with colleague Müller. I have no faith in him."

The young site foreman Sommer, who also has no party affiliation, expressed himself in similar terms. He described comrade Müller's approach in the following words: "Colleague Müller likes people to stand at attention when they speak to him."

And What Do the Comrades from the Production Department Have to Say?

The Secretary of the Party Organization at the Ostseestrasse building site, comrade Stampe, stated: "Comrade Müller adopts an uncritical attitude towards his own work. He has forgotten that we have our own party organization on the building site. That is why he never discusses anything with me. He appears on the building site without letting us know in advance and creates unrest by the way in which he talks to the workers. That is what happened in the discussion with brigade leader Rocke. We don't object to his visiting us. Only, when he does, we expect him to be helpful. But the kind of discussions that he conducts don't help, they simply destroy the workers' faith in the party."

The head of the trade union organization on the building site, a candidate member of our party, formed a similar assessment; and the activist, comrade Scherpinsky, who was awarded his high distinction for outstanding work on the Stalin-Allee, said: "The building workers would sooner see comrade Müller's back than his face because he shouts at them for the slightest thing instead of trying to win them over."

It is the duty of every party functionary and every party member to convince all workers, especially manual workers, of the correctness of our party policy by providing enlightenment at all times, thus encouraging them to collaborate more and more actively in the peaceful development work on which we are engaged. Comrade Müller does not do so.

The autocratic and arrogant attitude adopted by other officials—especially comrades Rank and Lemberg from the Department for Quotas—is, of course, no chance phenomenon. These men have modelled themselves on Party Secretary Müller.

But, then, comrade Müller's autocratic and arrogant attitude is no accident either. He believes that he is acting correctly when he rejects persuasion in favor of the bludgeon, for he has never been criticized for this by his party organization. Not even the district party headquarters has taken exception. On the contrary, comrade Müller's "methods" received official backing when comrade Baum, speaking as a member of the Secretariat of the SED District Headquarters for Greater Berlin, stated in the course of a discussion with party functionaries of the Berlin building industry that, if there were further incidents like those at the G-North building site, they would have to set a strong example: one of the building workers' brigades that had disrupted work discipline on the site would have to be dismissed without notice.

In other words, the building workers, who acted because they wanted to improve administrative procedures and consequently production (which neither the party nor the works management was prepared to do) are to be punished. This, of course, will not do at all.

If a works party organization and leading economic functionaries, who are also members of our party, abuse the workers' confidence, they can hardly expect the workers to take it lying down.

What Lessons Are to Be Drawn from This for the Future Conduct of the Party Organization at the VEB Wohnungsbau?

1. The party organization at the VEB Wohnungsbau must ensure that there are no more shady dealings in the Department for Quotas and that the officials there stop juggling with the quotas once and for all. Only then will it be possible to remove the justified suspicion with which the building workers regard the industry and party leaders.

2. The party organization at the VEB Wohnungsbau must try to ensure that the resolutions passed by our government and party are not implemented dictatorially by administrative order. Higher quotas can only be made legally binding for a brigade after its members have been convinced of the importance of such a measure in the fight for a better standard of living. Every other way of raising work quotas prejudices the work program. The greatest danger is that, when measures are introduced by administrative order, we alienate the workers instead of binding them to us.

3. The senior comrades at the VEB Wohnungsbau must rid themselves of their arrogance and self-deceit and stop painting things in glowing colors. (The "good" reports

which they compiled on the voluntary efforts to raise the work quotas are a case in point.) But this can only be achieved if criticism and selfcriticism are rigorously applied, if the comrades of the party leadership remain mindful of the men on the production line when they frame their resolutions, if these resolutions are informed by a genuine concern for those workers whose allegiance is indispensable if we are to achieve our political aims: the building workers and technicians.

Siegfried Grün
Käthe Stern

Das Neue Deutschland, June 14, 1953.

5. *"On a Number of Harmful Phenomena Attendant on the Increase of the Work Quotas"*

The resolution passed by the Central Committee of the SED at its thirteenth session and the subsequent resolution of the Council of Ministers of the German Democratic Republic of May 28, 1953, in which it was proposed that work quotas should be raised by an average of 10 per cent, are of major importance for increasing productivity, reducing production costs, raising the purchasing power of wages and improving the standard of living of all workers and employees. These resolutions furnish the organizational framework for the important voluntary movement towards higher quotas. They provide for a general review of the quotas in our nationalized industries with a view to raising them in accordance with the code numbers allocated to the different works so as to produce an overall increase of at least 10 per cent.

Because of the concern and responsibility which they felt for the workers the members of the Council of Ministers recommended in their resolution that certain measures should be introduced, whose provisions would come into force at the same time as the higher quotas. The object of these measures is to provide assistance for our working colleagues through the industrial trade union managements.

The most important provision of the resolution passed by the Council of Ministers states that by improving work organization and work skills, by introducing new working methods and improved techniques and eliminating time losses and strengthening work discipline the existing quotas should be raised in all works in accordance with their code numbers for purposes of increasing productivity.

In many works both the works and the trade union managements have conscientiously observed the terms of this resolution. But there are not a few works which have either failed to implement the resolution of the Council of Ministers or have violated its provisions. Thus, a dangerous "theory" has been evolved, which poses a threat to our successful campaign for higher productivity and which assumes that higher quotas must lead to lower wages. The trade unions are firmly opposed to this view, which grossly abuses the authority vested in the resolutions of the party of the working class, the Council of Ministers and the presidium of the executive body of the Federation of Free German Trades Unions and so prejudices the interests of all workers in the most outrageous way.

The work quotas are not being raised in order to force down wages but in order to produce more, better and cheaper goods for the same amount of work but with more economical working methods. This hostile "theory" of a drop in wage levels must be eradicated. The sooner this is done and the more thoroughly it is done, the more actively and the more consciously the workers will identify with the campaign for an average increase of 10 per cent in the work quotas.

But in this connection we must also oppose the positively outrageous methods employed by certain industrial managements who think they can establish new quotas by administrative order. The code numbers to be allocated to our industrial plants must be discussed by all concerned so that they can be correctly determined with the approval of the workers before being ratified and introduced by the management.

Although many industry managements perform their duties in a responsible manner, there are those who consider that the ten per cent overall increase in work quotas proposed by the party and the Council of Ministers after careful deliberation does not apply to them. Using their own judgment, they establish code numbers for their plants which are often twice as high as those envisaged by the appropriate ministry. These arbitrary measures are, of course, extremely harmful and provoke discontent and opposition among the workers. This is what happened in the Lehesten slate quarry in the Gera district, in a number of departments of the "Wilhelm Florin" Steel Works and Rolling Mill in Hennigsdorf and in various other works. Without exception, the managements concerned had to revise their code numbers. In the end quotas were established for these works with the participation of the workers, which were in complete accordance with the terms of the official resolutions.

In such cases that is the only way of strengthening the workers' confidence, thus ensuring the implementation of the resolution providing for higher quotas. For then every colleague will be prepared to identify with the call for higher quotas. Higher quotas can only be introduced in collaboration with the workers, never against their wishes. This is a point to be noted by all those works and trade union managements that have violated this principle. One of the really bad things in this connection is the fact that many trade union managements failed to take prompt action by pointing out to their industry managements that they were behaving improperly. Incidentally, it is such managements that are the advocates of the theory that higher quotas can only, and must, be introduced at the workers' expense. It does not occur to them that the time has come to mobilize all forces in order to exploit our internal resources by improving our work organization, introducing new working methods on a large scale, improving our work skills and eliminating all time losses from our production program. By doing this they could create the necessary conditions for the fulfillment and overfulfillment of the new higher quotas under the new conditions. In other words, by increasing productivity and reducing production costs they could enable the workers to earn as much as in the past and perhaps even more.

It is, of course, possible that, despite the new technical and organizational procedures, industrial workers or groups of workers will not receive their full wage during the first one or two ten day periods, but when they receive their third or fourth wage packet—by which time they will have been able to increase their productivity as a result of the higher quotas and the new technical and organizational methods—they will once again have reached their old wage level. The sooner and the more effectively the new organizational methods are implemented, the sooner the workers will be able to obtain their old wage by achieving higher work quotas and even to exceed it by higher productivity.

It is an undeniable fact that, whenever the works and local union managements have acted in accordance with the resolutions passed by the party and the government and the local union managements have acted in accordance with the resolutions of the presidium and the directives of the executive of the FDGB in the execution of any duties concerned with the raising of the work quotas, quite exemplary results have been achieved. The crucial factor in all cases is the active cooperation and good will of the workers.

The hero of labor Senior Foreman Lutzemann, from the Hettstadt Rolling Mill, roundly condemned the misconceptions which have been so prejudicial to the campaign for higher quotas, when he said:

"If the people in a works say that higher quotas mean lower wages, then there is something wrong with that works, for where we are, in my department, we have raised our quota on three successive occasions this year, increasing productivity by 40 per cent in all, and we have not only got back to our old wage levels again, we have passed them. Why were we able to do this? Because our works management has a technical and organizational plan, because this plan was implemented at the right time and because, as a result, we are able to work with less interruptions and more economically. And what we can do in Hettstadt can also be done in other works, provided that the managements all remain aware of their high responsibility towards the state and towards the work personnel."

This is the reason for the successes achieved in Hettstadt and other works. These managements were successful because they conscientiously and patiently explained to their workers the need for higher quotas on the basis of the resolutions and directives issued by the party, the government and the trade unions and because, with the cooperation of their workers, they carried out a careful review of the organization and technological methods used in their works and then proceeded to improve them. As a result important measures were taken at an early stage, which created a viable basis for the introduction of higher quotas. This is the only way in which this responsible task can be undertaken. Consequently, it is the duty of every works and trade union management to act in accordance with the resolutions and to correct any lapses which may occur without delay. This means, of course, that it is impermissible for works managements to transfer whole groups of workers from one wage group to another on their own initiative. For this they have no authority.

The publication of the communiqués issued by the Politburo and the Council of Ministers on June 9 and 11, 1953, respectively, has prompted a number of people to ask to what extent the resolutions calling for higher quotas are still valid. The resolutions calling for higher quotas are completely valid. Counting on the absolute trust placed by the population in its government the Politburo of the Central Committee of the SED and the government of the German Democratic Republic have openly confessed before the whole people to a number of past errors and have taken immediate steps designed to bring about a marked improvement in the standard of living of all sections of the population of the German Democratic Republic. But since all this depends on our being able to achieve the great tasks set out in the five-year plan on the basis of a steady growth in productivity coupled with strict economy, it is incumbent upon us to do our utmost to implement the resolution of the Council of Ministers calling for an overall increase in the work quotas of 10 per cent by June 30, 1953.

The industrial and trade union managements must regard this as their guiding principle and endeavor to carry out the resolution of the Council of Ministers so as to bring about a large scale improvement in the living conditions of the working population.

Otto Lehmann

Die Tribüne, June 16, 1953.

6. *"Politburo Statement on the Quota Question"*
   (*June 16, 1953*)

As a result of enquiries received from a number of factories and construction sites concerning the question of higher quotas the Politburo of the Central Committee of the SED considers it necessary to issue the following statement:

1. If we are to build a new life [for ourselves] and improve the living conditions, not only of the workers, but of the whole population, we can only do so on the basis of higher productivity and increased production. The revival and speedy development of the economy of the German Democratic Republic after the war was made

possible only by the realization of our old party slogan: "Produce more—Live better." This was and is the only proper course.

For this reason the Politburo regards the initiative shown by the more progressive workers, who have voluntarily gone over to higher quotas, as an important step towards the building of a new life and one which demonstrates to the whole population the way out of our present difficulties.

In this connection, the Politburo considers that one of the most important tasks facing the works managements and the party and trade union organizations is to take any measures needed to improve work organization and increase production, thus ensuring that the wages of those workers who have raised their quotas can be increased in the near future.

2. The Politburo nonetheless considers it quite wrong to effect a 10 per cent increase in work quotas in the public sector by administrative order.

The raising of the work quotas cannot and must not be implemented by administrative methods but only on the basis of conviction and voluntary cooperation.

3. It is recommended that the mandatory increases in work quotas ordered by individual ministries should be withdrawn. The government resolution of May 28, 1953, should be examined in conjunction with the trades unions.

The Politburo calls on the workers to gather around the party and the government and to unmask the hostile agents provocateurs who are trying to sow discord and confusion in the ranks of the working class.

Dokumente der SED, Vol IV, pp. 432–3.

7. *Appeal for Caution: The Evening of June 16. Broadcast by the Minister for All-German Affairs, Jakob Kaiser*

The demonstrations staged by the people of East Berlin will not come as a surprise to those who are aware of the intolerable conditions in the Soviet zone. I am nonetheless appealing to every single East Berliner and to every inhabitant of the Soviet zone not to allow themselves to be rushed, either by their own distress or by acts of provocation, into rash actions. Nobody should place himself or his neighbors in jeopardy.

Any really fundamental change in your living conditions can only be achieved, and will be achieved, by the restoration of German unity and freedom. At this present time, when our reunification policies have at last started to make progress, nobody should allow himself to be induced to dangerous actions. Do not think that we have forgotten our obligation towards you. We are constantly aware of it. We will now impress on the great powers the urgent need for a speedy solution of the German question. It is, of course, hardly necessary to point out that everybody in the Federal Republic and in the whole of the free world feels a sense of solidarity with you. We appreciate your reasons for demonstrating and the courage that this demanded; but we ask you to exercize caution, placing your trust in our sense of solidarity.

8. *A Call for Solidarity: Broadcast by the President of the Berlin Branch of the DGB, Ernst Scharnowski*

For months now, the Federation of German Trade Unions has been anxiously watching the retrograde social development taking place in your zone. The democratic actions that you have taken in your own defence, which are the birthright of every oppressed person and which were inspired by spontaneous and completely genuine feelings on your part, have led to events, whose scope and force have amazed us in West Berlin. As the longest serving democratic trade unionist and President of the Federation of German Trades Unions east of the Elbe I am not able to issue directives to you in the eastern zone and East Berlin. I can only give you good advice, which is inspired by a sincere sense of solidarity.

Your demand for a reduction of the work quotas to a tolerable level must be accepted by your socalled government, not simply as a temporary measure but on a permanent basis. On the next payday the wages should be paid out in full on the basis of the old quotas while at the same time current prices must not only be contained but brought down so that you can maintain your strength, on which your work depends.

The steps which you, the construction workers of East Berlin, have taken on your own responsibility and without outside interference have filled us with admiration and satisfaction. You are fully justified in making your demands by virtue of the fundamental human rights granted under the constitution of the Soviet zone of occupation. Your government passed the resolution granting these fundamental rights and, by doing so, authorized you to fight for better working conditions.

For this reason the whole population of East Berlin may justifiably place its trust in the strongest and most successful groups in the East Berlin workers' movement. Do not abandon them. They are fighting, not only for the social rights of the workers but also for the human rights of the entire population of East Berlin and the eastern zone. So join the movement of the East Berlin construction workers, transport workers and railwaymen and assemble on your own Strausberger Platz. The greater the number taking part, the more powerful, disciplined and successful the demonstrations will be.

The workers of the Federation of German Trade Unions welcome your fight for the most elementary rights of the workers, we assure you of our brotherly affection and firmly believe that you will carry the struggle in good order to a better conclusion.

9. *Government Statement Made by the Federal Chancellor Dr. Konrad Adenauer to the German Federal Parliament on June 17, 1953*

The events in Berlin have elicited a response both from the German public and from the world at large. The Federal Government wishes to make the following statement on these incidents:

No matter how we may assess the origins of the demonstrations staged by the construction workers of East Berlin, in their final form they undoubtedly constituted a powerful manifestation of the desire for freedom felt by the German people in the Soviet zone. The Federal Government sympathizes with the men and women in Berlin who are now demanding freedom from oppression and hardship. We assure them of our heartfelt concern. We hope that they will not allow themselves to be provoked into thoughtless actions, (Laughter from Deputy Renner) which might endanger their lives and liberty.

Any real change in the life of the Germans in the Soviet

zone can only be brought about through the restoration of German unity in freedom. (Deputy Dr. von Brentano: Hear, hear!) The right way of doing this, as the Federal Parliament recently reiterated in its resolution of June 10, is by holding free elections throughout the whole of Germany, forming a free government for the whole of Germany, concluding a freely negotiated peace treaty with this government, settling all outstanding territorial questions in this peace treaty and ensuring freedom of action for an all-German parliament and an all-German government in accordance with the aims and principles of the United Nations.

The Federal Government will act in accordance with these principles and will also do its utmost to improve communications between the different zones and between Berlin and the Federal Republic as a first step towards the restoration of unity.

The Federal Government is following the development of events most attentively. It is in constant and close contact with the representatives of the western powers. At this auspicious point of time we must all stand together irrespective of political differences for the sake of our great and common goal.

Verhandlungen des Deutschen Bundestages: I. Wahlperiode, 272nd session, p. 13449.

10. *The RIAS-Interview with Deputy Minister President Otto Nuschke*

Rep: Herr Nuschke, you are here in West Berlin. How did you come to West Berlin? Voluntarily?

Nuschke: I was kidnapped. My car was dragged into

West Berlin from the eastern sector by a crowd of excited West Berliners.

Rep: How do you assess the situation in the eastern sector?

Nuschke: Favorably.

Rep: Why favorably?

Nuschke: Because lots of people understand.

Rep: Understand what?

Nuschke: Because lots of people understand that what has been done is madness.

Rep: You mean the raising of the quotas in the eastern zone?

Nuschke: That was rescinded long ago, by a legal decree.

Rep: But then how do you account for the fact that the whole population of the eastern zone took part [in the rising]?

Nuschke: Because the trade union newspaper wrote something to the contrary.

Rep: What did the newspaper write?

Nuschke: Why it wrote—that it wasn't true, that the higher quotas were to remain in force.

Rep: And you consider that to be the only reason for to-day's demonstrations?

Nuschke: That is what sparked off the wave of unrest.

Rep: And when do you think you will have the situation in the Soviet sector under control?

Nuschke: We already have it under control.

Rep: Have you? What makes you think so? There is a state of emergency.

Nuschke: I drove through the whole of the eastern sector and nobody laid a hand on me. I drove past demonstrators. Nobody even tried to do anything to my little

car. It was not until I arrived at this critical border—
there were no people's police on the eastern side but
excited West Berliners were standing there and they
pushed my car across.

Rep: What do you say to the fact that the population of
the eastern zone is calling for the deposition of the
government?

Nuschke: It is not the population that is calling for it but
a section of the demonstrators, many of whom are West
Berliners.

Rep: Were you driving through the eastern sector all day?

Nuschke: I was.

Rep: And does it consist entirely of West Berliners?

Nuschke: No, by no means. I drove for hundreds of meters
past the Hennigsdorf demonstrators, who . . . me.*

Rep: And, as you see it, they were all West Berliners who
were simply (?) offering provocation?

Nuschke: No, but there were West Berliners there. That
was an orderly demonstration.

Rep: But then how are we to explain the fact that this
"orderly demonstration" had to be contained by gunfire and by tanks of the Soviet army of occupation?

Nuschke: That was the mixed demonstration—you know
—which smashed windows and broke in doors and so
on. I don't know, well of course—the people don't
differ from one another in the sense that those from the
eastern sector have a different sort of face or different
colored hair than those from the West. And so it is not
possible to be absolutely certain on this point.

Rep: Does the government approve of the deployment of
Soviet tanks in East Berlin?

* Three words were inaudible.

Nuschke: Naturally.

Rep: Why naturally?

Nuschke: Because it has an interest in the restoration of law and order. If this cannot be achieved through the police, then the army of occupation—every army of occupation—must naturally deploy its forces. That is perfectly natural.

Rep: Does that mean that these tanks are justified in using their guns?

Nuschke: They did not use their guns, they were also demonstrating.

Rep: How do you know that?

Nuschke: Because I was there.

Rep: Where precisely?

Nuschke: On the streets. I watched them drive past, the tanks.

Rep: And where are Herr Ulbricht and Herr Pieck and Herr Grotewohl at this moment?

Nuschke: Herr Pieck is convalescing in the Soviet Union, and where Herr Grotewohl and Herr Ulbricht are is beyond my knowledge.

Rep: Are they in Berlin?

Nuschke: Naturally, they are in Berlin.

Rep: And how will you defend yourself before the Politburo after your return?

Nuschke: I do not have to defend myself before the Politburo.

11. *The SED View of the Events: Resolution of the Central Committee of the SED of June 21, 1953, "On the Present Position of the Party and the Tasks Facing It in the Immediate Future."*

At its session of June 21, 1953 the Central Committee of the German Socialist Unity Party took stock of the situation in the German Democratic Republic and drafted the following resolution:

I. The Development of Events

The events that have taken place in the German Democratic Republic are intimately connected with the development of the international and national situations. The crucial feature of the international situation in recent months has been the enormous growth of the world peace camp. In Korea an armistice is imminent. In Italy the people have won a great victory over the forces of reaction. In England and France the opposition to governmental support for America's war policies is growing. In West Germany the patriotic movement for the reunification of Germany is also growing. Thanks to the initiative of the world peace camp a worldwide popular movement for the solution of all matters of dispute by peaceful negotiation has now been launched. Because they represent the people's interests, the peaceful policies of the Soviet Union, China, the German Democratic Republic and the other countries in the world peace camp are clearly gaining approval on all sides.

As a result the American and German warmongers find themselves in a difficult position. They now see their plans breaking down. The Third World War, which they wanted to unleash as soon as possible, is receding into the distance.

In their anxiety they are resorting to fantastic measures. One of these is their D-day plan, which was fixed for June 17, 1953, when they were hoping to infiltrate the German Democratic Republic from Berlin. By exploiting their bridgehead in West Berlin they want to rekindle in Germany the conflagration that the peoples of the world are now trampling out in Korea. They will not succeed.

Why did the warmongers choose this particular time to offer their fascist provocation to the German Democratic Republic? On June 11, the government of the German Democratic Republic introduced new measures which will strengthen the German Democratic Republic and lend a crucial impetus to the struggle for German unity and a better understanding between Germans. These measures, which were designed to bring about a marked improvement in the living conditions of the workers, especially the manual workers, of the German Democratic Republic, provided among other things for an increase in the production of consumer goods and for the allocation of credits and any necessary raw materials and commodities to freelance craftsmen and the proprietors of small and medium sized industrial firms operating in the private sector. Those who have fled from the republic, including the big farmers, are to be allowed to return and to have their property restored; thousands of prisoners have been released, teachers and pupils, who had been banned from the higher modern schools, have been readmitted; and the zone and sector borders have been thrown open.

The effect in all parts of Germany of the resolutions

passed by the Politburo and the government made the warmongers' position still more difficult and persuaded them to move forward their long prepared 'D-day' plan and provoke unrest in the German Democratic Republic at short notice.

The party and the government had started to correct the political line previously pursued by the German Democratic Republic because it had not led to a speedy improvement in the standard of living of the population of the German Democratic Republic and was not conducive to the all-German struggle for unity and peace. When the Politburo reviewed the general situation, the old line, which had been thought to be correct, appeared in a new light. In its capacity as the leadership of a Marxist-Leninist party the Politburo made its findings known in an official announcement, drew attention to the errors committed in the course of the past year and recommended to the government a number of measures designed to correct those errors. It then began to work out an overall plan for improving the standard of living of the workers prior to submitting it to the Central Committee for its approval. And at that very moment the western agencies decided to mount their D-day in order to frustrate this initiative for improving living conditions in the German Democratic Republic. The enemies of the people have themselves spoken quite openly about the preparations for this D-day. Jakob Kaiser stated: "It is within the bounds of possibility that this D-day will come sooner . . . it is our duty to prepare ourselves as well as possible for every contingency. The plan of the general staff is more or less complete!"

In West Germany there were, and still are, American

agencies evolving contingency plans for war and civil war on orders from Washington. In West Germany and West Berlin Adenauer, Ollenhauer, Kaiser and Reuter supervised the immediate preparations for D-day. Thus, in Jakob Kaiser's ministry a special section was set up to organize acts of sabotage and civil strife. This section, which was camouflaged as a "research advisory body," received millions of marks from the secret funds of German and foreign imperialists. In West Berlin, Kaiser and Reuter systematically recruited, trained and armed war criminals, militarists and criminal elements for service in terror organizations. Traditional fascist murder techniques were supplemented by American gangster methods. And so the fascist scum were reared once more. Between them Adenauer, Ollenhauer, Kaiser, Reuter and the foreign warmongers bear the full responsibility for the blood shed during the suppression of their fascist venture.

Our enemies launched their campaign to provoke unrest by exploiting the discontent felt by certain sections of the population, which had arisen as a result of our policies during the past year. By infiltrating the steamer excursion held by the VEB Industriebau on June 13, 1953, with their agents, who were employed in various large concerns, they organized a strike of construction workers for June 16, 1953. They then sent groups of bandits armed with guns and phosphorus, sulphur and petrol bombs across the sector borders to incite the crowds, thus transforming a perfectly genuine work stoppage into an antigovernment demonstration, which they tried to invest with the attributes of a popular rising by means of gunfire, arson and looting. Meanwhile, other groups of agents at other places in the republic were instructed to organize similar incidents for the next day or—in some cases—the next day but one. The fascist brats, who were smuggled into the republic and whose activities were directed from West Berlin, organized raids on food stores, apprentices' hostels, clubhouses and shops and tried to assassinate party functionaries and officials in the large administrative organizations and the departments of state, who were bravely defending our democratic order. Fascist and common criminals, whose names appeared on the lists prepared at the agents' headquarters in West Berlin, were temporarily released from prison. One of these was Erna Dorn, the SS Commandant of the Ravensbrück Concentration Camp for Women, who had been found guilty of bestial crimes against humanity by a democratic court. Clearly, these western agents were intent on setting up a fascist power in the German Democratic Republic, thus blocking the path to unity and peace for Germany.

Thanks to the timely intervention of broad sections of the population, who were heroically supported by the People's Police, thanks also to the intervention of the Soviet army of occupation, which declared a state of emergency, this scurrilous attack on the German Democratic Republic, on Germany and on world peace collapsed ignominiously within twenty-four hours. As a result, the blood bath that had been planned by the West was averted.

II. The Present Situation

All is quiet in the republic. The country is working normally. A large number of agents provocateurs have been arrested. The rest have been forced to lie low. But there is no guarantee that these peaceful conditions will prevail. The enemy is still trying to stir up trouble. The sorties flown by foreign aircraft during the past few days over Thuringia, Sachsen-Anhalt and other districts are continuing and bandits armed with weapons and radio transmitters are still being parachuted into the republic. Lorries loaded with weapons for other groups, who have yet to be discovered, have been stopped on the Leipzig-Berlin autobahn. Our enemies have gone over to acts of large scale sabotage. With the active participation of Adenauer, Ollenhauer, Kaiser and Reuter, who have taken personal charge of these subversive groups, the RIAS radio station is working round the clock, transmitting inflammatory broadcasts in a desperate attempt to put new life into this bankrupt venture.

As the situation has changed, so our enemies have changed their tactics. They have now instructed their remaining agents to lie low and try to provoke further unrest by launching a whisper campaign. And since large numbers of workers have now seen how their discontent has been exploited, our enemies are trying to incite the people of the countryside. By provoking them they hope to sabotage the supply of foodstuffs to the towns, thus creating a fresh source of grievance that will enable them to sow discord among the workers. It is essential, therefore, that we should now inflict a lasting defeat on our enemies, who have already suffered a severe reversal, thus eliminating their fascist bands once and for all so that we may build our social order on firm foundations and ensure the implementation of the new line announced by the party and the government. What does this necessitate?

III. Our Party and the Working Class

In the first place this necessitates new measures to ensure that those sections of the working class who allowed themselves to be duped by the enemy are roused from their delusions, that those who unwittingly and unwillingly came under the sway of their sworn enemies, the monopolists and fascists, are freed from their subservience, that the relationship of trust between the working class, the party and the government is restored.

How do things stand today?

The vast majority of industrial concerns did not take part in the strikes. In many concerns, where groups of strikers suddenly appeared to urge the personnel to join them, they were sent packing and the workers then demonstrated against the strikes by carrying on with their work. In other concerns the personnel spontaneously undertook to raise their output so as to show their allegiance to our party and the republic and to help make up for the production losses incurred elsewhere. But in many of the concerns which did take part and which are now working normally certain sections of the work force have become embittered. These men feel that they have been deserted by the party and the government. They have not yet realized that the suppression of the fascist provocation also helps them, that it provides the basis for their future life. Because they have not yet succeeded in forming a comprehensive picture of recent events, they see only their own local demands, the demands made by their own particular factories. Consequently, they have failed to grasp the one really crucial factor, namely that the fascist provocation began *because* and *after* the government had decided on a series of measures that were designed, not only to satisfy the justified demands being made by the workers, but also—and that is the whole point of the new line—to create a new kind of economic life and new working conditions in the industrial concerns and in all sections of the German Democratic Republic, which would make it impossible for justified demands to be overlooked ever again. Above all, these workers have failed to realize that their worst enemies are the big capitalists of America and Germany, who trample their own workers underfoot, throw millions out on the streets, let them starve, demoralize them and exploit their demands for their *own* ends, which undoubtedly pose a threat to the security and way of life of the workers in the German Democratic Republic. The great majority of the workers who had been misled by the agents provocateurs realized this when they saw the fruits of their labor—club houses, apprentices' hostels and factory canteens—going up in flames as a result of the petrol and phosphorus bombs thrown by these western agents. "That is not what we wanted," they said. "That is not the right way."

At this moment of time, which calls for action, the party does not intend to play into the enemy's hands by holding a postmortem to establish how one section of the working population could come to labor under such a complete misapprehension. That would be a terrible waste of energy. What is needed now is action. Consequently, the Central Committee has only one comment to make at present on this crucial issue: if large numbers of workers do not understand what the party wants, the party is to blame and not the workers.

It is essential, therefore, that all our party members and functionaries should distinguish most carefully between the honest workers, who are rightly concerned for their own interests and so listened for a time to the blandishments of the agents provocateurs, and the agents themselves. Honest workers, who err temporarily, are still honest workers and should be respected as such. This is equally true of those who have still not recognized the error of their ways; they too are honest workers and must be respected. In fact, they have the greatest need of the help and patient understanding of the party, they have the greatest need of the German Socialist Unity Party, even though they themselves are unaware of the fact. The Central Committee expects all its members and functionaries to demonstrate their intellectual maturity and their heartfelt concern by their passionate commitment to this section of the working population.

The Central Committee also expects all members and functionaries to keep a sharper watch for the real agents provocateurs, to unmask them in public and, with the help of the workers, hand them over to the security departments. Because it is determined to defend the workers' interests against fascist provocation with the utmost rigor, the Central Committee recognizes that the party must adopt a new approach to the working population. This essential step must be taken immediately.

The need for change is clearly demonstrated by the present attitude of many party members and functionaries. While tens of thousands of our members and functionaries have been, and still are, in close touch with the masses, there are also tens of thousands who sit in their offices, composing documents and biding their time. The party belongs at all times, but especially in times like these, with the masses! It is essential that the whole party should be mobilized for the painstaking task of convincing the masses. Consequently, the Central Committee expects all functionaries in all grades—the functionaries in the central administration, the functionaries in the districts and precincts—to visit the industrial works from tomorrow onwards. In every works, party and personnel meetings are to be convened at which our functionaries will be expected to answer any questions put by the workers and employees openly and directly and to work consistently *for* the interests of the workers, *for* the welfare of the works personnel, *for* the elucidation and implementation of the new line, *for* the correction of erroneous views genuinely held by honest workers, but against the agents provocateurs.

Our project will have succeeded if the workers resolve, from a sense of inner conviction, to support the new political line put forward by the party and the government and acknowledge the need actively to oppose all agents provocateurs, whether disguised or undisguised.

IV. The Immediate Measures

The Central Committee will not allow itself to be diverted from the implementation of the new line by the foreign and German warmongers, however much they may demean themselves by their sabotage attempts. It regards these attempts simply as further confirmation of the correctness of its policy. It will continue with the systematic implementation of the new line.

The resolutions passed by the Politburo of the Central Committee on June 9 and the government of the German Democratic Republic on June 11 listed the initial measures to be taken within the general framework of the new line which, in conjunction with reductions in the targets set for heavy industry in the economic plan, is primarily intended to bring about an improvement in the living conditions of the workers, the farmers, the intelligentsia, the craftsmen and the other sections of the middle class.

Today the Central Committee has resolved, in view of the great economic changes that have to be achieved, to introduce a second series of measures to facilitate the implementation of the new line. These are:

1. From today onwards wages are to be calculated on the basis of the work quotas in force on April 1, 1953.

2. From July 1, 1953 all workers and employees with a gross monthly income of up to 500 DM will be able to buy workmen's return tickets subject to the old reduction of 75 per cent.

3. The minimum rates payable in respect of old age, disability and accident pensions will be increased from 65. DM to 75. DM per month. The minimum rates payable in respect of widows' pensions will be increased from 55 DM to 65 DM per month.

The maximum allowance payable to those on social assistance will be increased from 45 DM to 55 DM per month.

Where the wives of men receiving old age, disability or accident pensions are not themselves in receipt of a pension and are unable to work or where they have reached pensionable age, the additional allowance granted in respect of a wife is to be increased so that the combined pension and wife's allowance reach a minimum level of 95 DM per month.

4. The practice of withdrawing the annual holiday entitlement of workers who receive hospital or convalescent treatment under social insurance schemes is to be discontinued.

5. The decree of March 19, 1953, authorizing the segregation of voluntary insurance schemes from the state social insurance scheme is to be withdrawn.

The annuity schemes, annuity schemes with options and burial schemes in force up to March 31, 1953, are to be revived at the old premiums and with the old benefits and will be available to all citizens.

The policies of persons insured against sickness under the state social insurance scheme will be taken over by the Deutsche Versicherungsanstalt, whose premiums will be fixed in accordance with the tariff introduced on April 1, 1953.

6. The construction and renovation of dwellings is to be intensified, especially in big cities and industrial centers. Additional investment funds and license credits of up to 600 million DM are to be allocated for the provision of dwellings (new buildings, conversions, renovations) and the repair of roads in excess of the targets laid down in the economic plan for 1953. The necessary revenue will come from the savings made as a result of the reduced investment in our heavy and essential industries.

7. A further 30 million DM will be set aside for the improvement of hygiene and sanitation in publicly owned industrial concerns in the year 1953. The local trade union managements are to submit appropriate recommendations to their central executives, who will examine and then forward them, together with their own comments, to the competent ministry for action. In the case of publicly owned concerns under regional control the recommendations are to be submitted to the appropriate districts.

8. Additional investment funds to the value of 40 mil-

lion DM will be provided in the year 1953 for the construction, reconstruction and conversion of buildings belonging to the cultural, social and health services, such as old people's homes, convalescent homes run by the vacation service of the trades unions, Kindergartens and nurseries.

9. The provision of working clothes, working shoes and protective clothing is to be improved in accordance with the recommendations made by the executive of the FDGB.

10. The daily domestic power cuts will be discontinued in the third quarter of 1953 by reducing the amount of power used in our heavy and essential industries. The Secretariat of State for Energy will be required to submit suitable proposals to the government by August 1, 1953, to ensure an adequate supply of domestic power during the coming winter.

The Central Committee will shortly reconvene—after working out a number of further necessary measures—in order to provide both the party and the general public with a comprehensive report on the problems posed by the new political and economic tasks. Meanwhile, the Central Committee wishes to draw attention to the fundamental fact that the far-reaching initiatives taken by the party and the government for improving the standard of living of all sections of the population can only be successfully implemented if, having been convinced of the need for a constant increase in productivity, our workers and employees acquire a more competitive spirit, make more extensive use of modern methods and bring the management and organization of the publicly owned industries to a proper level of development. For this reason the Central Committee welcomes the resolutions passed by the personnel of numerous works calling for greater efforts to make good the considerable production losses sustained as a result of the vandalism and abuses to which we have been subjected.

Let us hope that every party member, every worker and every employee is aware of the fact that the maintenance of peace and the establishment of German unity depend to a large extent on our ability to raise the standard of living in the German Democratic Republic, strengthen our democratic system and build a truly exemplary democratic state on German soil.

Adenauer, Ollenhauer, Kaiser and Reuter are aiming at war. That is why they are attacking us, that is why they are transforming West Germany into a stronghold of fascism and reaction. Our party and our government stand for peace. That is why we have adopted a policy designed to create an exemplary peace economy. Our new line is the most powerful weapon for all Germans against any act of warlike provocation on German soil.

To work, comrades!

With greater insight, renewed energy and firm discipline!

Long live the German United Socialist Party, the flag bearer in the struggle for peace, unity and democracy!

Long live the government of the German Democratic Republic, the government of peace and labor!

Long live the President of the German Democratic Republic, Wilhelm Pieck!

Dokumente der SED, Vol. IV, pp. 436 ff.

TIMETABLE OF EVENTS
NOTES
BIBLIOGRAPHICAL ESSAY
INDEX

Timetable of Events

1952

May 26, 27. The German Agreement with the Western Powers ending the occupation and the European Defence Treaty were signed in Bonn and Paris. The Council of Ministers of the GDR issued a decree authorizing new measures to be taken at the frontier separating the GDR from the Federal Republic (decree setting up prohibited areas).

July 9–12. Second Party Conference of the SED; announcement of the "establishment of socialism."

July 23. The Volkskammer (first chamber of parliament in the GDR) passed legislation reorganizing the territorial divisions within the GDR. The former provinces were abolished and replaced by districts and precincts.

July 24. The Council of Ministers of the GDR announced special privileges for the Agricultural Collectives.

October 10. Paul Baender (SED), Secretary of State in the Ministry of Trade and Food, was relieved of his post.

November 6. Minister President Otto Grotewohl censured the Ministry of Trade and Food for serious deficiencies in its work.

November 27. Due to the shortage of supplies in the GDR the municipal council of East Berlin prohibited the sale of food and industrial products to West Berliners.

December 15. The Minister of Trade and Food, Dr. Hamann

(LDP) and Secretary of State Albrecht (DBD) were relieved of their posts and arrested.

December 19. The government of the GDR published specimen statutes for the Agricultural Collectives (Types I to III).

1953

January 15. The state Planning Commission pointed to "alarming deficiencies" in the state-run industrial concerns. The SED press office attacked the unions for disregarding the urgent question of higher norms.

February 3. The Central Committee of the SED passed a resolution calling for a "campaign for strict economy" in the public sector.

March 5. Stalin died.

March 19. The German Treaty and the Treaty for a European Defence Community passed their third reading in the Federal Parliament.

April 15. The Soviet leaders advised the SED to adopt a softer line.

April 16. In a foreign policy speech the President of the United States, Dwight D. Eisenhower, put out feelers to probe the possibility of a detente. *Das Neue Deutschland* published a speech by Walter Ulbricht calling for the continuation of the hard line.

April 21. The political adviser to the Soviet Control Commission, Vladimir Semyonov, was recalled to Moscow. The bishops of the Evangelical-Lutheran churches in the German provinces protested against the persecution of the church in the GDR; they were particularly severe in their condemnation of the measures taken against the *Junge Gemeinde.*

May 11. In a speech in the House of Commons the Prime Minister of Great Britain, Sir Winston Churchill, called for a summit conference to resolve all matters of dispute between East and West.

May 14–15. The Central Committee of the SED met for its thirteenth session. It first considered the further ramifications of the Slansky trial and as a result of this discussion Franz Dahlem was relieved of his official responsibilities and dismissed from both the Politburo and the Central Committee of the SED. Subsequently the Central Committee passed a resolution "On the Raising of Productivity and the Introduction of Strict Economy" which called for the imposition by administrative order of higher quotas in all publicly owned works.

May 28. The Soviet government dissolved the Soviet Control Commission and appointed V. Semyonov, who had been political adviser to the Commission, High Commissar of East Germany. The Council of Ministers of the GDR ordered a general minimum increase in work quotas of ten per cent.

May 29. The Federal Chancellor Dr. Konrad Adenauer submitted to President Eisenhower a memorandum dealing with the question of reunification on the basis of free elections and with the further question of a German peace treaty.

June 5. V. Semyonov arrived back in East Berlin.

June 9. The Politburo of the SED decided to adopt a new line which would take effect immediately.

June. 11. The Council of Ministers of the GDR gave its approval to the measures proposed by the Politburo of the SED for the implementation of the new line.

June 14. In an article in *Das Neue Deutschland* the previous methods used for establishing higher quotas were severely criticized.

June 16. From an article in *Die Tribüne* it became quite apparent that the higher quotas called for by the SED were to be retained under the new line. This article triggered demonstrations by the construction workers of East Berlin.

June 17.   Strikes, demonstrations and mass meetings were staged in over 250 places in the GDR.

June 21.   At its fourteenth session the Central Committee of the SED passed a resolution "On the Present Situation and the Immediate Tasks Facing the Party."

June 26.   Lavrenti Beria, the First Deputy Minister President and Minister of the Interior in the USSR, was dismissed and relieved of all his responsibilities. This was first reported in *Pravda* on July 9.

July 16.   Max Fechner, the East German Minister of Justice, was dismissed and arrested.

July 24–26.   At its fifteenth session the Central Committee of the SED passed a resolution on "The New Line and the Tasks Facing the Party." The Minister of State Security, Wilhelm Zaisser, and the chief editor of *Das Neue Deutschland,* Rudolf Herrnstadt, were expelled from the Politburo and the party. Anton Ackermann, Hans Jendretzky and Elli Schmidt were not reelected as candidate members of the Politburo.

1954

January 22–23.   At its seventeenth session the Central Committee of the SED passed a resolution expelling the former chief editor of *Das Neue Deutschland,* Rudolf Herrnstadt, and the former Minister of State Security, Wilhelm Zaisser, from the party. The former Secretary of State in the Foreign Ministry, Anton Ackermann, was expelled from the Central Committee and reprimanded for supporting the Zaisser-Herrnstadt group. The former First Secretary at SED District Headquarters in Berlin, Hans Jendretzky, and the former First President of the German Democratic Women's League, Elli Schmidt, were also reprimanded on this account.

Notes

(In order to reduce the notes to reasonable proportions references to works listed in the bibliography have been omitted save in the case of direct quotations.)

1. *Dokumente der SED,* Vol. IV, p. 73.

2. Fred Oelszner, "Die Übergangsperiode vom Kapitalismus zum Sozialismus in der Deutschen Demokratischen Republik" in Deutsche Akademie der Wissenschaften zu Berlin (Eds.) *Vorträge und Schriften,* No. 56 (East Berlin, 1955), p. 30.

3. For information on the different phases of the process of social change in the GDR see Hartmut Zimmermann, "Probleme der Analyse bolschewistischer Gesellschaftssysteme: Ein Diskussionsbeitrag zur Frage der Anwendbarkeit des Totalitarismusbegriffs" in *Gewerkschaftliche Monatshefte,* April 1961, pp. 193 ff. (200 ff.). In addition to this excellent article there are also two East German works which should be consulted: *Grundriss der deutschen Arbeiterbewegung* (East Berlin, 1963), Chapters XII and XIII and Walter Ulbricht, "Vergangenheit und Zukunft der deutschen Arbeiterbewegung" (Section entitled "Zur neuen Periodisierung der fünften Hauptperiode der Geschichte der deutschen Arbeiterbewegung"), *Das Neue Deutschland,* April 14, 1963. Part of this article was reprinted in the *SBZ-Archiv,* May 1963, pp. 159 ff.

4. Gerhard Haas, *Der FDGB 1954* (Bonn, 1954), p. 11.

5. "Der Kollege Zschau und der Kollege Brumme," *Das Neue Deutschland*, October 15, 1951.

6. Werner Wolf, *Die Tägliche Rundschau*, March 26, 1953.

7. *Einheit*, No. 5, May 1953, p. 661.

8. *Einheit*, No. 12, December 1952, pp. 1306–7.

9. Otto Grotewohl, "Die gegenwärtige Lage und der neue Kurs der Partei" in *Der Neue Kurs und die Aufgaben der Partei* (East Berlin, 1953), p. 9.

10. The General Secretary of the Czechoslovakian Communist Party, Rudolf Slansky, was condemned to death and executed in 1952. The SED had already assessed the implications of this trial in December 1952 (see the Central Committee resolution of December 20, 1952 in *Dokumente der SED*, Vol. IV, pp. 199 ff.), but within a few months it became apparent that its resolutions had been disregarded in many quarters. Consequently, it reconsidered the Slansky trial at its thirteenth plenary session. Slansky was rehabilitated in the late summer of 1963.

11. "Über die Auswertung des Beschlusses des Zentralkomitees zu den 'Lehren aus dem Prozess gegen das Verschwörerzentrum Slansky' " in *Dokumente der SED*, Vol. IV, pp. 394 ff.

12. "Über die Erhöhung der Arbeitsproduktivität und die Durchführung strengster Sparsamkeit" in *Dokumente der SED*, Vol. IV, pp. 410 ff. See also Document 1.

13. Fritz Schenk, *Im Vorzimmer der Diktatur* (Cologne and Berlin, 1962), p. 186.

14. *Das Neue Deutschland*, June 24, 1951.

15. "Wie mit Hilfe sowjetischer Erfahrungen der Bürokratentrott in der Bau-Union Berlin überwunden wurde," *Neuer Weg*, No. 24, 1952, pp. 46–47.

16. "Wie kämpfen wir um die Verwirklichung des ökonomischen Grundgesetzes des Sozialismus?" *Neuer Weg*, No. 7, 1953, p. 26.

17. "Die Partei ruft die Bauarbeiter der Stalin-Allee zum

Kampf für höhere Normen," *Das Neue Deutschland,* April 10, 1953.

18. "Es ist Zeit, den Holzhammer beiseite zu legen," *Das Neue Deutschland,* June 14, 1953. See also Document 4.

19. The judgement of the East Berlin Municipal Court has been reproduced in Untersuchungsausschuss Freiheitlicher Juristen (Eds) *Unrecht als System: Dokumente über planmässige Rechtsverletzungen in der Sowjetzone Deutschlands* (published under the auspices of the Federal Ministry for All-German Affairs) Part II 1952–1954 (Bonn, 1955), pp. 127 ff.

20. Otto Grotewohl, *op. cit.,* p. 32.

21. "Die Menschen vom 17. Juni: Soziologische Untersuchung einer aktivistischen Minderheit" (study kept in the KgU-Archiv as part of the Material der Kampfgruppe gegen Unmenschlichkeit), p. 3; Winkler, *Warum 17. Juni?* (Berlin, 1954), p. 5; "Materialzusammenfassung des Bundesministeriums für gesamtdeutsche Fragen" (Extracts kept in the Archiv Friesdorf), Appendix IX.

22. Otto Grotewohl, *op. cit.,* p. 32. See also *Statistisches Jahrbuch der DDR* (East Berlin, 1955), p. 94.

23. Hans Köhler, *Zur geistigen und seelischen Situation der Menschen in der Sowjetzone* (Bonn, 1952), p. 38. For a more detailed account of Köhler's arguments see *ibid.,* pp. 30 ff., 38, 23 ff., 36 ff.

24. P. H. Seraphim, *Die Heimatvertriebenen in der Sowjetzone* (Berlin, 1954), p. 96.

25. Willy Brandt, *Arbeiter und Nation* (Bonn, 1954), p. 36.

26. For the text of the resolution of May 19, 1953 on "The Transformation of Magdeburg into a major socialist city and the Tasks Facing the Party" see *Dokumente der SED,* Vol. IV, pp. 418 ff; for the quotation from Otto Grotewohl's speech see Otto Grotewohl, *op. cit.,* p. 32; for the reference to the former SPD members see *Dokumente der SED,* Vol. IV, p. 454.

27. *Neuer Weg,* No. 23, 1952, p. 45.

28. *Dokumente der SED*, Vol. IV, p. 455. These changes in the composition of the East German work force have also been noted by western observers; see Karlheinz Meiler (pseudonym), "Standen die Bürgerlichen abseits? Der 17. Juni soziologisch untersucht" in *Deutsche Monatshefte für Politik und Kultur*, July–August 1962, pp. 31 ff. The other assertions made by Meiler in this article, which are based on limited statistics and, above all, on a problematical conception of an East German "élite," have been questioned in *Der Spiegel*, No. 15, 1963, pp. 30 ff.

29. Fritz Schenk, *op. cit.*, p. 204.

30. See "Die Menschen vom 17. Juni," p. 9, in the KgU-Archiv and the Communiqué issued by the Council of Ministers of the GDR after its session of June 25, 1953, which was reproduced in *Das Neue Deutschland*, June 26, 1953. Much higher casualty figures were given in the article "Juniaufstand" in *SBZ von A—Z* (8th ed.) and in *Parlement*, No. 24, June 15, 1955. But these appear to be incorrect. The author of the article "Juniaufstand" has told me that he no longer stands by these figures.

31. Quotation taken from Heinrich Siegler, *Wiedervereinigung und Sicherheit Deutschlands*, 5th ed. (Bonn, Vienna and Zurich, 1964), p. 38.

32. Quotation taken from *Der Spiegel*, No. 26, 1953, pp. 6 ff.

33. Andrew Tully, *C.I.A. The Inside Story* (New York, 1962), pp. 163 ff.

34. See *Dokumente der SED*, Vol. IV, p. 469. This quotation also appears in an excerpt from the resolution passed by the Central Committee at its fifteenth session which has been reproduced in Hermann Weber (Ed), *Der Deutsche Kommunismus: Dokumente* (Cologne and Berlin, 1963), p. 596.

35. See Erich Loest, "Elfenbeinturm und rote Fahne" in *Börsenblatt für den deutschen Buchhandel*, No. 27, July 4,

1953; Wolfgang Harich, "Es geht um den Realismus" in *Die Berliner Zeitung*, July 14, 1953; and Günther Cwojdrak, "Schreibt die Wahrheit" in *Die Neue Deutsche Literatur*, No. 8, 1953.

36. *Dokumente der SED*, Vol. IV, p. 467.

37. Hilde Benjamin, "Unsere Justiz: Ein wirksames Instrument bei der Durchführung des 'Neuen Kurses'" in *Neue Justiz*, 1953, pp. 477 ff.

38. *Protokoll des IV. Parteitages*, Vol. I, p. 219.

39. See N. S. Khrushchev's speech to a meeting of writers and artists on March 8, 1963; *Das Neue Deutschland*, March 14, 1963; and Ilse Spittmann, "Wollte Moskau die DDR wirklich aufgeben," *Die Süddeutsche Zeitung*, March 16 and 17, 1963.

40. See Robert Vincent Daniels, *Das Gewissen der Revolution: Kommunistische Opposition in Sowjetrussland* (Cologne and Berlin, 1962), p. 457.

41. V. I. Lenin, *Gegen den Revisionismus: Sammlung ausgewählter Aufsätze* (East Berlin, 1960), p. 219. This quotation also appears in Wolfgang Leonhard, *Sowjetideologie heute: Die politischen Lehren* (Frankfort on the Main and Hamburg, 1962), Vol. II, p. 115.

42. V. I. Lenin, "Was Tun" in *Ausgewählte Werke in zwei Bänden* (Moscow, 1946), Vol. I, p. 277. See also Wolfgang Leonhard, *op. cit.*, p. 36.

Bibliographical Essay

The events of June 16 and 17, both in Berlin and in the towns of the GDR, have been described by various popular authors, who have given good and highly dramatic accounts of the rising but whose reports are necessarily unreliable on points of detail. These include: Stefan Brant (alias Klaus Harpprecht) and Klaus Bölling, *Der Aufstand: Vorgeschichte, Geschichte und Deutung des 17. Juni 1953* (Stuttgart, 1954); Joachim G. Leithäuser, *Der Aufstand im Juni: Ein dokumentarischer Bericht* (Special Reprint of Articles in Issues 60 and 61 [September and October, 1953] of *Monat*, Berlin, 1954); Rainer Hildebrandt, *Als die Fesseln fielen: Neun Schicksale in einem Aufstand* (Berlin, 1956). My principal source was provided by several hundred eyewitness reports which I was able to consult at various institutes and associations in West Berlin. I also had recourse to two particularly important accounts by former SED functionaries. In the early summer of 1953 Heinz Brandt was Secretary for Agitation and Propaganda at SED District Headquarters in Berlin and he recorded his experiences in a commemorative article which he later incorporated into his memoirs: Heinz Brandt, *Ein Traum der nicht entführbar ist: Mein Weg zwischen Ost und West* (Munich, 1967; pp. 207 ff.). As personal adviser to Bruno Leuschner, Fritz Schenk was able to observe the events

186

both inside and outside the House of Ministries and described his impressions in his memoirs: Fritz Schenk, *Im Vorzimmer der Diktatur: Zwölf Jahre Pankow* (Cologne and Berlin, 1962). Schenk also dealt with the East German rising in an earlier work: Fritz Schenk, *Magie der Planwirtschaft* (Cologne and Berlin, 1960). An indispensable aid to the understanding of the part played by RIAS in the rising is: *Der Aufstand der Arbeiterschaft im Ostsektor von Berlin und in der sowjetischen Besatzungszone Deutschlands: Tätigkeitsbericht der Hauptabteilung Politik des Rundfunks im Amerikanischen Sektor in der Zeit vom 16. Juni bis zum 23. Juni 1953* (contains the texts of all transmissions made during the critical period). Information on the opposition to the SED regime in the GDR is to be found in: Karl Wilhelm Fricke, *Selbstbehauptung und Widerstand in der Sowjetischen Besatzungszone Deutschlands* (Bonn and Berlin, 1964) and Martin Jänicke, *Der dritte Weg: Die antistalinistische Opposition gegen Ulbricht seit 1953* (Cologne, 1964; a particularly well documented study). Both of these books might easily lead the reader to exaggerate the significance of the opposition forces within the GDR. Further bibliographical references will be found in my master's thesis "June 17th, 1953" (Columbia University, New York 1957), which appeared in an abridged German version on several occasions prior to 1959 as a "Bonner Bericht" (Report from Bonn). Thilo Ramm expressed misgivings about individual points in this report—Thilo Ramm: *Der 17 Juni: Tag der deutschen Einheit* (Neuwied, 1963)—which I have since clarified.

I have only been able to hint at the general development of the GDR before and after June 17. As yet there is no standard work on the GDR to which the reader might be referred. Ernst Richert, *Das zweite Deutschland: Ein Staat der nicht sein darf* (Gütersloh, 1964), a book written for the general public, is a collection of intelligent and stimulating essays on different aspects of the GDR. In the early 1960's Richert also published an interim assessment of the development of the GDR: Ernst Richert, *Die Sowjetzone in der Phase der Koexistenzpolitik* (Hanover, 1961). But for the period under discussion in this present study we still have to turn to a number of older works, such as Horst Duhnke, *Stalinismus in Deutschland: Die Geschichte der sowjetischen Besatzungszone* (Cologne, 1955)—which is, unfortunately, not very well arranged—and J. Petr Nettl, *Die deutsche Sowjetzone bis Heute: Politik—Wirtschaft—Gesellschaft* (Frankfort on the Main, 1953). A typical East German work is Stefan Doernberg, *Kurze Geschichte der DDR* (East Berlin, 1964).

Georges Castellan, the French scholar, produced an informative anthology in the mid 1950's: Georges Castellan (Ed.) *DDR: Allemagne de l'est* (Paris, 1955) and later published an extremely interesting, if biased, paperback: Georges Castellan, *La République Démocratique Allemande* (Paris, 1961). A similar work is Alfred Grosser, "Was weiss ich vom besseren Deutschland" in *Monat* 163 (April, 1962; pp. 84 ff.). Other useful sources of information are the quick reference books published by the Federal Ministry for All-German Affairs (Eds.) *SBZ von A—Z: Ein Taschen- und Nachschlagebuch über die Sowjetische Besatzungszone Deutschlands* (9th edition, Bonn, 1965) and the *SBZ-Biographie: Ein biographisches Nachschlagebuch über die Sowjetische Besatzungszone Deutschlands* (3rd edition, Bonn, 1964). There are also a number of important publications on specific aspects of life in the GDR. One highly instructive anthology is Peter Christian Ludz (Ed.) "Studien und Materialien zur Soziologie der DDR" in *Kölner Zeitschrift für Soziologie und Sozialpsychologie* (Cologne and Opladen, 1964). There is also a comprehensive and objective account of the whole machinery of government in the GDR: Ernst Richert, *Macht ohne Mandat: Der Staatsapparat in der Sowjetischen Besatzungs-*

zone Deutschlands (with an introduction by Martin Drath; 2nd edition, Cologne and Opladen, 1963). Siegfried Mampel has written two complementary works in which he makes a careful comparison between the constitutional law and the development of the constitution in the GDR: Siegfried Mampel, *Die Verfassung der sowjetisch besetzten Zone Deutschlands* (Text of the East German constitution with a commentary; Frankfort on the Main and Berlin, 1962) and "Die Entwicklung der Verfassungsordnung in der sowjetisch besetzten Zone Deutschlands von 1945 bis 1963" in *Jahrbuch des öffentlichen Rechts* (Vol. 13, 1964, pp. 455 ff.). Mampel has also written a short introductory study on the East German constitution: Siegfried Mampel, *Die volksdemokratische Ordnung in Mitteldeutschland: Texte zur verfassungsrechtlichen Situation mit einer Einleitung* (Frankfort on the Main and Berlin, 1963). An old book that is still well worth reading is Martin Drath, *Verfassungsrecht und Verfassungswirklichkeit in der Sowjetischen Besatzungszone: Untersuchungen über Legalität, Loyalität und Legitimität* (4th edition, Bonn, 1956). Carola Stern is the leading authority on the party apparatus, the history and the leadership of the SED. Her works include: *Die SED: Ein Handbuch über Aufbau, Organisation und Funktion des Parteiapparates* (Cologne, 1954); *Porträt einer bolschewistischen Partei: Entwicklung, Funktion und Situation der SED* (Cologne, 1957); *Ulbricht: A Political Biography* (New York, 1965). We also have to consider the documents published by the SED itself. The most important of these for the period discussed in this book are: Dokumente der Sozialistischen Einheitspartei Deutschlands: *Beschlüsse und Erklärungen des Zentralkomitees sowie seines Politbüros und seines Sekretariats* (Vol. IV, East Berlin, 1954) and the *Protokoll des IV. Parteitages der Sozialistischen Einheitspartei Deutschlands* (2 vols., East Berlin, 1954). An account of the economic development of the GDR can be found in Guy Roustang, *Développement économique de l'Allemagne orientale depuis 1945* (Paris, 1963). The social structure of the GDR has been dealt with in various works including Werner Bosch, *Die Sozialstruktur in West-und Mitteldeutschland* (Bonn, 1958) and Kurt Lungwitz, *Über die Klassenstruktur in der DDR* (East Berlin, 1962). An introduction to the industrial law and social policies of the GDR has been provided in Siegfried Mampel and Karl Hauck, *Sozialpolitik in Mitteldeutschland* (No. 48 of the series "Sozialpolitik in Deutschland" published under the auspices of the Federal Ministry for Work and Social Order, Stuttgart 1961).

June 17 can only be understood against the general background of the home and foreign policies pursued by the Soviet Union following Stalin's death. These are dealt with in Wolfgang Leonhard, *Kreml ohne Stalin* (3rd edition, Cologne and Berlin, 1963), Leonard Schapiro, *Die Geschichte der kommunistischen Partei der Sowjetunion* (Frankfort on the Main, 1962) and Robert Conquest, *Power and Policy in the U.S.S.R.: The Study of Soviet Dynastics* (London, 1961, pp. 195 ff.). Conquest's book is remarkable for its probing analysis of the shifts of power within the Soviet leadership. Two books which deal specifically with Soviet foreign policy are David J. Dallin, *Sowjetische Aussenpolitik nach Stalins Tod* (Cologne and Berlin, 1961) and J. M. Mackintosh, *Strategie und Taktik der sowjetischen Aussenpolitik* (Stuttgart, 1963). The restructuring of the eastern bloc that has taken place since Stalin's death has been analyzed in considerable detail in Zbigniev K. Brezinski, *Der Sowjetblok: Einheit und Konflikt* (Cologne and Berlin, 1962). William E. Griffith, *The European Thaw* (Cambridge, Mass., 1961) should also be consulted. Until now this work has been available only as a manuscript but it is shortly to be published in book form. Richard Lowenthal, *Chruschtschow und der Weltkommunismus* (Stuttgart, 1963) deals with the period from 1955 onwards but the epilogue, which analyzes the various stages of the international communist movement, also casts a revealing light on the events of 1953. Other earlier studies of Lowenthal's are also important, especially: Richard Lowenthal, "Am Ende einer Epoche: Die Umwälzungen im russischen Grossreich" in *Monat* 60 (September, 1953).

Imre Nagy, *Politisches Testament* (Munich, 1959) provides the best comparative study of the new line in the GDR (beginning of June 1953) and the new line in Hungary (end of June 1953). Further comparative studies, which are indispensable for an understanding of the links between the East German rising of 1953 and the Hungarian and Polish risings of 1956, include: Melvin J. Lasky (Ed.) *Die ungarische Revolution* (Berlin, 1958); Deutsche Gesellschaft für die Vereinten Nationen (Eds.), *Der Volksaufstand in Ungarn* (Report of a special committee of the United Nations: Investigations, Documents, Conclusions; Frankfort, 1957); *Der Fall Imre Nagy: Eine Dokumentation* (with an introduction by Albert Camus; Cologne and Berlin, 1959); Wanda Bronska-Pampuch, *Polen zwischen Hoffnung und Verzweiflung* (Cologne, 1958); Hans-Jakob Stehle, *Nachbar Polen* (Frankfort am Main, 1963).

Index

Uprising in East Germany
June 17, 1953

Designed by R. E. Rosenbaum.
Composed by Vail-Ballou Press, Inc.,
in 11 point linotype Caledonia, 3 points leaded,
with display lines in Weiss Series III and Weiss italic.
Printed letterpress from type by Vail-Ballou Press
on P & S Offset, 60 pound basis.
Bound by Vail-Ballou Press
in Interlaken book cloth
and stamped in All Purpose foil.

Library of Congress Cataloging in Publication Data
(For library cataloging purposes only)

Baring, Arnulf.
  Uprising in East Germany.

    Translation of Der 17. Juni 1953.
    Bibliography: p.
    1. Germany (Democratic Republic, 1949–   )—
History—Uprising, June, 1953. 2. Germany—History—
Allied Occupation, 1945–   I. Title.
DD261.4.B37 1972   943'.1087   70-38284
ISBN 0-8014-0703-6